River Terek
RUSSIA
EMPIR
SEA
Batum
Artvin
Tiflis
River Kur
Baku
Lake Sevan
Gumri
Kars
Erivan
River Araks
Erzurum
Lake Van
Van
Bitlis
Mush
Tabriz
Lake Urmia
PERSIA
Diyarbekir
Mosul
DESERTS
Deir El-Zor
River Euphrates
River Tigris

The Promise at the Sea

The Promise at the Sea

Vitali Ianko

VANTAGE PRESS
New York

This is a work of fiction based on actual events. Any similarity between the names, characters, and places in this book and any persons, living or dead, is purely coincidental.

The recipes contained in this book have been selected and written down by the author.

Recipes herein have not been tested by the publisher.

Cover design by Nonna Kazanskaya

FIRST EDITION

Published by Vantage Press, Inc.
419 Park Ave. South, New York, NY 10016

Manufactured in the United States of America
ISBN: 0-533-14870-7

Library of Congress Catalog Card No.: 2004090944

0 9 8 7 6 5 4 3 2 1

To Gregory and Hayk

It is better to go to the house of mourning,
than to go to the house of feasting.

—Ecclesiastes: 7.2

. . . . the dead know not any thing,
neither have they any more a reward;
for the memory of them is forgotten.

—Ecclesiastes: 9.5

Contents

Preface

> "Today, I am not sure that what I wrote is true.
> I am certain it is truthful."
>
> —Charlotte Delbo

This book is a result, though a belated one, of a commitment which the author took upon himself a long time ago, in a place far away from America.

From 1975 to 1991, the last year of the existence of the Soviet Empire and the year my wife and I left the country, our family vacationed many times in Sukhumi. At that time, this cozy town on the east shore of the Black Sea was the capital of the Abkhazian Autonomous Republic within the Soviet Republic of Georgia. It was during these years that I came to know Nargiz Zhamkochian whose adventures and experiences are recorded in this volume. For a short time after my first meeting with Nargiz she was, to me, just one of those local women who leased rooms in their houses to vacationers coming to "sunny Abkhazia," with its famous beaches, citrus orchards, cheese pies, and young wine made of sweet Izabella grapes. However, very soon I discovered that our kind landlady, an elderly woman with a thick-set, but not bulky, frame and a round, genial face, had experienced a chain of incredible events with narrow escapes from death and miraculous survivals. She was a survivor of the Armenian Genocide in Turkey from 1915 to 1922. She needed a listener, and I found myself fascinated by stories of her childhood. Each time in Sukhumi, I rented rooms in her house. She recalled more and more. I began taking notes while listening to her and then examining other sources on the extermination of the Turkish Armenians, Assyrians, and Greeks. During my last summer in Sukhumi, when the conflict between the Abkhazians and Georgians started turning ugly—soon it became a bloody war between the neighbors—I gave my word to Nargiz that I would write a book about her and her family's experiences. Unfortunately, my own family's wanderings and late settlement in our new country (USA) slowed my work; Nargiz did not live long enough, may she rest in peace, to see this book.

However, the book, with its characters, now exists, and it is up to its readers to follow their riveting journeys.

If a reader will be incredulous that one young girl could live through so many chilling experiences by the grace of miracle or by simple chance, I can only say that Nargiz' story is just one among thousands of similar stories of other Armenian children in Turkey who survived through years of persecution, exhaustion, starvation, diseases, and loss of family, and not one of these young survivors managed to stay alive except by virtue of fate or simple fluke.

This collection of Nargiz' memories is written in story form. Although Nargiz kept no diary and relied only upon her memory, brilliant in recalling realistic and chilling details, her narrative is true in substance and fact and is very consistent with the timetable of major historical events in the region.

The dialogues as they appear in this book do not pretend to be the actual words spoken at the time, but are intended to convey the meaning and emotions of the characters as they were remembered by the narrator, Nargiz Zhamkochian. A few real names have been altered and some nameless characters and places have been given names by me. I also condensed the time of Nargiz' narration to one summer month in 1991, setting it against the start of the collapse of the former Soviet Empire.

Although my first intention was to write a documentary account of a genocide survivor, I somehow ended up with fictionalizing her story. The material transformed itself. I had little control. Often, like many other authors, I questioned myself, "Why turn to an artistic form, to the novel, in order to dramatize an already extremely dramatic factual story?" Apparently, we who have not experienced the horrors of genocide cannot grasp the whole picture of it, even knowing all the real facts and events. The exact names, numbers, and places are not enough. The only way to understand the complete story is to imagine and co-experience it. And the only way to do so is through giving flesh and voice to its characters.

In writing this book I was fortunate to have the great support of my wife, Ana, who not only bore the brunt of my daily writing and of acquiring more and more expensive books needed for my writing, but was also constantly encouraging me to continue these activities. For this I thank her in a very special way! I am also very grateful to Chris Hurst for his valuable assistance during the preparation of the final text and to Penny Parsekian for her thoughtful suggestions.

The Promise at the Sea

Part One
Thorns of Memory

Black Sea, Bad Sea

My dear, I never walk to the beach. I hate this sea. The *Tachiks* used to say: *Fena Kara Deniz*. In Turkish it means "the Bad, Black Sea." They were quite right. In truth, they were good-for-nothing and absolutely clumsy sailors. During the frequent storms, when the sea truly was black, their boats sank with all hands; their boatmen went down like stones. The foolhardy Greeks were best along our entire coast in *Tachkastan,* from Sinop to Trebizond. So, the Tachiks had grounds to be afraid of this sea . . . and I have my reasons, too.

Why do you ask me about the reasons? May not an old lady have a secret? Moreover, all the same, you will not believe that the sea smell scares me. The pungent, sticky smell of seaweed and fish remains decaying under the sun terrifies me; it drives me mad, and gives me headaches and nightmares. Sometimes, occasionally, when I find myself in the seaside streets, this damned smell suddenly overtakes me and inexorably carries me away to the days of my childhood, which I never want to remember.

In my bad dreams, I again and again find myself sitting in a heap of totally cowed Armenian children. Some of them have been beaten up, many of them sick, and all of us are hungry, tormented by thirst, and longing for our parents.

Parents, grandparents, our lovely family; they all disappeared. We had not seen them for a very long time, ever since Grandma had given up my little brother, Hakop, and me to unknown people. *Why did Grandma, always caring and protective, do such a thing? Why did the people who had been sheltering us throw us out in the street that morning?*

You know, my dear, in that time, in the summer of 1915, I was four years old, and my brother, Hakop, only two. Of course, we were unable to understand that Grandma had hoped to save our lives by hiding us from the proclaimed deportation, fatal for the Armenians of our town. But the Turks were on the alert: they shortly declared a new order that all hidden Armenian children should be turned in under threat of severe punishment. So, many little fugitives were thrown into the streets. They were picked up, like poisonous mushrooms in a garden, by *zaptiehs* and flung into a heap in the open space near the port pier.

Let me stop here . . . it is a real torment for me to re-experience that day . . .

The children press themselves to one another. Hakop seizes hold of me. A few Turkish women surround our group, and a zaptieh, with stick in hand, walks around us. The women lament and quarrel with him, trying to pass the children a piece of bread and a mug of water. When they move toward us, the zaptieh opens his eyes wide, roars at the women, and knocks the bread and mug from their hands. In fury, he jabs his stick into the children and whips it over our heads.

The mug falls; we press closer together, and the water soaks into sand. "*Effendi,* they are *giavour* children, but let them at least have a drink," plead the women.

"Wait a little, and you will see them drink a lot of water," he guffaws in reply and points at the sea with his stick.

"Yes, yes, yes!" whisper the waves of the sea impatiently, as they smack into the stone wall of the pier. The sea cannot conceal its treachery; its waves sparkle and play under the sun like the scales of an enormous reptile.

The second zaptieh brings a few more children in a creaking two-wheeled ox cart and throws them down on top of us. I notice that two of them are naked. Somebody shrewd had robbed them; they would not need their clothes again. The ring of spectators increases, and our zealous watchman bursts out with damnations and uses his stick more and more frequently.

I often see all this in my dream. Always, my dream breaks at this point, but if I am able to fall asleep again, the most terrible part comes. *What kind of apparatus is inserted into my poor head?* It works like a movie projector which I cannot control—to destroy or even just to stop it. Maybe I am being foolish, but there must be a reason why I have been watching this dream thousands of times during my last seventy years. Someone is in charge of this machine and wants something from me. I am old, yet I must know.

Over the past few years, I have frequently woken up in the morning feeling as if I am getting close to something essential and I am just about to grasp it . . . anyway, now I have to continue.

The sun burns me mercilessly. There is not even a little breeze off the water. The stench of fish heads and offal littering this place after the morning catch overwhelms me, and my head is spinning. My brother, Hakop, cannot sit anymore; he lies on his side with his heavy, hot head on my thigh. His eyes are closed. He trembles. This small tremor frightens me. Big flies from the fish offal buzz around us and land on Hakop's face. I do not drive them off; in fact, I am so scared that I unwittingly begin to move away.

A mysterious, unconscious feeling of great danger shoves me away from my brother and the other children. Something urgently forces me to move. I crawl away from the children, who only weakly flounder and squeak in the heap like young, abandoned whelps. The zaptieh uses his stick to drive me back, but I persistently crawl out again. Such animal obstinacy and insensibility to his strokes save my life.

Sorry Hakop-*djan,* sorry for that. I was too young to realize that, as your older sister, I should have protected you to the end. I was like a brainless little donkey just struggling to survive. That moment lies heavy on my conscience . . . forever.

Now, do you understand, why I detest this sea?

Yes, you are right, they drowned all the children. They drowned them as useless puppies, not very far from the pier, without even bothering to sail farther into the sea.

How I was saved is another story.

“Lord” Pogos

I wish you could explain something to me: I clearly remember that terrible day in the small, dirty square near the pier; I even remember the puffy face of the growling zaptieh, the smell of the sea, and my brother’s trembling. However, the face of my Grandfather Pogos Aleksanian is a blank.

I was his first grandchild, and he loved me so much. My mother and grandmother used to talk about how much he adored me and always spoiled me, but I cannot recollect his face. I only remember someone strong, carefully lifting me in his confident hands, and me, closing my eyes in anticipation of something very pleasant. Suddenly—it was always suddenly, and that was why it was exciting—a wave of the strong, refreshing scent of eau-de-cologne washes over me. I feel the tickling touch of a mustache against my cheeks and forehead and hear some very funny words that make me laugh.

Sometimes I become confused. My father, Nishan Zhamkochian, had a mustache, too, which he thoroughly combed and perfumed every morning. However, at that time all men kept mustaches. I have my father’s photo and I am certain that this is not the man who lifts me up and makes me laugh. Instead, I see in my head a shadowy outline, like the reflection in an old and darkened mirror. Grandfather Pogos?! I am sure that if I could have his photo, I would recognize him in my dream-like memories.

My grandfather Pogos Aleksanian was an unusual man. His name was striking—“Lord” Pogos. Among Armenians, a nickname is very significant. It is more than a given name. One may have the name, for example, “*Khor*” Aram or “Blind” Aram, but at the same time have very sharp sight. Of course, in this case, something is wrong with the man. Perhaps the whole neighborhood, except Aram, knows that his wife takes up with his apprentice, or maybe this Aram is a rude, selfish man who does not see other people’s troubles.

There was also “Bytheway” in our town, a barber with a delicate nature who persistently tried to draw into grave conversation his wrapped-up-in-the-lather customers. His annoying efforts, in their great part, began and ended, got entangled in that peculiar interjection, and rarely produced any worthy thoughts.

In our ancient town of Kutora all people, rich and poor, Armenians and Greeks, and Tachiks called my grandfather "Lord" Pogos. He was under sixty years old then, and looked like a man of large consequence. Maybe he was a little pompous. Grandma used to say, "Importance was just dripping from his nose." Yes, she had a sharp tongue, my grandma.

Grandfather liked to promenade in the evenings along the main thoroughfare with one of his numerous friends and to receive the inevitable parade of homage from passersby. Dressed in European frock coats, waistcoats, and trousers, with a low and stately gait, the two men would graciously support each other as they negotiated the little puddles that formed after the short, summer rain.

"My compliments, 'Lord' Pogos!"

"What a day, *paron* Aleksanian!"

"Prosperity to your family and great success in your business, Pogos *Effendi!*" Then my grandfather would tip his beautiful *fez,* the only traditional item in his attire, and exchange bows. Tip and bow, tip and bow, again and again.

My dear, it is not difficult to understand him. He was sincerely proud of his garment and carpet shop on the ground floor of his almost three-storied home, proud of his wise wife *Iughaper,* who handled with confidence the whole household. His two sons, Levon and Simon, worked with him in the shop. His daughter, *Pietzar,* married a very decent man, although native to another town, yet very educated and clever, making her the envy of all the town's maidens.

"Lord" Pogos was especially proud that he had purchased from Germany four Singer sewing machines, by his words, more than any other tailor on our coast. *Was it four or three?* Sometimes my mother changed those numbers while telling me about provincial life in our town. These remarkable machines never broke. Maybe one of them is still being used by a Turkish woman.

"Lord" Pogos's shop occupied the entire ground floor of the house. The entrance door led to the carpeted fitting room furnished with chairs, coffee table, desk, folding dressing screen, and shelves with bolts of wool, tussore, and cotton. In this room "Lord" Pogos received the clients himself: local merchants, doctors, teachers, goldsmiths, and foreigners, who, for one reason or another, visited our seaside town. Also among the clients were the *kaimakam,* the police *mudir,* and other officials. A few tailors, Armenians and a Greek, worked for my grandfather. They sat in one large room behind a long wall adorned with the carpets for sale. My grandfather obtained these beautiful Persian rugs, Turcoman kilims, and carpets of Caucasus from his dealers around the country. Some were brought by camel caravans and the others were bought during his trips as far as to Urfa, Tabriz, Malatia, Kars, and Tiflis.

From the moment the clients entered the shop, a smiling owner hastened to them, helped them to sit down on an ottoman, prepared the table for coffee and smoking, asked about their well-being and inquired about the news from *Polis,* Trebizond, and the borders. Only then did he broach his main duties.

The door to the tailoring room endlessly opened and closed. Grandfather called his favorite tailor Aristotle or in common parlance Greek Nikos, to improve this or that—to adjust, to tuck, to fold a seam, a dart, a hem. As the door opened, the din of the tailors' loud talk and singing, mixed with the buzzing of the machines, bursted into the fitting room. Fresh cups of coffee were poured, one more *nargile* fixed, and new town gossip exchanged. Nikos's perspired bald patch made one more appearance. He made the last run with the client's trousers in his hands, and finally the front door was closed behind the guest. "Lord" Pogos, wearing a contented expression, counted his coins and uttered, "A very worthy man!" Then he used to add, "My sons, watch and learn how to serve such gentlemen." Nikos and the middle son, Levon, obligingly nodded their heads. His youngest son, Simon, looked out the big window onto the street. "Lord" Pogos fended off sad thoughts about his oldest son. Haroutiun, the one who had fled the country and who was so far away as to seem irrevocably lost.

"But then I was right to buy a tobacco plantation," "Lord" Pogos reassured himself. "Today's guest said the harvest promised to be of rare abundance."

Do you know why Pogos Aleksanian was an unusual man? He was rich, yet at the same time, he was benevolent. There were many rich Armenians in the town, but only one was named "Lord" Pogos. His generous hospitality and cheerfulness were well known. People came to him: someone to borrow money, another for advice, another for a favor. He fixed one with a job and put the second one's affairs in order, arranged audience with the police mudir or *kadi* and helped to keep young Armenians out of the conscription.

Suppliants and spongers beat a path to his door, but they tried to keep clear of Grandma. For Grandma, "Lord" Pogos's cordial generosity might have ruined the family. She used to remind him frequently: "Pogos Effendi, think a little more about your children. Be thoughtful about their future." However, my grandfather hated to worry about the future. He had his own idea: intense reflection about what lies ahead would only disturb the present. After the long evening-party with his friends, he used to hire a few coaches and arrive home sitting in the last of them while the first coach carried only his fez and the second only his cane.

"Iughaper-djan, *tsavet tanem*,*" he would say to her. "Try to understand that the future always prevents one from enjoying today's happiness. Who said that a day in the coming year should or could be better than this peaceful evening? Who promised this to you, my poor wife? Look, our children are healthy, doing well, and live nearby, except for your favorite Haroutiun, your *hent* boy. Let's enjoy these beautiful days and evenings together. Also, try to believe that the more I spend, the more God gives me. Money is useful only to spend on friends and relatives—less on the latter—or to bribe greedy officials in order to help our people."

Thus was Grandfather's usual response. Then he would change his clothes to slippers and a blousy shirt to his ankles and sit in the garden. A cold brook that ran down from the nearest mountain gurgled through the back yard. Grandfather's favorite place was a low bench under a fig tree, just beside the stream. He would lower his overworked feet into fresh water.

"Oo-hi, oo-hi, what a day, what a day!" he would exclaim with satisfaction. "Thank God for not forgetting us. Who knows what will happen tomorrow. Nobody knows, and today is just fine."

Grandfather, grandfather . . . I still call him this. Years have passed, but we remain the same—a grandfather and his little granddaughter. Somehow funny and sad, I have lived to be much older than he was. I am eighty, and he did not even reach sixty. Today, I agree with him completely. Nothing hinders true happiness like the stupid habit of waiting for something from the future. People waste years saving their

* "Let me take away your anguish." (Armenian saying)

living for more sunny days, depriving themselves of a deserving life. I am sure of that.

Not so many peaceful years were given to my cheerful grandfather and my people. Thus, "Lord" Pogos proved to be even wiser than his shrewd wife.

Imam's Advice

Winter storms have rushed over the coast. Easter has been celebrated. Then the cherry orchards all around became covered with a white-rose shawl of blossoms, and the chestnut trees adorned themselves in candelabra blooms. The dreadful summer of 1915 was moving nearer.

Alarm and disquiet settled into the homes of Armenians. My father, Nishan, and Uncle Levon have been driven away to the Turkish army. Gone and never seen again. One evening, "Lord" Pogos came home earlier than usual, and for a long time, sat under the fig tree. The babbling stream was his only companion. Anxious Grandma could not tolerate such inactivity.

"Pogos Effendi, people in the harbor are talking about very strange things happening."

"I know. These idlers in the harbor, always, for as long as I have lived here, drivel more than they work. Instead of fishing and selling their catch, they prefer to tittle-tattle, and then silly women spread rumors through town."

"They are conversing in whispers that many important Armenians have been arrested in *Pera.*"

"I know that, but who can understand these games? They are all politicians there, in Pera. These people made deals with the leading Tachiks."

"And what can you say about Trebizond? Fishermen and smugglers in the harbor are talking about Armenian killings there. They saw corpses in the sea."

"Iughaper-djan, I think these could be hent revolutionaries. Look, the Russian border is too close to Trebizond, and . . ."

"So many revolutionaries? Do you sincerely believe that murdered teachers and doctors, priests and ministers are all rebels?" Grandmother was insistent. She wanted clarification, not just calming, not at all.

"Lord" Pogos fidgeted on his bench. "This country, as ever, is a stepmother for our people. I hope it is no more than regular Tachiks' loss of mind. They were killing us everywhere twenty years ago, and they were killing us in Cilicia just a few years ago. They never change. Sultan or nowadays Young Turks, no difference; for us the outcome is the same. I hope it will be just another episode of their recurrent madness."

"Anyway, what are you going to do? Would you talk with one of your important clients? What about Police Mudir? He appreciated your work so much," said Grandma, trying a bribe of her own.

"Oh, no," responded "Lord" Pogos, shaking his head. "This man always deigned to underpay me, and I closed my eyes and accompanied him to the door with, 'Visit us again, Police Mudir *Bey*!' And he smiled graciously. Just a few months ago I sold him the rare Afghan kilim and he paid only half of the price that beauty deserved. 'Pogos Effendi,' he said, 'a perfect carpet is like an interesting book or a young girl, full of hidden treasures. You look for sugar but may find honey!' Pah! Now he became so hostile like a mad dog on the loose. I am afraid to go to his office because he will be furious thinking that I came to remind him about the due money."

"Pogos-djan, maybe you will try to meet with somebody else?"

His persistent wife was not used to giving up, and with hearing more and more news about Turks' atrocities, "Lord" Pogos himself realized that he should go, even if it meant getting himself in the thick of it. One day, having a suit ready for the kaimakam, he departed to do his dangerous reconnaissance.

Grandma remembered clearly that it happened a couple of weeks before the death of my grandfather. For some reason, she told and retold us the last of her conversations with him, especially what he said after his return from the kaimakam's office. She seemed to be trying to grasp, at last, a meaning of her husband's conversation with the kaimakam that eluded her at the time.

If you have time . . . if you want . . . here is the story of "Lord" Pogos and kaimakam as it was told by Grandma.

On that evening, "Lord" Pogos came back home in a good mood. Hardly waiting for him to change his clothes, Grandma began the talk. She immediately understood that her husband had spoken with kaimakam. Yes he had, and he was satisfied. Grandma gave him the first cup of coffee. Then a significant conversation followed.

"First of all, wife-djan, I met kaimakam. He received me . . ."

"Good! Did you ask him about it . . ."

"Secondly . . . let me go in order . . . secondly, he was polite with me as always. He suggested I have a cold sherbet and a cigarette."

"Good! And then?"

"Then I showed him my work, and he was very pleased as always, and he paid me as ever."

"Good, very good! But did you ask him about our matters?"

"Yes, of course. We were sitting in chairs, and I asked him very straight: 'Kaimakam Bey Effendi, you have been to Trebizond recently. I am sure that your visit was very important and successful. What news have you brought back to your town? Is there anything of interest for our people? We have always been loyal and respectful to the government. My own son and son-in-law are serving in our valiant army . . ."

"And how did he answer you? Talk about his answer, please."

"Well, he said that our success at the front is great, and we, thanks to Allah, will destroy all the enemies and win the war soon . . . look, he was so friendly with me. He even joked with me and told a funny story."

"A story? What kind of story?"

"A very funny one. Let's agree, Tachiks have incredibly sharp tongues. Their sayings and stories are very, very amusing, and this one is really something. It is about an *imam*, a holy man, and a woman.

"This woman had a son who frequently gorged himself on persimmons. He ate so many that his entire face became covered with boils. Neither this fool, nor his mother, could understand why. So, they turned for help to the imam. They went to him, and the mother described her son's troubles. The imam heard her out, thought for a while, and ordered the woman to return the next day. The woman came back exactly as requested, and the imam explained to her that her son must stop eating persimmons. The woman left. After a while, she returned to the imam to thank him for the advice. The son had gotten over his habit, and the boils had disappeared accordingly. She asked him, 'But why did you not give your advice the first day? You already knew the answer, did you not?' The imam replied to her: 'Yes, of course, but on that day, I ate persimmon myself.'

"It is a good story, lughaper, is it not?"

"No, it is not. It is bad, Pogos-djan. I cannot yet explain exactly why, but I do not like this story. Why did kaimakam not answer with some specifics? Why did he tell you this story? I have a feeling this is a kind of allusion or even mockery."

I see them in the garden. Grandfather is in his long, white house-shirt. A cup of coffee, half-finished, is in his hands. His once bright mustache is wilted. Sitting on his low bench and looking at Grandma, he is waiting for her interpretation. In his roomy shirt, he looks like a big confused and aggrieved child. Grandma is standing over him in her strict dark dress. Her hands are crossed and strained. Her intent look is directed into the water of the brook. She is trying her hardest to catch a glimpse of the answer there, to detect the hidden meaning in this story.

Her efforts were inconsequential. Everything was already predestined for them. Perhaps the kaimakam, to avoid giving a direct answer, gave notice in parable to "Lord" Pogos, or indeed simply mocked my grandfather. It does not matter. A deadly lot had been drawn for our family, as well as for every Armenian in the town, in the country.

Soon, my grandfather Pogos was taken away with his last son, Simon. Zaptiehs drove them along in a big group of Armenian men from the town to an abandoned inn at the foot of nearest mountain, known as *Harab Caravansaray*. The next morning, a band of Circassians slaughtered those men with axes and hatchets. They robbed the dead and threw their naked bodies into the deep hole between the rocks. Only my Uncle Simon, youngest in this group, survived.

Naked Souls

Why do you spend your vacation listening to an old woman's tales instead of walking on the beach or enjoying ice cream with your family on the quay?

You want to know how my life had been saved. Will you accept, instead, the story of my Uncle Simon's escape? Simon's survival is more miraculous than mine. I will serve you a cup of real coastal Armenian coffee. It is not Turkish coffee, as everyone nowadays calls it. The sherbet drinkers, they have even stolen the name of our drink. Perhaps some dull foreigners, who visited prosperous Armenian or Greek homes in Tachkastan, were served the rich, dark coffee in little cups and gave it the name of the country.

"Lord" Pogos and Simon were arrested together. It happened because Grandfather needed to stay busy. After his visit with the kaimakam, he stubbornly continued to work in his shop, in spite of the absence of clients and his own workers. As usual, early one morning he came directly downstairs to the shop. He brought Simon with him. They unlocked the front door. Shortly after, Greek Nikos, Grandfather's only remaining worker, arrived.

The gendarmes came right into the shop and took "Lord" Pogos and Simon away. Nikos went running to tell Grandma. She was ready. All the recent ugly events with the Armenians in Pera, Trebizond, and in her own town had paved the way. On that summer day, she was visiting my mother. Grandma's duty was to take care of everything. She worried about her powerless daughter, obviously already a widow, who lived separately with two little children. Now, after the men's arrest, there were two half-deserted households, suddenly filled with useless things. But her deepest despair was over Simon, who was only fifteen. She always believed that if she had been in her house when the gendarmes came, she could somehow have saved him. In the group of a few tens of arrested Armenians, he was the only boy among mature men. So listening to Nikos, Grandma succumbed to despair, while at the same time, holding on the slim hope for her son's release. Nikos kept repeating "Lord" Pogos's last words: "Nikos, please, do whatever my wife will ask you to do." My terrified mother stood by, benumbed.

Uncle Simon often told us what happened at the old, abandoned caravansaray out of the town. Maybe these memories ruined his life, for he could not get over them.

There were five or six zaptiehs, and none of them were from our town. "Lord" Pogos knew almost all the police staff, even regular zaptiehs, in the town, but these were the worst, specially recruited thugs. The most savage was a sergeant who incessantly cursed the cowed people and rained blows on their bowed heads and backs with his rifle butt, or jabbed them with his bayonet. Lame in one leg, he hobbled madly about, his malicious shrieks piercing the air.

"Keep moving! Keep moving! Don't look around! You damned Armenians, always look to the other side. Your Armenian soldiers betrayed us to the Russians. Due to their treachery, those cursed Cossacks shot through my leg." In a freakish display of anger, he spasmodically charged at the group. "Get cracking! And don't gloat over my leg, giavours. Thank Allah, we made short work of those traitors and shall do the same with you, too. Then we will beat the Russians and drive them right up to the very feet of their czar!"

The bandit tore the gold chain and watch from Grandfather's waistcoast, but he was unable to remove the old ring growing on Grandfather's chubby finger. He grinned at "Lord" Pogos's desperate attempts to pull it off, then shoved him into the inn with the rifle butt.

Poor Uncle Simon. Every time he told this story, he spoke with some shame and astonishment about the people there, on the threshold of their inevitable end; solid, capable men who cherished the fantasy of their personal survival, but did nothing to escape.

Squatting next to his father, Simon listened to the brief, passing talk which came out in spurts as the daylight faded. The doomed men sat on stones that had fallen from the inner walls or on timbers from the decaying roof, and tended their wounds. Only two of them paced about. "Senior" Zaven and Babken Mangasarian were fidgety.

Babken Mangasarian was a familiar sight around the town—not the man himself, rather a fleeting glimpse of his dumpy figure in the streets, in the port, around the shops and in the market, from early morning to late evening. He was always buying, selling, trading, of course, in small quantities, and arranging things. With his fast, mincing, half-walk, half-run, he visited tens of houses, and executed hundreds of rush orders and special missions, often very private. Catching sight of him, the townsmen made a game of trying to detain him.

"Babken Effendi, stop for a minute. How are you? Let's sit and have a drink and a cigarette!"

"Thank you, Effendi! Sorry, Effendi! I have to run. My commerce is in my feet."

The womenfolk said about him: "Babken's mother gave his birth in haste, at the double." Babken could not sit without a reason. So now he paced back and forth, inspiring mirthless jokes from the exhausted men who preferred to rest undisturbed after the long march.

"Senior" Zaven created a more pitiful picture. He seemed deranged. A native of the town, he was sent by his father, a rich man, to Italy to study at a university. He graduated and then stayed in that country for many years. Because his parents had died recently, he had returned to sell the family house and the rest of the property. But there was nothing he could do. The Tachiks had duped him for a while until eventually he found himself in the Harab Caravansaray among the arrested men. In a white linen suit and a white, flat hat with a narrow brim, which miraculously still remained on his tussled hair, he loudly muttered in a strange language and gesticulated. He frightened young Simon.

Suddenly, "Senior" Zaven approached "Lord" Pogos, who sat lost in thought against a wall. The eyes of the unlucky man were sparkling behind the cracked glass in his spectacles. Bowing to "Lord" Pogos, he said with a quivering voice: "Excuse me, sir! Nobody here wants to explain clearly to me what is going on. You have such a good-hearted face. Please, would you be so kind as to answer me. You see, they are wrong, I am an Italian citizen. The policemen should not hold me. I showed my passport at the police station when I came into the town."

"I think, my dear," replied "Lord" Pogos, "they consider you, in the first instance, an Armenian. Your father paron Vardkez was an Armenian, your mother *tikin* Gohar was an Armenian. I remember them. Both were respectable people, may they rest in peace. They were not guilty that they were Armenians."

"No, no! I came here from Milan. I live there. My wife is Italian. My daughter, Sylvia, is Italian. We live there together. My passport is somewhere here . . . oh no, it was with me today, and I showed it to our sergeant. I think he kept it. Sir, may I ask him to return my passport? I would appeal to the Italian consulate in Trebizond or in Constantinople."

"I think it would be better to do it in the morning." "Lord" Pogos tried to calm the dismayed "Senior" Zaven. "Sit down, please. Take a rest. They are tired too, our gendarmes. Better do not disturb them. Better in the morning."

"Thank you, sir! Thank you very much! Without fail, I shall tell my wife about you, how kind you have been to me," exclaimed "Senior" Zaven, slightly raising his white, flat hat.

"Wife, wife," "Khor" Aram grumbled into his hanging mustache. "The blockhead believes she is waiting for him. She is waiting for his father's money. They remembered the old guy only after his death. I stake my bald head that she has sent this duffer here, into thick of . . ."

"It is a sin and a shame, Aram Dourian, what you are saying," interrupted "Lord" Pogos, raising his voice. "Leave the man in peace."

"It would be better to look after your own wife," omnipresent Babken lashed back at "Khor" Aram.

"What a cattle!" attested Rouben Shaghbazian, the haughty owner of the biggest meat store in the town.

"Khor" Aram fluffed up his mustache, squirmed in his corner, and said: "I fall silent only out of respect for you, Pogos *Eghbair.*"

Darkness fell. A splinter of wood was lit. The talk abated, as if the prisoners feared disturbing the fragile flame. The indefatigable Babken contrived to find a little piece of candle in a cleft of a wall. He lit the candle. Probably some tramp or smuggler, who had whiled away the night in this place, had left the candle. Maybe he left in a hurry at daybreak, forgetting it in the wall. He was free, this stranger, free to go into the town or to the sea, but where would the captives be driven in the morning? Such were the thoughts of young Simon as he tried not to fall asleep.

The mouth-watering odor of grilled mutton began to percolate the chinks and holes of the old building. The hungry people grew restless. Babken pressed his face against the crack in the front door.

"These scums are making kebab. They are grilling meat on their bayonets. What bastards! Insatiable bellies!" he said, tearing his sharp nose from the crack and quickly returning. "Oh-ho, there are four more bandits, and the new ones are Circassians. Those who live in the nearest village of *Yeni Koy*. I am sure they brought the lamb for the gendarmes. When did they have time to become such good friends?"

The presence of the savage Circassians feasting with the zaptiehs did not bode well. The smell aroused the anxious men. Even the butcher, Arshak, a giant who had taken a vow of silence, perhaps right from birth, began to show signs of life. He moved the little figure of Babken aside and put his eye to the crack.

Guffaws and snatches of songs penetrated the darkened room. The shrill voice of the lame sergeant rose above the rest. He hurled picked mutton bones at the door, sealed from the outside by a few big stones. Furious, the butcher turned around and, clenching his heavy fists, exclaimed: "The world is my witness! I will take them all, right now. I will smash their empty heads, break the sergeant's other leg, and . . ."

Those nearest to Arshak tried to restrain him, and the others implored him to calm down. Noble-looking Vigen Petrosian, a teacher in Simon's school and deacon of the church, in the grip of terror, held out his hands: "Arshak! Arshak! My son, you are ruining us. Come to your senses." The deacon turned to Rouben Shaghbazian. "Say something to him! Save us!"

Shadows rushed about on the walls. The candle died out as the moon rose and illuminated the interior through a few breaches in the roof. Flushed, Arshak took a seat near his master, Shaghbazian, just opposite Simon. The boy looked at the butcher with delight and hung on his every word.

"I am waiting for the morning. I am on tenterhooks for the morning," Arshak muttered.

Simon believed that the butcher could destroy an army of Turks and Circassians. Absolutely. The butcher had unbelievable strength. When he worked in Shaghbazian's meat store, a huge axe played tirelessly in his hand. With one hand, he threw a whole carcass of a ram onto the block. The axe cut the air with a whistle and always landed in exactly the right place. It was pure theater. People came to watch his mastery. Grandma said that sometimes spellbound customers stayed at the store, forgetting to make a purchase, or if they had already bought something, forgetting to leave. The butcher's giant figure in the street would make the young boys shudder. There was a rumor among them that in his younger years, Arshak had been invited to Polis to the court of Sultan Abdul Hamid, to be his personal butcher and cut robbers' heads off.

The silence was broken by the town pharmacist, Najarian. "Paroner, I have just realized something important for us. The Turks cannot hurt everybody. For example, me, because I am the only pharmacist in town and in the area. If they . . ." he could not say the dreadful word. "So, anyway, my presence will help to prevent diseases among their people. Imagine what could happen in the town and villages if there is no pharmacist. The Turks will die themselves, from an epidemic. It is very logical, isn't it?"

"Forgive me, Pogos Eghbair, but I have to say a word to this man," "Khor" Aram, spoke up. "Listen, you dusty dirtbag. If you are right that the Tachiks would die without your presence and your medicines, I will kill you right now with my own hands."

"Indeed!" sniffed cattle dealer Shaghbazian, ignoring Aram and livening up for a minute. "Some people have much more to offer than others. Everyone knows our family has rendered a great service to the authorities. We also supply the army. I have personal gratitude from vali of Trebizond . . ."

"I beg your pardon, paron Shaghbazian! *Dzer hoske meghrov ktrem.**" apologized the pharmacist for his interruption. "Certainly, one must decide each case on its merits."

"Rats!" concluded "Khor" Aram from his corner.

"By the way." The thoughtful town barber tried to develop the topic further, but was cut short. At this moment, everyone's attention switched to Babken Mangasarian. He had left his observation post at the door and was now standing in the center of the inn's hall. His arm was raised, and an index finger pointed to a hole in the roof. The ghastly pale light of the moon fell on his face.

"This one has gone mad, too," whispered "Khor" Aram. "Maybe he is a sleepwalker, and we did not know."

"Babken, are you alright?" asked "Lord" Pogos, standing up from his stone. "Wait a minute, Aram. He is wanting to tell us something important."

"They are sleeping. They have gorged themselves and are sleeping . . . and here," Babken again pointed to the hole, "is a way to escape."

People raised their heads. The hole seemed narrow and too high to reach. Nobody, except "Lord" Pogos, agreed with Babken. But then

* "I am cutting your words but with a honey." (Armenian saying)

the little body of Babken Mangasarian revealed its great heart. He had already thought it all out.

"Come on! We can widen the hole and get up there using these logs, the logs right under your buttocks. Your ends are sitting on the means!" he exclaimed.

Escape . . . is it possible to escape from this dark, cold barn? wondered young Simon, now completely awake. *What a clever man Babken Mangasarian is, and we did not know.* Simon gazed raptly at his father, the roof, and the rest.

"Do not do that, Babken!" lowly cried the portly pharmacist, clutching his log. "Can you imagine what will happen to the rest of us when the sergeant figures out that somebody is missing? I am surprised at your behavior, *paron* Aleksanian. You were always so loyal."

"Pogos, my son," implored deacon Vigen, habitually holding out his hands. "Remember, Christ endured and ordered us to endure."

Why are they saying these things? worried the boy. *Such an excellent plot. Teacher Vigen always was a pain in the neck. Father must explain to them that they are wrong.*

"Paroner, as you can see, with my stoutness, I cannot escape," "Lord" Pogos began, "but most probably some of you can."

Simon did not believe his ears. Did his father say that he would stay? *Please make this a mistake, a joke,* he thought. *We cannot stay here till morning. We must run with the others.*

"I do not see anything wrong with some being saved, anyone who can climb through the opening," "Lord" Pogos continued. "By the way, please, paron Vigen, do not call me 'my son,' again. You are not my father in any sense."

"You, as always, want to give orders to the people around," exploded Rouben Shaghbazian, the arrogant cattle dealer. "As always, you strive to be a leader!" Shaghbazian's voice broke with rage. Usually he spoke without emotion, through clenched teeth. His speech softened only when he spoke with his beautiful wife, Suzanne, a tall blonde. Aunt Suzanne, or originally Shoushan, and her three girls, Simon's cousins; he remembered the tightly buttoned corset and an aureole of perfume, girlish giggles and white, pink, and yellow dresses, gossamer layers like buds—Nelli, Noyemi, Naane. Shoushan was "Lord" Pogos's younger sister, and then became Suzanne Shaghbazian. There was constant rivalry between her and the brother's wife, Iughaper. Her husband tried to outstrip "Lord" Pogos in everything. Now Shaghbazian lost control.

"All this is happening because of people like you, people who are never able to stop and lead regular lives. They are so agitated, they endlessly annoy the authorities. They even poison their children with revolutionary tastes. You think nobody knows where your elder rebel son, Haroutiun, took refuge? In Russia! You sent him there!"

Now the word was out. People fell silent. The escape hung in mid-air.

Song in the Night

I would prefer to stop here, my patient listener. The words are sticking in my parched throat. I will make more coffee.

My dear, I trust you, yet should you be writing down these words, spoken in such dire circumstances? It is not that I doubt their truthfulness. Uncle Simon was much afflicted by what happened there, in the Harab Caravansaray. He recounted it all, in detail, with faces and voices, many times. However, I worry that someone who reads it might feel contempt for those doomed people's words.

But you are right. We never know how we would behave in such conditions. Predators are always much more of one mind and organized than their confused prey.

Initially, "Lord" Pogos kept silent. He seemed confused. A family secret had been betrayed. He had been bluntly hit on an unhealed wound. Shocked Simon rolled up in a ball. Finally "Lord" Pogos spoke.

"People, what is happening to us? In our last hours, we have forgotten that we are human beings, Christians, Armenians. We were friends, neighbors, and even relatives. Rouben-djan, you are my sister's, Shushan's husband. I cannot blame you for your words. I am only thinking that my sister was happy with you and your girls. Why should I argue with you in such a place?

"However, now I can openly say to all of you that my elder son, my Haroutiun, was forced to flee from our town. Yes, it is true that he is not studying in Europe, as we used to say. It took so much from us to hide the terrible truth, so much shame to tell lies and dodge to everybody curious. . . . Haroutiun is really across the Russian border. My son killed a Turk. He took vengeance for his best friend's, Ara's, suffering and death. You all know the sad story of that hopeful young man.

"Now, although it is too late, I am proud of my son. My body for his soul!"

"Pogos Eghbair, surely you can be proud of your Haroutiun. We know, he was a just and brave boy," port mechanic Ovannes said weakly from his spot on the ground. Ovannes had lost a lot of blood. His sides, back, and shoulders were covered with stab wounds inflicted by the zaptiehs when he tried to resist.

"My second son, Levon, and son-in-law, Nishan, obviously perished in the Tachik army," "Lord" Pogos continued. "You heard what the lame sergeant said about our soldiers there . . . so, I have to save my last son, Simon. He is only fifteen, and, after all, he is the only boy among us, an absolutely innocent young boy."

Prisoners began to nod with understanding. But deacon Vigen would not hear of it. "It is fate; with dry branches, green branches also burn."

"Maybe everything is not so bad as we think. Why the Turks have brought us here instead of simply drowning in the sea?" asked pharmacist Najarian miserably.

"Just because they wanted to salvage our clothes," explained mechanic Ovannes with frightening calmness.

At these words, the giant Arshak woke up again. "Enough! I have borne too many stupid words. 'Arshak do not do this! Arshak do not do that!' Get out! I will wait for the morning, but tonight, I shall rescue this boy." He yanked a long log out from under a row of seated men, toppling them in all directions, and set one end in the hole indicated by Babken. Babken danced around him. Simon cuddled up to his father. Mechanic Ovannes instructed from the ground.

"At first, Arshak-djan, knock off the earth above and between the beams of the roof. Clean off all the beams near the hole, and only then try to move them aside."

The giant handled his lever playfully. The earth poured down from the roof, and the heavy beams squeaked and cracked under his mighty probes and thrusts. The men watched the slowly widening opening while holding their breath.

Finally, Arshak came to a stop. He firmly held the log at one end and leaned the other against the edge of the opening. "Come," said the giant to Simon. His dusty face was smiling contentedly upon a job well done.

"Lord" Pogos prodded his son toward Arshak, but Simon did not want to go. He was afraid to be found alone. He shook his head: "*Hairig** come with me, I beg you very much, come with me." Tears brimmed in his eyes.

* "Daddy." (Arm.)

"It is impossible, Simon-djan, let me take away your anguish. I cannot go with you. The opening is too narrow for my body, even if I could climb up the log."

"I promise you, boy, I shall come, too. I shall climb up, somehow, but you go first," consoled Babken Mangasarian.

"It will not be so difficult for you, son. You are as agile and adroit as a lizard. You shall slip from the hole easily," explained mechanic Ovannes, confidently. "Just listen to me. When you reach the hole, grab the nearest beam by one hand, then the opposite one with the other hand and pull yourself up. At this point, our Arshak will pull out his log to give you more room, and will use it to push you from below."

"Yes! Arshak will push your arse. And how!" cheered "Khor" Aram from his corner.

"Maybe you will need to pay for some help outside. Take this with you," said "Lord" Pogos, struggling to pull his ring from the swollen finger. The massive gold ring, with the square black stone, did not budge. Simon watched with tears as the blood dripped from the stripped skin. His father wanted to get the ring off at any price. Someone's hand stopped his desperate efforts. It was Rouben Shaghbazian.

"Keep it." From a hidden pocket in his trousers, Shaghbazian removed a few gold coins. "My emergency ration. It was useful for bribing Tachiks, for business purposes. Tie them into a handkerchief so you don't lose them. Also, please tell my dears that I love them and I am praying for them."

"Simon-djan, my son, be *jarbig.** You must reach your mother and sister, little Hakop and Nargiz; my body for their souls. You must take care of them. You are man now. If you see Haroutiun some day, tell him I loved him and that I was angry at him for nothing. May all go well with you!" "Lord" Pogos, for the last time, clasped his son to his bosom.

"Avoid Turkish and Circassian men, especially if they are in uniform," counseled the mechanic. "Beware also of their lads. It's best to appeal to women or to old people. Tell our people about us. Also, keep as far as possible from the Yeni Koy, it is close to the Harab Caravansaray."

"Don't trust any of them. Bitch's tribe," advised "Khor" Aram. "Keep as far as possible from the *Sheitan Delik,* this Devil's Hole is

* Smart. (vernacular)

also close to Harab Caravansaray; in the darkness, you may fall into it. Tell my wife I . . . to do a better job looking after my trees."

Arshak encompassed Simon with outstretched arms and helped him mount the log. "I am waiting for the morning," he whispered.

"God bless him," said deacon Vigen. "Senior" Zaven waved his white, flat hat.

In no time, Simon found himself on the roof. A fresh breeze quickly cooled his body, sweaty from the scramble up the slippery log. He began to shiver uncontrollably. Below, a stone's throw away, was the bonfire and the dark forms of sleeping gendarmes. Simon hugged the earthen roof, trying to suppress his breathing and the unavoidable trembling. The boy turned his face away from the gendarmes back toward the opening. He wanted desperately to go back to his father, to mighty Arshak, mechanic Ovannes, and others.

Babken did not appear as he had promised. An urgent whisper came from inside. "Jump, Simon, jump!" Simon started slowly and carefully to creep along the old roof. Bits crumbled through chinks washed away by the rains. *Surely the guards can hear my every motion. They are just amusing themselves, pretending not to,* the boy thought. *A little further, and the repulsive, gloating sergeant's face will suddenly appear in front of me.*

Finally, the boy reached the edge of the flat roof. Now he needed to jump, but he could not see the ground. The moon threw its light indifferently on the inn's roof, but the ground under the wall was lost in inky darkness. Again, Simon was paralyzed with fright. He did not have the strength to jump. Yet there was no one to help him.

A sound came from within. A long, thin, drawn-out note. It was a song. A song was taking shape. The sound rose from below and ran through the roof, right into him. Pressing himself to the roof surface, Simon felt each of the voices join in as the song became stronger and more harmonious. Simon could not make out the individual voices or words. He was stunned. He felt as though he was reunited with those left behind. They were bidding him farewell.

Loud laughter erupted from the bonfire. The awakened zaptiehs heaped ridicule and abuse on the singing, and the lame sergeant quickly whipped himself into a fury. Standing near the bonfire, he bawled at the captives, demanding silence. The singers did not hear him, or ignored him.

The sergeant seized a rifle and ran to the entrance door. He shot at the door until the people inside began to scream, and the song turned into moans and cries. But Simon had already jumped into the darkness.

I think we should stop now. Your family has come from the beach. I know you have to go for dinner with them.

You want to hear the end of Simon's story?! But I do not want to be the cause of a family conflict. Your spouse already looks askance at me. '*Indeed, what a strange landlady this old woman is,*' she must think. '*She should tell these stories to her own relatives.*' Even my house is full of close relatives—my son, his wife, and my grandchildren—so what? They are very busy. Who needs an old woman's stories in this day and age? Nobody. We, a few similar old bags, sometimes meet together, mostly at funerals, and recall . . . oh, these recollections, they are all the same. We exchange them so habitually that we don't even listen to one another. It looks as if we said, "Please pass me a cup of tea or a piece of cake."

It's quite different, the way you listen to me. So, I promise to tell you tomorrow about the fugitive Simon in a Circassian village, Yeni Koy, a lamb among wolves. In exchange for it, you have to promise me at first to go with your wife and kids to the beach. All vacationers come here for the sea, not for some sad stories. Promise?

Run Simon Run

Good afternoon! You have returned early, my curious vacationer. How were the water and the beach today? Too warm and too many people?! It can't be helped. August always is hot and crowded here.

I also finished my home assignment earlier; early sow, early mow. I should do an errand for my daughter-in-law. She is too busy, she says. I was also a wife, with a husband and two children, but I always had time to do my shopping. Besides, the marketplace today disturbs me. At our town's bazaar, the prices are exorbitant. Wasteful vacationers feast at the taverns and restaurants, but we, the locals, have a hard time dealing with our indulged merchants.

What is Gorbachev thinking? At least with Khrushchev and Brezhnev the prices were much more reasonable. Gorbachev's freedom is freedom for drivel. People did not work hard before; now they work even less. In the middle of the day, young men in their prime are holding mass meetings about independence. Abkhazia demands independence from Georgia, and Georgia wants the same from Moscow. We old people know from experience that idlers can never be independent. Sooner or later, they will hold out their hands. Meanwhile, what will become of us. We are about 50,000 Armenians in Abkhazia. The oldest ones escaped from the slaughter in Turkey and live here, together with their children and grandchildren. When the fight for total independence begins here, shall we have to flee again?

Meanwhile, are you ready for running Simon?

The short southern night ended quickly. Tired and scratched by the bushes, Simon propped himself up on his elbows in a thicket, hugging the side of a road that wound up into mountains. Disoriented, he did not remember how he got there, how far he had run and then stumbled along in darkness, driven on by shouts and moans of the people wounded in the Harab Caravansaray ringing in his ears. *Had the sun, ant bites, or birds awoke him? Or was it a sharpened sense of danger*? He crawled deeper into the tangle.

The snort of horses and murmur of voices warned of the approach of a small detachment of Circassian horsemen. Four men, looking similar in their foppishly embroided jackets and lambskin hats, rode in front. They silently proceeded in single file past the frozen Simon. He could see their soft leather boots, rifles, and sabres with ornate silver handles, and he smelled the sharp odor of the horses' sweat. The boy held his breath as the row of swarthy, sunburned faces, with screwed-up eyes, filed past. Behind them rode a few more horsemen. These were dressed more casually and conversed freely as they moved after their chiefs. Hurrying after them was a couple of the carts pulled by pairs of jades. At the very end of the procession ran a dog and a ragamuffin.

The dog with yellowed, snarled hair, covered with black and brown spots, stopped and raised its nose. Fortunately for Simon, its owner, a tall, skinny man in terribly rugged clothes and with a bizarre, narrow-shaped, hairless head, angrily hailed the dog. It put its tail between its legs and ran ahead growling, undoubtedly wary of the large club wielded by the freak.

Simon got out of the bushes as soon as the Circassians passed and went just in the opposite direction from them. The town's boy, he had already forgotten all the exact directions he received in the Harab Caravansaray. After a couple of hours he reached a fork. "Left or right?" Simon feverishly tried to remember what mechanic Ovannes and "Khor" Aram had told him at the departure. Nothing particular came to mind. He chose the road that was less steep.

The ways we choose, willy-nilly it seems, are a response to the voice we hear at the time. *Is it a divine voice? Or unlucky stars?* I believe in predestination. If not, why does one die at birth and another become a witness to a unique chain of events in his life? Why does one live through a revolution, and a war, and then a prison and torture, and all these misfortunes one after the another? Why, after all, did some survive the total massacre, The Slaughter? Perhaps there is only one reason: to testify. A survivor is obliged to remember; an eyewitness must never forget. For that, they are being saved; for that, more and more is being revealed to them—against their will.

Almost fainting from fatigue, Simon finally came out at a small village. It was situated on a flatland. The road abruptly sloped down to its ramshackle dwellings. Simon stayed on the rise, in the underbrush, and circled the village cautiously. He recalled the words of the adults at the Caravansaray: "Beware of the Circassian village Yeni Koy; beware of its men and lads." "And dogs," he added to himself, remembering the serpentine-colored dog he had met on his way. However, Simon decided to look for a house where an old woman might live, and then ask for a help. Due to exhaustion his mind could not think up anything else. He was also afraid to move during the night because of the danger of falling into the Devil's Hole lurking somewhere in these places.

From his natural shelter, the village was clearly visible. Nothing was happening. A few hens scratched in a heap of dung, and two or three emaciated dogs wandered about the backyards like lost souls. Thin, bluish puffs of smoke were the only sign of human life. The aroma of newly baked bread, wafted by the hungry Simon, awakened pictures of the *lavash* baked at his grandparents' home. Every Saturday, about 300 snow-white sheets of thin, flat bread bearing the brown and black scars of the fire were made to feed their entire clan. How dexterously his mother and grandmother played with the layers of dough, whirling them in their hands, tossing them in the air, gradually giving them the shape and thickness of a towel. Sitting on the ground, mother quickly leaned over the hot opening of the *tondir.* For a moment, her torso and face were directly over the red-hot charcoal at the bottom, while she swung the wooden paddle holding a layer of dough and sealed the flat dough to the hot, massive clay wall. Baked sheets were removed from the smooth walls by a hook and laid out on the table. In the evening, "Lord" Pogos, with his son-in-law, Nishan Zhamkochian, and Rouben Shaghbazian, with Aunt Susanne, came in their coaches. The innocent scent of the fresh bread instantly mixed with the exciting fragrance of the woman. Then the lavash, like a newborn infant, was wrapped in wide linens and carefully loaded into each coach with all sorts of good wishes. In the darkness, en route home, Simon would furtively shove his hand into the pile of lavash sheets and tear off a long strip. He would hear the husky laughter of Aunt Susanne as his fingers felt the warm, soft skin of the bread.

Simon lost track of time. Suddenly he noticed a woman's figure at the nearest house. By her relaxed, confident gestures, he decided she was the mistress. The boy had no choice. He could not return to the parents' home by himself. He had no idea about the way to his town. At the same time, he feared leaving his shelter in the bushes. Simon took out the gold coins given to him by Rouben Shaghbazian. The boy made an effort not to think about the fate of the people in the Harab Caravansaray. He counted and re-counted the heavy pieces, little yellow disks that might save his life. He decided to present them at once to the woman, before she would send out a call.

Between the village and the fugitive was a shallow ravine, but to reach it, Simon had to cross about twenty paces of open ground. The boy gathered his courage. As soon as the woman entered into her hut, he dashed out of the bushes and dove into the ravine. Terrified, he waited for the shouts of pursuit, but all remained still.

The ravine was deep enough for the boy to stand upright without being seen. Quickly he made his way to its opposite tip and then to the slope closest to the hut. There he crouched to catch his breath in the slimy refuse, broken pieces of pottery, bones and waste dumped from the nearby dwellings. He again took out the coins and held them tightly in his fist, then raised his head above the ravine edge. To his horror, he found himself almost face to face with a woman he had failed to notice before. *Obviously she had been watching my stupid moves the whole time, but why didn't she scream for her villagers?* Such thoughts flashed through the boy's head.

The woman was small and hunched and old. Seated as she was, with her back to the sun-drenched wall of the hut, she apparently sought its warmth. The boy warily searched the features of her mossy face for signs of good-naturedness. She had a face as brown and shriveled as a year-old apple with a thousand wrinkles. This pause saved him from big trouble, for suddenly, around the corner of the hut, appeared the same detachment of the horsemen Simon had met on the road at dawn. With a terror, Simon realized that the road he had chosen at the fork has brought him to the Circassian village of Yeni Koy.

However, now the horses were laden with bulging bags, hanging down on both sides. Slowly and silently, the procession passed the hut and disappeared deep into the awakening village. The cart and a few men turned in and stopped. The noise brought out the mistress of the house and, shortly, barefoot, ragged children came running from all directions. The old woman awoke and hobbled toward the arrivals.

The men lifted a male corpse off the cart. The head was wrapped in a bloody rag. The younger woman reached the body and began to shriek. Then the old woman fell to her knees, her wail joining the lament of the first woman. One more lifeless body remained on the cart. The men gesticulated madly, trying to explain. "*Boyuk* Arshak,

Boyuk Arshak," they said, repeatedly. *They are talking about giant Arshak, butcher Arshak,* thought Simon mechanically. The younger woman scrambled to her feet and cursed the men, stretching her hands to them and to the heavens. The men shoved the strange creature with the eggplant-shaped head toward her. Now there was something even more forbidding about him. Simon could not realize exactly what it was. The man's yellowed dog stood by him.

With a silly grin, the freak lowered his bag to the ground and squatted to remove its contents. Simon eventually recognized what was strange with this man. He saw the white flat hat of "Senior" Zaven, resting on his ugly head. Although Simon's eyes had already grasped what had happened, some part of his mind held the understanding in check. Lying in the muck of the ravine, the paralyzed boy watched how the freak took a man's head from the bag. Holding it by its thick, long hair, he lifted it in front of the woman. Simon did not need to see the face. He knew that it was the butcher Arshak's.

The woman, who must have been the dead Circassian's wife, spit in the butcher's face. The small crowd started to laugh approvingly, but the new widow fell in fury upon the freak. To escape her blows, he covered his face with his hands, letting go of the head. The white hat flew off freak's hairless pate, and the severed head hit the ground with an inexpressible, horrifying sound. Men bolted away. The idiot stood motionless, sobbing loudly, the tears rolling down his muddy face. His dog let out a menacing growl.

Simon had had enough. In a daze, he slipped back into the ravine and dragged himself away, tripping over rocks and stumbling in and out of the eroded stream bed. Tears blurred his sight. He crossed the open space on the opposite side of the ravine and plunged into the undergrowth. All had collapsed around him: his hope to reach home, his fragile dream to see his father again—all destroyed. Now there was no stopping for the images of the bloody party that he had kept from his mind. He saw the pack of Circassians—the invited guests—and the sergeant with his zaptiehs—the hospitable hosts—with the prisoners as the main dish at the Harab Caravansaray. As furious as a charging bull, butcher Arshak crashes through the unsealed inn's door, wielding a huge log and, trying to get at the sergeant, swipes at the Circassians with all his might. He smashes their heads and ribs. The gendarmes hiding behind the mob of stricken dumb thugs shoot him and the giant falls on his knees. Encouraged killers, with shouts "Bismillah!" or "In the name of God!" press on him as wolves. They bend his powerful neck to the ground, and raise their axes and hatches over his head. Then they rob the corpses of the slaughtered prisoners and stuff the bloody clothes and shoes into the prepared sacks. Someone lifts the lifeless hand of Simon's father. It is the lame sergeant, armed with a knife. He is looking for "Lord" Pogos's gold ring with the black stone.

The Gold Ring with a Black Stone

Yesterday my daughter-in-law gave me a dressing-down. I forgot to buy basil for the dinner salad. Big deal! Even the best of us can slip up. Besides, every Armenian mistress should grow her own herbs. Look out the window, please; the entire lot is under tangerine trees. Now, these trees bring real money. Gone are grapes and apple trees. Can you believe that two dozen of these rather short trees may generate a year-round income for the family? People in northern Moscow and Leningrad are crazy for these fruits. So, there is not a place for even a small herb corner in our garden.

However, hand upon heart, for the first time my daughter-in-law turned out to be absolutely right. I was in a hurry to talk with you and forgot about all small fry.

You do not have to worry; Simon was rescued. By a Kurd. His name was Bakro. Simon lived for four years with Bakro before he was reunited with Grandma and my mother, but I also want to tell you that his survival did not bring him normal life. Uncle Simon remained forever a broken, isolated person, filled with intense shame and guilt. He never married, and he often talked to himself. People usually took him for crazy. He was so obsessed with the time spent in the Harab Caravansaray and then in the mountains, that he could not stop thinking about all these things, you know. For example, he could not erase from his mind the image of his father's gold ring. While talking with men or when even walking down a street, he unwittingly stole glances at men's hands as if searching for this ring on their fingers. He could not control this, even with people he knew intimately.

I remember one day he came home out of breath from running. At the time, the end of 1919, Grandma, my mother, Haroutiun, Simon, and I—the only survivors in our family—were living together in "Lord" Pogos's tumbledown house. After the years of separation we managed to return under its roof, each of us in his own way. Uncle Simon was already a young man, but he and I understood each other better than anyone else. I had lost my childhood and, at the age of eight was not just a little girl any longer. Quite contrarily, Uncle Simon's mindset remained the same as that of a fifteen-year-old boy who was driven away from home by the Turkish gendarmes. So he came to me first with the shocking message. He had seen Topal Chavoush or the lame sergeant, that torturer and murderer, near the town's bazaar gate where the beggars and cripples gathered for alms. Before telling Haroutiun, who was quick with his fists, about this bastard, we decided to double-check the sergeant's identity.

We ran to the bazaar. Many frightening characters surrounded the square at the gate. From a distance, Uncle Simon indicated a man sitting on filthy rags. "Do not look at his eyes. Just look on his hand for the gold ring with a black stone. It has to be on it. It's definitely Topal Chavoush." Poor Uncle Simon. He believed he had seen the ring, but who would sit in such a place with a piece of gold on his hand? Slowly I passed the beggar, keeping my eyes to the ground. "*Para, para, parays sorlum var.**" The man held out his hand to me. There was no sign of a ring. I saw only dirty, blackened, trembling fingers.

Uncle Simon could not believe me. "It's him. I saw his eyes," he said repeatedly, as we stood for a long time in the piercing wind. Finally the beggar stood and snuffled off into the bazaar. "No, it's not him. The sergeant was lame in the left foot. How could I be mistaken?" asked my shaken uncle, weakly.

We returned home, cold and discouraged. Besides our small, white-hot stove, made from sheet metal by Haroutiun, we became lost in thought. Grandma, as usual, tinkered behind with simple housekeeping. She proffered us a field-basin with a few washed potatoes and saltcellar. The tin basin, slightly rumpled on the flanks, was perhaps left by the Turkish *askers* billeted in "Lord" Pogos's house. The china saltcellar, with two separate sections for salt and pepper, and little flying angels around the sides, was an object from our former life which had somehow been left in the house.

Uncle Haroutiun took a seat near us. With his sharp pen-knife, he sliced the potatoes into thin circles and sprinkled them with the coarse, gray crystals (I have never since seen such dirty but unusually tasty salt) and set the slices in rows on the scorching surface of the oven around the vent pipe. Then my mother sat down next to me. I livened up. My

---

* "Money, money, I need money!" (Turk.)

favorite time began. The baked slices came off the metal easily. I burned my fingers and lips . . . and ears as I listened to the tales and adventures, new and old.

To make a long story short, can you imagine what Grandma did to stop her son's obsession? She "found" the ring. Yes, the same gold ring with a square black stone. Years later, my mother told me that Grandma, who knew the ring very well, described it to a jeweler and had him make one. She sacrificed a pair of gold coins from the cache she had hidden before the exile. Of course, she made up a story for Uncle Simon—that she had recognized his father's ring in a jeweler's store and bought it because the ring was a family heirloom filled with memories. The family decided that Simon should wear the ring to signify that he was the last to see "Lord" Pogos.

At the time, I believed the story headlong, as did childish Uncle Simon. At first, he was very agitated, but then he became more relaxed. He seemed relieved for a while, but not two or three weeks had passed before he again started seeing things. Now my uncle claimed he had seen Babken Mangasarian. He insisted that he had distinctly noticed Babken's slight figure and mincing gait crossing the square near the port. Simon ran toward him joyously, but the figure disappeared in one of the narrow crooked streets off the square.

Grandma tried to bring her son to reason by saying that if Babken had survived, he would, first of all, without fail, have come to visit her, "Lord" Pogos's wife and his customer of many years. Simon instead was merely discouraged. *How could he have lost sight of Babken in that street?* "But it was him, mayrig-djan," whispered my uncle Simon. "This time I am sure. Babken is so smart. He could have escaped. Moreover, in the Harab Caravansaray, he promised to follow me. I am sure he twisted the lame sergeant and his zaptiehs around his little finger."

Impatient Haroutiun left the house heatedly; Uncle Simon was incurable.

Well, nobody really could knock that nonsense out of his head. Nobody could bring back his lost soul. Even the *aralezes.*

Aralez? Oh, of course, you have no idea about that creature. Only very few old Armenians like me may know the *aralezes.* I heard about them from my grandmother, and she maybe from her grandmother.

In very ancient times, when Armenians were not yet Christians, they believed in many various gods, goddesses, and evil spirits. It was an interesting time because instead of one God people had many—major mighty gods, some less important ones, and also very simple ones who were at the others' beck and call—and everyone of them was assigned to his own department. It's now that people bombard our only God with their requests, rarely vital. They usually divert his attention with their cheap wishes.

So the aralezes were not major gods, but they possessed some specific power. They could revive people fallen in battle by licking their wounds.

Do you know why some such ancient stories are so truthful? It is because of the details! Aralezes were sacred dogs; they had doggy faces and maybe tails, and also wings because they lived in the heavens. But you see, people have always known that a dog's licks are indeed a good cure for bruises and scratches. People say, "Don't worry, your wound will be healed soon as one on a dog."

In Armenian, to lick is "liezel." So the ending of the word "aralez" shows how those gods performed their duties. One can understand the first part of their name, "ara," as coming from the Armenian word "aryun," that means blood. However, I prefer to believe that it comes from another of our old legends: Ara the Handsome. He was an Armenian king. His nearest neighbor was Queen Shamiram, who ruled the powerful Assyria after she got rid of her talentless husband. She was a woman in the prime of life and she needed a deserving man. The exciting news about the very good looking king of Armenia reached her ears. Shamiram sent her ambassadors with wonderful presents and the word of her love. Unfortunately, Ara, very handsome but apparently a bad diplomat, did not return her love. Now, we cannot know exactly why he did it. Maybe he was already married, or perhaps he just knew the gossip that Shamiram had hairy legs. Nobody knows. Armenians always proved to be bad in diplomacy, anyway. Importantly, as a result Shamiram went to war in which Ara was killed. When Shamiram saw what she had lost, grief-stricken, she prayed and besought to those half-human, half-canine aralezes to fly down and revive her fallen love.

Of course, he did not raise from the dead. It's just a beautiful legend. Also, my young and handsome Uncle Simon did not ever return to a normal life . . .

Oh, here is my son, Nishan, coming after me. He must be wondering why I am not in my regular places. Ara, Shamiram, and their matters, they made us to forget about the present. Let's return to our time and our daily bread.

Grandma Iughaper Against the Fate

May I ask you, my diligent recorder, what you are going to do with all of this scribbling? You see, my son is worried about your vacation time being spent in such a way. My Nishan said to me yesterday: "Mayrig, these people came to our town and rented an apartment in our house to have fun, to enjoy the sun and the sea, and you are depressing them with old, tiresome stories. Stop telling these stories! Please!"

He also said: "What will change, Mama, if one more person becomes familiar with your dead relatives? At one time, you tried to tell me about them. So what? I just became needlessly pained by those terrors. Once again, I urge you to stop telling those tales. Let people live their own lives."

I know what he meant. Indeed, such sick stories can disturb the heart. Instead of thinking about their own business, people suddenly begin to ponder the past and question how this or that could happen. Anyway, what are you going to do with these notes?

You will try to publish this story?! You are sure that it should be done? So, not only you, but many others will be disturbed, won't they? This will really make my son glad.

Jokes aside, now I must do my utmost to be honest. For instance, last week, in a flash of temper, I mentioned that the Tachiks did not drink coffee. So, they did. Of course they drank coffee, just like all the other folks in our old country. I was simply indignant. Why people do say, namely Turkish coffee? Why not Arabic or Greek coffee? All for them, always in their favor. Lucky tribe.

It's unbelievable that they lost the war with Russia, but ended up with a big piece of Russian territory. The loser got the winner's land. Fortune smiled on them! As the war was ending, Lenin started the revolution and overthrew the czar, Nicolas. He detested Nicolas because the czar's father had ordered the death of Lenin's terrorist brother. Immediately, when Lenin came to power, he fell out with the czar's allies in France and England. Instead, he made friends with the Turks, Russia's old enemy. Lenin gave Kemal Pasha or Ataturk (the

Father of the Turks) the lands where the Armenians had lived from time immemorial. Funny; those lands were in Russia's possession for a long time, even before the war. Kemal Pasha played with Lenin in the guise of a revolutionary. Nobody can deny that the Tachiks are the best diplomats in the world.

At that time, my Uncle Haroutiun was with the Russian army and grieved over the revolution which ruined all the last expectations of Armenians . . .

Yes, my dear, you are right. This is not so important, Arabic coffee, Armenian, or Turkish; the major thing is that it must be good coffee. Anyway, here they are, your cup of the Armenian coffee and the continuation of my story.

During the time when Uncle Simon, saved by Bakro, was suffering of shock and fever in the Bakro's summer tent, there was a last family council at his home in the town. It was very quiet and brief. The council just of two people. Only Grandma Iughaper and my mother, Pietzar, remained in the family house. They were sitting in the big room above Grandfather's shop. It looked out onto the street in front and, through the veranda, onto the garden in the backyard. My brother, Hakop, and I were sleeping in our room on the third floor. Perhaps we dreamed of something pleasant and funny that last night in the family home. We did not understand the approaching end of our world.

Sevouk, our black, dumpy mongrel, did not understand anything, either. For the first time in his life, he was allowed to lie on the carpet at the threshold of the big room. This dog, Grandfather's pet, earnestly destroyed rats all around the neighborhood and, in the morning, when he reported back to his master, he would lay out their corpses on the veranda stairs. Grandma endlessly reprimanded him not to do that, but Sevouk's passion for his master's approval was stronger than his guilt in the face of Grandma's admonitions.

The deportation order had been declared by the criers in our town. Since almost all the Armenian men had been destroyed, it only concerned women and children. Informants with gendarmes went around to the Armenian houses and notified the inhabitants that nobody would be allowed to sell any belongings. To some households the Turks offered the option of converting to Islam to avoid exile. If not, the Armenians were given a couple days to arrange for departure.

The two women sat in silence, until Grandma shook off her deep pensiveness. "They have wiped out our men. Now they want to do the same with us. Indeed, why would the Turks tolerate the presence of Armenian women and children in this land; to be thorns in their eyes?" She turned to her daughter. "Out of sight, out of mind! They want us dead. They want us dead, and we must come through. The zaptiehs will whip us up until we give up, but we will go lightly clad, and must be prepared to hold up to the end of the route. They will deprive us of water and bread; we must learn to subsist by eating roadside herbs and drinking dew. Our former countrymen want us dead, but we will not stand for that; we shall both scramble out and return to our home. Amen!"

Grandma resolutely stood on her feet. "Let's prepare for that, my daughter. Each hour now is worth its weight in gold. To that point, we shall begin with the gold."

Grandmother Iughaper divided the family money into two piles. One pile contained the gold coins, which she put in a clay jug. Then she took out two old, worn dresses, two dark shawls, and four canvas sacks. The smaller coins from the second pile were sewn into the folds of the clothes and tucked into the corners of the sacks.

"Don't forget all the places where we have sewn the coins," Grandma said to my mother, "so along the way we can pull them out quickly, a little at a time. Even if some coins will be taken away, there is a chance some will remain with us."

"What about the coins in the jug? Should we put the jug in a sack or someplace else?" inquired my mother.

"Pietzar, dear, I told you that we shall return home. I am sure of it and I know, at that time, we shall need money. That is why we should hide this jug here. Help me, my daughter."

Grandma carried the jug, holding it across the bottom, and ordered my mother to kindle the oil lamp and follow her to the garden. At the veranda wall, my mother was to pick up a spade and carry it to the fig tree. They set the jug and spade down and walked to the fence where there was a water gate. Together, mother and daughter used their strength to lower the heavy plate. Then they returned to the jug of gold.

The brook quickly disappeared from its channel, its habitual bubbling cut short. Grandma tucked the bottom of her skirt into her belt and stood barefoot in the stream. She dug a pit for the jug, easily carving out the wet soil from the bed. Sevouk tried to help her, but was immediately driven away. Pietzar kept the lamp above Grandma's shoulder. By the time the brook's low murmur had been completely interrupted, the dark garden was enveloped in silence. Shadows of Grandma's bowing and straightening figure flickered about the grounds and trees. Although there was a high stony fence around the garden, my mother shook and her hands trembled.

"Don't be afraid, my girl," Grandma kept repeating. "There is nothing to be afraid of now. The real fright is ahead."

She lowered the heavy jug into the prepared pit, filled it with the stones she had unearthed, and covered it very thoroughly with dirt. Finally, she trampled down the little mound. Then the women opened the water gate, and water ran again through the channel. The stream began to sing as if nothing had happened.

Grandma Iughaper was satisfied. No trace remained of her work. She sat on the low bench under the fig tree and washed her feet.

"Mayrig, please, let's go inside. The children are alone," my mother pleaded. Grandma looked at her with incomprehension. "This was his favorite place."

Then she dried her feet, and they went into the deserted house.

Inside, there was no time for sad reflection. Grandmother made my mother sit down in the garment shop on the first floor, and sew wide straps into the sacks, so it would be easy to carry a pair of them by placing the straps across the shoulders. My mother could not understand why they needed to do this, since they had a coach and a strong horse in the barn.

"We are not going to use the coach at all. I'm sure you will agree with me. Consider this: if we decide to take our coach, we must hire a coachman. At this point, I cannot find a single reliable man among the Turks, Kurds, Circassians, or even Lazes. Any of them would be glad to have the opportunity to throw us out of the coach and disappear with all our belongings. What will we do then?" inquired Grandma to my short-sighted mother, who was nodding her head. "The coach with many goods inside will be easier prey than these sacks and the old clothes we are wearing."

"Since we have decided to return home—after all—we must brace ourselves for every conceivable type of Tachiks' perfidy." Grandma was leading her daughter to the most difficult part of her plan. "We need to be able to walk a long way and, if needed, to run and hide somewhere.

Could you do that in a coach? The thugs will turn their attention first upon the coaches and carriages."

My mother nodded her head once more. "I am worried only about the children. How can little Nargiz and Hakop walk with us? It is impossible to carry them along with these sacks of provisions. We need the coach just for them."

"Pietzar-djan," Grandma began gingerly, "we should leave them here with . . ."

"For God's sake! What are you talking about, mayrig? I will never part with my little ones. Wherever they are, I must be with them."

"Pietzar, my heart, let me take away your anguish; do you really think I did not consider this? We do not have any choice. If we take the children, we shall die, all of us."

"Oh yes, better to die than to bear such things. *Astvatz! Astvatz!** Why did you leave us? Nishan, my soul-mate, how could you leave me? For whom have you abandoned your children and wife, my beloved Nishan?" My mother sobbed. Time was flowing away.

"Die! You cannot bear this ordeal? You want death? So take it!" Iughaper was standing over Pietzar's head. In her outstretched hand was a sharp knife. "Go upstairs and kill your little Nargiz and Hakop, then kill yourself." The tear-stained young woman recoiled. "The Tachiks will be happy. They will laugh. You want to see them laughing? I don't. I already told you that we shall survive, in spite of their will."

Suddenly, Sevouk ran to the shop front door. The dog listened attentively. Pietzar leapt to her feet, wiping her face. A scratching sound came from outside. Grandma Iughaper watched the dog. He sat silently, his tail moving from side to side.

"You see, Pietzar, Sevouk is not growling and the hair on his nape is as usual. Clever dog. He is showing us that it is a friend. I know, it is Nikos. The Greek has come for the children as promised." With these words, Grandma quickly opened the solid door. A strange figure slipped into the shop. The women hardly recognized Nikos, dressed as a tramp. He wore a soiled, torn robe, belted with a bit of cord, and the likeness of a turban pulled over his head. In agitation, or perhaps, in fear, he shifted from one bare foot to the other.

"*Kalisperasas kiria Iughaper, kiria Pietzar,*"** whispered the street wanderer. "Sorry for the delay. The whole town is packed with bands of arrant rogues and thugs. I crept through the backyards to get here."

* "God!" (Arm.)

** "Good evening, Mrs. Iughaper, Mrs. Pietzar." (Greek)

"Carrion crows fly together," said Grandma. A bead of mucous hung under Nikos's nose. *The man is really scared,* she thought, as she invited him to sit down and catch his breath. *At the same time, how brave he is to leave his home and family and come here.*

However, Nikos would not sit. He was in a hurry to finish his dangerous mission before sunrise. With pangs of memories reflected in his black eyes, he looked around the shop. "Can you use our coach, dear Aristotle?" Grandma used the man's real name.

"No, kiria Iughaper. It will do too much noise. All these bastards will come running. You can see, dear; I even came barefoot."

"But we would like to give this coach to you. Leave it at your house. Also, you can take all you want from here—rugs, china, bed linen, and . . ."

"No! No! Please don't offer such things. Of course, my wife, you know her, she is a simple woman and would not be averse to showing off all these beautiful things, but in our poor house, such riches will only bring the fiends' anger upon us."

"At least, take my ring. You can sell it in need," insisted Grandma. Her daughter also tore off her wedding ring and begged the man to take it, slipping it into his hands. She was dissolving in tears.

Nikos indignantly shook his head. The improvised turban slipped down over one ear. Despite the women's reproaches, he responded with only one phrase: "Do not forget, dears, you are giving me the most precious thing in your home: your children."

Nikos left, carrying Hakop and me, still in our serene sleep, in the wheelbarrow which usually was used to deliver the sold rugs and carpets to "Lord" Pogos's customers. The deflated women lost the power to continue preparing for the deportation. Alone in a big house, which had quickly cooled down without loved ones, clinging to each other for warmth and comfort, they tried to sink into sleep.

In the morning, a loud knock at the front door, shouts from the street, and Sevouk's bark raised the women to their feet. When, under this incessant noise, they opened the door, two zaptiehs burst into the shop. A young police officer followed them. A brand new uniform harmoniously sat on his well-proportioned figure. His face with youthful fluff and a small, closely cropped mustache expressed disdain and aversion.

On the officer's imperceptible signal, the other figure came a little forward from behind him, rustled something, and again went back respectfully. An informer. Iughaper looked at him with amazement, the blood rushing to her face. She could not believe her own eyes. *How could he, especially he, bring them to my home? How bold he is to come here,* thought my grandmother in disarray. The first time Pietzar had seen her in such confusion, but it very quickly changed to disgust.

"Tailor Aleksanian's family . . . so then, how many of yours are here?" asked the officer with artificial indifference, looking around the quite impressive furnishing of "Lord" Pogos's shop. Sevouk began to growl. The officer and the gendarmes gazed at him with interest. Apparently they were surprised by this single act of resistance. "*Kuchuk kopek, amma pek darghin*"* They did not know the power of the dumpy's jaws.

"Look," the suddenly livened-up young Turk exclaimed, addressing his subordinates. "Their dog, an Armenian dog, is barking not at us, but at the informer, an Armenian too. *Korkak khalk*."** The youth looked at the women with a grin, and the gendarmes began to guffaw after him.

The figure behind him hushed the dog and then hissed to Iughaper: "Hey, woman, shut that dog's mouth." Grandma took Sevouk in her arms and explained to the officer: "The dog is barking because he is smelling a rat, a big rat." The gendarmes roared with laughter as if they had understood the hint. With these words, Grandma passed by them to the entrance door, put Sevouk out onto the street, and closed the door. Then she answered the young officer: "Now, *Zabit* Effendi, there are four of us remaining in this house: I, my daughter and her two children." He was pleasantly impressed with her perfect Turkish, which she had learned sometimes associating with the wives of her husband's high-ranking customers. None of those women remembered her in these hard days, but Grandma contrived to mention a few of their names. Although the youth again took a haughty tone, she succeeded, for a while, in excluding the embittered informer from the conversation.

The officer, with a triumphant air, took an official proclamation out of his service jacket and read out some excerpts out loud: ". . . in attempt of Armenians to destroy the peace and security of the Ottoman state . . . they have to be sent away . . . Armenians forbidden to sell their property and belongings which they are unable to carry with them . . . if anybody will shelter or give food and assistance to Armenians, such person will be sent before court for execution. . . ."

---

* "Small dog, but very angry." (Turk.)
** "Slave people." (Turk.)

"Zabit Beyeffendi," Grandma moved her hand around. "We as very humble servants of the Sublime Porte understand your order and will leave all these things as they are." Obviously, he was a newly fledged officer, perhaps, the most junior, and Grandma, each time she addressed him despairingly flattered him. She was ready to empty all rooms only for that to get rid of the zaptiehs as soon as possible. She and my mother were on pins and needles due to the fear of being asked to show the children.

The gendarmes, their eyes shining lustfully, examined the reception room with the "Lord" Pogos's collection of rugs and the shelves still filled with rolls of fabrics and then the tailor room with his favorite Singer sewing machines. They touched the weighty rugs and rolls, and spun the nickel-plated wheels of the machines. Only the presence of their serious chief restrained them from committing immediate robbery. The youth was extremely interested by the bronze ink-pot on "Lord" Pogos's desk. Its cover was adorned by a skillfully made figure of an eagle with outstretched wings. "He is discerning the bird like a child. He is just a boy, approximately my Levon's age. God, where is my boy? Is he alive? Or does he lie somewhere unburied?" The woman sighed, unable to contain herself. The young Turk put aside the knick-knack. In a minute of unbearable silence, the informer turned out to be near him and whispered something in his ear, after which the newcomers went up to the big room.

There Grandma tried to divert the gendarmes' attention, showing in detail all the valuable things which had to be left in the house. The informer's grimaces scared her. In a desperate move, she suddenly ordered her daughter: "I am hearing a noise in the children's room. They have awoken. Go up and dress them. Meanwhile I will show the Zabit Beyeffendi what kind of a coach and horse we are leaving behind us."

On the bending feet, my mother went up to the empty room where we were sleeping before Nikos took us to his home. Grandma managed to take away the gendarmes and the informer to the courtyard. He was not keen to leave the house, but he could not say a word to stop the officer, who had a burning desire to see the coach and the horse.

In the stable, my shrewd grandmother asked the officer about our horse's points. "*Kuvvetly at, guzeldir haivan*!"* admitted the youth. His

---

* "Strong horse, magnificent animal!" (Turk.)

mates loudly agreed, yet the informer could only make a distrustful face. So, when Grandma cordially suggested they be driven by the coach instead of walking under the sunbeams around the Armenian quarter, they accepted without a moment's thought. She even had the courage to ask the officer for a piece of paper certifying this requisition.

"*Hayde, kapuyu ach,*" commanded the officer sitting with his zaptiehs in the coach. "*Ishidiyormusun, boyuk sichan?*"* he shouted at the dumbstruck informer. The gate onto street was opened and the coach departed. The informer began to run aside, clinging for the coach handrail. Grandma only managed to say to him: "Farewell, Missak!"

The beautiful ink-pot disappeared with the guests. Only a spot of ink that had been splashed out remained on the wall. The women let in Sevouk. The blackie became flighty and has lashed himself by the tail right up his shiny nose and happy eyes. He felt that his dog's small sins have been forgiven and he could continue to enjoy the recently granted privilege of staying inside the house, where many places smelled so entrancingly of his absent master.

"Have you seen, mayrig, how Sevouk did growl on the informer? Isn't it strange, how the dog was able to recognize the traitor, he has seen the man never before, hasn't he?"

Pietzar stood still. She looked at her mother. An idea, a terrifying surmise simultaneously stabbed both the women.

"Oh, then, he has been here before. Obviously with the other gendarmes. In that black day when they took away father and brother Simon. That's why Sevouk growled at this man; our faithful Blackie remembered all that happened here on that day, in our absence." My mother was talking, taking looks at Grandma whose silence only confirmed the story.

"My God! And this one also bears the name, Armenian. This man could come here twice, his snake eyes not at all look down, his stone heart not at once was embarrassed . . ."

"Embarrassed? Of course not. This man does not know embarrassment, he never felt it. He was just very angry when he realized that he could not embarrass me. However, I am almost sure that he made our boy Simon be driven away with the men . . ."

"Mother, do you think he was making all that because of you, out of spite? Why?"

"Because many years ago he was my first, my unfortunate groom-to-be."

---

* "Go and open the door. Do you hear, big rat?" (Turk.)

Emine

They never told me. . . . Grandma and my mother never told me . . . never told how exactly they survived the route, the death march from the cozy seaside town to the lifeless sands of Syrian deserts.

The total exodus: the draining of blood. Groups of Armenian women and children from all around the country merged into streams, then into floods which flowed down, through the entire body of country, straight to the end. . . .

They crossed the mountain passage to Tokat. The place was lavishly fertilized by the flesh and blood of the Armenian soldiers. They have been disarmed by their Turkish comrades-in-arms and brought here to build the military road. *Did my mother feel that she was shuffling on her husband Nishan's bones?* That which had remained of the calm, reserved man who knew five languages and liked his books. *Did Grandma notice her son Levon's skull, gleaming on the roadside?* The only remains of the young, cheerful man who played drums and flute and already was looking for a bride. *How could these women climb the mountains on the route to Sivas and Kharberd? How could they escape the death in the cold waters of the Euphrates river?* There were so many women and children murdered and thrown into the water, and groups of disgraced girls who, binding the hairs together, had jumped into the river, that the Kharberd Bridge was dammed by their bodies and bloody water left for a long time a red mark on his piers.

They never told me details of that march. Sometimes they suddenly fell silent when I entered the room. Maybe they were ashamed of what had happened to them . . . but how do I know?

My head is spinning round. I am sick. These pictures are flying by my eyes. Very fast. Where are they from?

I feel giddy. I barely can see you, my dear. It is not good day for listening to my ravings. Open the window. It feels so hot, as if I am trailing by that road, too.

I am seeing the people drag themselves. Silent, they are passing by the cities and towns, leaving behind nameless villages. The columns of people are blazing new trails through the hills, rocks, thickets, and country wilderness.

Grandma Iughaper is pulling me by the hand. My mother is next to me. "Please, don't fall behind, Nargiz, my girl." But I know that I am not a little girl. I am a woman, a grown-up woman, tikin Nargiz. How did I come to be here, among these tacit, at their last gasp people. Darkness.

Now, new vision. Our column, like a very long caterpillar, creeps out from our town and leaves behind its shady cherry orchards and hazel groves. The marchers with bags and children on them or wheelbarrows move by us. Familiar faces and those I saw once. A long procession of the Armenians whom I have met during my entire life.

An open coach drives by us. I recognize the tear-stained face of the woman under wide-brimmed hat and sad faces of three girls near her. They must be Rouben Shaghbazian's wife, Susanne, and their daughters: Nelli, Noyemi, Naane. They do not see my grandma and my mother who walk with their heads down. One of them weakly waves at me by her white hand. A man sitting on the coach-box turns round and winks at me. It is the zaptieh from my bad dreams. *Am I dreaming?* Is it the old, red-mug zaptieh who guarded me and my brother, Hakop, near the pier? I want to stop the coach. I know all beforehand—I am not a little girl. "Do not ride with this coachman! Do not ride that way!" I am trying to cry, but nothing comes out of my dried-up throat. Grandma and my mother, for some reason, do not want to help me. They stubbornly go forward, looking down.

Now, I see the Shaghbazians crucified on the trampled down ground. Side by side, with tender, snow-white arms and thighs stretched, they look vacantly on the serene sky. Here they are, a few feet from each other: Nelli, Noyemi, Naane, and their mother, plump Aunt Susanne, husky voice frozen behind her quitened lips. Grandma carries me further. "Do not look, Nargiz-djan, do not look."

Am I a little Nargiz? Or a ragged girl Emine? Or an old woman, tikin Nargiz Zhamkochian? Now, I am getting confused—even more. The sun drives me crazy. It is the beginning of August. I sweat. Grandma helps me to continue the pace. She urges on my mother, too. But my great-grandparents, "Lord" Pogos's parents, come to a halt. I am noticing them in the column near us. Stout "Lord" Pogos's father cannot breathe; he sits flabby on a roadside stone. Great-grandmother stops by him, tiny as a sparrow, with small bundle in hands. She is waiting as two gendarmes hurry to them. I know what will happen. In terror I hopelessly move my feet. I cannot find my grandma near me. Perhaps she is already ahead of me. I am unable to make any advance.

Another gendarme slowly approaches me. I try to go with other people, but I fail. The gendarme grins. Here he is lifting his rifle. I am covered in sweat, and he begins to guffaw. Now, instead the rifle, he is holding a stick. It is again the same gendarme from the square near the pier, the laughing coachman of the left-behind Shaghbazians. He has harrowed them and now came for me. He lifts his stick; I press myself to the burning sand, I close my eyes and . . .

Have I woken up? How has it happened that you are here? How long have you been sitting here, near the bed of such silly woman like me?

Aha! So you could listen to her miserable muttering.

I do not feel so good. I am really sick. It is because of the sun, its heat, and the sea's humidity. About every summer there are a few such terrible days when I cannot tolerate stuffiness. I take cool showers and then sit in a draft.

I know, I know perfectly well that it is absolute foolishness. Often after that I collapse in fever. I feel bad for my son's family, they have a really hard time with me. The only consolation is that they do not lend an ear to my gibberish.

You will not believe me, my dear, when the fever drives me mad, it usually drives me back to exactly the same place, the small square near the port pier. Again I am pressing myself to the burning sand. Once more time I am stubbornly crawling away from the hipe of children burnt by the merciless sun. However, today I saw myself in that column of deported women and children. Really sick imagination!

What did happen then at the dusty square at the pier? Well, at that time a *mollah* happened to be near the square. He knew my grandfather very well. Both men liked getting deep into lofty matters together. Mollah's gaze from under the round spectacles hooked me, nestled up against the ground, like a little animal still trying to grasp onto his life. The mollah told the women gathered at the square that it will be a great shame for all of them if the grandchild of such kind person as "Lord" Pogos lost her life like a useless puppy. He prompted the women to divert the zaptieh's attention, and when they had succeeded, he snatched me and ran away, covering me with his wide black robe.

My mollah—don't remember his name—when he brought me in his home said to his wife: "We had three kids, this girl will be the fourth. Take care of her before somebody come for her from Pogos Effendi."

I just mentioned that I don't remember his name. "The mollah" or "our mollah"—that's how my family used to call him. I am also unable to recall something about my life in his home as well as in the Greek Nikos's home. Maybe it is because those happened to be short periods of time. After two or three weeks of living with Nikos's family, Hakop and I were found on the street. However, neither Grandma nor my mother ever said a bad word about Nikos. The man had his own kids and it was really mortally dangerous pursuit to continue hiding the Armenian children. By the way, Tachiks did not spare the Greeks, either. After the Armenians, their turn came. When my mother and grandmother returned to our town there was no one who could tell them what had happened with Nikos, his clamorous, grumbling wife, and his children, big-nosed as their father. The terrible time had swept them away as surf does after a big storm with articles forgotten on the beach.

Shortly after, the mollah's wife died. Poor man, he could not take care of his three children and gave them out to kinsfolk for a while. He carted me away to his acquaintances in a Turkish village, on condition that somebody will come for me from "Lord" Pogos. The man truly believed in that and it happened. However, before that, I had to live four years as Emine. The Turks of that village gave me this name, although most often they called me simply a giavour *kiz*, i.e., infidel girl.

Strangely, I remember my life in this wretched village with some latent tenderness. Perhaps because of the absolute freedom I had there. I always was completely on my own. I had to work every day, always hungry as a wolf, chilly, and dirty, from my bare feet to my tousled hair. My owners, without any ceremony, could make a slip on the back of my head. They did that without any particular malicious anger. I am sure they merely were treating me like one of their goats or sheep. In general, I also was left to find food by myself. If Emine had died, not a single soul would have been concerned. However, this giavour kiz was strong, tenacious of life. I was sick only once. Who knows what has happened with me. I just was laying in my corner . . . I remember only that when I came to my senses, I took my legs from under a short sheep's skin (my blanket), and was surprised that they became so leggy and so thin, like two straws. Initially, I thought those were someone's else legs. I was afraid to stand on them.

As you see, I lived these childhood years as a weed in a field. I was among people, while at the same time absolutely at my own accord. Nobody tried to pry in my feelings, nor devoted a single piece of attention to me, and I paid them back by living there as an alien. They were quite right calling me "infidel girl." The girl with the Turkish name, Emine, lived those years like a butterfly pupa.

At daybreak, I drove my little flock of goats and sheeps to the nearest pasturable slope. I tied a small cloth bag with newly soured yogurt to my belt. While I ran after those willful goats, and stupid sheep who fecklessly followed these yellow-eyed rogues, cool liquid seeped out from the bag and flowed down my leg. When puffed and tired we rested somewhere on the sheltered spots. I untied the bag and slowly emptied it by using the rolled leaves of mint or another edible herb, carefully biting off pieces of separately kept flat bread. I then turned out the bag and continued the pleasure, clearing away the remains of yogurt by the fingers. Not one piece of bread or drop of yogurt would be left for the dog, accompanying me in the mountains.

No, it was not the second Sevouk. I remembered our family's Blackie, but I could not call this one Sevouk because it was big light-browny shepherd dog, and already had a Turkish name—Arslan—which means "Lion."

So, during the work, Arslan had to feed himself. The yogurt in the bag was enough only for Emine. However, sometimes, during the sunny afternoons, when small grey fish with short mustaches gathered under the shadow of mossy boulders in the stream, I contrived to catch them with my hands. At that time my head got scorched and the feet swallowed after cold water. The following feast made worth while. I threw a few barbels to Arslan, wagging his tail. The others I grilled on a bonfire. Little Emine was able to do so many adult things. I never had matches, but could handle tinder and flint. As a gratitude, Arslan let me lie down near him, when a heavy shower drove us in a cave or under a crag. If two lie together then they have heat. One cannot be warm alone.

We spent a lot of days together. Interminable days. Every one, from its daybreak to sunset, contained a series of very important happenings and unexpected independent discoveries: a loss of a lamb, getting stuck in a cleft, and a tryout of unfamiliar black berries on lengthy thorny twigs, or a sense of puzzled disappointment and chagrin when looking at the beautiful, colorful, round stones from the stream bed, quickly fading under sunbeams just in my hand; then bathing in warmed dams, followed by finding frightening black spots, birthmarks, on my smooth girl's belly—the everyday adventures which alternated by sudden periods of serenity, when everything around, and white clouds, and big lone trees up to their smallest leaf, became stiff in some benumbingness, and even larks and grasshoppers fell silent for a minute as if they felt the grand significance of that moment, and my biblical animals stopped to nibble grass and fixed their gaze upon nowhere, as well as Arslan who stretched out near me with his heavy head on his front paws, staring at the same invisible point far off.

All around was prepared for a revelation. However nothing happened. Apparently, the little girl Emine could not hear. It was such a great time for reminiscing about something innermost. A remitted opportunity. A lost chance.

Sometimes I, that little girl, noticed a sheep flock above me, a flight of milky-white fleecy clouds in clear sky. I craned my neck toward the sky. *Who is the shepherd that drives this folk? Does he see me from there?*

Eh-eh, my patient listener! Instead of getting some important find, I was forgetting my native language, and dear faces were fading within me. By the end of those shepherd years the town girl Nargiz completely dissolved into Emine. I spoke only Turkish, as everybody around me. Even the dog, Arslan, the goats and sheep spoke that language. Silly folk; they did not understand the Armenian commands.

I converted images of my mother and little brother, the two whom I most used to play, into small primitive dolls made by myself. I recreated them as two faceless figurines, pieces of the intricately formed roots of heather or maybe fragments of the gnarled oak branches. Hidden in a secluded place, they amused me one entire summer. Then the fall rains carried them away, and Emine was all alone. And at last, but much later, a rescuer came for her from "Lord" Pogos.

Scraps of the Old Dress

Not so many days of your vacation remain, my dear.

Oh, just a week! So, I have lost a couple of precious days not talking with you because of my banal fever. Getting old is no picnic. However, be condescending, please, I need to finish my story. If you pledge, don't hedge. Know that saying?

At least, I must tell you how I was found in the Turkish village and brought back to my family. Actually, to the few survivors of the family.

It was a regular day, although not exactly. I wasn't out with my sheep, and it was crucially important that I was present in the village at this particular day. Thanks to the village mollah who taught local children to pray. He took me into his barn with the other ragged fellows. The man was a hadji, meaning that he had made a pilgrimage to Mecca and my owners wouldn't go against him. That is why they let me spend the working time by learning "*La illaha een Allah, Mohammed rasul Allah*."*

The barn door opened. My mistress entered and said some words to the priest. I remember them as if it were just today:

"*Giavour kyzin nene gialmush*."**

With a wild animal's flair I understood that somebody had come for me who wanted to take me somewhere. Of course, I had no idea about that somebody with the strange name: "grandmother." A confused little girl, I fell on the earthen floor at the feet of my Tachik mistress and begged her not to give me to a giavour. By that time I was Emine and no longer considered myself an Armenian. The village children behind my back were giggling at me.

Grandmother Iughaper began to talk with me in Armenian, and I replied in Turkish: "Don't want to go with you. Go away." She was silent and only looked at me. In the evening, before the sunset, I knelt and prayed to Allah, and she did not say a word.

---

* "Allah is only God and Mohammad is his prophet." (Moslem sacral phrase)

** "The grandmother of the infidel girl has come." (Turk.)

Nevertheless, Grandma got her way; in the morning we went to the town. My happy mistress accompanied us, riding an old, pensive donkey. Grandma had bought the woman's consent. My owner was tempted to return me in exchange for two pairs of used men's shoes, a few shirts, and a little money. The woman wanted to indulge her master, her stern husband. After all, it was a really good deal for them living in that dejected and indigent village. Usually, it was very hard to locate and bring back such Armenian children as me. The Turks did not let them go. For instance, my grandmother found also her grand-nephew. Three times she forced her way to the Turkish village where he was taken in after his entire family was slaughtered. She promised money and goods—everything she had, but the Turks of that village were deaf to her entreaties. They hid him and then began making threats to scare away my stubborn grandmother. Eventually she gave up. What could she do, even her somber persistence had an end.

That long trip to home. When I became tired, my Turk woman let me sit behind her on the hardy donkey. The donkey's back under the woman's broad, sprawled skirts was in a pungent sweat. The animal's gait reverberated in the endless, monotonous recitative of the rider. "We're riding, riding, riding. Down, down, down"—drawled the woman in anticipation of a good profit. The donkey was nodding its heavy head. Sometimes thorny lashes of blackberries scratched my bare feet. I glanced back: Grandma held the pace, always behind us, but not so far, often disappearing on the turns of serpentine road and catching up with us at the watering-places.

How did she do it? You see, as a matter of fact, she was not so old as grandmothers today. She was in her middle 40s. Also, she had proved that she was a tenacious walker. I mean, she survived the death march through mountains, rivers, and deserts.

No, I do not believe that some kind of excitement related to my rescue, joy or happiness—whatever you may call it—had inspired Grandmother Iughaper. It could be quite the contrary, just because I knew what words she had repeatedly drummed into my mother's head during their death march. My mother told them to me, unwillingly admitting their worth, like women hand down an old family recipe.

Then, during that deadly march, Grandmother Iughaper persistently admonished her daughter not to rely on hope or another inspirational, but rapidly wearing out means of survival. The very essence of her everyday exhortations directed to my passionate, volatile mother was that in their inhuman condition, the hope for survival, returning home, and seeing their children again could turn out to be like irons on their feet. Such a feeling could easily vanish with any step while witnessing more and more acts of the gendarmes' cruelty. The hope could melt away rapidly when there were nothing else around except the constant sufferings of the doomed victims. Grandma used to whisper to my mother, matching her words with her breathing: "Don't think about what will happen. Not after two days. Not today. Or even before the next stop. Divide up the route into pieces. There, a tree ahead. Let's make it together. Under the tree, stop for a second. Good girl. Lean on the trunk. Have a rest, Pietzar. Good girl. The gendarmes are busy . . . with the ones who dared to drop behind."

You are listening to me, but you maybe disagree with my grandma's words about hope. Yours is a natural reaction, I suppose a very human one, but only in the light of this current delightful day. We are both just sitting now in straw chairs, drinking coffee, and jabbering. Today, my grandmother's words seem so extraordinary to us. However, let's do not forget that she survived the march—one of a thousand—and made my mother do the same. After all, what Grandma had forecasted during that time all came true.

She outwitted their guards by saving a few gold coins for when a rare chance turned up, and she managed to harbour my exhausted mother in a friendly Kurdish village near Kharberd. Grandma continued her perilous journey much further. She walked with the wretched remnants of other dying away groups of Armenian women and children right up to Urfa. The menacing heat of the burning sands from the Syrian deserts where their lives were fated to end rolled up onto the city streets. The railway station square and the nearest alleys were filled with cadaverous figures; naked or covered with rags people were blindly awaiting the final transportation. The gendarmes almost abandoned their surveillance over the half-dead bodies. Only Grandmother Iughaper could not sit and wait in such a prostration. Beyond all her powers, she sneaked into a side alley and dragged her feet along. Iughaper was trying to find the house where she and her husband, "Lord" Pogos, spent a couple of days during their visit to Urfa. The house owner, also a rug dealer, sold to her husband, a camel-load of carpets. Both men thought they did a very good deal, so the rest time in Urfa was spent on entertainment. The Urfa merchant, Musa *Agha,* was found to be a devoted gourmet. Now, Iughaper feverishly strained every strength to find his house with familiar tile ornaments over the gate. Hard to believe, but she eventually found it before being caught by gendarmes or ordinary Turks, their voluntary assistants. She convinced this rich and powerful man that she would be his best cook, the most skillful he had ever had. Indeed, later, Musa Agha became fascinated by her dainty feasts. He used to invite his influential friends and officials to boast of his dinners. Grandma had to create a new dish almost every day to surprise her gourmet protector, and every such day was the day reconquered from the death. Her "kitchen tale" deserves a special time to be told.

My unbelievable grandma! Her frequent refrain, which she used after every battle with fate so merciless to her family, was: "Among all animals, man is the most hardy one. And that is his main misfortune." The more dangers she managed to escape, the more new ones seemed to arise. Grandma could not enjoy her triumphs, even a little, because she was always expecting the next blast at any moment. Her face maintained expression of clear understanding that an unjust game was being played with her and the family. It looked as if she were saying: "Want to try one more time? Well, I shall do my best again. I shall not surrender. But why us? We did not deserve such treatment."

Sorry, my dear, enthusiastic listener. You have not stopped my distraction from the story of my return, and I went astray too far. Obviously, you have realized that this old woman is not a good narrator.

No, no, no. Do not disclaim that. I do not remember well dates and names related to even very important events. When was Turkey defeated? I do not know exactly. When did I return home? In the end of summer or maybe in the autumn of 1919. I was a small girl. I remember what I saw, felt, or heard from my people. Now, my memory is a broken jug. The wine or, maybe, the sour vinegar is gone, and I am just trying to reconnect the jug's fragments. My fingers run over the pile of scraps. Suddenly some of the fragments sting me. . . .

Well, let's continue the story. Besides, that distraction line can make you feel that some time had passed, riding the donkey, and here we are, almost home. On the outskirts of our town, Grandmother bought a *simit* for me. I took one half of this bagel with poppy seeds and gave the second to my Turk woman. Grandma said nothing. The town turned its lights on. In amazement, I exclaimed to the woman in

Turkish: "Mother, look, the big village is on fire!" This time, Grandmother could not stand it: "*Shan lezy thogh!*"* Little Emine understood what the old woman meant.

When our short caravan entered the backyard of "Lord" Pogos's house, Uncle Simon noticed us from the veranda window and cried out: "Mairig, did you find her? Where is she?" A young woman in a white dress and with strangely very light skin, smiling eyes and soft hands, softer than newborn lamb wool, embraced me and moistened my face and arms with passing, redolent kisses. Grandma tried to hold her back: "Do not scare the child, Pietzar. Oh, how right I was leaving you here. With your inconsiderate gusts of emotion you would have ruined this deal. That's for sure." My mother loosened the embraces.

Here I did something that the adults would never forget and would retell many times with laughter and delight. They were all very consistent in describing my odd reaction to the impetuous "welcome home." After freeing myself from my gentle mother's hands, I deeply sighed, looked around, and made for the nearest bush of oleander. Behind the bush I pulled up my mercilessly lacerated dress and squatted for the minor call of nature. In suddenly secured silence the sound of the spurt was heard as a victorious overture.

In the morning, I woke up from a long sleep. Clean pillows and linen in my bed pleasantly cooled my body. It was only later that I found numerous darns all over the old and thinned-out bed linen, meticulously made by my mother.

By that morning, the Turk woman, previous owner of my body and soul, had already left. In great joy, due to my return and despite my grandmother's muttering and sarcasms, my mother and Uncle Simon awarded her with threads, ribbons, and laces into the bargain. In the afternoon, sage Grandma told me to put on my fantastic scraps, which I arrived in yesterday, and took me with my mother to a photographer. Now, I understand that Grandma intended not only to establish the fact of our reunification, but also to demonstrate our victory to that mysterious one who had designed and led the dreadful game for us. Sadly, she was completely unable to express herself through words or emotions as did my mother, overflowing with tears, smiles, kisses, and caresses. Had Grandma let herself speak she would have said: "*Djanes varvetz, mohir darav.*"**

---

* "Give up this dog's language!" (Arm.)
** "My soul burnt to the ground, only ashes remained." (Arm.)

The town's former photographer was slaughtered with "Lord" Pogos and other Armenian men in the same carnage at the Harab Caravansaray. The new owner of his pillaged studio, also an Armenian, from nobody knew where, with startled face and nervous hands, was ineffably glad to serve my terse grandmother. The man bustled around, clicking with his tongue and, as he glanced upon me, his eyebrows flew up like small birds. There was not enough light in his studio, so he led us out into the empty yard and arranged us just near the wall.

Here, I have brought this photograph: chip of the past, my grandmother's unspoken reproach and the inaudible outcry of her rebellion. Look at it; seeing once is better than hearing ten times. Is it really a picture of the lucky winners of the greatest prize? No one among us even slightly resembled a victor who had received her life back.

Unfortunately, our frequent wanderings and time itself have left dents on the photo surface. However, you can see my decrepit dress. It consisted of maybe ten separate pieces. The original base was almost gone and its remains were buried under the new additions which I found here, there and everywhere. Like a snail I always carried my greasy dress on me, fitting in new pieces of any (even in the slightest degree) appropriate materials. There were scraps of a holey bag for flour, a men's garment sleeve, and even a sheepskin which I adjusted in the back side of the dress. Some parts of that "shell" were linked to each other with various kinds of strings.

After the studio, Grandmother burnt this dress in our backyard. Rich, black smoke rose for a moment, accompanied by the crackles of burning insects.

Turkey, 1919. My grandmother, Iughaper (sitting), my mother, Pietzar, and I, in my old dress. You may call us "the survivors" but definitely not "the winners."

Adults' Secrets

Excuse me, generously, but I recommend that you do not go to the beach today. I know that it is your last swimming day here. However, do not go.

Why? Just because you and your noticeable wife and kids would pass through the streets near the central plaza. The guys who have mass meetings at that place are becoming more and more rampant; as always, the people's spiteful madness begins with their foolish words. Just this morning, my son told me that at yesterday's meeting of these town bawlers, some Georgians beat up an Abkhazian man. Or quite the reverse. It really doesn't matter. But now, the insulted party is eager to pay the offenders in their own coin.

Do not understand me wrongly, my dear. My advice has nothing to do with your staying at home and listening to my story. Honestly, I care more about your safety . . . and also know that even some very simple, negligible deed can lead to fateful consequences. Like it or not, our deeds are pregnant with the after-effects.

Yes, of course, we also can have an unexpected luck.

Talking about the luck, when my grandmother and mother returned to their town, shortly to be joined with Uncle Simon, they all were sure that the number "three" had become the allotted surviving quota for our family. They were told by a Turkish neighbor about the Armenian children being drowned near the port pier. This woman had heard from some others that "Lord" Pogos's grandchildren had been seen in that group. There really remained nobody whom my folk could ask about me. The Greeks were gone. The Armenians remaining in the town were those who, at the time of deportation, had chosen to be converted into Turks. My family did not mix with them.

So, one day, my women decided to go to *hammam.* Since their return they had avoided it. Firstly, it was far from the home and, besides, there were no familiar faces around to gossip at odd moments, as in the good old times. Anyway, they went. Native cleanness overcame sad feelings. Reaching the hammam they bumped into an old friend, the mollah, who, four years ago, had saved my life. The women and the man fell into each other's arms and burst into tears. The mollah was in even worse shape than the women: a long widowhood, indigence and several illnesses had stolen up on him and had plagued his face. Only his kind eyes were still shining brightly from under familiar round spectacles with cracked glass.

*"Dagh dagha kavushmaz insan insana kavushur,"** the mollah could only say.

"You, see, Effendi, there were seventy of our clan in this town. You knew them. Now we are only three who remain." Grandmother again established the fact of this special number.

"Terrible, terrible times! Believe me, hanum, some days I was so ashamed of us humans that I could not even look into an animal's eyes. What could I explain to my donkey, the witness of the people's atrocities? He was my only companion in those days of disgrace, when I beat down doors of the town Beys and Aghas. I looked callous in their eyes, and nobody, not even my former students, wanted to hear my entreaties to stop the killings. I was praying to Allah much more fervently than ever before . . . and again, what could I answer to the puzzled, sad eyes of your Sevouk?"

Poor mollah was so glad to find the cordial listeners. He replied to the women's unspoken question. "Sometimes I met your Sevouk wandering down the streets, but then he disappeared . . . However, I beg your pardon, hanum, who is the third one living with you now?"

"My son, our Simon. He found refuge in a small Kurdish village at that 'terrible time'."

"May I make you and Pietzar Hanum very happy by saying that you are wrong?" Mollah felt guilty for not mentioning about me from the beginning. "You two and Simon are not the only three alive in your family; there is the fourth. I will point out another small village where your dear granddaughter, Nargiz, is living now. Oh, my sluggishness! For some reason I was sure you had already found her, I thought she was that third one. You should forgive me, I was so ill and did not leave my bed for so long time! I even did not know about your return to the town!"

So, I am asking you, what would have happened to me if, on that day, at that hour, my women had not decided to go to the hammam?

* "People may meet but mountains never." (Turk.)

Even the more so, as our mollah died soon after this accidental encounter. Man supposes, God disposes!

After my return to the family, I was coming to my senses rapidly. Everybody's love and caress, native speech, and my grandparents' spacious house itself were not strange for me. All that had been with me, in me; it was just frozen for a while. The dim, faceless shadows and vague whispers, which sometimes disquieted little shepherdess Emine, all those were now regaining clearness and articulation. I recognized the aroma of cooking coming from the kitchen, and the stupefying pink abundance of the oleanders, wildly spread in the courtyard. Uncle Simon again showed me how to make small boats using this plant's thick, lustrous, stretched leaves, and I rediscovered the babbling brook and other secluded spots in the abandoned garden, the tiny pockets between the bushes which I used for hide-and-seek games still fit my body perfectly, as if I had never left the house.

The joy, the fun of recalling one's own native language; it is almost impossible to describe these feelings. It very likely cannot be understood by anyone who never took a return journey to his first words and names. My every day was like: "I knew it! I heard that before! Sounds right!"

Maybe my renewed Armenian fascinated me because it turned out to be all about pleasing things, delights and gratification, and, of course, my grandmother's delicacies. This second time I learned Armenian, I was not that inert infant; I was a hard-working girl. My mind was opened. I could make fun of recognizing that the frequent mother's "my sweety"—in Armenian, "*kahzres*"—really sounded like a very sweet, blueishly white piece of lump sugar, slowly crumbling under my teeth. KAH-ZR-RES!

Or "*TZH-VZH-HIK.*" Does this word not sound exactly like small pieces of lamb entrails, with masses of onion rings, sizzling and fizzling in a big pan together with splashing around grease from the fatty tails of sheep? A gleaming hill of shredded liver, heart, guts, and spleen—all of excitingly different textures—disappeared from my plate much faster than the teasing steam. The brown gravy was being thoroughly cleaned off the plate by many pieces of lavash, making white rounds and triangles on the plate surface.

How wonderful was "*djur,*" an Armenian word for water. It has a purling, even growling sound. It means not just water, but the running water, brooks and rivers coming down through rocks and narrows. The word of our mountains and valleys. The Turkish "*su,*" or SOO-OO is plain and drawly, like the slow water of the flat steppes where these people came from.

I can say to you that Turkish did not occupy a significant place in me. My Turkish was rather the tool of surviving, the language of orders and means. All the memories of my life in the Turkish village always were just pictures: paths on slopes, grass and clouds, sheep and my dog, Arslan. I always saw them in my dreams as a silent film.

No, I did not think that my Armenian somehow constricted my Turkish. They are in different parts of my memory. I usually say "*kay-iun*" and "*koepek*" instead of Armenian words for "sheep" and "dog," and also definitely will say Turkish words "*odun*" and "*balta*" for "fire-wood" and "ax." However, what I learned in my family, from my people, I have remembered and spoken only in Armenia. "Kahzres!" I learned it from my mother.

One discovery followed another. Meals could be hot and eaten at the table, and it was possible to do nothing during the entire day but bathe in a wash-tub—under the four, pouring, soaping, rubbing women's hands—must be done every evening, before bedtime.

Then, the adults' secrets began to reveal themselves.

Grandmother Iughaper made *rakia*; its strong anise scent bursted out from the coach-house every time the door opened. The scent mixed with the smell of the previous tenant, our horse, who had lived there before the exile. Now, Grandma spent long hours in his empty barn, withcrafting near the fire and the gurgling coppers. She tasted the product by adding a little water in a tumbler of cut glass. Good rakia immediately acquired a milky color. A bottle or two of that "explosive" was being rolled up in clean rags and placed into a small knapsack. I smuggled it to some of Grandmother's customers, devout boozers. Their money was not enough to make our living and pay for my comeback. One by one, Grandmother was spending the coins from the jug she had buried in the garden brook.

When she and my mother returned to the town they found that my parents' house had been completely pilfered away right up to its base stones. "Lord" Pogos's house survived such ravage simply because, during the war, it had been quartered by various military units. Of course, many fruit trees had been cut down for heating, and our dog,

Sevouk, had disappeared. Without him, rats became a menace. The brook left untended by the house occupants became shallow and almost dried out, but then the jug with the coins remained intact. "What idle people," muttered Grandmother Iughaper, re-hiding the coins in another safe, but more accessible place. "Could not find time to treat the brook, such a treasure of fresh, cold water. So, how would they find this treasure, this gold, just under their noses?"

When Uncle Simon came down to the home from his mountain refuge, the first work they did was to clean up the trashed stream bed. Soon, the brook began to babble to them about the years of neglect and its desperate efforts to keep the trusted family secret.

My Uncle Simon was a mystery. I saw a young man, just eighteen to nineteen years old, tall and slightly curly-haired. He was the tallest in our family, both his brothers resembled thickset "Lord" Pogos. Simon was much better-proportioned, and had jet-black eyebrows and a thin mustache which made the refined features of his pale face more prominent. A confused smile disturbed his lips. Even with me, a slip of a girl, he talked with some confusion, as if he were making excuses. He never seriously worked. I mean by his own, always preferring to be on catch up with somebody. However, even strict and just Grandmother Iughaper never mentioned this to him. My mother used to stroke his head caressingly when passing by him, idly sitting near the veranda window looking onto the courtyard. Also, Grandma asked my mother every morning how he had slept during the night. My mother used to sigh very pitifully and shook her head. Initially, I was just lost in conjecture for why the women made a fuss of such a loafer.

When I returned home with some smuggling money, my uncle was waiting for me like a boy, my peer, to continue our interrupted discussion of the remarkable dogs we saw in our lives. I extolled my wolfhound Arslan's merits, and Uncle Simon told our family's sagas about Sevouk's battles with rats (unfortunately, I did not really remember our short, black warrior) and described the extraordinary abilities of the Yellow Beast, the Circassian dog he observed when he lived in the mountains.

Bakro, his savior, often visited us. "Presents himself as if he is a light in our eyes," Grandmother Iughaper used to say when seeing the Kurd. Uncle Simon looked more confused than usually. My mother brought a clay carafe of cold, diluted *matsoon* to the regular, but always unexpected, guest. Bakro did not eat or drink rakia in our house, but

Grandma did not even suggest her "dynamite" to him. The Kurd just sat on the floor, bending his legs. He fetched a pipe somewhere from his belt and silently emitted fumes out of his pendent mustache.

"His wolfy eyes were blazing, just sweeping around," began Grandmother, after Bakro also silently left the house. "Pietzar, please, no more bustling in the room, I do not like how he looks at you. What else does this bandit want from you, my son? Why does he come and make us waste time?"

"He is not a bandit, majrig. The man is a hunter. After all, he saved my life . . . he also told me that you appeared in the town, brought me here . . ."

"Yes! But for what a price! Son, you have already paid for all he did for you, and too much; even more than we paid for our return."

The words had been said. Uncle Simon's head bowed lower, his eyes were filling with moisture. What possible could happen to him? Something so bad that it makes Grandmother really mad. She should appreciate Bakro if he really saved her son. At least she have to be polite with him as with a guest. I was thinking.

My mother, of course, could not contain herself: "Whatever it was, mairig, our Simon found shelter in this man's house. For four dreadful years . . ."

"Kurd Bakro, what a hero! Eagle! An eagle does not kill a pitiful sparrow hiding in the chink of his nest. He is a hunter, he likes to pursue. I don't want to see his wolf eyes anymore, nor his eagle nose in our home. Cut his feet off here." Grandma persisted.

Then ten days or a of couple weeks later, Bakro again dismounted at our gate and tethered his horse under the surviving tree. Again the grandmother grumbled at my mother who served him a cold drink.

Uncle Simon guiltily tried to dispel my doubts. He repeatedly told me that Bakro really was hunting when he had come upon his, Simon's, almost lifeless body stretched on the ground. I imagined how this "sparrow" must have been scared when he opened eyes and saw the Kurd Bakro, who was sitting on his horse with the rifle in his hands. In the last act of desperation, Simon had reached out to give him the coins, those few gold coins that people in the Harab Caravansaray had given him before his escape. The strong hand of Bakro had lifted Simon onto the horse, behind the rider, who then brought Simon to his house. His village, not even a village but rather an summer encampment was situated higher in the mountain that the Circassian village of Yeni Koy, where Simon saw the freak with Arshak's severed head. (Would Simon take another road on the fork he ended in Bakro's village.)

Bakro returned all the coins to Simon when the boy came to his senses. "Those coins," grieved over Uncle Simon. At that time I could not understand why my uncle was so obsessed with "those coins." Looking at my puzzled face, uncle Simon blurted out his "terrifying secret," but because my age I hardly realized his concerns. "The stubborn tribesmen, they whispered into tribe chief's ear that 'an infidel could not stay in their village,' they said the Turks and Circassians would not like it. They were afraid that Turks and Circassians would not allow the tribe to set up its tents in *yayla* during the next summer. The yayla had really good pastures for Bakro tribes's sheep and horses. So the alarmed chief ordered Bakro to take me to the town. Bakro brought me to the town, right to the mosque. *Mufti* read something from Koran and made me repeat 'La Illaha il Allah' . . ."

". . . Muhammad Rasul Alah." I finished instead of him. "Uncle, I know this too."

"Yes, Nargiz-djan, tsavet tanem. You were repeating the words as a child: a clean, innocent heart, and no ideas in your mind. But I, saying those words, had accepted *Hak Dini* or True Faith. I became a Turk, and I had paid for that with those coins. Not me, exactly; Bakro did, but you see, namely the coins which they gave me there, in the Harab Caravansaray . . . my late father, and others, Mighty Arshak, mechanic Ovannes, Shaghbazian, and Babken . . .

"On the other hand, they wanted me to escape and tell everyone about their end. However, to whom can I tell such things? Even my mother is embarrassed of me. I feel it."

"Simply do not tell anybody that you were a Turk," I quite arrogantly instructed my sorry uncle. "Nobody knows, except my mother and sister. There were Bakro, me, and that Turkish priest in a green turban. We met only one woman on the stairs to the mosque. Her face looked familiar, but I am not sure. I remember her glance . . ." Poor Uncle, he was not sure of anything.

Old hidden secrets were coming to the surface.

One day, after Bakro's usual visit, Grandmother was again inquiring about such strange tenacity. Uncle Simon was sluggishly defending himself. He again adduced that Bakro's nomadic tribe had been settling their camp in nearest mountains since time immemorial and has always been extreme rivals to the Circassians from Yeni Koy (New Village).

They did not respect these newcomers who ran headlong from their native land in the Caucasus during the bygone wars with Russians. Bakro and his tribesmen called them "Rus cadgers" and "barefoot czars." Mountaineers from Bakro's village always joked about their faint-hearted neighbors, Uncle Simon told us.

"One New Villager is eating supper. A candle is burning on the table. He notices his wife's shadow on the wall: 'Somebody snuck into our house.' 'The other one is just behind you,' replies the wife seeing her husband's shadow on the opposite wall. In fear, they crawl under the table. Later, their son comes. 'Be aware son. Dangerous strangers have come to eat our supper.' 'They ran away, I do not see them,' says the 'brave' son from the door. The parents get out from under the table and the family runs away from the home because the shadows appear on the wall again."

Grandmother was certain that Circassians had expressed something similar, maybe even more trenchant, about the Bakro's tribesmen. Uncle Simon alluded to the fact that the Bakro's tribe was not responsible for the slaughter of the Armenian men that morning at the Harab Caravansaray. Grandmother replied that if Kurd Bakro and his people had been invited by the Turks "to help" them in that bloodbath, they would not have missed such an opportunity to live off the victims' corpses.

Uncle Simon had lived for about four years with the Kurds and he knew that she was right; Bakro's tribe had considered itself passed over in that deal. Kurds were offended because they were sure they would finish off those unarmed Armenian men much faster and without losses from their side. "Just think, Boyuk Arshak alone had crippled a few slow New Villagers and had sent two these white-livered braggarts to the Angel of Darkness." Many times Simon had heard such talk between Bakro's tribesmen.

However, in attempt to somehow defend his savior, Uncle Simon played his last trump card. He told the story that Bakro himself had suffered because of the Turks. His younger brother, Meho, had been executed by them. The Turks had unfairly accused his brother of murder. "Since that time Bakro hates the Turks," stated Simon.

"How did it happen?" asked my compassionate mother.

"Bakro was with his brother in our town. For some reason they stayed too long. They were returning home almost at night. In a dark street their horses lingered at the man's body."

"Oh, of course, as always they were ransacking the streets and looking for stealing something," murmured Grandma.

However, Uncle Simon was encouraged by the obvious interest showed by his mother. "Bakro's brother, Meho, immediately dismounted to rummage through the man's clothes. So, according to Bakro, there certainly was a robbery (everybody would to do that in such an appropriate place, considered the Kurd) but no murder. Somebody had killed this Turk just before their appearance. At that moment, the town's guards ran into them; Bakro, being on the horse, managed to escape unrecognized, but poor Meho was caught near the body with money and other belongings of that dead Turk in his hands. Under such circumstances, he had no chance to vindicate himself, so the Turks executed him."

"Did your 'innocent' Kurd mention when that had happened?"

Uncle Simon was not paying enough attention to notice that the story somehow disturbed the women. My mother glanced at Grandma's strained face. "Bakro did not mention the exact date, I had an impression that it did happen many years ago. However, imagine, mairig-djan, how he was touched when I told him that my brother also suffered because of the Turks. That story about our Haroutiun's friend, Ara, his ruined love and his death at the hands of a Turk, and Haroutiun's revenge for Ara's death, and also about . . ."

"What? You told him all about Haroutiun? How could you?" My grandmother was shocked, I had never seen her in such disarray and anger. "How did you learn about 'Haroutiun's revenge'? You were so young at that time. We never took the risk of letting you into your brother's crazy deeds."

"Mayrig, I never knew that before father revealed it when we were in the Harab Caravansaray. The last night we were together, he told to all Armenians there that Haroutiun was a hero because he had killed a Turk in vengeance for his friend's death. All the people there—butcher Arshak, the mechanic Ovannes, and "Khor" Aram, and the others—were listening, too."

When the name of the "Lord" Pogos was spoken, my mother rushed to Simon and then to Grandma with composing embraces.

Now, my grandmother had a clear picture. All the figures did tally. She needed only a few details.

Soon, Uncle Simon, provided with complete instructions on how to question his Kurd, had a talk with him. He was trying to find out the exact time when Bakro's brother was caught and executed in our town. The Bakro's answer bore, accordingly to Grandma's opinion, mocking character. "It happened in the year when my best horse died, too." My mother repeated Bakro's words again and again, wondering if they meant the same year as when her brother, Haroutiun, did his 'crazy' deed.

However, Grandma became confident that the Kurd, this harboring eagle, had selected our house as the place for an ambush. She told my mother that Bakro was waiting for Haroutiun, the man who was responsible for his brother's death. Indirectly, insisted Grandmother, but for the "blood-thirsty" Kurd it might be enough to brood the plans for his own vengeance. She thought that Bakro was sure that sooner or later this Armenian would return to his family nest. Strangely enough, Grandma looked happier due to such conclusions. "Such people have unbelievable animal sense. He feels that our Haroutiun is not dead. He is alive, and will come back, to his father's home that he left a long time ago. The Kurd is waiting for him, so we shall wait, too!"

The Red Thread

Here is the day of our parting. I wish luck to you and your family. Have an eventless trip back home!

Look, my dear, what a chubby capon I have fried to keep your family busy during those annoying train stops. I know, I know, your assiduous wife has prepared all provisions, but be patient one more time. You can never find such naturally grown poultry in our Soviet stores. What they sell is ugly chicken, blue and emaciated as if after a chicken labor camp. Those long-legged creatures, smelling of fish due to their feeding, with incredibly stretched out half-feathered necks and closed, pale eyes, look like an eternal reproach to any woman who gets down to clean them for soup. There is almost nothing on them to fry.

Now, take a look at my joyful bird. It is shining like the dawn sun and has a crisp brownish skin because it was fried in its own grease with well-pounded garlic. Your kids will like it.

Tell your wife that I have wrapped it in waxed paper; my daughter-in-law works in the drawing office of a plant and she takes out rolls of that paper for home use. A Soviet engineer, who brought in a college diploma instead of a decent dowry, she receives only 100 rubles a month. Besides, now everybody steals something from their working place; that is why this country is collapsing. The government shams that pay people their salaries, the people, in their turn, sham that they work for the government! Who began first? How it will end? Nobody cares!

However, it is all vanity. From my experience, if one sincerely wants to live a righteous life he must follow "red thread." Best of all—the red thread of love. Not of justice, not even of truth, but namely love.

Where did I hear about "red thread"? Recently, our local church priest, Father Mesrop, spoke some marvelous words. Sometimes he does, when he is slightly tight, just three sheets in the wind. That day, he was talking about the tempters. Nowadays, they confuse people's heads and insert dangerous thoughts of inborn primacy. "One man deserves more than another; this people are superior to their neighbors, and so on." Most of all, I liked the Bible story in his speech. "A pregnant woman had twin brothers in her womb. The time came for her to give birth. When one of the brothers showed his hand, the midwife marked it with scarlet thread, saying, 'This is the first!' However, he took his hand back. Then the other came out and, after him, this one with the scarlet thread." So, who is the first? Or senior? Or superior?

Oh, you know the other story?

You are saying that "red thread" comes from England; the red thread was braided in all ropes belonging to the English Military Fleet to prevent their theft. Interestingly, English sailors also stole, made off with heavy ropes, and I blame my daughter-in-law for the waxed paper.

Nevertheless, I think that the red thread of love must direct us through our entire lives. Love, and its younger sister, compassion, should be the guiding stars in all decisions and deeds we make in dealing with people, alive and dead.

Yes, even with those already gone; I mean the way we remember our dead.

It is so simple: love feeds memory. I love those people who have since moved away: my mother, uncles, Grandma, and little helpless brother, Hakop, and the others. I know that nobody in the entire world will remember them if I stop recalling. When I think about my family they are around; their voices, laughter, worries, and favorite sayings. I even feel touches of their hands. If I stop associating with them, they really will disappear. They will be forgotten, lost, hopelessly dispelled into the air, and finally, irrevocably dead. It is my obligation to keep them alive. To whom else could they ask for such a favor? I am the sole attendant at this transit station. My memory is the only thing, the thread of love, that links us and them. Only imagine, dear, if that thin thread, rotting with time, will snap. For a moment, fear chilled my bones . . .

If talking about love and compassion, my mother, Pietzar, was most talented in sharing the mishaps of others. She just dissolved everything in tears and soothing words. Grandma was quite different. She liked to help through action. "Sometimes I am envious of you, Pietzar. You are always ready to weep and cry instead of seeking a way out." I was astonished by how one can be in envy of another's tears. Now, I perfectly understand how difficult it is—silently finding ways out from one desperate situation after another. Nevertheless, someone in family has to do it, the one capable to carry such a burden. However, crying, and particularly crying together, "alongside" or in support of a sufferer also is very important. But you know, people are different. So, to each his own. As my Russian neighbor, Natalia, says, "One likes watermelon, another pork gristle."

My mother spent hours listening to Uncle Simon's reflections, and always with such co-emotion that it looked as if he were confiding in her for the very first time.

"Nature is so indifferent! You drop down on the ground, exhausted and desperate. Then, for a moment, you notice ants running in and out of their hill, and you are so defenseless and lonely that you wish to run in with them and hide yourself underground, in that quiet, invisible place. But what does it matter to them? They run and run, doing their own ant business, but you must stand up and go further . . . Or another time I was struck. We entered our town, that day when Bakro and I were riding to the mosque—I already told you, sister, about that cursed day—until I looked around from behind Bakro's back and was just stunned. The town was without its Armenians who had lived in it so many years. However, the town did not know about that, and did not care. The same streets stretched, orchards continued to show green and bear fruits, and birds sang to their utmost."

"Right!" caught up my mother. "It was very similar with me when, during the nights, mother and I lay on the bare ground, only bags under our heads, and I stared at the stars. They were so beautiful and so far from the people's torments . . ."

"But then, no stars, no birds, and no ants can ever harm you," Grandma said briefly.

May I ask you where you are going? Oh, to catch a taxi on the street! Well, this is not a good idea, my dear. Firstly, no one taxi driver is so crazy to ride around the streets right now, when the groups of incensed men are just scouring the town. Abkhazians are looking for Georgians on that street to beat up, and the latter are after Abkhazians on the next street. They all are seeking a chance to be free with their fists, so scarcely will they look into and recognize your Slavic face.

Secondly, you should not worry about the ride. I already told my grandson, and he will be here in time to take your family to the train station. He was born here, my Movses. He knows every back street, and will bring your family to the station right at your train departure time.

Did Haroutiun return home? The answer to your "last question" is, "Yes, he did."

When? Well, my insatiable listener, your previous question was not your final one! However, I will tell you that Haroutiun came back shortly after my grandmother made *matah.* Usually, the Armenians make matah after their solicited wish or favor becomes fulfilled. Tenacious in her purpose to see her son alive, Grandma could not wait. She had already showed so much patience to The One who had spun a web of our mixed up lives. Without any doubt, she would loosen her purse-strings for that occasion and buy a lamb, but there were not enough Armenians in our town to share the sacrificial animal. All the Armenians who still lived in our town were *shurtvatznere*—in Armenian, the turned over or those converted into Islam. At least seven families must take their portions and give these words of blessing: "Let your matah be accepted!" There were not seven Armenian families in the whole town who were still Christians. Only two; our family and the butcher Archak's wife with three daughters who survived their death march and subsequent slavery at the hands of the Arabs. All familiar Greeks also were gone.

Grandma bought a rooster. A matah bird should be a rooster, not a hen, and best of all of red color. Grandma's rooster, a genuine leader of poultry nobility, had a fiery red and crimson feather with a shot of blue steel on its puffed-up chest and fluffy tail. For a couple of days this fiercely pecking bird was pacing out in our backyard and garden, trying to call together his lost harem, when he was given the grain. The feeding did not help. Boiled, according to the old rules, in plain water, the rooster had lenten, hard meat.

In her previous life, during the good times, Grandmother Iughaper would not have asked the butcher's wife to come for dinner. But now, the situation required evasive action. Desperate Grandma suggested counting Arshak's wife and two of her elder daughters of marriageable age, as three separate families. Grandma, herself, Uncle Simon, and my mother with me made three more families. After deliberating with my mother about those important numbers, Grandma rested on the candidacy of the Armenian photographer, a newcomer in our town and a stranger to her (he took our picture with me in my "famous" ragged dress) to represent the seventh family.

So, seven families were finally assembled, albeit barely; seven families totaling nine people. After my grandmother's brief explanation, all said the sacred words and wished the return of Haroutiun. The rooster was unyielding. Hungry people valiantly worked right up to its bones. In breaking the rules of matah, Grandma and mother served an additional meal, large *midias* stuffed with rice and herbs, a common dish on our coast. It was not prestigious, because a couple of dozens prune-like midias and handfuls of rice were affordable for everyone. However, this dish requires certain cooking skills. In the early morning, under the intent women's supervision, Uncle Simon cleaned and polished the shells glimmering in water and looking like black stones. Their subtle scent was disturbing to me. I was afraid to help my uncle, and then ate only a bit of the spicy rice, but not from inside the shells. My fear of the sea had not fully awakened yet, just raised its ugly head.

There was nothing left of old furniture in our house. We sat around the tablecloth, a double-folded piece of linen, laid out on the wooden floor. The voice of butcher Arshak's wife filled the dining room. For an Armenian woman she was very tall, and had a deep trumpet voice. Of her seven children, three daughters had escaped death in exile. Beatings, starvation, and typhus took away their brothers and sisters, one by one. However, even years of slave labor, humiliation, and hunger could not choke the blooming physical beauty of the creations of Mighty Arshak and his wife. Uncle Simon was overwhelmed and confused by the extravagance of their young feminine contours. Two younger sisters had bluish marks on their foreheads, made by their Arab owner. The girls frequently shifted the kerchiefs to conceal these ugly stamps of their endured slavery. Their hair, cut very short, did not hold the kerchiefs which, time and again, slipped back, exposing the smooth arches of their black eyebrows framing huge dark eyes with long lashes, almost like buffalo eyes. The third sister differed from her siblings; she was older but slender in complexion, and her face was not distorted by the forehead marks that her sisters and mother had. Her hair was long, and her entire look and moves were more delicate, maybe because she was pregnant.

"Tikin Iughaper and you, tikin Pietzar; I want to say something secretly. We are going to Russia! Our legs are still strong. They crossed the entire country twice. To hell and back. We will reach Russia." This woman could not hide anything. Her confident voice rumbled between the bare walls of the big room and rolled up onto the listeners. The giant daughters nodded assent. If they had join their loud mother resoundingly, the molded ceiling of the dining room would have crashed down on our heads, my Grandma used to recall.

Arshak's wife proposed to my grandmother that they journey to Russia together. Grandma explained that our family could not join them because we were waiting for Haroutiun. Many times after our family returned to the town, she sent letters to his address in Sukhumi. There, before the war, Haroutiun had a tailor shop set up for him by his father, "Lord" Pogos. There were no answers from him, yet. However, Grandma explained, she believed he was still alive and could find his family at his parents' home. "We should just wait for him here!" Of course, Grandma did not tell Arshak's wife what nourished her hope the most: persistent visits from Kurd Bakro.

"Easier to find him by yourself over there, Iughaper, my sister. What about us, we will definitely go. The further from this land, the better. Tiflis, Baku, and even very cold places in Russia. Anywhere. There will not be any life for us here anymore. Believe me, my sister. Here Tachiks finished us off, Armenians."

"We were in Tiflis just before the war. We could stay there, but my wife and I did not like it: seven taverns to one church. How stupid we were!" awoke the photographer, with his eyebrows, like frightened birds. The memories and self-reproaches had completely ruined the man. It was easy to guess what had happened with his family, so nobody asked. My mother had to bring him a small tumbler of rakiia (again in violation of the matah rules) and later, at his departure, my grandmother slipped a bottle into his fidgety hands.

Also, a couple of coins from the "brook cache" moved into the grateful hands of the butcher Arshak's wife. The woman caught my mother's glance upon her daughter's protruding abdomen. "The young Turk. He was *chavush* in our convoy. Took her to live with him in his house, but sold the rest of us to an Arab. Somehow she held out, but eventually got pregnant. We hope Arshak does not see this from there." Arshak's wife looked up for a moment and the daughter guiltily cast down her eyes. My mother embraced the bowed young woman and sighed with her.

"But then, when the Inglezis came, I went with their soldiers to his house and took her back." The voice of Arshak's wife thundered again, resounding victoriously with a hint of gloating. "Initially, the Turk rode the high horse, shouting at me and the Inglezi soldiers. However, very shortly, he was begging my daughter not to leave. He promised her gold bracelets and other jewelry. Then he began talking about love.

He spoke real rubbish, something about 'drinking honey from the navel,' and other such nonsense. A cunning fox! He tried to move the Inglezis—duffers I would say, between us—to pity. They even asked my daughter if she would like to stay with him because she was pregnant. No way! Arshak's daughter would never do such a thing! She went with us. The Turk and his parents cursed us incessantly. They called us 'ungrateful Armenians!' Be grateful for what? For sparing our lives? For not killing me and my daughters as my other children and my Arshak? The hell with this Turk and all his family. We left their village immediately. Then eventually we got here. My Arshak is here . . . somewhere. Also it was on the route to Russia."

Arshak's wife ended her roaring monologue. Any passerby on the street could easily have heard her story. We were all moved. My mother was still embracing the young pregnant woman who hid her wet face in my mother's shoulder. The two families were a long time parting. Apparently, the people suddenly realized that because they were the last Armenians of the town, with their final farewell the entire old world, the entire past life they lived in this place would vanish forever. Some invisible thread would break. Even I, a slip of a girl, felt the great sadness of that moment.

Finally, our guests left. The rooster's bones were carefully collected and buried deeply in a secluded place of the garden, far from the evil eye. Then came the days of waiting for Haroutiun. The adults avoided talking about his return, letting the Supreme Instance decide when it should happen. Often my mother worried about Arshak's family and their journey to cold Russia. Grandma used to assure us that Arshak's wife would break through all possible obstacles. My grandmother gained a lot of respect for that *zoravor* woman. She admired the woman particularly because of her coming back to the town after her long exile in order to find out how her husband, Mighty Arshak, had ended his life. My grandmother even expressed her regrets at not knowing this simple, but strong woman better in the old, pre-war times. Uncle Simon was pleased by how loudly the woman thanked him for telling the story of Arshak's last heroic battle at the Harab Caravansaray. (Many, many years after, the youngest daughter of Mighty Arshak found my mother and me in Sukhumi. She told us that after long and hard wanderings her mother had led her and her sister to Astrakhan, a city in Russia, and they had all settled there. They both married, had children, and lived quite successful lives. Her other sister, who was pregnant, did not reach Astrakhan. In the small transit train station, where there was no doctor or mid-wife, not even warm water, she died when her labor went wrong.)

The matah worked out. One gibbous day, when sparse passersby were getting soaked under the rain, which had kept on drizzling from the earlier morning, a stranger in ragged dervish-like clothes was spotted at our gateway. There was absolutely nothing to do for me in the yard or on our lane on such a downcast day. From the window of our veranda I watched the man with idle curiosity and then with caution. Slowly he took off his ragged robe, showing his feet in the trampled boots and jodhpurs and the lengthy, double-breasted jacket. The man was touching the gate stones, slowly patting them from up to down. The iron lattices had been uprooted from the walls and taken away a long time ago. The way to the courtyard was opened wide, but the inert stranger was just staring at those stones, and the yard, and the chopped-up garden.

I called my mother. She nestled up against the next window and then ran out to the man, screaming, "Haroutiun, Haroutiun has come!" The barn door in the garden flew open. Uncle Simon and, behind him, Grandma, both soaked with the odors of anise and alcohol, also rushed to the newcomer's embraces.

It is impossible to tell you in brief what happened thereafter with my family. Do not take it wrongly, but it somehow sounds ridiculous to me. My tongue is unable to describe in a few words even the reunions of Haroutiun with his family. Words are futile here. Just a useless peel against the genuine feelings.

Moreover, I am already hearing the call signal of my grandson's car. He will help you with the luggage.

I do not know why, but I have a feeling that we shall come across each other one more time. Come here again for your next vacation. Let's believe that people's madness in this place will fade, the sea will be calm, and the old lady will still be alive to resume her story . . . about hent Haroutiun and his adventures, about Kurd Bakro and their encounter, and about our escape from our town to Constantinople and then, eventually, to this current place in the Sovietland. Good-bye, my true listener!

Part Two

Take My Memories

St. George with the Scarlet Cloak

Welcome back, my dear. I am so sorry I foretold on our departing that our next encounter would be soon. I should bite my tongue. God is my witness that I did not mean it would be in a few hours. Nobody knew that the railway station would go on strike. Now, this word is so popular, even old women have learned it; people are protesting, demanding, frightening, and—to put it bluntly—wringing out everything by threats. Sovietland will not swallow this so easily. . . .

Calm your wife and put the kids to bed. They did not deserve such an end to their summer vacation. You may continue staying in your rooms until this commotion abates.

My tongue should fall off for saying those words. I mean if I really brought the failure of your departure . . .

Are you telling me that it was a simple coincidence and that your delay did not happen according to Supreme Will? I am not so sure about that, nor about our encounter. I really hesitate to think of our encounter as purely accidental. Why, among hundreds of summer houses, did you choose mine in which to spend your vacation? Why should you, an absolute stranger, so readily become captivated, almost seized, by the events of my past? There is something or somebody who dragged you in.

Oh, I am trembling because of the power of fate. Don't you see? The story of my family, which began more than seventy-five years ago in Turkey, on the opposite side of this sea, this intricate story, full of forced partings and unexpected encounters, somehow found you, light-heartedly vacationing here, on the Soviet shore of the sea, kept you listening for days about all its moves and turns, and now did not let you leave by your own will.

Don't you realize that the return of Haroutiun was decided beforehand, as far back as when my "hent" uncle was carrying out revenge for his slain friend, Ara? Not without reason at that midnight hour two Kurds, Bakro, and his younger brother, were riding through our town and came to that exact point where, a minute earlier, the mortal fight between Haroutiun and his friend's slayer, Mehmed, had ended. By the tragic turn of events, Bakro's brother was accused of killing Mehmed and executed; years later, as we know, Bakro saved Simon's life, having no idea that Simon was Haroutiun's younger brother.

After all, what a strange plan it was to bring them both together, Haroutiun and Bakro, and tie them in such an odd way in a tight knot, despite their never having seen each other. How dare we doubt the thoroughness and refinement of that plan? It would be a kind of blasphemy to dismember this whole plot into some sequence of casual and banal accidents.

Why would you not consider that today, you have been given a sign, an order, to stay? I think this additional time has been granted to both of us to finish the story.

So, should I serve you a cup of coffee? Let's hope your wife and kids are having sweet dreams. After those distressing hours, waiting futilely at the train station, they deserve it.

Upon Uncle Haroutiun's appearance, our hushed house became filled with new sounds and odors. It seemed like a new life had been breathed into its interior, the space that had been wounded and intimidated by years of outsiders' invasions. All-penetrating, pungent waves of the inferior tobacco and shoe polish spread around the house each time the door of Haroutiun's room opened. I liked those new, exciting, and intriguing odors; they were also accompanied by the unusual—loud and confident—sounds of Haroutiun's voice, and his crooning of funny-hissing songs he had learned in the Russian army. I also heard some mysterious metallic inklings and tinklings coming from behind his closed door.

Haroutiun, my so-called "hent" ("crazy") uncle, with all his extraordinary qualities, was so magnetic that I committed a treachery. I betrayed my best friend, Uncle Simon, by not playing or talking with him as much as I did before. I spent hours waiting for a moment to slip into Haroutiun's room. He let me see his pistols. He had two; a black one with a long barrel, which he hid in his haversack, and a small one that he carried on him, which I liked better because it had ivory brackets on the handle. Every day Uncle took them to pieces and oiled them, making those inkling and tinkling noises, and then aimed at dark spots on the empty wall. He screwed up his eyes. His face and arm were like stone. But his lips cursed somebody on that decayed wall. To the sincere horror of my mother and Grandma, Haroutiun cursed and swore a lot; but always in Russian, particularly while being tipsy. Truthfully, he searched for any right moment to gargle, although he had never been seen drunk. He used to say that flowery, verbose Russian curses were the best; in Armenian they lost their discouraging cogency.

Uncle Haroutiun also named his pistols in Russian. The big one he called "The Cannon"; directing it at the empty wall, he whispered through his lips, "Only one shot, only one bullet from my faithful Cannon, and your foul remnants could not be picked up even by spoons." Caressing the small, toy-like pistol, Uncle pensively sighed, "My Maria!" and his shining protuberant eyes moistened. Sometimes he answered to my surprise, "What do you know, kid? She was so tender, my Maria, so kind, as, as . . ." and I could not keep back my laughter. Here, my uncle pretended to be furious at my silly laughter. He picked me up with his mighty hands, threw me in the air and picked me up again, and jokingly pulled my ears. Then, after all that, he tucked me under his blanket and pillows on the floor where he slept, while my mother came running into the room because my crocodile tears, and feigned squeals and yelps. He convinced her that he had not seen me around for a long time, while I was trying not to breathe or move under the crumpled blanket. Of course, my mother always played along by repeatedly asking where I might be and where my squeals had come from.

I considered that fun to be a kind of betrayal of Uncle Simon. Gripped by the demons of his past, pursued and afraid of the shadows of the lame Turkish sergeant, whilst simultaneously looking for and avoiding a confessing face-to-face talk with his irascible elder brother, my poor Uncle Simon was no fun at all. The best adventure he could offer me was one more search for the ghost-sergeant, the aimless voyage to the bazaar square when the cold wind was chilling us to the marrow.

Haroutiun appeared as a new character in our reserved family, very strong and confident, unlike the other, crest-fallen figures. He was not tall and looked rather like his late father "Lord" Pogos. He was shorter than Simon. However, you would never notice that difference should you see them next to each other. Talking briefly and loudly as if in the trenches, looking straight into anyone's eyes, Haroutiun dominated. His thickset frame conveyed extraordinary strength; with his iron fingers, Uncle easily bent coins. His protuberant eyes stuck out and the thoroughly shaved cheeks on the round weather-beaten face reddened slightly when he performed this trick.

Sadly, my mother and Grandma could not enjoy to such an extent that sense of security and confidence inspired in me by Haroutiun's thunderous presence. The women were expected incinerating outbursts from him if he were ever to learn all about the Simon's conversion into Islam. Here, the women disagreed: my mother favored gradually letting Haroutiun into his brother's secret, while Grandma Iughaper was point-blankly against that "deathly" idea. "Aman, Aman! God, have mercy! Your brother will not accept this. He was always madly furious when it came to the Tachiks' bestialities against Armenians, even when he was young. Now, if you have noticed, he has become more hent than before?" Grandma was referring to the new Haroutiun's escapades, unprecedented in our town; without any particular reason he would walk along its streets, hands in the pockets of his lengthy military jacket, pointing a vacant stare at Tachik men. No one Armenian could dare to do that ever in our town. However, after their defeats inflicted by the Inglezis, Franks, and Russians, the troubled Turks could not withstand my uncle's crazines. They preferred to just let him pass.

Haroutiun's provocative boldness scared Grandma, who strained her every nerve to devise plans for avoiding possible troubles. She feverishly thought of how to assuage the storm that was drawing nearer with each of Haroutiun's more and more obstinate questioning of poor Simon about the circumstances of their father's death and Simon's survival among Kurds. The stumbled and confused stories of his brother perplexed Haroutiun. He wanted more and more details. As if that wasn't enough, each occasion Haroutiun went out was fraught with his fighting some Turks and their inevitable harsh retributions against all of us. There was also that Bakro who, by Grandma's reckoning, had been waiting for Haroutiun's return. With heavy heart she thought about their encounter. Fortunately, it was winter and Bakro's tribe did not brought their sheep and tents yet to our mountains. However, the spring was approaching and Grandma was afraid of Bakro's inevitable visit. Apparently, she was already considering the necessity of moving out from the town to some safer place, but there was not so much energy left in her small body for such a big change. Besides, everywhere we could go—Armenia or Russia—there were hunger, typhus, and continuing hostilities.

Our family's frail boat was floated down to the crushing bow-waving rocks. My "hent" ("crazy") Uncle Haroutiun was swinging it and seemingly even Grandma, our skillful navigator, could not handle the dangerous ride.

My mother rushed about between her brothers, both crazy in their own ways. She made every effort to be next to Simon in his quandaries when Haroutiun's questioning began. Naively, she tried to digress from Haroutiun's inquiries by asking him about his battles and other adventures. Sometimes this ruse worked and then we heard some of the warrior's stories. More often, Haroutiun used to leave the house because he would lose his temper.

At those times, my mother would come and sit in our wretched kitchen which, then, was the warmest and driest place in the house. She would come with her big black eyes dimmed with tears, and a deep fold wrinkled her pure brow framed by the modestly combed hair. A light blush adorned my mother's harmoniously rounded face, and her tender, inquiring voice pinched my little coarsened heart. She would try to find out the reasons for Haroutiun's abrupt manners and provocative intolerance.

"This terrible war has changed him so deeply, really turned him over. He was such an affectionate boy, maybe a little hot-tempered, maybe too straightforward, but always just; always. Do you remember, mayrig, how much he wanted fairness for everyone, for all the people around him? How funny was it when he used to knit his brows on hearing that somebody had been hurt unjustly? Oh, my dear brother, my Harout!

"And now my Harout cannot be simply happy that his brother, Simon, survived; he is questioning him like a kadi does with some petty thief. This terrible war has indeed embittered his feelings!"

Grandma kept silent, pealing as usual with the sounds of crockery.

Incidentally, my dear, it is amazing how much time both my women spent treating our empty kitchen. They had only a few odd bowls and plates, but I remember them swabbing those pieces, rubbing, and polishing them again and again as if an ineradicable dirt marked their dented surfaces. During the night, I would wake up because of thirst or bad dreams and hear the same sounds from the kitchen.

Grandma would be there, mechanically drying the same dishes or dusting the table. I never saw those women sleeping; whenever I would suddenly awake, at the very first moment when the ugly sea monsters of my dreams were floating away and my eyes began to open, my mother's or Grandma's still vague faces were already looking above me, and their careful hands were ready to bring me out of my nightmare. However, I am unable to remember a moment, even one single episode, when I could find them asleep. Later, after many years of living here in Sukhumi, far away from Turkey, my mother remained the same sleep-avoiding person. She hinted at an explanation once, blabbing out to me, "Why go to sleep when you know you will see again the same terrible scenes you have experienced in real life? My mother, Iughaper, let me sleep during those nights when the Tachiks were driving us like sheep to the slaughterhouse. Then, the real events during the daily marches were much more gruesome than any nightmare my mind could produce."

My mother continued tormenting herself over Haroutiun's striking transformation. Her barely restrained sighs compelled even firm Grandma to break her silence.

"Your brother is about the same as when he left this house. In my opinion, he has not changed at all. He is the same reckless soul. Since I have already opened my mouth I will tell you one more thing: the longer I live in this world the more I become convinced that nobody changes. Traitor remains traitor, and hent remains hent! Look into the essence: if it walks like a duck and quacks like a duck, it's most likely a duck."

"But I am feeling," worried my mother, "that he is hurt, deeply in his heart, and is also shattered and confused. Just imagine how many inhospitable places he must have crossed while fighting, how many strangers he must have met on his way here. Some of them became his friends (he said he lost his best comrades), others maybe tried to hurt him, and also all those combat hardships and atrocities. . . ."

"Ah, Pietzar, Pietzar, my pure daughter, did you not walk through such similar places, alien and hostile, by your own worn-out feet, and did you not see with your own eyes how mercilessly people can treat other human beings? Was your slavery in that Kurdish village a sugared life? Don't force me to speak longer because your little daughter is here. However, all that did not change you, did it?

"And you, Nargiz, stop eavesdropping on the adults' conversations. I told you that your curious ears would grow and grow, and one day would become the size of a donkey's ears."

Then Grandma would turn again to her bowls and plates. I would stay in the kitchen next to my still-thoughtful mother, resting my body against the wall. The dim light of a winter day concealed the crying shame of the wall, whose single decoration was a small lithograph of Saint George defeating the Dragon. The dragon was huge; its green wavy joints consumed the greater part of the picture space. Much smaller Saint George on his stallion (which looked rather like a pony) was bravely galloping up to the gigantic snake, trying with all his might to pierce the snake's head with his harmless pike. Saint George's scarlet cloak was flapping and streaming in the air. The pale face of the rider was indiscernible, even though it was directed not forward to the monster, but awkwardly twisted to my side, and even a little bit back. As a young girl, I always racked my brains because of the hero's such careless tactics. It might have been that he was looking for help. Some anemic figures of people were milling behind a rather low white town wall in the corner of the picture, but nobody was going to lend a hand to Saint George. Gloatingly grinning, the ugly, fat dragon lay in wait for the hero. Poor, small Saint George!

I liked his scarlet cloak the most in that lithography. Its fiery, resilient flourish was exploding the prevailing feeling of doom, conveying swiftness of the attack, yet with some hope.

Keenly feeling for Saint George, I innocently sighed. It immediately alarmed both women.

"Don't upset the child, Pietzar. It will be better if you tell her a funny story about her uncle. Do you remember what he did to 'Frank' Markar and his chickens?"

"Oh yes, Haroutiun's prank was really funny." My mother livened up. "But wait a minute. I will bring Simon here. I hope it will cheer him up, too; we should not leave him alone."

So then my Uncle Simon came into the kitchen, his eyes glassy and shoulders drooped. He cast glances at me with stealth. There was anguish and some reproach in his eyes. He knew that I had found a new object of interest: Haroutiun. However, very soon, my mother's dulcet voice, the artistic play of her arms and even shoulders, and her flushing face and sparkling eyes, had completely enchanted us both.

We were seeing, as if with our own eyes, a dark silhouette of "Frank" Markar, sitting at the opened gate of his house. Despite the warm summer weather he is in black trousers matched by a buttoned-up shirt and waistcoat of the same color. The chair, with a twisted back and a small flattened pillow just the size of his scraggy, incessantly fidgeting buttocks, is pulled far enough into the street so that he can look over the entire long fence of his cherry orchard. Its numerous branches with ripening fruits are hanging across the fence. It is an irresistible bait for neighboring lads.

My mother showed how desperate "Frank" Markar was bending his lean body in various unthinkable angles in order to have the better view of the street and the fence, and how the man was screwing up his eyes behind his spectacles that had slipped down his nose, trying to identify people appearing at the top of the street. Of especially crucial importance was detecting Haroutiun, the leader of the local boys. One should never let him out of one's sight. However, to the contrary, if it was just a neighbor, "Frank" Markar would pretend to be simply enjoying a good summer day. He would look down and polish his boots with a piece of flannel, until the neighbor would start speaking, "Paron Markar! How are you doing? Guarding as always?" Giving no ear to the gibe, "Frank" Markar would reply, burring diligently, "Mer-r-rcy, mer-r-rcy! How are you, paron?" "What about your wife, madam Zabel?" "Mer-r-rcy, gr-r-rand mer-r-rcy! She is fine, just magnifique!"

You should know that Markar Simian, one of our town's ordinaries, had brought his wife, Zabel, from Polis. She cut her hair short, knew genuine French (she actually spent her youth in France) and, not enough, she was Catholic. Soon Markar Simian began letting garbled French words fall here, there and everywhere, and mostly out of place. Also his madam called him "Marko." The Armenians of the town, all of them—and simpletons, and haughty pomposities, and even local cranks—could not tolerate all those oddities. The nickname "Frank" Markar stuck to this man like a leech. However, that pair managed to stun the virtuous town-dwellers further: Madam Zabel initiated home production of the French cherry brandy. It was a secret recipe she had brought from her favorite country, a memory of her sweet fragrant childhood.

You know, nowadays, this Madam Zabel could be a very successful businesswoman; she could open a liquor store somewhere in a popular seaside resort and flourish. However, back then her persistent efforts found only annoyance, irritation, and jealousy in the Armenian community. The town's bigwigs accepted samples of her delightful product of noble dark red, almost purple, color with cheerful aroma. However, they would not spend money buying it by themselves. Meanwhile, "Frank" Markar was assigned to keep Haroutiun and his friends off the cherry orchard. His madam did not want any kind of fruitless expenditures, not even traditional treats for passersby. This was too much *savoir faire.* Even "Khor" Aram, the town-wide recognized boor, used to bring out from his beautiful fruit-bearing garden a peak-cap full of apples and plums, or apricots, and entertain everybody who would agree to stay for a couple of minutes with him listening his crude jokes.

For Haroutiun, such unconcealed stiginess of Madam Zabel represented an obvious major disparity with human nature, an almost bellicose unfairness which had to be somehow corrected before ruining other beliefs of the world's benevolence. During that particular summer, none of his group of boys was able to treat himself to "Frank" Markar's juicy cherries. The man did not leave his observation post until all the fruits, the entire harvest, had been jammed into bottles whose necks were then tied up with gauze bandages. The bottles were standing on the tables in the garden; some of them were hanging from tree branches, looking like small gallows-birds with identical white scarfs around their heads. The cherry juice was already fermenting and gathering strength under the bright sun.

Now content, "Frank" Markar spent more time inside the house, and Haroutiun, with his pals, could observe the garden by climbing onto the top of its clay fence. There the young boys tittle-tattled about Markar and his wife, trying in their childish way to explain the amazing miserliness of this couple. However, forbidden fruit is sweeter. So, little by little, the boys came to a tempting idea. They decided to examine the contents of the bottles after all, because of the fuss in the town about those Madam Zabel's cherries. Haroutiun ventured to smuggle a pair of bottles from the table to the fence. Suddenly, something scared off his accomplices at the top of the fence. The children's hands that had begun shivering could not hold the heavy vessels while Haroutiun was climbing back from the garden. With a muffled sound both bottles fell and crushed on the ground. The confused boys ran away. Departing at the gate of Haroutiun's house, his friend Ara said, with slim hope, "Maybe they will not notice the missing bottles because they had so many? Will they, Harout?" "They certainly will! Such misers like them apparently count and re-count all their things several times a day."

Haroutiun was right. A few hours later, Greek Nikos, a tailor from "Lord" Pogos's shop came for Haroutiun. The time of reckoning had come. Earlier, furious Madam Zabel, wearing a hat with artificial flowers and a close-fitting gaudy dress, and accompanied by the mournful "Frank" Markar, appeared in the shop, demanding full compensation.

"With all profound respect to you, sir, I am completely shocked by such a barbaric act from your son." The strapping, big-bosomed Madam Zabel pressed against the rather short "Lord" Pogos.

"Such losses, such huge losses," assented "Frank" Markar from the side. "Seven good laying hens and two bottles of magnificent cherry brandy." It turned out that these stupid, greedy hens had stuffed themselves with the drunken cherries from the broken bottles and then had dropped dead here and there in his garden.

"Lord" Pogos was really ashamed by his son's action, unseen in the town. However, he also was manifestly trampled by the fact that this woman did not send her husband alone for negotiations, but instead presented herself in his shop, and, in an unprecedented scene, she was now pressing upon him. Haroutiun's father did not know where to rest his eyes, fascinated by Madam Zabel's outstanding bust while she was chasing him across the waiting room. (Here, my mother also made a great deal of portraying their strange dance. I was roaring with laughter, not even fully detecting the piquancy of the presented situation, but happy at our joint excitement: the vibrant voice of my mother, the brief smiles and elaborative comments of my usually sober grandmother, and my Uncle Simon's puerile joy, so rare for those days.)

"Lord" Pogos felt a big relief when Haroutiun appeared before him. Haroutiun did not deny his guilt in destroying the bottles of cherry brandy, but was unaware of the tragic end of Madam Zabel's hens that resulted from his actions. However, "Lord" Pogos was eager to pay for all the damages; and the bottles, and for "the innocent birds killed in such a gruesome manner." At that time, confused by Madam Zabel's invasion, he even forgot to establish a proper punishment for Haroutiun. Being saved from Madam Zabel and "Frank" Markar, he could only repetitively exclaim: "That was not a woman; it was a ship, a whole battleship!"

The story did not end; it had one more twist. The very next morning, puffing Madam Zabel and mournful "Frank" Markar revisited my grandfather's shop. Through their inconsistent groans it became clear that yesterday, after discovering their dead hens, this too thrifty pair had decided to use, at least, the dead hens' fluff. Before throwing them into the rubbish heap, "Frank" Markar very diligently picked through them, leaving only the rough wing feathers. Unfortunately, the hens were not really dead, but simply dead drunk due to having eaten the fermented cherries from those broken bottles. The morning chill refreshed their lost souls, and there they were, meeting their greedy owners at the usual place in the courtyard for the morning feeding. Their disfigured bodies were covered by pathetic sparse feathers, shamelessly displaying to the astounded eyes of Madam Zabel and "Frank" Markar the ugly-looking bluish skin with pimples of cold.

"This was a total embarrassment," Madam was moaning. "What would people say if they saw our birds shivering of cold and shame?" But this time, "Lord" Pogos was much firmer. Barely containing his laughter, he could only suggest to Madam Zabel an abundance of small pieces of cotton and silk, the waste from his tailoring work, which she could use for "hens' suits, jackets, or shirts, whatever would be appropriate for the birds in their desperate situation."

The end of this town's legend is rather vague. (Such a thing usually happens to the other similar, many times told and re-told stories.) Some people have said that Madam Zabel left my grandfather's shop in a such great anger and dissatisfaction that even her husband preferred to escort her in rearguard, while other towners have assured that "Frank" Markar was carrying a package with him, and thereafter they saw with their own eyes the hens wandering around his courtyard in small, but elegant waistcoats. My grandfather, "Lord" Pogos, who unexpectedly became a key figure in this story, kept a significant silence. What was known for certain was that Madam Zabel and "Frank" Markar eventually left the town. It could be due to the total failure of their cherry brandy venture or because of towners' unending gossips.

The house door gnashed suddenly, and closed with a bang. Uncle Haroutiun was returning from his wanderings by the town's streets. . . .

"Avenge Me, Haroutiun"

Heavy footsteps stopped at the door, closed to keep the kitchen warm. My mother jumped from her chair.

"Here is our Haroutiun!" she anxiously exclaimed while opening the door wide. "Come in, come in, Haroutiun-djan! Nargiz, move a little bit and give your uncle some space near the stove. Let's bake potatoes while there is still heat in it."

Every time, upon returning from his walk, my uncle would utter some strange phrase, a wreckage of his inner discourse, such as "All the streets of this town lead nowhere." Those words, spoken in the sticky silence, were so strange that I still remember them.

Passing fresh-cut potato chips to Haroutiun, who was putting them on the red-hot surface of the stove, my mother (the pigeon of peace) tried to direct his thoughts in a more mirthful direction.

"We were just talking about our former neighbors, Madam Zabel and 'Frank' Markar. Surely you remember them, their famous cherry brandy and their drunk chickens? There was so much laughter in the town after your prank that madam and her husband moved to Polis and then to her favorite France."

"But then they have both survived. The entire town laughed at them. Oh yeah, our towners were so talented at deriding and ridiculing each other. However, after all, those two misers proved to be smarter than their scoffers. Now where is the laughter of the townspeople? It was axed, shot, drowned in the sea, burned and hammered! Look around the town; there is not even one Armenian left here. Of course, I mean the real Armenian, not those who became Mussulmans. Converted bastards! Where are those Armenians ridiculing 'Frank' Markar? They have been slaughtered like brainless sheep. No one fired back and killed any Turkish gendarme, not even the goddamn weakest, oldest, most disabled zaptieh, or one of the most bedraggled Circassian. No! Nobody even tried to run away and then laugh at the Turks, and all this makes me sick!"

The woman usually kept silent during such bouts from Haroutiun. Sometimes, very briefly, my grandmother, Iughaper, ascertained that the Armenian women and their children alone could not have resisted the armed Turks and Circassian bands. The devilish Tachiks destroyed all the Armenian men beforehand, group by group. In our family, in the beginning, they sent my father and my middle uncle, Levon, to build military roads, and the two most capable men of the family disappeared forever. Then the Tachiks took my grandfather Pogos and teenager Uncle Simon to that Harab Caravansaray to kill them too.

"Well, it was easy with defenseless crowds of women and children, but what about those bright and clever Armenian heads in Polis, those Armenian members of Medjilis* and the leaders of the Armenian parties? Instead of arming their people against the deadliest enemy, they sang the hymns of romantic friendship with the Tachiks. Soon the world saw the shameful end of that meek love and trust! What a shame!" My uncle uttered his Russian curses so thickly that it was hard to tolerate, despite the fact that nobody else among us knew even one word of the Russian tongue.

My mother caressed and compressed the trembling Haroutiun's hand, "Harout-djan, listen to me. It is absolutely wrong. I cannot explain my thoughts right now, but I am sure that you should not feel any shame or feel somehow responsible for what has happened to us here. You should not burn yourself down . . ."

"Eh," responded Haroutiun. "Nowadays, in this unjust world, everybody, if he is not a scum, is burning like the logs in this stove. You, my gentle sister, are burning by giving light and warmth around, and my obliged mother is burning with an even, stable fire, and in such a way she will burn herself out. And I am burning myself, too, burning with the crackling of fire and frequent sparks. Move away or you will be scorched! For me the cracks and sparks are much better than a slow smoking smouldering."

Once, Uncle Simon was courageous enough to say that there was an Armenian in our town, the mighty butcher Arshak, who stood up bravely to the killers and destroyed two Circassian marauders and crippled a few more during his fatal battle at the Harab Caravansaray. That was enough. Haroutiun stuck to him like a bear to honey, and deluged him with a barrage of questions. Confused, Simon told him almost every detail of his escape from the Harab Caravansaray. He painted the picture he saw in the Circassian village while he was in nearby

* Turkish Parliament.

hiding, the scene when the village freak brought severed Arshak's head to a woman whom Arshak had made a widow just a few hours earlier. Poor Simon was stumbling, yet feeling relief while uncovering some circumstances of his survival that my grandmother had previously forbidden him to tell Haroutiun. However, he did not have yet more courage to confess to his brother, breathing heavily and noisily through Simon's entire explanation, about those ill-starred gold coins of Rouben Shaghbazian that had been spent for his, Simon's, conversion.

Haroutiun's reaction was exactly what both my grandmother and mother had been terribly afraid of. Immediately, Haroutiun declared to his brother that the moment had come to pay a tribute to the people who had saved his life: giant Arshak, Simon's father, Pogos, Babken Mangasarian, and the others. "Everyone who has survived is in deep debt to the hundred or maybe more who did not."

"Babken could be alive, maybe . . ." Simon dared to whisper. Such diffident words inflamed Haroutiun even more.

"No, they all are dead, remember that once and for all! Instead of expecting to see Babken walking down the town's streets you must climb the mountains and find that place where our people fell, and where their bones have been laying without any care. After all, we two sons must bury our father. Instead of carrying his ring on your finger go there and pay your debt to the man."

Poor Uncle Simon! He was so afraid of going back to that place where the massacre he had miraculously escaped had taken place. He was also sincere in not remembering that desperate path to the Harab Caravansaray, and he had no idea about the location of the Sheitan Delik, where the robbed bodies of the Armenian men had been dumped. He knew about the name of the Armenian towners' last destination only from the Kurd Bakro's words. Other Kurds from Bakro's tribe were terribly afraid of this dismal place inhibited by the malicious *jinns.* Only the inveterate hunter Bakro dared to appear in the forest surrounding that haunted place.

Simon's memory incapabilities, the daily tears of his mother and sister, and their laments and implorings did not stop Haroutiun from developing his "crazy plans." Now, they not only included two brothers, but also Bakro, who would lead them to the Sheitan Delik. When the spring came, he urged Simon to hasten a meeting with this mountaineer. "Go to the bazaar *meidan,* find out whether your 'friend' Bakro has already returned to his yayla?"

That was the kind of man my elder uncle, "Hent" Haroutiun, was. He was not really crazy, or extraordinary. Not at all. I think he was rather a simple man, a man of few but unbending principles, one of which was: "Worship a hero and punish an offender or a traitor! However, the traitor must be treated first." Did it sound crazy at that time? Perhaps. His intense dark eyes, slightly protruding, were shining with fire when he appealed to Simon. Haroutiun was very eager to inspire courage in his delicate brother. So, one day he told him and us his own story of duty and revenge.

It happened before my birth, at the time when my parents, Pietzar and Nishan, had just asked for a blessing from "Lord" Pogos. Nishan Zhamkochian came to our town from Kirason. He was exceptionally well-educated, knew languages and finance, and got two jobs, one at the port as a translator and the other as an accountant in a local bank. My grandfather was proud of having such a promising son-in-law. The preparations for the wedding were going at full speed. About that time, a new, very strange, breed of Tachiks appeared in the country. Those Turks, mostly young people, were talking about things unheard of. They advocated freedom and equality for all people of Turkey. The most clever Armenians, the intellectuals and politicians, were the first to swallow the bait. Such tricks always happen to us Armenians. For some reason our know-alls, with astonishing ease, presuppose in other people they are dealing with ideas and intentions that actually never existed in the minds of those people. The more clever an Armenian is, the more naive he turns out to be. In reality, the idea of genuine freedom and equality for Armenians never entered the Tachiks' heads, neither the old, nor the so-called Young Turks. So then, Manouk Libaridian, a nephew of "Frank" Markar, came to our town from Polis. He came to wind up all the remaining affairs related to his uncle's house and land. (I told you that "Frank" Markar and his wife left our town for good.) Meanwhile, Libaridian Effendi and his family were spending pleasant vacation under the shadows of the blooming cherry and apple trees, far away from the crowded capital.

Although this well-to-do man was very informed and tempting company, the old generation of Armenian towners did not spend much time visiting his open evenings, namely because those assemblages were open to anybody. There, one can meet heatedly arguing youths, graduates of the town's Armenian school with their teacher Aram Manukian, who was viewed in the town as "a revolutionary," along with laconic, reserved mechanic Hovannes, mixed visitors from Trebizond and other neighboring towns, and a group of the "new" Turks cajoled by the smooth-tongued host, and then be greeted by his attractive wife in her stylish attires. The town's elder Armenians, having learned from their long experiences of dealing with the local Turks, were hesitant at becoming involved in such informal talks with Turks and, save God, arguing with them.

In our town, from time immemorial, the Armenians and Turks lived in two parallel worlds. In great part there were only two occasions when Armenians entered into some private discussions with Tachiks. That was either when an Armenian in legal trouble asked for leniency from a Turk in an official position or if a Turk wanted a loan from an Armenian. On both occasions, the final result might be that the unlucky Armenian would take a punishment. This definitely occurred in the latter situation if the Armenian had enough impudence to ask for his money be repaid. This happened as sure as night comes after day. Haroutiun saw that for the first unforgettable time when an elderly Turk, dressed in frayed trousers and a turban which once was of white color, was beating the owner of a neighboring kerosene shop who dared to demand that the customer's debt be paid. The Turk just took off his crumpled galosh and struck the strapping shopkeeper a few times on his shoulders and lowered head. A minute later the hot-tempered customer was holding a funnel over his can while the grown quiet shopowner was pouring kerosene from the heavy churn in his big hands. Haroutiun, then a young boy, had gotten the idea, for the first time, that something was wrong in an otherwise fascinating and alluring world.

During that summer when Libaridians were in our town, Haroutiun was reluctantly visiting their salon in "Frank" Markar's house. While telling the story to Simon, he admitted that, at that time, he did not understand much of the discussions. He also did not like the Tachiks' presence there, particularly the face of young Mehmed Jemal. A son of a rich landlord and a powerful tribe chief, Jemal Bey, he had been sent to Europe by his father who was trying to establish friendship with that new breed of Turks claiming more and more popularity and power in the country. However, young Bey soon returned under the father's wing. It looked like political conversations did not attract much of Mehmed's attention; he rarely squeezed out a smile when hearty hosts talked to him. His face, with its regular features and thoroughly greased black mustache, markedly livened up when he directed his gaze upon their daughter. In her evening gown or even in a modest day dress, Takouhi Libaridian was always pretty, charming, and the center of attention. Haroutiun's best friend, Ara, was ready to spend every evening in "Frank" Markar's former house, just to hear Takouhi's joyful voice and natural laugh. He begged Haroutiun to accompany him there. In his loyal friend's presence, he, a usually shy and sensitive person, felt more confident and relaxed. Upon returning home, Ara continued expressing his admiration: "Did you notice her eyes, Harout? They are amazing; grey and green. I have never seen such beautiful eyes. Her hair, smooth and curved around her tender face, was like a frame of a divine picture. She speaks, moves, and smiles with such grace, absolutely unfeigned, the total opposite to our town's affected and pretentious, marriageable girls. I think she is more interested in you that in me, the unfortunate one who fell in love; she asks you about this and about that, yet you are not burning with the desire to express yourself, not like me, not at all. I am dying to show my total obedience to regal Takouhi!" (He was saying those words because in Armenian Takouhi means Queen.)

The three young souls were the same age, recently graduated their schools. Ara, the pride of his class, enthusiastically discussed with Takouhi his plans of going to study philosophy and literature somewhere abroad. She had definitely decided to study medicine in Paris where her family had relatives. Haroutiun was not such a brilliant student as Ara (nicknamed in their school and even around the town as a "walking encyclopedia") so he held his tongue when Ara and Takouhi were weighing the advantages of universities in Germany and France. However, a boring career in his father's garment shop did not lure my uncle either.

Only the very possibility of being with Takouhi in the same university made Ara euphoric, particularly in contrast to Haroutiun's seriousness. Ara liked everybody and looked to everything with trust and fervor. He liked the elevated tirades of Paron Libaridian, the sober, down to earth question of mechanic Hovannes, controversial arguments of his favorite teacher, Aram Manukian, and the presence of Turks in the Libaridians' house, even Mehmed's wry face. "Dear Harout, I am completely with paron Libaridian and Doctor Rasim for they both are right in that the Turks, Armenians, and Greeks should unite around one common idea, in order to bring their country to peace and prosperity.

Listening to them, an Armenian and a Turk, both extremely enlightened persons, I believe that our country can become as civilized as others in Europe. We have great potential, and I, myself, would be happy to study harder, to bring back my knowledge, and to contribute it into the resurrection and prosperity of this country. By the way, do you know that paron Libaridian saved Doctor Rasim's life? He was hiding the doctor in the cellar of his house in Polis when the sultan's bloodhounds were after the doctor."

My uncle tried to sober up his friend: "I did not know about the doctor's story. However, I did notice he became visibly angry when our teacher, Aram, very politely asked him why, in order to reach that unification, oppressed Armenians should go a long way down by restraining their striving for immediate reforms rather than Turks making steps up toward establishing normal human relationships and abandoning centuries-old abuses of power. Really, it is logical. It is so simple that even I, not a politician or philosopher as the others in there, can understand this disparity. Our teacher is a wisely polite man; he used words like 'oppressed' and 'abuse of power.' I would ask the doctor straightforwardly: 'Why should the Armenians, better educated people, all those thousands of mechanics, clerks, merchants, builders, and peaceful hardworking peasants go down the road to darkness and savagery, sacrificing more of their already wounded pride and rights, instead of doctor Rasim, and others of his ilk, encompassing his people, the Circassians, and the Kurds to stop their barbaric treatment of Armenians?' "

Apparently, Ara was surprised by such a lengthy speech from his taciturn friend. Usually, Haroutiun would walk silently with his hands in his pockets or clutched together behind his back. At these moments his figure resembled that of his father, "Lord" Pogos. Taller and leaner, Ara would constantly run ahead of him, then turn to Haroutiun and walk for a while backward, impulsively gesticulating, blurting out his considerations and simultaneously avoiding passersby.

"Understand, Haroutiun, we are talking here about a very long and painful process, and our teacher, Aram, despite all my respect toward him, is just showing his impatience. Paron Libaridian mentioned that this man is a typical revolutionary, and it was bad that he stopped to come for the discussions. Even in this matter he expressed that he was not tolerant . . ."

"Tell me about the kerosene shopkeeper. Explain his options. Should he continue to put his head under his Turkish customer's punches?" insisted Haroutiun.

"Again your kerosene shopkeeper! Well, here is his program: patience and understanding, understanding and laborious work! Don't smile. If the store owner is more educated, he obviously should be more able to understand than that ignorant Turkish peasant who, by the way, is a victim of the existing conditions, too, because he cannot afford to buy kerosene and light up his dwelling . . ."

"Beautiful words! Dangerous words! I prefer to remember our old saying: 'You may make friends among Tachiks, but do not forget where your weapon is.' And you had better watch how Mehmed snorts when you approach him and Takouhi talking," concluded Haroutiun against the Ara's fervent objections.

Thus, arguing between themselves, the two youths reached Ara's house. Then Ara volunteered to escort Haroutiun to his house, where their roles changed again. Their houses in the Armenian quarter were within a short distance of each other, so they really did not have enough of a walk to resolve all the burning problems.

As I told you, at that time, my future parents were going to marry. There were a lot of preparations in "Lord" Pogos's household, and Haroutiun was more often called for help. Ara was informing him about his, Ara's, visits to the Libaridians' evenings. A couple of times he came with Takouhi and her mother to buy something in "Lord" Pogos's shop. Her openness and joyful spontaneity made quite an impression on all the members of my family. "*Maral agchik*,"* agreed even my critical grandmother, Iughaper. Ara was in a state of bliss.

Then came that terrible news. Ara, mercilessly beaten, was found in a dark alley not far from his house. Haroutiun knew this narrow passage hidden among tall clay fences very well. They both used this for many years as a short cut. Apparently, somebody also found it very suitable for an ambush.

For two days Ara was unconscious. His previously refined, slightly hook-nosed, face had swollen up and turned purplish-black. Ara's lowly lamenting mother moistened it with diluted vinegar, trying to reduce his fever, wiping up the blood being hawked from her son's lips. Haroutiun spent much of his time near his friend's bed. Ara's father, the

---

* "Beautiful, gracious girl." (Arm, word-by-word "deer girl.")

town's doctor, periodically came upstairs from his office on the ground floor of the house, bringing drugs, and quietly stood next to his son's bed. Ara was his pride and admiration. Ara's teenager brother rolled himself up into a ball next to Haroutiun.

On the third day, Ara looked at them and tried to speak. He did not know who had attacked him. In darkness, under only the moonlight, he did not recognize their faces. Meanwhile, in the town, rumors began circulating that some "strange thieves," perhaps nomadic Kurds from the nearest mountains, were responsible for the robbery attack. Haroutiun told us that from the very beginning he realized that no stranger to the town would wander by that narrow hidden street, only locals, and particularly those who knew this route frequented by Ara. Sometimes, left alone in the room with Ara, he tried to discover the details that would confirm his suspicions. But Ara could not even recall the number of the bandits—"two or three." Everything happened suddenly and rapidly. The attackers did not demand money, and they did not say a word. To Haroutiun's frustration, Ara was more worried about Takouhi; he wanted to see her and was desperate to warn her about something bad that might happen to her. However, at the same time, he was ashamed of his frightening appearance and helplessness. Takouhi, herself, was eager to see him, but Ara asked Haroutiun to postpone her visit until the next day, then one more, and so on. Unfortunately, he was not getting better. Finally, Takouhi came herself. She cried and caressed his hands, describing how her family was shocked by this brutal event, how her father was missing the Ara's presence during the evening meetings, and how her desire to be a doctor was becoming stronger while seeing him, Ara, in such pain. So, after his recovery they would both go to study in Paris.

That night, Ara's temperature increased. Often he fell into a drowsy state, then talked to Haroutiun feverishly. He recalled that evening when, upon returning from the Libaridians', he saw two figures approaching him on that dark alley. Before he could greet them as regular passersby somebody else struck him on the head from behind and knocked him down. So, there were three of them, and they definitely were not Kurds because something in Ara's mind was convincing him that he was preparing to greet them in Turkish. Ara desperately tried to catch some vague pictures which glimpsed fleetingly in his wounded head.

"Maybe you saw their clothes, or could it be that you heard them speak just a few words of Turkish?" Haroutiun was trying to help his struggling friend with his own assumptions.

"Paris! I heard one shout out 'Paris.' " Ara even raised himself a little from the pillows, but then fell back from exhaustion. "He was kicking and shouting 'Come and get your Paris! Take that, and that. This is your Paris!' "

"I suspected it! I already knew it! Damned Mehmed!" gnashed Haroutiun. "Wait a little, you fat snake. I will settle our accounts with you."

Uncle Haroutiun said that it was exactly at this moment that the first thought of vengeance struck his mind. But what a great difference there can be between people in the same situations, even between two close ones; while my uncle was already thinking about Mehmed's punishment, his wounded, dying friend was inquiring: "Why did he do it to me? What did I do to him?" There were no clear answers or explanations (hatred? jealousy? envy?). Nothing could save innocent Ara. Something very important was broken inside him. Pain and anguish absorbed him and took him away. My uncle's best friend died. His last words were: "Please, try to help Takouhi—and also, find the truth . . . and if the truth is yours, avenge me, Haroutiun."

Thus, suddenly, my uncle, then just a seventeen or eighteen-year-old youth, was left to face this obligation that could be too huge even for an adult. He was absolutely alone in running the whole matter: an investigator, a judge, and a punisher. Ara's parents were crushed by their grief, they both frenziedly clung to Ara's younger brother, their only remaining child. They heard the words Ara spoke about his murderers, but were too afraid of Mehmed's father; this powerful Bey would make short work of their family. (By the way, their silence did not save their younger son. When in 1915, the *Yeghern* began, he was taken away by the Turks, along with my father, my middle uncle, Levon, and many others, and nobody ever saw those Armenians again. On the morning of the deportation day, Missak the Informer and zaptiehs found the dead bodies of Ara's parents sitting in chairs in their home. They had continued their routine work to the last day, treating their patients, be them Greek, Armenian, Turk, or Laz. Then they had prepared poison for themselves. For them, death came much more quickly and comfortably than for their Armenian neighbors.) Haroutiun's father, "Lord" Pogos was up to his neck with his daughter's coming wedding. Teacher Aram and mechanic Hovannes, approached by

Haroutiun, although listening to him with sympathy and understanding, pointed out that those few words spoken by Ara would be taken by the Turks as simply as a dying person's ravings and would, after all, result in a new round of humiliation and even abuse for the local Armenians.

Haroutiun decided to visit the Libaridians. Firstly, he had promised Ara that he would warn Takouhi against Mehmed. He also needed to see the murderer's eyes. My uncle said to us that he already knew that the entire plot of Ara's assassination was created by Mehmed. Who else, with so much ease, could have tracked down Ara's regular route from "Frank" Markar's house to his home? Who else knew about Paris, often discussed by Ara and Takouhi during their talks at the evening gatherings? Also, that malicious grin of Mehmed, twisting his lips each time Ara talked about his and Takouhi's future study plans. Nevertheless, Haroutiun wanted to see the enemy once more time, to examine him closely.

Initially, he called the sad Takouhi into the courtyard (the former garden of "Frank" Markar, now fairly well thicketed with weeds), the place of Haroutiun's and Ara's pranks and adventures. There, he found out from her that during that ill-fated evening, Mehmed left the Libaridians' salon immediately after Ara. It was exactly what he had expected to hear. Haroutiun did not want to scare Takouhi and reveal his own plans. So, he only mentioned that their friend's death was not a result of his encounter with some vagrant Kurds, but most likely with someone from the town. In tears, Takouhi ran to the house. Haroutiun followed her. After a very short exchange of words with her parents, Takouhi proceeded to her room. Haroutiun found himself in the midst of the usual group of habitues. Manouk Libaridian, with exaggerated conviction, turned to him, telling him that the Chief of Police had been making considerable effort to find the persons responsible for the death of Ara, such a promising youth, and that he, Libaridian himself, and also Doctor Rasim, a dear friend of Police Bey Effendi, would additionally remind him about this matter. "He speaks like he spreads butter," a sullen Haroutiun thought, taking a look over the guests' faces. The doctor's spectacles were flaring up under the bright light. Mehmed was disdainfully staring at Haroutiun and openly grinning from ear to ear. He obviously did not feel any danger. Barely concealed irritation could be heard in Libaridian's voice. Haroutiun felt that it was because of his silence. He said good-bye and left. "Many, too many people of yours,

Libaridian Effendi, still continue to show their age-old annoying mistrust and stubborn suspiciousness. . . ." These words spoken by the doctor were the last of what Haroutiun heard in "Frank" Markar's house.

However, his warning took effect. The Libaridian family urgently left the town and returned to Constantinople. Before that, Takouhi made her last visit. She recalled how happy the three of them had been just a couple of weeks before. She timidly questioned Haroutiun's plans, trying to articulate something very important. He failed to see Takouhi's desperate and worried look during that visit. He never noticed her special attention to him. (For years, my mother and grandmother had often reproached him for that. For a young girl of her age, to come alone to their house was quite an unprecedented action for the customs of our small town. Obviously, such an extraordinary deed of Takouhi had a very important cause and the both women recognized its delicate nature. Haroutiun did not.) Other problems excited his heart. He was thinking about a weapon. Mehmed was taller and heavier than him. My uncle realized that even if he managed to seize an opportunity to fight with the Turk face to face, the necessary result would be in jeopardy. He promised Ara to slay his murderer and he should do it for sure.

But my uncle could not find a weapon. There were no pistols or rifles in the Armenian households to which he had access. He had already discovered a couple of secluded places where Mehmed spent time—cards and hashish—with a bunch of his friends, the similar idle rich, surrounded by arrant knaves and spongers. Haroutiun did not care that maybe among them Mehmed had recruited two of his accomplices in Ara's murder. My uncle wanted the young Bey's life. Haroutiun stole a big knife from the butcher store belonging to his aunt's husband, Rouben Shaghbazian, and then re-grinded it into a short narrow dirk. He began carrying the dirk with him in a leather sheath.

Haroutiun was so obsessed that he hardly noticed the departure of Takouhi from his life. My parents' wedding party made a brief stir and passed. My hent uncle continued his "hunting" until eventually he struck.

Why are you asking me about his dreams? My uncle never mentioned any dreams he might have had before the fight with Mehmed. There was nothing significant or extraordinary; nothing at all.

Well, one thing he recalled was that before going in that day for his routine of shadowing Mehmed, he stopped at the kerosene shop for some reason. The shopkeeper was busy with a tight-fisted customer, showering praise on the quality of the grease for wheels. Haroutiun did not find anything special in the kerosene shopkeeper's quite ordinary, Armenian face, nor in the grease he was selling either. The shopkeeper caught up with him at the turn of the street.

"I know you. You are 'Lord' Pogos's sön. Did you want to buy something? No? Maybe something for your father? What were you looking for in my store? Nothing? Anyway, good luck, and please, convey my most sincere regards to your father."

With difficulty, Haroutiun broke away from that man. He cursed himself for that useless distraction. Toward the evening he found Mehmed in his favorite place, playing cards and backgammon. Haroutiun patiently waited until a group of the last players emerged from the entrance door. Very soon, Melmed parted from the noisy companions and walked alone deep into narrow and winding streets of the market quarter. Haroutiun followed him, not believing in such a fortunate progress of events. After twists and turns they came onto the street which was used to drive cattle to the market. Now, at night, it was deserted. Haroutiun slowed his pace to deaden the sounds of his strides. Suddenly, he lost sight of Mehmed. In confusion, he entered a small square between a huge plane-tree on one side of the street and a long cattle water trough on the other. The tree shadow obscured the scene. Moonlight sparingly revealed the ground and high clay fences guarding the nearest houses. Suddenly, the enemy's dark figure came off the tree trunk.

"*Hosh geldiniz Parisiye*!* I spotted your vile squatting figure from the very beginning!" The Turk broke the night silence, approaching Haroutiun. "So, do not cherish any hope in your blockhead that you have caught me here. It is you, an Armenian microbe, who now has no chance running away. Only don't squeal as your friend did, and try to extend my pleasure."

Haroutiun forgot about his dirk and rushed to the enemy. A few times Mehmed's merciless punches threw Haroutiun on the ground, yet each time, Haroutiun attacked him back with doubled fury. Mehmed was heaping abuse and egging on Haroutiun, promising him a much easier death than that which struck Ara. He was talking and laughing through the fight. However, he was aware that somebody from

* "Welcome to Paris!" (Turk.)

the nearest houses might interrupt the fight and prevent him from finishing off the young stubborn Armenian. Mehmed underestimated my "hent" uncle's stubbornness. Soon, his breathing became heavy and broken, and his punches lost strength and accuracy. Perhaps his sweet rakish life had taken a toll on his fighting endurance, or maybe he had talked too much trash and it had spoiled his breathing rhythm. A few minutes later, Haroutiun brought him down, and they fought at the foot of the tree.

Each time this story was retold, usually to inspire his younger brother, Simon, my uncle, Haroutiun, at that particular point, showed some kind of respect toward Mehmed. In moments of candor, he obligingly mentioned that his enemy, while being down, never shouted for help. Apparently the Turk could not imagine, or maybe was ashamed of, being saved from a beating by the younger and shorter giavour Armenian. Perhaps, he still did not believe that my uncle could kill him. However, then my uncle managed to reach for his self-made dirk and plunged it into Mehmed's chest.

Haroutiun quickly came to his feet. Mehmed was wheezing in agony. My uncle's friend, Ara, was avenged. Haroutiun did not say a word during the entire skirmish. Now, he wanted to say something important: tell Ara that his promise had been fulfilled, or to shout out something to wake up all the sleeping souls in the town. But his bleeding, rapidly swelling lips could not move. He realized that instead of any sounds from his mouth, he was hearing a clattering of horseshoes coming from the part of the street adjoining the market. Mehmed's wheezing died down. The clattering and also the vague sound of voices were approaching the small square with the plane-tree as Haroutiun was leaving the place.

The Crooked Cucumber

Tell your wife not to weep. Very soon the strike will calm down and your family will be able to leave our town peacefully. For the time being, Gorbachev, this pendant in Moscow, has enough power to stifle the railway strike. More importantly, one need not weep over such a thing as a train delay. Your wife should believe me. I know crying. Armenian women have cried their eyes out, made a whole sea of tears. I have wept so much in my life, it would be enough to free a hundred young butterfly-like women, such innocent souls as your wife, from crying. But I also know, after all, that the caravan of daily life carries away all our sorrows.

These words about the caravan are from an old Armenian cradle-song my mother used to sing to me, sitting at my bed:

Sleep, my baby, lying in your cradle;
I have wept very much, you need not weep.
The blind cranes fly crying over our country,
And I have wept very much; you need not weep.
In the black forest the wind is mourning,
Mourning for bodies the wild dogs devour.
Don't weep, my baby, I have wept very much.
Far in the desert the camels are kneeling,
The caravan carries away all our sorrows.
I have wept long enough; you need not weep.*

Let me tell you, in general, the Armenian women preferred tears. They did not speak; they wept and cried. The Armenian women did not tell personal stories (though anyone among those martyrs might tell amazing adventures and miracles of survival). They just cried. For an outsider, this was without any apparent reason. Suddenly and uncontrollably they would cry for themselves, sometimes even when doing household chores. Their hands in soap water or in dough, they tried to stop

* From: Mabel Elliot. "Beginning Again at Ararat." Fleming H. Revell, 1924.

the tears by wiping their eyes with their shoulders. A great shame overfilled their hearts, but stoned their lips. The Tachiks made with them such terrible things that the women could not talk about those things. A wife would not tell her husband, nor would a daughter to her mother, nor a sister to her brother. This haunting, all-consuming shame, I think, was the Tachiks' major intention. It was their utmost achievement. Maybe the major plan was to kill as many Armenians as possible, and then leave a handful of survivors to vegetate in a scab of guilt and self-disgust.

To the contrary, the Tachiks, in their mass, never felt shame or pity when seeing the herds of Armenians, their former neighbors, mostly women with young children, being driven to the slaughter places. The Tachiks looked through our bodies and faces, our begging hands and eyes. They had no pity. Oh, yeah! The Armenians were so dirty, in rags or half-naked, exposing blackened scaly skin and bones impassively protruding everywhere. Hair on their heads moved because of flocks of lices. One may feel pity for those who look like human beings or, at least, useful domestic animals. The exiled Armenians were neither of these. The women and children ate grass and waste. They belonged to a garbage dump. It was easy to look through their hideous figures. No mercy, no shame.

I also think that not only shame, sticky as hot tar, kept the Armenian women silent. There was also a bitter realization in the women that they would be unable to convey their terrible experiences using usual, normal words. What are the "terrible experiences" for others? For instance, for you, my patient listener? Writing words such as "hunger, terror, rape, humiliation, killings, death, and despair," can you feel by yourself and express to others exactly what those women went through?

A peel of words! A feebleness, dumbness of man's tongue! I know what torture it is to be unable to express feelings burning inside. When my brave grandmother found me in the Turkish village and brought me back to our home, I discovered my mother anew. All by herself, love and tenderness, she immediately became my deity. Grubby child Emine, I loved and worshiped her so much. I loved my mother, but could not say a word to her about what I was feeling. After a few years of living among the Tachiks I had forgotten Armenian, and for while spoke only Turkish. However, I knew no Turkish words about love.

Emine had never been told, and never learned such words. My speechlessness was the most painful part of becoming Nargiz. The proper words were coming to me slower than the dirt eaten into my skin was being washed away from my hands and feet. I did such odd things; I kissed my mother's dress that wore her scent, bit off a piece of bread that had touched her lips, or sang something that I believed slightly resembled the rhythm and melody of her gentle words.

The first time I told her, "*Es siroomem kes, mayrig-djan*!"* I irrevocably became Nargiz. I was finally saved, and it was a great relief and joy for all of us. A rare one for those times, had come.

I assure you that when the sense of humanity is completely lost, man's speech has no value; it does not work. Words, even the most colorful and extraordinary, do not sound; sentences, though very keenly twisted, fall flat. A story of an incredible survival becomes dim as the moon in a well. The Yeghern or The Massacre of the Armenians was beyond anything that could be related by usual words. This catastrophe needs another language, maybe one without words at all. Perhaps we should use a language which instead consists of raw sounds of suddenly bursting sobs, moaning pains inhabiting the defiled body, screaming nightmares, mad outcries for the lost children and doleful muttering of remembering the deaths of loved ones.

Now you understand why my women did not talk about their death march. They walked the entire length of Tachkastan; for weeks they dragged themselves from the Black Sea shore to the Arabian deserts. Of the big crowd of Armenians who left the town with them, only a few have survived. With the exception of my mother and grandmother, I saw only butcher Archak's wife and their three daughters come back to the town after the war. There was nobody else, as far as I know. Thus, one might have expected a lot of incredible stories from my women, but in reality, this was not so. Some vague fragments. Here and there accidentally dropped remarks and short phrases, or a brief re-telling of the other fellow-marchers' fates. But mostly there were just wet eyes, sighs, and shaking hands during the day and moans in sleep. Though my mother buried the life she had lived in the Kurdish village—where she was left to survive by her mother—inside herself, she could listen others' life stories. My mother persuaded my uncles to

* "Dear Ma, I love you!" (Arm.)

share their memories, but she never told them about her life in that Kurdish village.

I am telling you, there was so much shame in the Armenian women!

As for my grandmother, Iughaper, wild horses could not drag a word about her ordeal from that slight woman. "You must look forward, you are young; let us keep quiet about our sins," Grandma used to say upon hearing my questions. She always hated all that women's tittle-tattles, even in better pre-war times. At those times, when in need, she preferred to send for Babken Mangasarian, to get a brief, but capacious summary of the town's news. Such restraint of words, very strange among the town's women, was apparently developed in her after an old incident with The Crooked Cucumber.

Oh! It was a love story that ended with humiliation and empty gossips.

The Crooked Cucumber was a man with a quite common name, Missak Gazanchian. Somebody in our family, maybe my grandfather, "Lord" Pogos, or more likely my grandmother, Iughaper—believe me, she was short on words but long on meaning—gave this man such a strange nickname. She knew him very well. They were both from the same small village near the town of Shabin-Karahisar in the *vilaiet** of Sivas. You should know that this town has a special meaning in the heart of every Armenian. From time immemorial, the soil of Shabin-Karahisar gave birth to Armenians of a special kind—proud and freedom-loving spirits. Our Armenian hero, General Andranik, a terror and a punishment for the Turks, Kurds, and Azeris, was born there. Shabin-Karahisar was one of a few Armenian communities which put up fierce resistance during the massacres of 1915.

However, sometimes unexpected wrong things happen, exactly like with cucumbers. You plant a hundred seedlings on the same lot and in the same soil, you give them the same amount of sun and water, provide them equally with manure, and you thoroughly clean the seedlings' beds from weeds. Now, if you have taken such proper care of all of them, you would expect a good harvest. One after another, you would collect from the beds even, well-matched, sweet-scented and tasty cucumbers. However, among those hundred cucumbers you could suddenly run against a crooked one, for some reason twisted at an angle and bitter to taste, one that is absolutely inedible. A useless product!

* Province. (Turk.)

Missak Gazanchian was a tall man with regular features, a shock of curly hairs and, despite his young age, a fluffy mustache. Of course, Iughaper, six years younger than Missak, was pretty much charmed by him. Moreover, for many years, she was his intended bride. When she was still in her cradle, and Missak played his young boy's games, their fathers, two village friends, decided to marry their children as soon as they reached proper age. The elder Gazanchian had paid one gold coin to seal the deal. Thus, every villager knew that, sooner or late, Iughaper and Missak would marry. In this way both families did not need to resort to the services of a *meechnord* in order to find a suitable bride or groom, nor did they have to carry out long negotiations. Also, they avoided possible embarrassment if the negotiations had failed. The groom's family already had *khosk kap** or the acceptance of the bride's father.

Of course, Iughaper could not talk with Missak, even if they sometimes accidentally met each other in the course of daily living in that small village. The old Armenian customs did not allow for that. So, my Iughaper was imperceptibly growing, turning into a thin, seemingly frail girl, but very quick and jumping at any work around household. Missak had an elder brother who looked after family's sheep and cows and naturally would become the next *tannoo-ter*** after his father. As usual in Armenian families, field work fell to Missak's lot.

However, Missak was not tempted by such simple peasant perspectives. With the permission of his father and brother, and the help of a relative in Shabin-Karahisar, he began a small venture. He traveled to the town, bought up all kinds of cheap things usable in country households, and resold them in his and in neighboring villages. Villagers paid repeated tributes to his enterprise. "Your son is shrewd, very shrewd," old village men used to say to Missak's father, when the women, visiting Iughaper parents' house, deliberately and significantly hinted, especially in her presence, how Missak's future wife would be lucky to have such an assiduous master. By and by, Iughaper's mother invited the women to feast their curious eyes upon the daughter's dowry which had been prepared for her over many years. A chest of walnut wood was opened, filled with Iughaper's beautiful handwork, made with the needle and

* "The word was tied." (Arm.)
** Head of household and extended family. (Arm.)

on the loom, a pile of gifts to the groom's family—scarves and handkerchiefs, warm winter stockings and embroidered aprons—as well as linens and bedspreads, and, of course, the bride's white and red silk veils, and a major feature of the presentation, a blue velvet jacket decorated with gold threads and small pearls.

The summer had ended, then fall; the busy days of gathering in the harvest had come to an end, too. Fall was the best time for a wedding, but nobody came after Iughaper with ring and gifts, followed by numerous trays of pastries and candies, sweetened nuts and fruits, music and dance. Surplus sheep and a steer were not sacrificed for the wedding feast. For some reason, the Gazanchian family was not in a hurry. Missak continued his shuttle travelings between Shabin-Karahisar and the village, except that he stayed in the town for a longer time. His confusing father evasively muttered something about some unexpected family troubles and circumstances. Iughaper's father concluded, with regret, that the animals set aside for the wedding should be fed through half of winter. On the other hand, he consoled himself that the wine from the grapes of the proceeding harvest would be fully ready to enjoy later.

But nobody came after Iughaper in winter, either. No ring, no trays, no music. The sheep and steer marked time in cattle-sheds. Iughaper's father was angry. Then Lent arrived, and everybody knew that no engagements nor weddings were allowed during that period of time. Then rumors began spreading around the village that the Gazanchians had broken their promise because there was something wrong with Iughaper. Supposedly, a woman of the Gazanchian clan had seen Iughaper in the village hammam and had convinced the groom's family that Iughaper could not bear children because her thighs were too small.

Oh, those women's hammams! They were their exclusive clubs, fortified resort places, an oasis where they did much more than merely wash themselves. Families of women arrived there with young children and an array of bags and baskets of linens, towels, camel's-hair gloves for rubbing bodies, and clothes, as well as fruits, pastries, nuts, and home-made cold drinks, anticipating with great pleasure day long talks, news exchange, and direct observations.

However, when Iughaper's furious father confronted his old friend, Missak's father, the latter was unable to produce the name of the woman who started the gossip about Iughaper. Instead, the elder Gazanchian blabbed out that he himself had first learned about Iughaper's thinness from his son, Missak. The man also candidly confessed that all initiative of postponing the wedding came from his son, too.

Meanwhile, village women were shouting the scandalous news on every street corner. New forces were becoming involved in the discussions. *Kavors* or godparents of both families were trying to find a compromise. At that time, a visitor from Shabin-Karahisar brought another stunning news. He said that since last summer Missak Gazanchian had been hanging around a daughter of one of the richest merchants in the town. The girl was not blind in one eye nor lame, but for some reason she was *toon-mnatzogh**. So, her father was obviously ready to do everything to please the suitor for his daughter who had lost her bloom of youth. To the merit of the village elders, after considering new facts, they required the Gazanchians to pay my grandmother Iughaper's family compensation for loss of face.

I have no idea how much it was, and whether it was even money, or part of a future crop, or animals. What my terse grandmother did allow herself to recall from her ill-fated marriage was that her father had returned to Missak's father the gold coin he had been keeping since that day when they had both promised to marry their son and daughter to each other.

Many years passed. Both of my grandmother's parents died, thank God before The Yeghern, but she always recalled her father with pride, gratitude, and tenderness; the latter was not usual for her. She was grateful to him for sending her to find her chances outside of the village, as far away from Shabin-Karahisar as possible. Despite any wrongdoing, her life in the village would be nevertheless a miserable one. An unchaste bride would be placed backwards on a donkey and paraded through the streets of the village accompanied by the shriek sounds of horns and drums. Of course, this was not the case with young Iughaper. She had been found innocent. Missak was the one blamed publicly for the ruined wedding. Yes, he left the village in disgrace, and it is true that his relatives reaped bitterness for many years where he had sown. Nevertheless, Missak was a man. That is why he was free to leave the village and go to Shabin-Karahisar to soon marry that old maid with the fat dowry, which he did not fail to do. My grandmother, at that time a young girl of maybe fourteen years of age, could not do the same and leave the village by herself. If not for her father's decision, quite

* "Left at home" or an old maid. (Arm.)

extraordinary in the eyes of his country-folk, she would have been confined to that small village world, spending downcast years mostly in her parents' house. The shadow of the scandal would forever trouble her life. As a rule such rejected girls would never marry other men.

I see your delicate wife winces when I describe such barbaric things. Oh, yeah, "betrothal at infant age" and "payment for loss of face" now sound ridiculous and stupid. And that "riding the bride backwards on a donkey" was an awfully brutal custom. Nevertheless, it was the way of life the Armenians lived at that time. All those old-fashioned rules and regulations, those which, at first glance, seemed strange orders and prohibitions, were in great part, measures of survival. Armenians hurried to marry their very young daughters in order to give them enough time to produce more children, future ploughmen and herdsmen, who, by the way, died very frequently of various diseases. Also, one more thing occupied the Armenians' minds. The earlier a girl was married, the less chance she would be kidnaped by Turks or Kurds who had a particular desire for virgins.

For me personally, it is not the old customs which are disturbing, but our present inability to grasp an exact understanding of young Iughaper's feelings. *What did my fourteen-year-old grandmother think about Missak? Could she, an adolescent girl really love him and miss him when he finally vanished from her sight? Was she mad because of the humiliation and suffering? Or was it like out of sight, out of mind?* There is a huge difference between what people felt then and how they react now in similar circumstances. I only can imagine a slender, quiet girl with damp, almond-like black eyes, wandering around the house, anxiously listening to vague sounds from the outside and the beat of her own heart. A wounded swallow!

Eventually Iughaper left the village. Her father sent her to a seaside town on the Black Sea shore. That was how she was found to be in our town. There, distant relatives gave her a refuge. There she met Pogos Aleksanian, her future husband and my grandfather. He was not "Lord" Pogos yet. He was just a tailor, a widower who had lost his wife and house in a big fire which had happened in the town a few years earlier. Together they have raised four children: three sons—Haroutiun, Levon, and Simon—and a daughter, my mother, Pietzar. Iughaper supported her husband in becoming "Lord" Pogos, a successful and generous man. She really vindicated her name, which means, in Armenian,

"The Bringing Oil," or, in other words, "The One Who Brings Prosperity." She helped her husband to build a new and bigger house with the garment shop on the ground floor. This shop had three big windows facing the street and four "Singer" sewing machines, subjects of my grandfather's innocent boasting. Thus, my grandmother, that former slender village girl with perplexed, almond-like eyes, became a zealous far-sighted houselady, Iughaper Hanum.

By the way, it is funny how my grandfather chose his second wife, Iughaper. One day he came to her relatives' house with a meechnord, a woman who was supposed to introduce him to a young woman in the house. If my grandfather liked this young woman, he was supposed to say these secret words: "I like this room!" so the matchmaker could then proceed with her next duties. During that evening young Iughaper helped in serving the table for the guests. My grandfather immediately fell in love with her. (God knows how it happened!) So, he said to the matchmaker, "I like this small room!" hinting on the younger and slender Iughaper. The woman could not understand why he had changed the agreed-upon words. She asked him to repeat. "Do you like this room, paron Aleksanian?" He said again, "Not this room. I like the small one with the pink curtains." My grandfather meant the silk shawl with an embroidery of pink flowers which covered Iughaper's head and shoulders. The people of the host family were in a quandary. They had no such room. However, this time, the crafty matchmaker understood a secret message of her client.

Iughaper crossed out Missak's name in her heart, never talked about him, and did not visit her native village for many years. As I know, my grandma went there only when her father died. How do I know? It is because from there, my grandfather, who, of course, accompanied her and covered some of the funeral expenses, brought that extraordinary phrase told by Missak's father at the funeral repast. Although the saying is obscene, it remained in our family's folklore as an odd, but funny, expression of genuine straight-forward sincerity, so very characteristic of the people of Shabin-Karahisar. You excuse me, but the elder Gazanchian, obviously in some late apology to Iughaper, bluntly admitted: "*Missak'i padjarov menk kakh kerank*!"*

---

* "Because of Missak we all ate the shit!" (Arm.)

Yeah, the Shabin-Karahisar folks were such boors. One more interesting thing about them was that whenever and wherever they met Iughaper, they felt obliged to inform her about Missak's condition. "Missak Gazanchian trimmed his head of hair and got a thin mustache," or "Missak opened his own store." Then, a couple of years later, Missak and his still barren wife moved to Trebizond, according to him, in search of more space and animated commerce, although everybody knew that this man simply did not get on well with the people of Shabin-Karahisar, who, by his words, were "uncouth blockheads." Things did not go well in Tribizond either. Missak worked hard, with obvious embitterment. Light-hearted and risible inhabitants of the big seaside town did not understand Missak's sullen obsession with immediate success. Customers avoided him because of his displeased, as after a gulp of vinegar, face. He worked much harder. He never met a deal, no matter how small, dirty or risky, that he did not like to try. However, everything failed in bringing profit. Missak acquired a quite visible bald patch on his head and muttonchop sideburns. Angry tongues were saying that he almost regularly battered his wife who could not become pregnant. The patience of the father-in-law in Shabin-Karahisar ran low, as well as his loans and credits. Maybe now Missak understood why this man's daughter "was left at home." She turned out to be a good-for-nothing wife, petty and bawling like a stallholder on the last row of a fish market.

Then Missak's father-in-law died, never seeing his grandchild from his daughter and Missak. The brother-in-law who inherited almost the entire fortune continued sending small amounts of money to his sister, but the credit line for Missak was shut tight. Trebizond became too much of an embarrassing place for him to live. Missak and his wife moved to the smaller and less fancy Kiresun. The famous cherry orchards there did not gladden Missak's heart. He managed to open a store, just a bit bigger than the one he had at the beginning of his merchant career in the native village. There was an island near the town of Kiresun which had a very old, half-ruined statue of a Greek goddess who, accordingly to the local people's belief, might have helped infertile women. Missak and his wife made tours to this island where she passed her empty belly between the legs of the statue. It did not help. Returning from the island, they like all others in the boat, threw pebbles into the sea, but their troubles would not go away.

Surely, you know, how powerful some human feelings can be, for instance malice and jealousy. Sooner or later these are going to get you, hit you right on the head, and then knock you off your feet. There was so much malice and jealousy in Missak that he could not stand up straight. At the time of his vegetation in Kiresun, my grandparents began receiving disturbing news. Some obliging tongues retold Missak's enraged remarks to them. He lumped the blame for his permanent misfortunes on my grandmother, telling anybody willing to listen to him that Iughaper's curses, because of his refusal to marry her, had poisoned his life and business. It was then that my grandparents renamed him "The Crooked Cucumber."

These words remained in our family. Up to the present days we have been using the words "Crooked Cucumber" as our secret code to attest a dishonest person. It suits. My mother would say, "The Cucumber with the Moustache" and we, just us, would know that she meant Stalin. These days, I say, "The Marked Cucumber" or "The Marked," and my household members know that it is Gorbachev with a big birthmark on his balding head. Two crooks, each in his particular way.

At this point, I allow myself to again be amused by the strength and weakness of the words we, people use. I imagine words as . . . sorry for maybe the clumsy comparison—butter churned from the sea of milk, the sea of people's experiences, generation after generation. Thus, there are words made and used by two or three generations of one family, exactly like our "Crooked Cucumber," but there are also "butter-words" which were used by whole nations, millions of people and through tens of their generations. There are all-human words. People say "Sun," and everybody understands it is life and harvest; everybody feels warmth and joy. When hearing such words as "Black Sun," people perceive them as a frightening sign; some of them think about it as an image of gloom and desperation, sin and punishment, while there are the others, in much less numbers, who will remember that they have seen such sun with their own eyes. Another vacationer, Doctor Isakovich from Minsk, my guest for many summers, told me that he witnessed a "black sun" almost every day through the smoke from the chimneys burning corpses of the dead prisoners in his concentration camp during the last war with the Germans.

Yeah, Black Sun is different from usual words. I would like people to call the Armenian massacre in Turkey "The Black Sun" or something like this. However, many Armenians of my age call it simply "Jart." In

Armenian it is for "Destruction." But the word "destruction" is so overused and worn out: "destruction of property" or "drinking was his destruction!" This word does not work. There is a great need for new words when conveying stories of tragedies never experienced before. The regular "butter-words" make the stories too smooth; they conceal the total meaninglessness and madness of the event. Some survivors, in despair of the weakness of such "butter-words," invent their own language, which sounds and looks absolutely crazy. All their wails and mutters, obsessions and rituals, doubts and self-isolation, bravados and rage; why would people not consider these as a most precise and convincing language of the survivors? Why expect normalcy if the entire world around them has broken all established rules and natural expectations? Thus, for both my uncles, Simon and Haroutiun, the world had lost its order forever.

You are asking me to continue. . . . Well, nothing good was expecting Missak Gazanchian. For a while, he and his wife disappeared. Surely, my grandmother heaved a sigh of relief. But then news from Kiresun came again. Missak and his wife had returned, and not alone. They had gotten a son. Rumor had it that Missak had begotten the child with another woman somewhere outside the town, and then had forced his wife to take the child in. By other accounts, Missak had bought this boy from a bunch of wandering gypsies who apparently had stolen the boy from Lazistan. Why Lazistan? Simply because the boy's hair had a strange reddish hue for an Armenian, and everybody knew that Lazes, the mountainous tribe of Muslim Georgians, stood out for their light hair. Of course, Missak's wife, while foaming at the mouth, fervently claimed the opposite, but her words were not worth a picked corn-stalk. Nobody had ever seen this woman big with child.

So then, his son's appearance did not bring pride and joy to The Crooked Cucumber. Not even peace of mind, not at all. He continued to batter his loud wife as if she were the one to blame for their son's red hair and more and more striking unlikeness. Malicious anger had built a huge nest in his heart. One unlucky day, just before the war, The Crooked Cucumber brought his family to our town. The newcomers settled in a hovel on the outskirts of the town. Missak and his wife worked here and there as day laborers, however preferring to work for Turks, Greeks, and only as a last resort for Armenians. The Crooked Cucumber hated my grandmother and her husband because they were rich and well respected in the local Armenian community. In moving to town, he apparently was driven by the wish to embarrass them, but the community did not buy his old stories. The unusual color of his son's hair amused and entertained the locals much more. So his hatred spread to all Armenians in general.

Shortly after The Crooked Cucumber's foot stepped on the town's ground, the war and then the massacres began, and the sun faded for the town's Armenians. Men were drowned in the sea or slaughtered in Harab Caravansaray. Women and children were driven to a slower death. Their bones were scattered along the roads from the town to Tokat, then Sivas, Malatia, Urfa, and farther to the Arabian deserts.

The Crooked Cucumber served at that time as the Turks' interpreter, informer, and messenger of death. (The Turks made him or he volunteered.) Who knows whether this man eventually felt like a powerful and influential figure when, with a group of Turkish gendarmes, he entered the Armenian houses and saw the eyes of helpless women and children? He did not fail to make the same visit to my grandparents' house. Even two visits; the first when he accompanied zaptiehs who took away my grandfather and young Simon, and the second when he came with zaptiehs to declare to my grandmother and mother the order of their deportation. Then, for the last time, my grandmother, Iughaper, saw her unfortunate groom-to-be. A salt-and-pepper beard covered his face while a fez barely concealed his full bald spot. She might have had a lot of difficulty finding in him the features belonging to that tall handsome young man, the former Missak Gazanchian.

So, you want to know what happened then with The Crooked Cucumber? Yes, he has survived, and his wife. And his bastard son, too. Unfortunately for us, for the remnants of our family. I don't want your wife to hear what happened when my Uncle Haroutiun met The Crooked Cucumber. I will tell you this particular story later.

Nothing to Do but Go

The cold, dark, dreary months ended, and spring burst forth first with the tender, newborn leaves of grass, and then with almond and cherry blossoms. However, our life did not become any brighter. Troubles, small, big, and very big, set in and hit like hailstones, all in the same place.

One day, when my uncles were somewhere out of the house, an old Turk, a gendarme, made an unexpected visit. About that time, the Turks packed around Kemal Pasha were engaged a life-and-death fight with the Greeks. The Kemalists desperately needed every single man capable of carrying a rifle to be sent to the front line. Though the old gendarme had a savage face and sinister drooping mustache, he turned out to be not so frightening. Initially hiding behind my mother I heard his weary, cracked voice explaining why Uncle Simon should be drafted immediately. I could tell that my mother and grandmother were stunned. Obviously, after all that had happened to their family, the women could have expected almost anything, but Simon's service in the Turkish army was beyond imagination. Grandmother tried to protest. "Zaptieh Effendi, my son is an Armenian. In accordance with the old law he is not allowed to bear arms." Surprisingly, the old Turk did not shout at Grandma, nor did he even interrupt her words. He replied with much understanding that he knew our Aleksanian family and, of course, remembered her husband, "Lord" Pogos, well. The gendarme would never usually bother such people, neither then, when "Lord" Pogos was alive, nor now. However, there was a snag! An Armenian woman had repeatedly informed him that a few years ago Simon had accepted Hak Dini, a True Faith, and become a Moslem. That's why he should go into the army. He would close his eyes to Simon's delicate situation, continued the old Turk. He was not even asking for money to do this favor, just a small *bakshish*, a present. What about a bottle of rakia? He had heard that Aleksanian Hanum made it better than anyone else. After the loss of his son in the Erzeroum battle with the Russians, life had become an aimless sequence of empty days, the old

Turk explained, trying to vindicate himself. "And the most important thing," pointed out the old man, hiding the given bottle in the pocket of his worn out greatcoat, "is that you should do something to this woman. She looked like a real *dishi koepek,* a bitch. Allah is a witness! Such a woman would not calm down just by herself. Instead, she would deliver the words about your son to my chief." Upon his departure, he provided my grandmother and mother with the description of the woman and also gave them the directions to her dwelling located in the Turkish part of our town.

Just as the gendarme left our house Simon stepped into the kitchen. My poor mother and grandmother did not even have a minute to give way to tears and grief. Uncle Simon lifted his hand to show two big flat fish threaded on a cord. "Look, Mayrig, look Pietzar! And Nargiz, you, too! I have been helping a fisherman at the harbor and he gave me these two great kalkans. These are so fatty, you may fry them now or smoke like the Greeks used to do it. Soon a lot of *barbunia* and *palamut* will come. The man knows the fish seasons so well!" I never saw my uncle so happy. However, when he was told about the gendarme's visit, the heavy kalkans slipped from his fingers and fell on the floor with a plop. "Now I am done for!" These were the only words he could say.

"No, no. Do not give up. You are not going to serve in their goddamned army. We will find a way . . . ," my mother rushed to console her brother.

"I did not even mean the army. I think Haroutiun will make short work of me before that. As soon as he learns how I became an apostate and paid for it with gold coins. And he will be right; his brother is a cowardly traitor, a mean Judas!"

"Stop it, Simon. You are not Judas. You were just a frightened boy. Who would not be? We all know that you were confused and alone. God also knows and forgives." Mother made the sign of the cross over his hanging head and continued. "Otherwise, why would the old gendarme bring the news when Haroutiun was not at home, especially since he often spends his days laying on his bed, right?" The ringing sound of my mother's words was so assuring. I believed her, and Grandma nodded in complete assent.

But as luck would have it, Haroutiun himself, in flesh and blood, appeared in the courtyard calling our names. Apparently, he was in an elated mood. My mother made a decision as quick as lightning. "Don't say a word. Just moan. You are sick. With fever. Caught a cold at the harbor." Near the stove, she put together a couple of empty wooden cartridge boxes, which we used as our chairs, laid a slightly resistant Simon on this improvised bed, and covered him with his jacket and blankets I rushed from the bedroom. She even managed to tie her head-scarf around his forehead in such a way that only Simon's rather long nose was visible.

"Do not be afraid. I have put you here in order to help you. Pretend you have a headache. The rest we shall do. And moan, moan."

Haroutiun entered the kitchen asking a bunch of questions about what had happened to our ears, why none of us had reacted to his shouts, and what we were doing instead? When told that we were busy with Simon, he became even more animated. He was angry because instead of looking for Bakro, his brother was resting in bed near the hot stove. Maybe his brother had forgotten that they were supposed to make a pilgrimage to the place where their father's life had ended? Simon was making very natural moaning sounds. My mother and grandmother tried to explain to Haroutiun that today Simon did his best to provide dinner for the entire family. They proudly lifted two kalkans from the floor as a proof of Simon's hard work in the face of the piercing sea wind and his current "fever."

Haroutiun's swoop had abated. Moreover he brought "very good news." Not relying much on Simon's efforts he had made inquiries to some Kurds, who appeared in the town's bazaar, by himself. Today he found out that Bakro's tribe arrived and set up their tents in the yayla as they usually did at the time when the young grass became juicy enough for their sheep. He also learned that one of Bakro's children had been sick and died recently. This apparently explained why Bakro did not resume his regular visits to our family. The good news, said Haroutiun, was that he had sent an urgent call to Bakro on behalf of Simon. Surprisingly for him, his brother's name was familiar among many Kurds. More doleful groans and moans came from under the blankets. "You should get him on his feet as soon as possible. The Kurd could be here any day now and guide us to our father's grave." With this Haroutiun went to his room.

The fish have been cleaned at the courtyard, as far from Haroutiun's ears as possible. Bending over the rather flat basin and close to each other, my mother and Grandma were holding secret council. Connecting some pieces of information provided by the old gendarme with

Simon's hazy recollections of that ill-fated day when he accepted Hak Dini at the town's mosque, they tried to identify that "Armenian woman" who knew my uncle's terrible secret. Next to them, I played with fish bladders trying to explode them between two stones. Meanwhile, I saw on their faces that both were frightened by their own strengthening stronger suspicions. Everything was pointing to Missak Gazanchian's wife! (Her name has been erased from my memory, by the way.) My grandma and mother had no idea that she was in the town, but apparently the woman knew very well that we came back and were living in our house. Most likely she had recognized Simon at the bazaar. You know, poor Simon wandered in there, obeying his brother's order. It was so strange; he was there looking for the Bakro who had actually brought him to the mosque for the conversion. He had not met Bakro, but instead had been spotted by Missak's wife.

Simon vaguely remembered the strange look the woman sitting on the mosque parvis gave him when he went downstairs, ashamed and repenting of his deed. *Did he meet the same fixed look when circling among the market stands?* A few minutes ago, in our kitchen, he was convincing his sister and mother that sometimes he felt he was being watched there. Who knows? He always floated in guesses and doubts. Ghosts of the past haunted him, and the shadows of Babken Mangasarian and the lame Turkish sergeant appeared dimly on each corner of the streets. Maybe he was just convincing himself, but it did not matter. The women had made a general decision. Our family should leave the town, disappear, move far away. We could not live in the same place where even one Gazanchian lived.

However, we needed a break, a time to prepare for our next exile. So my mother went to pay a visit to Missak's wife. She took money with her to *pagel otzi beran'e,* or "to shut the snake's mouth." She also took me with her. Grandmother stayed at home to explain our absence to Haroutiun. She told him that we had gone to find some medicine for Simon. Besides, my grandmother could not go because there was a real risk of encountering Missak. She thought that the Turks might have spared his miserable life as payment for his traitorous role during the deportation of the Armenians from our town.

I did not want to go. I was hungry and the fried kalkans would be just right. To my surprise, my mother was unusually persistent. So I agreed, but only upon Grandma's promise to keep fish warm until my return. Then we have left. Looking back at that time I understand that the women were very concerned about my tongue. Of course I could, absolutely unintentionally, have blurted out something, just a word, that would have fired up Haroutiun's anger. My mother also wanted immediately to explain to me the reason for making up her story about Simon's "sudden fever." Keeping my palm in one of her hands, she used the other to reveal her face slightly, covered with a dark shawl, and continually glanced at my face while trying to justify her recent actions. My loving mother! She also wanted me to understand that lying and deceiving were very bad things. She told me some stories from the Bible, but at that time I did not know much about this book.

You see, I had been living with my family for less than one year. It is absolutely clear that in that time we had no Bible, no icons in our house; everything was destroyed by the Tachiks. The town's Armenian church was burnt, its big round building stood shamelessly defiled on the empty, lifeless square. Only my favorite Saint George shook his thin spear on the wall lithograph.

So, as a little pagan, I did not pay much attention to my mother's words. Instead, I did notice a change in the appearance of the streets. Although there were still houses burnt and looted, and standing silent with their blind windows in our Armenian quarter which we already passed, its streets were wide and paved and many had elevated sidewalks. But now we were walking up the hill through narrow winding streets, earthen, dirty, and smelly. One-storied mud dwellings had flat roofs and some of them served as yards for the next higher-sitting huts, or as places for drying dung bricks. In the small street coffeehouse, under the canopy of an old grapevine, a few Turks sat smoking narghiles and enjoying *keif**, silently and motionlessly. Their prostration freed us of any inquiring looks. However, my mother tightly covered her face with her shawl and stopped talking to me in Armenian. Finally, after some roaming around this gloomy neighborhood (which reminded me of the Turkish village I had lived in) and a couple of questions to a friendly looking woman, my mother found the house she was looking for.

The house was strange. For such a small dwelling it had a massive door, made of thick tree-trunk halves secured with iron flat bars. The small windows by both sides of this incredible door were covered from inside by heavy dark curtains. Mother knocked on the door. Silence.

---

* Daydreaming or being up in the clouds. (vernacular)

"Maybe they are in the other half of the house?!" whispered my quailing mother. She picked up a pebble from the ground and knocked again, more insistently. Again the door did not open. We could not leave this place. My mother needed to talk with Missak's wife. A weird sense that somebody was in the house constantly watching our faces did not leave us. We then noticed an eye staring at us through the narrow opening between the curtains in one window, then in another. We heard hushed voices, followed by a short scream or exclamation after the sound of breaking pottery, and finally the door opened slightly. A tall woman with an angry face and disheveled hair stepped out and closed the heavy door behind her. A boy, maybe a couple of years older than me, slipped out after her.

"Nargis-djan, play with the boy for a minute," said my mother with a sugary voice I had never heard from her before. I immediately hated her pretentious way of talking, especially when neither the boy nor his mother showed any reaction to my mother's words. She also asked him his name; she asked in Armenian, then in Turkish, but he continued to stare at us with scarcely concealed irritation and malice. My mother turned to the woman, calling her "sister" and "Hanum" and using the same unnatural tone. I remained face to face with the young Gazanchian.

To tell you the truth, I had never met such an angry creature before. Even the boys in the Turkish village who regularly teased and called me "Pig-eater" and sometimes dealt me punches, were much less disgusting. This boy had red hair which stuck up in all directions, so his head looked like a wisp of straw. Having stolen up to me more closely, he kicked my ankle-bone. When I cried he gnashed his petty teeth in a contented smile. What a freak he was, this young Gazanchian! Better if we had never known him!

So he kicked me, and I swallowed tears of pain as if I knew that my mother had no time to help me. His mother showed no particular reaction, neither to her son's violence nor to my mother's assumed friendliness and pleading tone. She just took money and hid it under her clothes. We returned home downhill by an already familiar route. The Turks in the coffeehouse even did not change their relaxed positions. I hated this whole experience. My ankle-bone was smarting, and when we arrived home I found that the fried kalkans had grown cold and the fish skin was not crispy and crunchy. I saw that my mother also smarted from the insult of hearing her own sugary voice she was using to talk to "Gazanchian Hanum." Moreover, she was not quite sure whether the coins she had slipped into the woman's hand would be enough to buy her silence. She could not say anything for sure to Grandmother about the existence of Missak Gazanchian, either. Was he hiding in that dismal hovel behind the thick door and dusty curtains? Why would that man, shameless during normal times, be hiding from people when only a few of the helpless Armenian survivors, who remembered his meanness, remained in the entire town? And later, did he keep sending his wife for more and more money from my mother? My mother and grandmother struggled with the answers. At that time, they did not know anything about him. However, during that summer, in response to the demands of Gazanchian's wife, my mother secretly met her a couple more times and gave her additional money. They met at the bazaar. My mother would not go to the Gazanchians' lair again.

Naturally, our time in the town was running out. Grandmother Iughaper was feverishly seeking for a way to get out of there. Finally, Grandmother Iughaper found two Lazes, two brothers who somehow became owners of an old Greek *felucca.* These Lazes undertook the job of smuggling us away. What could be better? The two brothers, genuine rogues by themselves, did not ask questions. But there were a few obstacles, too. The old boat was leaking. The Lazes needed a few days to make some repairs, and, of course, they had to have an advance in order to buy some materials. Then they needed to have a few days more, and more, and so on. They were lazy workers and clumsy seafarers. We became certain of it later. The Lazes promised to transport us to Batum in Georgia. From there, according to Grandmother's plans, we could reach Sukhumi where, before the war, Haroutiun, using his father's money, had co-owned a tailor's shop. (The sea way seemed to be much safer than traveling by land along with throngs of other refugees ravished by hunger and diseases.) Meanwhile my grandmother was parting with the coins from her "gold jug."

About Haroutiun: he agreed surprisingly easily with the escape plan. Perhaps, he also had felt himself uncomfortable in the town. He could no longer walk around ignoring everything. After that Kemal Pasha came to Samsoun to organize the Turks' defense, over Greeks, the local Tachiks had grown more and more hostile. So, Haroutiun agreed to the trip to Batum. However, he did a grim joke that scared me a lot. He said that for those Lazes it would be easier just to take away Grandmother's money and then throw us from the boat. When he saw my fear he laughed and showed his "The Cannon" pistol, assuring me that those bandits would not dare to do such stupid thing in his presence.

Anyway, our women, occupied with their own secrets and preparations for the trip, underestimated Haroutiun. Soon it turned out that he also had secrets and was preparing for the departure in his own manner. He was an experienced, observant warrior, and for him it did not constitute a big deal to notice my mother's deceitful visits to the marketplace and her strange embarrassment when, upon her returns, she reported back at great length about what she had been looking to buy there. Of course, she never mentioned her encounters with Missak's wife. But when, accidentally or not, Haroutiun caught sight of his sister talking with that woman at the marketplace, which he frequented still seeking news from Bakro, it aroused suspicion in him. Maybe he had overheard my mother talking with the woman in Armenian, but with an unnatural, pleading voice, that sugary tone I hated when she spoke at the Gazanchians' den. Maybe he had seen the money that my mother was giving to Missak's wife. However, to make the story short, Haroutiun followed the mysterious woman to the place where she lived. The ugly hovel in the poor hillside part of the town with heavy door and curtains in the windows excited his soldier's vigilance. He felt a threat to his family emanating from behind this door. Haroutiun set up an observation post near the Gazanchians' lair. He studied this family's strange habits and rules. He noticed that the door was never left opened; always when the woman or red-haired boy went out, somebody inside bolted the door immediately to secure the entrance. Whenever the woman and boy came back and knocked on the door, the curtains slightly moved, making an opening for somebody's eyes, in the right window and then in the left one. Finally the patient hunter caught a glimpse of this somebody. Only at early dawn, a lean bold man would come out of his burrow. From his location, Haroutiun could not see the features of the man's face. The man shifted from one foot to the other, huddling himself for protection against the chilly air. The man would not stray far from the opened door; he simply looked around, peering intensely toward the sky or to the end of the narrow dirty street as if expecting a threat from everywhere. He snapped at the woman's angry voice apparently demanding that he close the door to stop letting cold air into the house. Haroutiun had spent too many years outside of our town; he could not possibly to recognize those people, he knew nothing about The Crooked Cucumber.

Here, there and everywhere Haroutiun made inquiries about that strange Armenian family living in a Turkish quarter, and the man hiding behind the thick wooden door and window curtains. He learned that the Gazanchians had a *vesika*, a Turks' permission to remain in the town instead of going to the "death march" with other Armenians. They had remained in the town all these years. Haroutiun even deigned to ask a couple of questions to one of the Armenians who had also escaped the deadly exile by converting himself to Islam. This man who always felt humbled in the presence of Haroutiun disclosed in detail all Missak Gazanchian's mean tricks carried out during the deportation time. "We know that you despise us, traitors of our fathers' beliefs. Many of us curse ourselves for our own weaknesses, but believe me, we are not as bad as Missak the Informer. We just bent under the Turks, he did crimes with them. Now, this mercenary creature is afraid of his own shadow. That is why he is hiding in his dark burrow like a scorpion, like a . . ." Haroutiun did not need to listen the man anymore. He learned enough about Missak. *What kind of connection had his sister, Pietzar, with the informer's wife?* This question nagged at him now.

The very next day, on the secluded street to the bazaar, Haroutiun confronted Missak's wife. When he stuck the barrel of his "Maria" pistol in her side, she cut short her yelping and began talking. She told my uncle everything about Simon's conversion. Haroutiun was so stunned that he let his iron fingers off her elbow. She could have run away, but the woman was so greedy that she decided to profit by "selling" the same secret of our family for the second time. She suggested to Haroutiun that she would not tell anybody about Simon's conversion. Haroutiun noted that his sister, Pietzar, had already been paying for this. However, he promised to give the woman some money for not telling his sister about their conversation. The woman assured him that nobody would know about it. Haroutiun insisted that "nobody" really meant just that, and that not even her husband or son would learn anything about him and Simon. Seeing how the woman grinned when he mentioned her husband, Haroutiun was assured of exactly what he had guessed in advance. This stupid, greedy woman apparently had been keeping all the money given to her by Pietzar to herself. Apparently, Missak, the Informer, never leaving his shelter, could not have even known that a few of our family had survived and were living in the town. Most importantly, The Crooked Cucumber had no idea that Haroutiun already took aim at him.

Unfortunately, my mother and grandmother, busy with their plans and secrets, did not understand the seriousness of the new changes in Haroutiun following that important encounter with the Crooked Cucumber's wife. Of course, they noticed that he did not stay home during the day and came back to sleep late after midnight or even at dawn. *The next oddity*, they thought. *Let him act that way because Bakro still has not appeared and our family's days in this town are numbered.*

Haroutiun was mad at his brother Simon, but he avoided any confrontations with him because Haroutiun was well aware that in a fury he might reveal his plan of vengeance against Missak the Informer. He was also aware that his mother and sister would do everything to dissuade him to do this. My uncle treated the duty of vengeance which had befallen upon him with absolute zeal. He could not take any risk that might compromise it. The plan was to destroy Missak Gazanchian precisely during our last hours in the town. After that Haroutiun would immediately join us and embark on the Lazes' felluca and he would be gone with the wind. Haroutiun was absolutely sure that Missak's wife would wait for the money he had promised for her silence. The Crooked Cucumber, being in a state of ignorance concerning Haroutiun, was doomed to the fate he deserved. The only obstacle to Haroutiun's plan was the exasperating lateness of Bakro. Haroutiun needed the Kurd as a guide to the Sheitan Delik where the bones of his father "Lord" Pogos lay unattended and uncommitted to the earth. Without such a pilgrimage, my uncle could not leave the town. The presence of Bakro would also serve as a protection against all kinds of thugs and pillagers wandering in the surrounding mountains as well as the Circassians who lived in the vicinity of that mysterious place (Devil's Hole).

The ultimate farewell to his father and revenge on the traitor; those two duties possessed Haroutiun's mind. At the same time, just the single thought that Bakro had brought his scared young brother Simon to the town's mosque for the conversion turned his head with wrath. The only way he could stop from exploding was to continue watching after The Crooked Cucumber beside his thick door to study his habits, collect some articles useful for the trip (for example, hanks of rope and tar for torches) and then clean and polish, again and again, his loyal pistols, "Maria" and "The Cannon."

One day, exactly when Haroutiun was knitting again his travel baggage, Bakro rode into our courtyard and dismounted.

Up and Down

I am telling you our family's tale so avidly. Unceasingly. Like a camel drinking water after a long hot crossing. The water which comes from the dark deep well.

I remembered I was studying the Armenian alphabet with uncle Simon. He put together a small board for me, wrapped with two-finger-high slats. Then we filled the space with clean sea sand. After it was moistened and smoothed it was ready for writing. Sharpened wooden stick made clear narrow furrows of ornate Armenian letters. A flat pebble readily erased my errors and cleaned the sand surface for new exercises. My stick drew "A-ee," "B-ee," "Gin," "Da," and then "Nargiz," "Mother," "Simon," and "Haroutiun." The last word was the most difficult to write; it remained unfinished because Bakro appeared in the courtyard.

Uncle Simon brought Bakro into the kitchen where all our household goods were concentrated, particularly those which people could sit on. Bakro took a seat on the only chair by the window, the same place he had sat months before, waiting for Haroutiun. Uncle Haroutiun stood leaning against the door frame, crossing his arms on his bulging chest. Everyone else sat around helter-skelter hesitating to initiate conversation. I felt more comfortable next to my St. George on the wall.

"Your big brother is shorter than you," Bakro said to Simon as he turned to him. Haroutiun grinned for a moment, then grew impatient. "Tell your Kurd about our plans," he reminded Simon. "Will he guide us to the place?"

Simon served as a medium between the men. At this moment the women started up. "Haroutiun-djan, give the guest some time after his journey," began my mother, who then turned to Bakro with the customary questions. Grandmother brought coffee for the men. In this way they selflessly tried to clear the air. However, it turned out that Bakro, who recently had lost his young son, was not in the mood for talking. Only when Simon recalled the youngster's tricks and how this lean, but dashing boy had protected him, "Infidel Seemo," from the lads' mockeries back there in Bakro's village, did the impermeable eyes of the Kurd strangely gleam, and he started smoking like a chimney.

Haroutiun was sarcastic: "Yeah, Simon, they really took you as one of their own." His words sank into the women's sighs. Mother and Grandmother pulled out their handkerchiefs for wiping up their tears. Their handkerchiefs were always ready for such use. Grandmother brought refreshing tan, a matsoon diluted in slightly salted cool water. She had no more coffee. Over the last few days, the women had not bought anything; they were finishing up their modest stocks before leaving the town.

"For God's sake, tell your Kurd why I called him here," exclaimed Haroutiun. For him, the prelude was over.

"Your brother is a very impatient man. He has always been impatient . . . he did not even manage to finish his most important work," noted Bakro, knocking out ashes from his pipe.

"What are you talking about?" It was the first time Haroutiun spoke directly with Bakro, in Turkish. Both men did not need Simon anymore. My younger uncle sat still in his place.

"One moonlit night, my brother Meho and I were riding here, in this town. In a small square behind the bazaar wall, under the shadow of the platan tree, we found the body of a Turk, with a dagger in his chest." Bakro began his story unhurriedly, glancing sidelong at Haroutiun, who did not interrupt the Kurd. "There was money on him. My young brother had never seen so many gold coins. He took them. Then the Turk opened his eyes. Freed of the coins' weight he felt himself better. The Turk tried to say something to my brother. Maybe the name of his killer. Or perhaps asked for help. We did not listen to him. We felt we should disappear with the money on the sly. So I ordered my brother to finish off the Turk and follow me. He did it. However, the townsmen from the neighboring houses then began running upon him with staves and stones. My Meho stumbled with his horse and was caught. Years later, from your brother Seemo, I recognized that on that night we had finished your work. You were impatient then. You left the Turk not only with your dagger in his chest, but also with your name on his lips."

Haroutiun was not stunned by Bakro's story, like the rest of us. Not at all. "I was young and Mehmed, son of Jemal Bey, was the first Turk I had sent to Hell," said Haroutiun. "After that there were more and more, and not one of them had time to say a word or a prayer, even let out a squeak."

"I don't care much about the Turks. And particularly about sons of their beys. But anyone who counts himself as a man should not leave any unfinished matters after him," Bakro noted weightily, again filling his pipe.

My poor mother and grandmother, who had observed the men's conversation with their throats dried out and hearts which had stopped beating, felt that the major storm had passed. They hurriedly spoke beautiful words of consolation to Bakro. Their glances desperately begged Haroutiun to say something appropriate about Bakro's brother and his untimely end at the hands of the Turks. Simon sighed and sighed, and uttered sorrows, but my stubborn Uncle Haroutiun did not follow them. One more time he showed that he had returned from the war changed. "Reckless when he was young, but now he has become *irakan hent,* really crazy. Doesn't think about life and death, doesn't care about the family," whispered the women in confusion.

It was funny, if one could find something humorous in our situation, that Bakro then expressed exactly the same opinion about my elder uncle. When told about Haroutiun's planned expedition to the Sheitan Delik the Kurd stared at him with sincere amazement. "Only a crazy person would go to this place by his own will. It is a horrible place. It is prohibited for people of our tribe to go there."

"If so, then who threw the bodies of my father and the other Armenians into this hole?" objected Haroutiun.

"The Turks," replied Bakro. "And the Circassians of Yeni Koy. These people are newcomers. Their tribe came to these mountains running from the Russians. My tribe has been using these yaylas from the very old times, so old that nobody can remember them exactly. My father was a boy when the Circassians appeared. These stupid scavengers from that lower village have no idea about the danger of the Sheitan Delik. No respect. Of course, they could go there. But they would pay. Sooner or later the spirit of Sheitan would haunt them and . . ."

"You are all uninvited invaders here, rogues and killers," muttered Haroutiun, in Armenian. Bakro stopped telling the tale and stared at Haroutiun with an inquiring look. Simon rescued the moment and smoothed over the interruption. "Indeed, Bakro's people are different when compared with the Turks and Circassians, particularly those who came and settled on the same slope of the mountain below Bakro's summer camp. Bakro's villagers are taller and, amazingly, some of them have light hair and eyes." Involuntarily, we all looked at Bakro. The hunter was tall, but his eyes and hair were as black as coal. Simon noticed our glances, "His son was blonde, exactly as the boy's mother, Bakro's wife . . ." The women emitted sounds of sorrow and astonishment.

"Tell me more about this devil's place. How does it look?" asked Haroutiun, and the Kurd continued his tale.

"It is a big hole. For example, an entire cart with two oxen would disappear in it without a trace. It is so deep! It should be deep because it is a gate. It leads straight to Sheitan's abode. Whoever goes into the hole falls straight into his clutches. There is no escape from Sheitan and his servants, the *jinns.* The unfortunate person dies in terrible torment. The jinns cut off belts of skin from his back and tie him to a pole. Next they make him lick a copper where tar is already bubbling. Then they pour the tar on his feet and make him walk and even dance on his smouldering feet, whipping the unfortunate with lash swaddled with his own skin belts. . . ."

A young girl, I was frightened by Bakro's vivid descriptions. I pictured the Sheitan as a fat green serpent, exactly the same as in the picture of St. George on the kitchen wall next to me. I also imagined that my Uncle Haroutiun would go to the Devil's Hole where the ugly serpent had tortured my grandfather and other Armenians, and there he would shoot the beast with his powerful "Cannon" pistol and save the innocent people, like the brave hero St. George did.

"Is this hole in flat surface? Are there big rocks near it?" Haroutiun was trying to find out the details which he was interested in.

"I don't know exactly. I already said that we never approached The Hole. The Sheitan can see any crazy person who dares to come close. Even if a man, hunter or traveler, stays a hundred *arshins** away from The Hole, the stenchful breath of the Sheitan can overtake him. Then that's it. This man is doomed because the breath is so noxious. He may be able to return home by himself, or perhaps his fellow hunters would help him to get home, but it doesn't matter. Soon, he would turn green as a fresh pod of pea. Anything he tried to eat would come back with

* Approximately hundred yards.

exhausting convulsions, and he would die soon cursing his own arrogance.

"Often the Sheitan sends his jinns out for lost souls. The people who were caught by the darkness near the place said that they saw small lights here and there, all around the Sheitan Delik. They saw the burning eyes of the jinns scouring near the surrounding cliffs for the lost people. The only way to escape them is to climb up a high tree and keep vigil all night until morning."

Haroutiun livened when heard about the cliffs and rocks. He asked more questions, apparently trying to create in his mind the exact picture of his father's unusual grave. But it appeared that Bakro had indeed never put his foot close to the Sheitan Delik. He flatly declined guiding my uncles to that place. His face and voice expressed genuine fear and respect.

I still remember, almost word for word, what the Kurd said: "Allah took my son. It was his fate. We could do nothing about that. I have a young wife, and maybe we will be granted another son. So why would Bakro go to the Sheitan Delik? Bakro is not desperate like you!"

"And we do not need your help," exclaimed Haroutiun. "We shall find that place by ourselves." With these words he left the kitchen.

Amazingly, help came from an unexpected side. My mother, who before that was against Haroutiun's expedition, allowed herself to intervene in the men's arguments.

"Excuse him, Bakro Effendi. You are right. My brother Haroutiun is impatient and desperate, and sometimes acts crazy. But there is not a *drachma** of his guilt in all these. The terrible things that happened in our lives changed him." My mother tried to choose her words very carefully. She spoke slower than usual, and her words resonated within the empty kitchen walls. Bakro, who was about to leave, sat down again.

"You have mentioned the fate of your son, but isn't it also fate or Providence that four brothers, Haroutiun and your brother, Meho, and then you and Haroutiun's brother, Simon, have been connected in such strange ways? *Allah severson*** Bakro, you have to help them! After all, visiting a father's grave, isn't that the most significant duty among your men, too? Do you visit the grave of your brother, Meho?"

"Yes, I do," responded Bakro, getting his pipe.

---

* About 1/3 ounce. (Turk.)
** If you love God. (Turk.)

"So you are luckier than us. We have no graves. The Turks did not give us back the bodies of our men. Their bodies were burnt, drowned, or thrown away like a garbage. We could not bury them. Now we are condemned to swallow our grief and drink bitter tears forever."

"They gave back his body the same morning. He was dead by then. Those townsmen have beaten him up with clubs and stones. They ran against him like a crowd of rats. A hundred against one. By the time old Jemal Bey arrived to enjoy his part of the torture my brother was dead."

"We are sorry, and I am sure that deep in his heart Haroutiun is also sorry for what happened to your brother." My mother spoke passionately and took a breath. "Haroutiun simply fails to show his feelings. Apparently, he also could not explain his plan very well. Now, I know that he is right. The place where our father's body lies should become a grave. The very one grave for all our men. However, this can only happen if my brothers can see it, pour a handful of earth into it, and shed tears over it. So now, Bakro, would you help them with this sacred journey? Would you help them to find the way to their father?"

Bakro did not show such shock as was displayed on the faces of Simon and my grandmother while listening to my mother. He did not answer my mother's last appeal. He was silent, deep in thought. Even the noise being produced by Haroutiun outside the kitchen could not distract him. The Kurd was weighing the possible dangers of the proposed journey with my uncles. One could understand what this man was considering. Wandering around the place haunted by the Devil, with two Armenians no less, could bring him nothing but trouble. During the journey they might come across savage Circassians from the rival Yeni Koy, or various trampling bands, or jinns disguised as vagrants. "In the scrape, Simon would not be of much help, and his brother Haroutiun—oh, this extraordinary Armenian, an interesting character of a very different type—his defiant look by itself would be just enough to cause trouble." Perhaps it was such thought that furrowed Bakro's forehead.

After thinking for a long time, the Kurd sent Simon after Haroutiun. The latter entered the kitchen knitting his brows. My mother remembered later that this was the same thing my uncle did when he was a young boy, displeased or intractable. Bakro stated his decision. He would take the brothers upward to the mountains by the shortest and safest route, but he would not accompany them to the point of their particular interest. He would stay with his horse and wait for their return, if they returned at all, in a secluded place about half an hour's walk from the Sheitan Delik. This was as close to that place as he could go.

Haroutiun's arguments and half-serious taunts did not shake Bakro's decision. However, after some additional consideration, which visibly irritated my impatient uncle, the Kurd suggested hiring one more guide, just for the very last segment of the trip. He succinctly mentioned that person to Simon and left him to explain the rest.

Simon, who had internally reconciled himself to the inevitability of the forthcoming journey, began describing the new guide-to-be. Baba, a "poor soul" in his thirties, lived in the Circassian village of Yeni Koy near the place where my uncles and Bakro were planning to go. The man knew the area around the Sheitan Delik perfectly. In addition, strong and remarkably hardy, he could be very useful in carrying Haroutiun's load, he would be happy to do it for a very small reward. My elder uncle had prepared a collection of bags and bundles, small and bigger and quite heavy ones. However, he said that he would not trust this fortune to some Circassian.

Simon tried to dispel his brother's doubts. Baba, in his words, had the mind of a child. He would obey the travelers as he always did when dealing with his villagers, old and young. Baba had no family of his own; he belonged to the entire village. Everybody could make jokes about him because of his childish way of talking and acting and also the strange shape of his hairless head. Some Turk called him Kabak, meaning Squash, and this word became his name. Nobody listened to Baba Kabak, except his dog, continued Simon. This would allow them to reach the Sheitan Delik without attracting the attention of Kabak's villagers.

Simon was painting a picture of Kabak's life and his strange relationship with his dog. Even Bakro who, of course, knew this freak very well from the neighboring Circassian village was listening to Simon's words with visible interest and sometimes nodded his head in agreement. However, Simon, who often got carried away by his own amusing stories, had enough sense on this occasion not to explain in the presence of Haroutiun how he had met Baba Kabak and his beastly dog for the very first time a few years ago.

He did not dare to tell his brother that, when hiding in the thorny blackberry bushes after his escape from Harab Caravansaray he had noticed that strange squash-head man and his notorious dog among the bunch of Circassians hurrying the road as for some seasonal peasant work, mowing or threshing. However, that time the work was slaughtering and looting the Armenians who had already been driven into the Harab Caravansaray. Simon did not mention seeing later the severed head of mighty Arshak in Baba Kabak's hands, and then its falling and rolling on the ground.

Later, before the women cooked a modest meal, Haroutiun and Bakro reached another agreement. My uncle asked the Kurd to find one more horse in order to make their ascent to the mountains faster and easier. Bakro was somehow hesitant, even when Haroutiun promised a tempting reward, causing a barely audible sigh from his mother's side. She was our treasurer. The Kurd was just unable to comprehend that an Armenian could and would ride a horse. In his mountains. He reluctantly agreed, but only if Haroutiun would take off his military jacket and put on some other regular clothes.

Oh, that Haroutiun's jacket! He had brought it from his tramples in Persia and the Arabian lands. He wore the jacket when he was looking for survivors of his family through all camps of Armenian refugees scattered in those regions. It was so worn out and greasy ("On hungry days I boiled it and made soup," Haroutiun used to joke) that it was practically impossible to recognize as a uniform previously belonging to an English or German officer. It took a great deal of talk and work for the women to wash it well. Haroutiun would not part with the jacket easily, because of its many deep pockets. He really needed those to carry with him many essential things every day. These were a tobacco pouch and a lighter made of a cartridge case, and a small book of German army rules with thin paper for cigarette wrapping; the "Maria" pistol, of course, and extra clips; a pen-knife, an object of my greatest desires, in addition to a much bigger folding knife; and also a compass with a small lively bubble, as well as many more other fascinating things.

Even after careful washing and darning, my uncle would still find in his numerous pockets a tiny handful of sand or small pebbles reminding him of the places far, far away where he had traveled, seeking us, his family's survivors. He would reminisce about the Bedouins who fed their camels with dried fish or the fire-spitting lands and fire worshipers' temple near Baku.

Nevertheless, my stubborn uncle had to agree with Bakro. So, when the Kurd returned the next week, he brought for my uncles some awful looking, bright colored garments and *shalvars**. Also, instead of a horse, promised for Haroutiun, the Kurd brought in a mule. Haroutiun was not happy. However, he soon discovered that those poor, ragged clothes were very clean, and had a pleasant scent. Bakro's women had washed them well in a mountain stream and had dried them out on the flowering banks. Upon putting on these clothes my uncles turned into two regular Kurds. The only disadvantage was that they had difficulty hiding the pistols under those rags. That's why Haroutiun liked his jacket; it covered both his weapons perfectly. He gave the small one, "Maria," to Simon to carry during the journey. Just in case. He also trained Simon in his room on how to use the pistol.

The men left before sunrise. For good luck, Grandmother Iughaper poured a mug of water on the ground where they walked as they left. We women stayed at home. It was our final day in our town. Grandmother went to make the last arrangements with the Lazes. According to Haroutiun's plan, at night we were to wait for him and Simon on the shore where the smugglers' felucca rode on anchor. My mother and I had to clear up our things around the house. It was easy work. We could only take a few things with us for the sea trip to Batum. I decided to carry with me my picture of St. George and the porcelain salt cellar with light-hearted angels around the edge. I made a mistake.

As you can understand, I remember all these details of our last days in our old town very well because I was there. However, the story of my uncles' adventures during the journey to their father's grave is based largely on Uncle Simon's accounts and a few of Haroutiun's remarks.

Using his hunting paths Bakro safely got my uncles through to the first stop, as he had promised. There, in the vicinity of Yeni Koy, they were supposed to meet Baba Kabak. This part of the trip was hard. Many times Haroutiun and Simon were forced to dismount and help their loaded mule to clamber up after Bakro's well-trained horse. At the other hand, the travelers did not encounter anybody along their route.

My grandmother worried a lot that the local Circassians would ambush my uncles at this point. She was afraid that Baba Kabak would prattle about his talk with Bakro and stimulate a dangerous curiosity

* Wide trousers. (vernacular)

amongst his villagers. Haroutiun was also well on his guard as they reached that pre-arranged place. However, he only found one man there, lean and tall. Haroutiun immediately changed his thoughts about the clothes he and Simon were wearing. Theirs were very decent in comparison to the couple of rags covering some parts of the stranger's body. His feet, blackened with dirt which went almost up to his knees, obviously never knew any kind of footwear. But the most remarkable feature was this man's head. His inflated skull bulged out, particularly at the back part. This erection was tightly covered by completely hairless skin. Glossy and darkened, in the sun it looked like the peel of a ridiculous vegetable, an enormous squash.

At last, Haroutiun had met Baba Kabak. A rustling and crackling in the bushes and a growl notified Haroutiun that Baba Kabak's inseparable dog was hiding close by. To Haroutiun's loathing, the freak expressed ingenuous joy and excitement on seeing his brother Simon. His eyes, which had no eyebrows, were sparkling, and his meaty lips were mumbling some words of greeting mixed up with spittle.

Bakro raised his voice at Baba Kabak and flung a stone at the bushes. The growl stopped for a while. The travelers sat on the trunk of a fallen tree to have a bite before continuing their journey. Baba Kabak immediately swallowed his portion, a huge horn of lavash rolled with cheese and fresh herbs. After that he moved closer to Simon and stared carnivorously at the lavash in Simon's hands.

Simon could barely eat. The closeness of the notorious Circassian village and meeting with Baba Kabak brought back all his fears and ghosts of the past. It was in this forest where he had wandered after his escape from the Harab Caravansaray. Somewhere around here he had been hiding in the roadside blackberry bushes when he had seen the band of Baba Kabak's villagers rushing to do their job at the Harab Caravansaray. Exactly in this village he had seen the same men returning home with the bloody clothes of the Armenians. And the haunting picture of Arshak's severed head! The shadow of the lame Turkish sergeant still inhabited these places. His zaptiehs appeared to be behind every tree. Simon felt that old fear again got to his bones.

Poor Simon could not eat. He gave his roll of lavash to Baba Kabak and the bread disappeared in Baba's belly before Bakro could snatch it back. Haroutiun reprimanded Simon because the brothers needed their strength to reach their goal. Bakro angrily dealt the glutton a good smack on his ugly head. Baba Kabak burst into tears, getting them all over his dirty face, but not forgetting to pick up crumbs of cheese by his other hand. A menacing growl came from behind Bakro. Haroutiun saw Baba Kabak's dog. The beast had a rather long yellowish trunk, painted here and there with brown and black spots and burdened with long teats. The mother-dog was defending her foolish child; its powerful paws inspired respect. Obeying Bakro's order, Baba calmed his guard. The travelers then took off to the Sheitan Delik.

This portion of their route was much easier. The path led them between big trees along the slope of the mountain. While on the plain surface Bakro's horse started to trot lightly. The mule carrying Simon and Haroutiun tried not to fall behind. Baba Kabak remained next to the stirrup. His long deer-like feet were indefatigable. Sometimes he left the horse behind and turned back his monstrous head to smile, as if urging on the horsemen. His dog's trunk glided after him, leap by leap.

Bumping along behind Haroutiun's back, Simon gave himself up to sad thoughts. Almost five years had passed since his miraculous escape from death, here in this place. After that he had lived with Bakro's tribe for about four years traveling inland for winter months and coming back to these mountains for springs and summers. Many times during these years he had met Baba Kabak of Yeni Koy. Among the Circassians of that village Bakro consorted only with the Squash-Head. On numerous occasions Simon had laughed loudly with Bakro at the freak's stupidities and pranks. Also, both, Simon and Baba had helped Bakro when he was hunting. Baba taught him, Simon, how to catch the small brisk fish in the ice-cold water of the stream dams. *So, why did the capers of Baba Kabak and his comic smiles not cheer his heart now? Why, even behind his brother's back, was he feeling the familiar fear?* He knew why. How could he completely forget during those years that the same Baba Kabak, perhaps with the same ardor, had helped the lame Turkish sergeant and his zaptiehs to dump the listless bodies of his father, Pogos Aleksanian, and other Armenians into the mouth of the Sheitan Delik?

The mule suddenly stopped. Simon and Haroutiun dismounted and approached Bakro who was watching something on the ground. The dog snarled lowering its snout. It was the corpse of a fox, dead for a while. "It's near," said Bakro sombrely, pointing with his whip-handle at the bared jaws of the animal with withered foam dried around its teeth. Haroutiun grimaced with irritation, but it did not help. Here was the invisible line which Kurd Bakro, a hunter and an occasional robber, could not cross. He hobbled the horse and mule near the huge oak tree and sat morosely under its concealing branches. From here Haroutiun and Simon had to walk accompanied by Baba Kabak and the dog.

Upon dividing the load, the wayfarers continued their route. Soon they left the forest behind and walked by the open slope with the separate clumps of trees. There was no need to hide anymore. Nobody could cross their path because they were already near the Sheitan Delik. Soon they saw the place, a rather shallow hollow. It was indeed strange and terrifying. The hollow looked like a scar on the green body of the mountain, a wound inflicted by a giant force. It looked like a bleeding wound because the reddish and brown rocks scattered within the hollow and the bare cliffs hanging on its edges resembled freshly clotted blood. Haroutiun noticed an old abandoned road on the opposite side of the hollow. This road meant that people used to come to this place. It apparently branched off from the main road connecting the town and the villages on the slopes of the mountain.

Haroutiun and Simon went down, stealing between the rocks. Baba Kabak followed them, despite his dog letting out a warning roar. At the bottom of the hollow, my uncles realized what was terrifying about that place: silence. There was no grass, no bushes, and no birds or grasshoppers. Not even a mosquito. There was only dark, sticky sand which made sounds after each of their steps. The sand creaked, and in the absolute stillness those lifeless sounds reverberated from the cliffs. The place did not like to be disturbed. Baba's dog climbed onto the huge boulder and urged its master to follow her. There they sat, on the flat stony surface warmed by the sun, and watched the two restless Armenians.

Haroutiun and Simon found the Sheitan's mouth, a deep rounded gap in the ground at the side of the hollow bordering the mountain's body. Behind the hole, the cliffs, the huge cylindrical pillars, formed a portal. The door which one might expect or imagine to be there was invisible, and only a black hole lied in the way to the portal.

Bakro was right. The hole was big enough to swallow up not just a human body but a whole carriage including its harnessed horse. Its walls abruptly snapped into an inky darkness. The stones thrown inside this darkness disappeared without a sound. Only some strange irritating odor rose up from there.

Haroutiun walked around the hole in order to find the best place for his descent. He lay on the edge of the gap, trying to distinguish something inside it. Simon was ordered to illuminate the walls with inflamed torches tied to the rope, but the flame emitted fumes and died shortly after being lowered into the gap. After a few attempts, enraged Haroutiun rose to his feet. His plan of reaching the body of his father was going to fail. The Sheitan Delik did not let go of its catches easily.

Suddenly, Haroutiun changed countenance. He felt dizziness. Simon rushed to his brother and supported him, helping him to lean over a rocky fragment. He gave Haroutiun a flask of water, but Haroutiun only brought it back with agonizing convulsions.

However, Haroutiun came to his senses after some rest. "Gas," he uttered to himself, or to Simon who was sitting on the same rock. "Goddamn gas," he explained, with regret for his sudden weakness. Simon wanted to say, "Let's go home or we shall die here, like the fox we saw on the way to this poisoned place," but he chose rather to keep silent.

"Look at them," continued Haroutiun, pointing at Baba Kabak and his dog who all that time had not left their spot on the tall boulder. The pair was growling, muttering, and squabbling with each other. "The animal is smarter than the man. This bitch is keeping him there, far from the gas." The dog was warming its teats under the sun, casting looks with open disdain at the brothers.

The presence of the dog and its conduct annoyed Haroutiun. He told Simon that the dog knew perfectly all about the poisonous gas near the hole, and she obviously anticipated they both would die there. He was so serious that Simon feared his brother had completely lost his mind; the Sheitan Delik had taken it away. Haroutiun thought that the dog was jeering at them. He wanted to shoot "the beast." Simon assured his brother that if Haroutiun killed the dog, Baba Kabak would leave them and they would not be able to find their way back. He had no time to explain to his brother that because of her magical abilities and unbelievable old age, this dog had gained an enormous respect among Baba's villagers. Killing this dog would incur the anger of the entire village of Yeni Koy. After such an insult, the Circassians would chase the brothers relentlessly.

Poor Simon had not managed to say even a quarter of these words when Haroutiun aimed his "Cannon" at Baba's dog. However, in the twinkling of an eye, the beast leaped from her stone bed and hid behind the boulder. "I told you she was gibing at us," shouted Haroutiun. Baba Kabak thought this hide-and-seek game was hilarious.

After failing to recover his father's remains, Haroutiun got down to the second part of his plan. Only then did Simon realize what his brother had been collecting in his room for the trip. In two small, but quite heavy bags, which were always in Haroutiun's care, Simon saw some bars made of a strange soft material.

"Explosives," Haroutiun briefly answered. "Very useful things, particularly when there is a need to close a matter, once and for all!"

It is getting worse by the minute, thought Simon, helping his brother to carry those bars to the hole.

When Haroutiun finished loading the cracked rocky pillars hanging over the Sheitan's mouth with the bars, he ordered Simon to hide behind a couple of large boulders standing far enough from the hole. Simon lay down behind that stone wall, but then remembered about Baba Kabak. He half-rose and showed himself, calling Baba to join him. Baba's dog was barking from her hiding place. The squash-head freak was laughing. He definitely enjoyed this hide-and-seek game.

Then Haroutiun appeared, running from the place where he had kindled the sparking cord. Unfortunately, the cord was short, so he was running with all his might. Baba Kabak was jumping on his flat boulder with a great fervor. Simon did not know where to look and whom to shout at. His brother's legs, strong but short, did not look fast enough. He might still have been feeling weak from the gas poisoning. On the other side, Baba Kabak was performing his deadly dance in accompaniment with the wild shrieks of his dog who was trying to pull him down from the boulder.

"Down, Baba, down," Simon shouted again. He nearly rushed to the freak, but Haroutiun's heavy body fell upon him and pinned him down. The ground shook, and thunder from the Sheitan's Delik drowned out all other sounds.

The hollow of the Sheitan Delik, that ghastly quiet place had never heard such an awful din as the one my Uncle Haroutiun created. When he and Simon stood up and the dust after the explosion cleared, they saw that there was no Sheitan Delik anymore. The rocky pillars which were guarding that yawning gash had fallen to the ground and completely covered the hole.

The brothers slowly approached the newly formed mound. Stunned and sad they looked at their father's tomb. For a few minutes they could not say a word. All the words they had been preparing on the long trip to his place seemed needless.

Suddenly, the silence was again interrupted: This time it was because of Baba Kabak and his heartrending wails. For a moment, Simon had absolutely forgotten about him. Now he recognized Baba who emerged from a pile of dirt and stones. Baba was grasping his head and wailing. His hairless head had been cut in many places by the sharp rocky splinters, and the blood was flowing between the fingers.

"Baba, poor Baba, wait a minute . . ." Simon went to help, but the freak, deafened by the blast, did not hear him. Frightened, he took off before Simon could reach him. Haroutiun couldn't help laughing while watching Baba Kabak scrambling between rocks and boulders, yet not letting his hands off his precious head. His dog followed him limping in one leg.

The wailing and barking faded behind the edge of the hollow. "Don't worry," said Haroutiun. "Such creatures do not die easily. From my experience. Good people die, heroes are killed in action. Creatures survive." He turned again to the father's tomb.

"Come here, Simon," said Haroutiun. "Before the ashes of our father, Pogos Aleksanian, and the other Armenian martyrs of our town, swear by your most dreadful oath that you will never betray the faith of our ancestors. Swear that you will be an Armenian forever, even if it brings only misery to you!" And Simon swore.

"At the tomb of our father, vow vengeance on our enemies and traitors. Vow together with me, Simon!" And Simon vowed.

Haroutiun said one more thing that stunned Simon. "One day these rocks will move aside and open a way out. Then all these people; our beloved father, and mighty Arshak, and shrewd Babken Mangasarian, and just mechanic Ovannes, and the others all will come out, to the terror of our enemies, to ride through their villages and cities, destroying them all as ours have been destroyed. That day will come!" Haroutiun cried out these words and shook his fist at an invisible enemy. The mountain echoed his words in confirmation, or maybe in a gibe. "Amen, amen, amen," Simon said, over and over again.

When the brothers reached the agreed place under the huge oak tree they did not find Bakro there. The Kurd had disappeared. Simon was hurt that Bakro could leave them without any warning. Haroutiun was not surprised by the Kurd's behavior. He decided to go back to the Sheitan Delik and follow the old road he had noticed at the edge of the hollow. It should take them to the main route leading to the town. Simon hesitated, afraid of walking down that route frequented by the local Circassians. He also knew that there, down the main road, Haroutiun and he would pass the Harab Caravansaray, the place where he had spent the last night with his father and other Armenians. The shadow of the lame Turkish sergeant was still hiding there in wait for him, the sole survivor.

The brothers were arguing when they heard a sound. They pressed themselves to the ground, lending an ear to it. It was a voice, unusually trembling, but that of Bakro.

"Is it you, Seemo?" inquired the voice coming from the dense bushes. Simon wanted to see Bakro, but the hunter's voice stopped him: "Stop or I will shoot. Are you really Seemo or a jiin in disguise?"

It took quite a time for Simon to convince Bakro that it was really Simon and Haroutiun before him, and not two jiins who were coming after him. Bakro asked a lot of questions, the answers to which he simple-mindedly believed could be known only to him and Simon. Meanwhile, with great irritation, Haroutiun lay down on the puffy layer of leaves and accompanied each of Simon's answers with his own loud comments. Arguably, it was Haroutiun's ridiculing remarks that finally convinced Bakro to leave his concealment. Then it took a few more minutes before he allowed himself to approach the brothers and make certain that they both were genuine human beings.

"There was a terrible sound, exactly from the place you had gone to. I began to saddle the horse and mule, Allah knew, just in case. Then Baba really scared me; he appeared, running and screaming. His ugly head was covered in blood and seemed to be dangling from his neck. It looked like . . . like it had been in Sheitan's mouth, and Sheitan had not appreciated Baba's head so he had spat it out. He and his limping dog flew by me as if a thousand furious *jiins* were pursuing them. So I hurried away, too." The Kurd did not say why he came back. Nevertheless, Simon was very grateful.

"What did happen there? Was it Sheitan's roar?" Bakro kept asking. "Did you see the jiins? Or other monsters?" Simon could not tell the truth. He talked some rubbish and quickly changed the subject to thanking Bakro for helping them to escape from the place indeed inhabited by the Evil Spirit. Bakro listened to Simon's fables with much attention and some new respect. "Good," whispered Haroutiun. "The fear will keep the Kurds and Circassians far away from the tomb." He held his tongue and only told his fellow travelers to make haste.

The same way down to the town was much easier and faster. This time, the travelers rode lightly. Haroutiun had with him only the water flask and his faithful "Cannon" pistol. On the outskirts of town he dismounted, giving Bakro the understanding that this was the point where they would part. After a few clumsy phrases of gratitude—my elder uncle had never been a voluble person—Haroutiun left Bakro and Simon and slowly went forward, letting them bid farewell alone.

Thus, my Uncle Haroutiun never knew—and never asked—what Simon and Bakro said to each other, but the rest of us did. Simon told us everything. Actually, because he was overwhelmed at that moment, he could not remember his own words very well. He said something about not being able to forget Bakro, his family, and their good times together. He remembered Bakro's words better. "Leave him," the Kurd had said pointing with his whip toward the leaving Haroutiun. "I respect the brotherly friendship, but around him you will never be safe and happy. Let him go alone. Here is your mule. Let's ride to our mountain meadows. We will hunt fall quails again and make shish-kebab. In spring we will drive sheep to yayla and fish trout in the lake. We will make jokes about Baba Kabak and you will tell people about the encounter with the Sheitan and his jiins. Everybody will have fun."

With tears in his eyes, Simon shook his head. "I have to go with him. I have promised." However, the Kurd was persistent. "Hey, I promise you a beautiful girl to marry. Kurdish women are the best. They don't put *yashmak** on their faces like the Turkish hanums do, but they don't talk too much in the presence of the men as the Armenian women do, either."

Simon realized that the Kurd bore in mind his sister, Pietzar, and her pleading speech a few days ago. Bakro interpreted Simon's silence as hesitation. "Well, brother Seemo, if you want a girl of your own kind, we can find one. I know one Turk, an old bundle of mischief, who keeps two young Armenian orphans for himself. We may try to save a plump one for you."

Simon knew he couldn't stay. "Farewell, Bakro-djan! Say hello to poor Baba. I really should follow my brother." Simon turned around

* Veil. (Turk.)

and hurried after Haroutiun. There was a short horse clatter behind his back, and then the hunter Bakro vanished from his life.

"You are late," noted Haroutiun when Simon caught up with him. "Their *muezzin** has already crowed. Get a move on. We should be there before darkness. We cannot afford to miss him." Haroutiun was speaking in unison with his pace. He led Simon by the unfamiliar dirty alleys and back streets of the hilly part of the town. They passed the small coffeehouse under grapevine and went higher and higher.

Simon thought that they had enough time to find us still at home and then at night to move together to the place where the smugglers were to pick up our family. He hoped for a short rest and a calming talk with his mother and sister. Instead, however, they continued to climb up, and Haroutiun would not distinctly explain who "him" was. A vague sense of alarm again began to rot Simon's heart. The only comforting thing was that the passing Turks did not pay much attention to them. They were just two ragged fellows. The brothers were wearing Bakro's clothes covered with the dirt and dust of the Sheitan Delik. The poor neighborhood itself was inhabited by similar-looking people.

You know what strange thing Simon noticed there? The evening sun was leaving the scene, setting behind the opposite mountain. The last sunbeams were still throwing light on the neighborhood's streets, but the night shadow was occupying its lower parts and moving up implacably. Thus, while the brothers were walking up by the steep streets, the darkness was falling behind them.

As they passed by a plain ramshackle house, Haroutiun slowed his steps to look around it and its curtained windows. Twenty or thirty steps further he suddenly dived into a breach in the clay wall fencing an abandoned garden. He carried Simon along with him. The brothers took cover in high burdocks. Only from there did Simon realize what was odd about the hut which they were watching: the thick, heavy door. It looked as if the rickety dwelling was tired of such a burden.

Only after taking up position next to the embrasure in the wall did Haroutiun tell his brother about the goal of their additional trip: to give

* A crier, who, with a melodious chant, summons the Moslems for ritual worship from the minaret five times a day.

short shrift to Missak the Traitor. Haroutiun reminded his bedeviled brother that during the gendarmes' raids in the town, this Missak had led the Turks from one Armenian house to another. Simon had dim recollections of a tall Armenian who followed the band of gendarmes bursting into his father's shop, just a featureless figure who bounced back from the door when the gendarmes drove his father and Simon out—to the Harab Caravansaray.

Haroutiun was satisfied by his timing; he had enough time for a short reconnaisance and preparation. Simon's heart missed a beat when his brother asked him about the "Maria," a small pistol that Haroutiun had given him this morning. Simon realized that he also had to shoot Missak. His palms and fingers came out in a sweat. The pistol trembled in his hands when he held it out to his brother.

"Keep it," said Haroutiun. "We should do it together. And don't you dare refuse. You have vowed vengeance, just today, at our father's grave!"

"But this man, Missak, he did not hurt anybody by himself," Simon risked uttering. "He simply accompanied the Turks, what could he do against them?"

"He is a traitor. A traitor is worse than an enemy. Much worse." The soldier lost his temper. "He is a poison, and poisoned bread is more dangerous than hunger!"

Simon fell silent. He was afraid that somebody would hear his brother's voice, but the street was on the point of being plunged into the darkness of the southern night, and was already empty. Haroutiun had been waiting exactly for this moment.

With more persuasion and threats of damnation, Haroutiun forced his brother to follow him to Missak's shelter. He explained to Simon that when he knocked on the door, Missak would draw back the window curtain and lock through the opening. Haroutiun also said that Missak always opened the curtain first in the window on the left side of the door, and then on the right side. "Like a badger, he always does the same thing. Now, we are going to use this habit against him."

Simon could barely hear or understand his brother's instructions. Haroutiun cocked Simon's small pistol and placed him against the right window. He hammered the heavy wooden door with the "Cannon" in his firm hand and then moved toward the left window. Simon thought that such a loud knock would draw the attention of all the neighbors around Missak's hut. He was looking at the window curtain and praying that nobody would answer the knock.

The curtain moved aside. Simon saw a face, or at least a part of it. The oil lamp inside the room threw light on a pale forehead, narrowing eyes, the gristly nose, and hanging mustache. He realized that it was the face of their target man—Missak the Traitor. He had to lift the pistol and shoot the man in his eyes, but he was lingering. The man inside was still peering at Simon. Perhaps he could not see him well, or was trying to see something very important in the face of the night messenger.

The fascination was interrupted by the "Cannon's" thundering shots. The man's face became distorted as he slumped back and disappeared from sight. Haroutiun, already standing next to Simon, grabbed his hand and began to drag him away along the street. A woman's cry followed them. The guttural shriek became even louder when they turned into an alley.

"Don't run, walk casually. His wife just leaped out of the house. It means we really got him." Haroutiun hid both pistols in his bosom. "Hawl hawl, greedy she-jackal. It was the payment which you have deserved." So down went the brothers and nobody stopped them.

Why Is This Sea So Salty?

Go to sleep my indefatigable listener. I could not help overhearing your wife's indignant whisper. She looks so woebegone because of this delay. Apparently she has already been picturing herself back home in her cosy kitchen or bedroom, but instead of that her family is suddenly stuck in the middle of an ugly melee. Who could expect this railway strike? So, you go and try to soothe your wife's worries.

Tell her that my grandson is doing his best in arranging your safe departure. Believe me, neither the Abkhazians nor the Georgians are very persistent in anything, even in fighting. Soon, these people will return to their daily routines, at least for while, and that break will be enough for your return to home.

She sleeps and you are back for the conclusion of my story! But my story has no conclusion. It has an end, but no conclusion. I am old. I obviously have had enough time to come up with some witty concluding thoughts, but I still have nothing in particular. For instance, about the people: there were some very good ones even among the Turks and Kurds who saved and helped us, and some really bad ones among the Armenians who betrayed their own people. So, perhaps I should say that there are no good or bad nations in the world, only good or bad people. Maybe this is true. However, it sounds too insipid to be my conclusion.

It is hard to derive a sense of what happened with us in Turkey? Well, the meat of it all was that they, the Turks, destroyed us, the Armenians, in many ways, imaginable and uninmaginable, and only a handful of our people managed to run away wherever they could. Now the Turks completely own the most fertile lands, eat the most delightful fruits, and enjoy the most beautiful views, while we, the oddments of the past, look back from this opposite shore, moaning in feebleness. You see, again nothing particularly wise comes to my mind.

Oh, you think there is something else? "Deeper?!" "The first genocide," "the second genocide," these numbers don't make much sense.

I am not well-educated, but I think there have been similar killings and deportations done to other peoples before us, the Armenians. Recently I realized that I didn't care much anymore that the Turks never admitted to committing the Yehern. Who needs their words? Here is a simple fact: we lived there, on that shore, and now we are here, on the opposite side of the same sea. You are much younger than me. Remember my words. Nobody and nothing will be able to persuade them to admit what they did. For the Turks, any words I say, or my mother and grandmother could say, are untrue. Some survivors, striving to keep their memoirs as pure as mountain streams claim to be, provided exact names, dates, and death routes . . . but in vain. The Turks will never admit anything. But they know . . . the names, the routes, and the reason.

Believe me, it is hard to remember and tell. For instance, I don't remember dates and I did not know what was going on outside of my small family. Sometimes I am not sure whether I saw things at the time for myself or heard about them afterwards from others. Some of their memories became mine. Now, my memories are like a hank of threads, separate threads pressed together. So, how a storyline will start, and twist, and end depends on what thread's tip you pull. It may be long or short, sad or terrifying; it all depends on the thread. It may also snap if pulled too abruptly. Each thread is not just a string of words; it is rather a tissue of animated pictures, still intense odors, and wild sounds; a living flesh of familiar and strange faces, pains, screams, and tears. Can anyone fully convey those things in obedient and accurate words? I am the first who would not believe it.

Thus, one may say that the story is a tale that has no moral conclusion, makes no sense, and possibly is not true. Nevertheless it happened to me and my people.

Continuing our talk about the human memory, I would like to mention that it may hide out not only in the head but also in other parts of our bodies, too. Sometimes it bursts out from such places, from such unlikely recesses that one would not believe.

I, myself, had a memory hidden in my skin or, more precisely—don't smile—in the soles of my feet. I am referring to a particular part of my life experience. That is what happened with me and my little brother, Hakop. . . .

You know, I told you about that day when Hakop and I were together for the very last time. After that day I never recalled my poor brother, neither when I was living in the Turkish village nor after my grandmother found me there and brought me back home. The girl Emine, who became Nargiz, never mentioned her brother's name, as if it had drowned in the sea with him. My relatives did not dare to ask me about his fate. They knew from the mollah, my savior, how Hakop's innocent life came to a tragic end. They did not want to awaken my memories of that terrible day spent under the burning sun on the sandy seaside square. However, it turned out that these memories were alive, branded on my skin. Or maybe they were buried in the hot sand along the Black Sea shore, just waiting for me to step on the sand.

When, at dusk, my mother, grandmother, and I came to the secluded spot where the sea-smugglers had promised to pick up our family, we found it was empty. We took our place behind the old abandoned boat, almost half hidden by the sand and crumbled shells. We sat there on our bags and packs. The sea was quiet, and the golden and reddish strips were gleaming under the beams of the drowning sun. A couple of sailboats at a distance were barely moving. One of them could be the felucca we were there for. My mother and grandmother were very anxious that Haroutiun and Simon had not appeared at the time my elder uncle had promised during their departure. Time and again my mother looked out from behind the boat's remnants. "Not yet," she answered to my grandmother's silent question.

The smell of the sea was worrying me. This had happened to me a couple of times before, too, when my mother or grandmother brought fish or mussels from the harbor fishmongers to our kitchen. On those occasions, I could not breathe and felt very anxious. However, during that evening, our last in the town, I was sensing not just light waves of the distinctive salty smell; the whole sea was in front of me. The huge living mass was lazily moving in languor, luring me in and pushing me away.

Grandmother Iughaper apparently noticed my unusual quietness and timidity. She suggested I take off my sandals and socks, and walk—"Do not go too far"—on the warm sand. She did not want to hurt me, my poor grandma, overwhelmed with so many troubles and concerns. She always had a thought of me or for me in her mind. I mean, it was like she never stopped thinking of what would be good or necessary for me.

As soon as my soles drowned in the still warm sand, a chain of vivid pictures in a chaotic order came to my eyes, and familiar sounds to my ears. The whole of my body was stricken. As if all at once, my body dwindled in size, time went back, and I turned into that small Nargiz, a dirty, thirsty creature, crawling away in fear from the pile of naked Armenian children swarming on the hot sand. Again I saw, very clearly, the old zaptieh with the punishing stick in his hands. I heard his gruff shouts and felt the scorching strikes of his stick. I also felt the trembling of my little brother Hakop's hand on my shoulder. I tried to throw it off and . . . and then I ran somewhere, screaming.

I ran because I was afraid of these pictures which were glimpsing fleetingly and uncontrollably in front of my eyes. I ran by my mother and grandma. Taken aback they did not attempt to stop me, and I disappeared into the darkness that had already crept along the beach. Only then did my mother run after me as fast as she could. Grandma remained near our bags, pacing around them in total disarray. The cold silver crescent was hanging in the sky, throwing some light onto the bizarre scene taking place down the earth.

I don't remember how long I was running. My sobbings turned into low squeals alternating with broken breaths. Suddenly I buried my head in somebody. Familiar strong hands and tobacco smell, along with confident voice, brought me round. It was my Uncle Haroutiun lifting me and pressing me to his mighty chest. Uncle Simon who, himself, was half-dead with exhaustion, was caressing my badly scratched feet. Soon my mother ran into us and I found myself in her hands. Then, a total failure of memory—oblivion. Apparently I kept repeating my drowned brother's name. Maybe something else. This was how my relatives recognized the reason for my great fear of the sea.

Nevertheless, at that time they had no choice other than to return to the place where Grandma had been left all by herself. They found her completely alone: our bags were gone. In our absence, the Lazes had appeared with the small launch-boat. Upon finding my grandmother alone and hearing her beg them to wait for a time until the others got back, the smugglers—did I mention to you that they were twin brothers—became furious. The Lazes did not want to change their plans and wait, even though they had delayed the date of our departure numerous times because of the endless felucca's breakages and repairs.

However, this time they happened to be very punctual. So they left, seizing up with them all our wretched belongings. Obviously the smugglers had well and truly brandished my grandmother, but did not find even a para on her. All our remaining money was thoroughly sewn into a cloth belt, tied around my belly. Because the women were going without my uncles to this place arranged by the smugglers, they came up with this idea that, as you see, proved to be very prudent. During all the scrapes I had created that evening, the belt remained safely sitting in its place under my dress. However, as I discovered the next day, I had lost my favorite things: Saint George's icon and the tiny porcelain salt-cellar ornamented with flying baby angels. It was not a good sign for our journey!

After short embraces and kisses, the joy of finding each other safe and sound gave place to confusion. Simon fell on the sand; he could not even speak. Mother kept me in her arms, firmly pressing my head to that sheltered place between her shoulder and tender neck. The aroma of her skin and hair broke the terrifying odor of the sea.

"Should we go back home?" asked my mother.

"No!" simultaneously replied both her brothers.

"I know the Lazes," noted my grandmother, settling down near her younger son. "They would not leave the bay without the promised money. There is nothing valuable in the bags they took away from me. Blockheads! I don't believe that any operation by such fools, smuggling trash from one place wretched by the war to another, will bring a profit. Maybe it will be a slim one. The money I have promised them was their best deal. They should return, just wait. . . ."

"Goddamn," exclaimed impatient Haroutiun. "I gave away my lighter to your friend Bakro! Now I cannot start a fire here and signal the Lazes. How many times have I told myself, 'Don't be a soft-hearted ninny. Don't be so slushy.' Now it's my fault. Any man is welcome to spit in my eye and rub it in with his foot if I ever do such a thing again."

"I did not even notice that you gave him a farewell present. That was nice," uttered Simon.

But Haroutiun did not hear his brother. "If these rogues are still out there somewhere," he was reasoning, peering into the sparingly moonlit smooth surface of the bay, "we can call them." He walked toward the water, put his fingers in his mouth, and let out a piercing whistle. Then again and again. Some dark low object slid out of the body of the darkness and moved noiselessly toward our place. "Haroutiun-djan, please, don't argue with them about the bags. Just let them take us away from here," pleaded my grandmother.

The felucca runs friskily. The water makes a hush-hush sound under its bow. It is morning. My mother asks me to see how beautiful the mountains are. I show myself from under my blanket and look at the motionless coast. "The mountains, the mountains." For some reason these words stick in my mind. "Are these the real mountains, the same mountains where I lived among the Turks and shepherded the sheep with the wolfhound Arslan? The mountains where my uncles and Bakro were preparing for days to travel to?" Not at all. These look so small with the cover of green trees and toy houses herded on the slopes and at the foot. Again I muffle myself in my blanket, cutting off the sight of the sea and its pungent smell.

Some time passed. Then, drifting back to the daylight from the bad dreams I recognized the voices of my mother and Uncle Haroutiun. Apparently I had caught the heated conclusion of a long conversation. Perhaps the conversation turned in that way when Simon told the women all that had happened with him and Haroutiun on the way to their father's grave and after. Most likely it was Simon's eagerness to relieve his mind. Haroutiun would hardly have revealed the fate of Missak the Traitor. This was not the women's business.

However, the avenger was now under the fire of my mother's words, expressing her deep misery. My mother must have really been desperate talking like that to her brother. She asked Haroutiun who gave him the right to punish Missak for his moral weakness. My mother believed that only God could judge humans for their deeds and most often he forgave the weak souls. Simon, who had quieted down next to me, moved, and his collapsing voice reminded Haroutiun that there, at Missak's dwelling door, he had said almost the same words to Haroutiun—but in vain.

"Even our mother forgave this unfortunate man," exclaimed my mother. Her voice was trembling, too, but nevertheless still sounded somewhat truculent.

Here Haroutiun started talking, and I could imagine how quizzically my uncle looked at his brother and sister. "I don't know what this coward did to my mother except bringing gendarmes to arrest her husband and son. My father, by the way. However, I did not punish him for my father's death only. I destroyed him because he betrayed all the Armenians of our town. Oh, of course, you both think that such misdoings are forgivable, but there is one thing, one reason why you cannot let it go. It is beyond your scope. You don't know if his victims forgave him at the gates of death."

"Our father was one of them. He was the kindest man we knew. He would never wish such a violent end on anyone."

"Pietzar, listen to me. You cannot answer for all of the victims. What about the butcher Arshak? Or the mechanic Ovannes? Did they forgive the traitor? If only one, just one among the Armenians of our town—a man, a woman, or a child—asked for revenge, I had to do it."

The loud and insistent voice of Uncle Haroutiun did not stop my mother. She wanted to prevent her brother from committing such reckless acts in the future. No, not "reckless." This is an improper word to define the Haroutiun's actions, which were planned and carried out so precisely, like military operations. It is better instead to use another word—which I have trouble thinking of right now—showing how much my mother was afraid that such zealous self-commitment to his all-consuming ideas would further harden and gradually destroy Haroutiun's own life. This was what my mother and grandmother were afraid most of all. Simon, who had taken only a small part in Haroutiun's actions, was already suffering. His best day was when he came from the harbor with the kalkans in his hands. He was joyful and full of the fresh sea air. The women doted on Simon and prayed for the full recovery of his mood. However, upon returning from the journey to the mountains with Haroutiun, he became the same Simon I knew, broken-spirited and prey to numerous doubts and guilt. The visit to the Sheitan Delik and the assassination of Missak the Traitor had brought back all the ghosts of his past.

The women were still nourishing the hope that Haroutiun could become a more regular person, marry a good Armenian girl or woman and have children. Perhaps, this kind of hope of seeing their sons or brothers married and with children dies the last in Armenian women. Besides, on a small boat, what was there to do but talk? So, emerging from my next dream, I heard my mother's voice again. She was continuing her selfless efforts to convince her brother to begin a new life. She also tried to obtain his word that he would not draw Simon into any more of his risky undertakings.

Uncle Haroutiun sounded bored with the long talk. He would speak only with reluctance, until he burst out with an unusually lengthy tirade.

"I took my brother on that journey so he would be able to cleanse himself. What he has done before or allowed to be done to him was so terrible that I don't even want to name it. This total disgrace meant that my brother needed not only worship at his father's grave, but also to commit the act of a reborn person, a deed of a new, strong man.

"You are a woman. You cannot truly understand our man's problems. Well, our particular problem with this creature, Missak, was simple: a jackal or a snake in his heart, he was, unfortunately, also an Armenian, and the people he betrayed were Armenians, too. In this case it became our duty, a responsibility of the Armenians who were still alive, to punish him. Nobody else would do our job. Of course, there are many among our people who still think the Russians will return and help us, or the English troops should protect us, or the French give us refuge. Wrong! It's our duty to do everything. After all, we should show that Armenian men are real men, not like that kerosene shopkeeper I have seen in our town. I hope that all Armenian kerosene shopkeepers are already dead!

"God created women to give birth to children. Women are all about life and love. But men are different. We men think about death, too. Death often solves our problems better than love and forgiveness.

"So, don't talk to me about love, sister, especially here on the sea, this sea. My love has been drowned here. My love, Maria, is somewhere under these heavy waves. How agitated they have become. Maybe she is calling me from there."

Actually, the surf became so high that splashes of salty water began to pour over us. The conversation ceased by itself. The hush-hush sound turned into a floundering and champing noise, as if the angry sea were trying to swallow our unyielding boat. I climbed out from under the blanket. This was the moment we saw why this sea was named the Black Sea. Its color, blue and green, turned before our eyes into dark grey and black.

We also realized to what danger we were exposing ourselves when grandmother struck a deal with the two Lazes. Just before the trip, she began questioning their buy-sell qualities, but now it became absolutely clear that their sailor skills were even worse—much, much worse. The smugglers were confusedly fussing around the deck, giving the same orders to each other and bickering about who should carry out those orders. They were trying to haul down the sails while the strong wind and rolling were making it more and more difficult. The brothers smugglers, had identical faces, like slices of the same melon, and had the same bright-colored Lazian clothes, so their chaotic actions and running began to make our heads swim. We got into a low booth on the deck, pretending to be a passenger cabin and cargo storage, too. The walls and roof of this awkward extension, rather like a dog house, were full of chinks and did not protect from the pouring water. The bales and bags of the smugglers occupied the greater part of the space. We pressed our bodies to each other and let the boat owners deal with the angry sea. However, it was not long until both of them also left the deck and squeezed us further into our humble shelter. At least it was warm.

Haroutiun asked the Lazes about the situation, but our skippers' evasive answers could not dispel our fears. Haroutiun was a good soldier, but not a sailor, so he could not help those oafs. The sea could have ended our trip right then, but for some reason delayed the execution.

When I woke up next time, the storm had already ceased. I did not know how long we spent in the cabin. Strangely, in that crowded state, and darkness, and with the crazy sea rolling, I felt better than the last evening on the shore of the bay.

Outside the cabin the sun was shining, and the rows of waves ran peacefully like sheep driven on by the boat. Those waves were everywhere my eyes could see. The storm had carried our boat away from the coast. The Lazes, who had navigated the boat just by following the coastal line, were now in trouble. Truly mountaineers, they came to own this felucca by chance. The war created many fantastic twists and turns in people's lives. Our unlucky skippers had no idea about the direction they should take. So, again we saw an already familiar performance. The Lazes were arguing loudly and fruitlessly, waving their hands at each other after every heated bout.

We laughed, my mother and I, at the smugglers' escapades. We were happy that the storm was over and the sun and emerald sea were so peaceful. Haroutiun fished out his compass, but could not din into the smugglers' heads what direction they should sail in. Besides, the sails had been torn by the storm, the small flat-bottomed launch carried in tow had disappeared, and soon it was discovered that the water was creeping into the under-deck space. Obviously, the carefree Lazes had not used the time on the shore to better caulk the boat, and it could not stand against the heavy surf.

We were drifting. To somewhere. The smugglers, this time with concerted efforts, dragged their soaked cargo onto the deck. However, more and more water was creeping into the boat. At the same time the supply of drinking water had run low. It was good that Haroutiun had his flask. "Never keep the flask empty . . . and cartridges, too, by the way," was telling Haroutiun to his brother. He let us drink water, but only a few gulps for each of us. The smugglers had their own source. My grandmother and mother refused to drink, letting me to have more, but Haroutiun was firm. Everybody had a water ration.

Then I suddenly found out that my treasures were not with me. I even forced my mother to open our bags and look through them all. We found neither the picture of Saint George nor the small salt-cellar. Where are they now? The picture, of course, does not exist, destroyed by the water and sun, but the small piece of porcelain may still rest in the sand of that secluded bay from our night embarkment, gleaming pensively under the lapping waves.

I cried, smearing the bitter moisture over my face. My mother and grandmother shared time consoling me and discussing Haroutiun's sad exclamation—"My love, Maria!"—that so unwittingly broke from his chest. I stopped my sobbing for a second just to inform them that Haroutiun had a beautiful small pistol he called "Maria." This detail only added fuel to the fire. The discussion now drew in Simon, too. He handled this small pistol but did not know anything about a woman with the name Maria. Simon remained so aloof from the present situation burdened by his own persistent reflections that the women soon left him alone with his thoughts. Haroutiun sat down far enough away not to hear my ugly whining and the women's talk. He grinned at the smugglers' desperate gesticulations.

The honest truth, at that time, the felucca's crew and passengers were a bunch of fools. Nobody fully realized the real danger of the situation. The boat was sinking in the open sea; we had a few gulps of water left, and no help on the horizon.

Upon becoming tired out in the sun, the Lazes found shelter in the shadow under the stern. The boat noticeably became bulky and circled around. We were forced to move from one side of the boat to another, in order to escape from the burning sunbeams. My lips were salty, and thirst made my head foggy. Maybe I had lost more liquid from my body from crying over Saint George's picture, so my thirst was just agonizing. Haroutiun gave me a little water, just to wet my cracked lips, and to wash out the salt. Finding a moment to talk, my mother shared her observations with him. She told him that when she had asked one of the smugglers about drinking water, the Laz had replied that the storm had swept away all their waterskins stored on the deck. However, she noticed that the smugglers did not seem to be suffering from the absence of the water. Not at all, at least, like their passengers.

Haroutiun went to find out the truth. Whether he talked to the same smuggler as his sister had or to his brother remained unknown, so much alike were the Lazes. The most important thing was that my uncle returned with water. Thus the drinking problem had been solved, at least for a while. However, we completely forgot about the water when a ship appeared at a distance coming fast in our direction. A small distant spot was growing and growing in size until it turned out to be a big white steamship. We all stood on our feet, joyously waving our hands and shouting something like "Take us!" or "Save us!" Nevertheless, the ship did not stop. Its enormous trunk roared past our shell-like boat. A few passengers on the ship's deck high up above us greetingly waved their hands and hats at our inaudible cries. Haroutiun was the first to realize what was happening and quietly sat back down in his place. For a short while the ship's rear stern remained in sight. The troubled water around our boat gradually calmed down. Only peels of fruits and a few scraps of paper floated in it reminding of the ship.

Everybody realized that our journey was about to come to an end. The felucca visibly subsided and the surface of the sea became dangerously close to our eyes. We avoided seeing such threatening closeness bunching together in the middle of the deck. The Armenians and the Lazes were praying, each to their own gods.

"God All-Mighty, forgive our grave sins! I have lived too long; my sins should be the most numerous and heaviest among all of us. Punish me, and show them your mercy!" My mother echoed my grandmother's prayer asking God to spare my life.

Why were my mother and grandmother thinking that the boat was sinking under the weight of their sins? What kinds of crimes those two women have possibly committed during their lives?

Their own survival in the Yehern? Was their strong wish to live that they showed an act of human revolt against foreordained fate? If that were true, then one should also accept the terrible, unimaginable idea that God was responsible for all that had happened with us there; God had taken a map of Turkey and a red pencil and had marked all those death-march routes for the Armenians, ending them in the deserts or the depths of the sea. Of course, he did not like that some victims had disobeyed his plans.

However, I think contrarily. God's hand was not behind the creation of these ordeals. Instead it was present in the miraculous salvation of some people who were almost doomed, such as, for instance, my mother, grandmother, and Uncle Simon, too.

You see, escaping death during the Yehern was not only the natural craving for life, the craving that for some outsiders, and even for the survivors themselves, seemed to be an egoistic, animal-like thing. It had a higher goal. Sooner or later each of the survivors should have found foreordained goal of his survival. Unfortunately, some of them couldn't do it.

My mother could not bear the desperation, particularly seeing that I, again, was stricken with terror. This time it was the sparkles of the sea water. Under the sun and mild surf its surface looked like the scales of a monstrous lizard or serpent. I cried and repeated the name of my little brother. Grandmother and Simon kept me in their soft arms. My mother crawled along the deck to Haroutiun. Later, she remembered that she had done this because she has been afraid of walking and swinging the boat, so it would take in water.

Crazy idea? Yes, indeed! The heavy, overloaded boat would not move under her light steps.

Even the cry of his favorite niece could not tear Haroutiun away from staring into the water. It was as if he were trying to penetrate the depth of the water and see his Maria. When my mother reached him she forgot for a minute why she was there. The expression on her brother's face made her believe that at any moment he was going to slide from the side of the boat and plunge himself into the water. She had no strength to speak. She simply clung to her brother and embraced his arm with her hands.

Should I talk now about Haroutiun and Maria? About how the love ended between the Armenian soldier and the Russian nurse?

Actually, Haroutiun began telling this story to my mother on the military ship that eventually picked us up. He spoke about it very briefly.

Many more details were provided by the front-line friend of his we met in Constantinople.

So, I should not break the "natural flow of the story." Unfortunately, I just did it by telling you about the military ship and getting to Constantinople instead of Batum. You may change the order of events as you think is better for your writing.

Well, well, we will now return to the sinking felucca in the Black Sea.

Uncle Haroutiun returned to life, and to action. He ordered the smugglers to throw their cargo from the deck. Whatever the Lazes had been transporting in those bales—wool, tobacco leaves, grain, or flour—the sea water had soaked into them during the storm and made them heavier. One of the Lazes greeted Haroutiun's words with much rage and resistance. By the way, neither my mother nor Haroutiun could recognize whether this Laz was the same one who had refused to give us water or not. However, the second Laz showed more understanding of the boat's desperate condition and contained his reluctant brother while my uncles dragged the bales to the side of the boat and threw them overboard.

When the massacre of the goods was over, the first Laz continued his crying, kneeling on the deck. Sometimes the man straightened himself up and rended the air with shouts. His brother, his double, comforted him by embracing his shaking shoulders.

It was hard to establish the real success of the rescue attempt. Maybe the reducing of the weight on the wrecked boat indeed extended its floating for while. Who could say exactly? Nevertheless, the felucca was still struggling to stay afloat when another ship appeared on the horizon.

The hope made the situation more frightening. The ship seemed to be motionless. Only the smoke line actually showed it was moving in our direction. My mother tried to prolong our end for a few more minutes. She decided to throw overboard our skinny bags, too. However, Haroutiun did not let her waste everything in there. He found his favorite "Ingliz" jacket and put it on instead of the garment given to him by Bakro. At that moment a saving idea dawned upon him. He salvaged my mother's white nightgown, tore it open from the neck to the hem, and laid it on the deck. Using his sharp penknife, he cut

Bakro's colorful garment and made a few strips out of it. Then he put the strips onto the torn dress and told the women to sew them on.

My uncle was an experienced soldier. He always had his tools with him: pistols, knife, compass, and so on. My mother and grandmother had also experienced a lot, in their own way. So they carried their needles and threads on them wherever they were forced to go. In ten minutes they hastily sewed the strips onto the white cloth. Then my Uncle Simon and one of the smugglers stood on the open deck, stretching my mother's nightgown between their arms. When the ship was close enough the sailors on it noticed this white flag with a cross of strange color. After the ship reduced its speed and came closer to us they saw the things thrown overboard still floating around the helpless felucca.

A launch was dispatched and we were all taken to the ship. I was in a drowsy state, and I did not remember the rescue part well. Later, Simon and my mother said that the Lazes gave the foreign sailors a hard time. The Lazes hesitated to get into and off the launch bobbing up and down on the surf made by the ship's propeller. Can you believe, the sea smugglers could not swim? Actually none of us could swim either, although we were born and lived on the sea coast. The smugglers could not understand the strange language of the sailors, but wanted to bring some of their remaining belongings with them. So there was a log of begging and cursing, shouting and gesticulating, and throwing things back and forth.

On the ship, Haroutiun talked with a couple of Russian officers who happened to be among the passengers and learned that this military ship was heading straight to Constantinople. One more time the route of our family had been changed, without our knowledge. At least Constantinople was in the arms of the allies.

Our luckless smugglers were more devastated than us by the news about the ship's route. With each hour it carried them further away from their beloved Lazistan. Rizeh, Trebizond, and even Kiresun had already been left far behind with their lower slopes of mountains dropping down to the sea in staircase-like terraces of gentle green plantations and orchards. During the entire trip on this big ship, the Lazes and our family stayed together. A small gypsy camp was pitched on the lee side of the upper deck, in a secluded corner where there were less chances to get under the crewmen's feet. Although these men were friendly, gave us heaps of blankets, and a couple of times brought us helpings of their tasteless meals, they were complete strangers.

"Look at this boiled grain—the utter slop. Who knows—it might have been prepared with pig fat." The Lazes complained to Uncle Simon, who had the patience to listen to them. "Look, everything here is made of iron." The Lazes banged their emptied basins against the surrounding surfaces. "How is it not sinking? It may sink at any moment. Plus, the same iron things are inside. Have you, Simon Agha, been inside of this Sheitan's creation?"

I agreed with the Lazes. It was a really frightening thing to go inside the ship's belly: the narrow booming stairs and corridors, endless turns, and a sharp, pungent smell from the men's room. Neither my mother nor I would dare to go there without Haroutiun, though we risked having our bladders burst.

"Simon Agha, ask your brother; he can understand these infidels. Ask whether this iron prison-boat will stop somewhere before Stamboul. Maybe at Samsun? Even from there we could somehow get home." Imperturbable Haroutiun stood alone leaning on the handrails, staring again into the water.

One Laz determined that my mother was the kindest and, in this way, the weakest member of our family. He began his siege by whining about their misfortunes of going so far and to an enormous city such as Stamboul. "Hanum, for you, the Armenians, the entire world is open. You go anywhere and you always find a bunch of Armenians, or even hundreds of your people, who arrived there before you. They will help you. Quite contrarily, everybody knows that we, the Lazes, do not like to travel. The others make jokes about us, saying that our rears became rooted to our mountains. You will see, Hanum, how many Armenians still live in Constantinople. They have churches, khans, food stores, taverns—everything where one can knock on the door for a bed and a piece of bread, at least for a night. Where would we find a Laz in that huge human anthill? Who would give us shelter?"

My mother's tender face turned pink. She was upset, but could not immediately find a proper refutation. "You, the Armenians, like to travel!" She should replied that the Armenians usually did not travel for plain curiosity, but were forced to seek a safe place, ran away for their lives, escaped their deaths, or were deported. However, my mother did not say these words. Thus, the Laz got to the point of asking for the rest of the sum of money that he and his brother had agreed upon with my grandmother. Grandmother Iughaper refused to pay for the failed delivery of our family to Batum. Uncle Simon shrugged his shoulders. My kind mother turned to Haroutiun.

"Why should we pay?" Haroutiun was indignant at the very fact that his sister had let her mind be occupied with such an arrogant demand. He immediately made for the Lazes who were afraid to move away too far from our "gypsy camp." Soon he returned from their negotiations.

"I don't know how you speak with people, but everyone who meets you sooner or later demands money. I told the Laz that he should expect his payment when he gets to hell, and the man understood."

"Perhaps it was another Laz, not the one I talked with," timidly pointed out Pietzar.

"Can be; they look so alike, like two peas in a pod. However, my Laz showed complete understanding. They could not get us to the point we wanted, so we would not pay the money they wanted. The sum our mother gave them in advance turned out to be even bigger than these scoundrels deserved. They should continue their fishing at the bay instead of sailing in the open sea. Where did our mother succeed in finding such a stupid pair?"

"A drowning man clings to a serpent. That's how the saying goes. The Lazes are not serpents, you are right—they are just silly."

"He confessed to me that it was their first trip to Batum without the man who had accompanied them before and had taught them to sail the Greek felucca. The greedy brothers, I suspect, dumped their teacher because they had to pay his share."

"Anyway I am sorry for them. After all, with their help we have escaped from the town."

Haroutiun looked at his sister with sudden tenderness, and then turned toward the sea again as if trying to hide his fleeting weakness.

"Are you thinking about her? About Maria?" asked his perceptive sister.

"Oh, don't. Bakro is absolutely right; you talk too much." Haroutiun tried to keep his voice firm.

"Your niece told me that you have a pistol named 'Maria.' She knows more than us, your mother and sister."

"This one." The soldier put a small object in the woman's palm. "One of her discharged patients thanked her with this piece. Apparently this person had taken it from a dead enemy officer. The Russians had no such toys in their armor. Look here—a natural ivory on the handle. Maria gave me this at our parting."

"How strange. Such a beautiful thing, real craftsmanship, yet it was made for killing. Why do people do that?"

"Oh, this is nothing. People have learned to build huge steel boxes, self-moving beasts with cannons and machine guns, and also boats that can go under water and fire special missiles. Imagine, deep in this water, that such a boat is following our ship. The ship's crew is working or resting in their cabins, the passengers are laughing and walking along the decks, and nobody suspects that the invisible enemy is getting closer and closer, and maybe has already fired the deadly missile . . ."

Pietzar shuddered and looked with fear toward the quiet waves around the ship. "That's what happened with Maria?"

"Yes. There was a Russian hospital ship. It transported seriously wounded soldiers from Lazistan to Batum. There it was supposed to pick up new medical supplies and other necessary materials and bring them back to our hospital and front-line aid posts. Maria was a nurse in that hospital. She was assigned to accompany her patients to Batum. I did not want her to go. However, her chief nurse thought that her patients would be more comfortable in her presence. Maria promised to come back as soon as possible. That day she gave me this pistol. We had nothing appropriate to give to each other for presents. We were waiting for a better time. But it was the last time I saw her, smiling and bright, and as assuring as always . . .

"Shortly. At the very end of her journey back, very close to the new naval station at the bay of Rizeh which, by the way, we had just cleaned up from Turks and bands of Lazes and Adjars, her ship was attacked by a German underwater boat. It was morning, and the white flag with the red cross on the mast and red crosses on the white funnels clearly showed that it was hospital ship. When the boat began to attack, the sisters of mercy in their uniforms were called on deck to demonstrate the ship's purpose. Vainly. The missile was fired exactly into the middle of the ship's body. The hull broke in two, and the bow and stern rose straight into the air, as if in a last salute, and then went down quickly. People, men and women, dead and alive, fell into the whirlpool, screaming in terror. Then, only broken pieces of wreck, boxes of medical supplies and dressing materials, nurses' headdresses, and a few survivors, mostly strong men, remained on the surface. How could a woman survive such violence? Maria was not found. . . ."

"Vah, vah, Haroutiun-djan! Tsavet tanem, Haroutiun-djan!" lamented my mother. "Tell me more about her, about your Maria. What kind of a person was she?"

"No. I cannot stand your tears. It makes me weak. I had better go and find the Russians I spoke with. They should have something to drink. . . ."

"Believe me, brother, tears are good, very good. It's okay when people are capable to bemoan their lost ones. Do you know anything about Maria's family? Is there a mother or sister in faraway Russia who is shedding tears over her?"

"Maria did not tell me much about her people. The only obvious thing was that she did not come from a rich family. I remember that her chief nurse said to me, on that day when, after receiving the devastating news, I appeared galloping crazily on the horse that my friends had borrowed for me from the Cossack regiment, that Maria had not much of education, but was her best nurse because of her kind heart and very caring hands. This was the very same woman who had sent Maria to that hospital ship. Why did she say those words to me? Was it to somehow excuse herself or read a short, unwritten epitaph for one of many victims of the war? I could not derive any sense of the event. I felt dead myself. There was only one thing I knew, was sure of: it was the end of my story. Whether my body would live or not, after Maria I could never love somebody else.

"Was she beautiful? A typical Russian? Did she love me? Yeah. For me she was the most lovely woman. She was not tall, but exactly my height. She had blue eyes and blonde hair, if you meant those of a typical Russian girl. Do you remember the color of the heavy unhurried honey our mother used to buy in spring from the upland villagers? That was the color of her hair.

"She was my first woman and I, *durachok,* or silly in Russian, used to become furious when I saw her joking or laughing with her patients, the Russian soldiers. I thought she was easy and they were all impudent. There were some skirmishes, before her chief chucked me out and forbade me from coming within a hundred archins of the hospital. So we pretended that my wound had not completely healed yet, and Maria was allowed to meet me outside the hospital to change my bandages."

"Oh, you *char balik**, you did not tell us that you had been wounded. Where? How bad? Of course, it was serious if you spent time

* Bad boy. (Arm.)

in the hospital." Pietzar looked over Haroutiun as if she could see his old wound through his clothes.

I am sure, it was the same penetrating look she, my mother, and also grandmother Iughaper, produced every time I was not myself, momentarily checking my face and body all over from my head to my feet. But they could not see those dreams that since the sea trip have been terrifying me as regularly as the sea creates storms and the moon turns into a crescent.

"Hah, my wound! It was not serious, but rather funny. You are my sister, so I can tell you why it was amusing. But first; let me explain that war is not a constant battle, fierce attacks and counterattacks. I wish it could be like this, but it is, unfortunately, in great part waiting for action, a long, annoying waiting. In simple words, it is sitting in trenches. The winter trenches, half-full of cold mud, are the worst. We—I mean the Armenian *druzhiny** and the Russian infantry men and Cossack regiments—had spent the previous year in trenches, sometimes beating off the attacks of the local bands of Lazes, Adjars, and Circassians, guided by their Turkish masters. The Armenian fighters were the most disappointed. Many of us had homes and families behind the enemy front line. We were dreaming about moving forward and liberating our people. Every day I looked at the mountains on my way home and hoped for the offense signal.

"Our waiting ended only after a new commander was put inn charge of Russian forces in Lazistan. 1915 began with the cleaning up of the lands between Batum and the Chorokh river mouth from the local Moslem bands. Then we took the port of Hopa and, in the spring, moved to Artvin that had been lost to the Turks during the previous shameful 'year of sitting.'

"Here comes my 'funny' wound. Because of the cold and dirt, I got terrible boils. At first, I did not pay attention to them, since there was no reason to spend time on such trifles. Understand, it was our first successful offensive campaign. We were moving toward our homelands. However, those ugly bumps grew more and more and hindered my moves. The worst of them nested right on my rear. During the marches my waist-belt would slip on them and would make me clench my teeth

* Detachment of volunteers. (Russ.)

in pain. I was young, stupid, and felt ashamed of showing this particular part of my body to somebody. So I endured it as long as I could, keeping my belt as far up as possible, until one day my trench-fellows, Hetoum Kilikia and Karo Bakvetsi, may the latter rest in peace, found me in a great fever and unable to bend. They both took me to our first aid post and then on its wagon to the hospital.

"That 'funny' wound! It made the Russian patients laugh a lot. Each time Maria came to change the bandages, they made jokes about me. Of course, now I understand that for them, some seriously wounded and some crippled, it was a rare chance to have some fun. While they were joking that a bullet had struck me in the butt because I was running away from the Turks like a hare, I was trying to escape from the soft but unexpectedly strong hands of Maria. I wanted to fight with laughing Russians who questioned my soldier's pride. I already spoke Russian well enough, but in feebleness and distress I shouted to them something almost inarticulate, mixing all the tongues I knew. It was my first time in hospital, and I was also ashamed of the young woman's seeing me in such a pitiful position. I wanted to ask that another nurse, maybe on older one, change the bandages, but at the same time I was afraid of missing those regular visits from Maria. I already admired her, her tender voice and kind, smiling face.

"However, I was then kicked out of the hospital because I fought with some patients. It seemed to me that they were very free with their hands in Maria's presence. After the Turks had been ousted from Artvin, our offense stopped again. We waited for a long time, until the beginning of the next year. The new delay made me angry when I thought about my family, waiting for me there behind the Lazistan mountains. On the other hand, I got a chance to spend all my free time wandering near the hospital and trying to see Maria's face or hear her voice. Soon I discovered that often Maria would go to a neighborhood fountain for some fresh water. I saw her bringing two pailfuls on a wooden shoulder stick with hooks on the ends. I cannot remember the Russian word for this tool. Anyway, taking heart, I approached Maria and her fellow nurse at the fountain and offered help. I found that Russian stick and hooks to be difficult to handle. On Maria's soft shoulders, when she took her graceful steps, the pails behaved quietly. On me, as if on purpose, the pails swung crazily and wet me from both sides. Maria laughed and called me 'durachok,' but I was not offended.

"You know, Pietzar, she liked to laugh, but she also was very smart. She put wide leaves of burdock into the pails and that kept the water from spilling on the way to the hospital. Those minutes together were precious. Everybody in the hospital got used to seeing me around. *'Tvoy chernoglazyi prishel!'** shouted the nurses and old patients to Maria. The strange Russians! I think I still do not fully understand them. One day they were making rude jokes about me and then kicked me out, yet the next day they were smiling when they saw me and were candidly happy for me and Maria. Even her chief, a stern, dry woman, tall and lean as a poker let Maria treat 'the wounded Armenian volunteer' outside the hospital. Of course, she knew that my wound already has been closed up.

"Strange thoughts occurred to me during that summer. I was thinking about how my family would meet Maria. She did not see much in her life in Russia. She told me that the soil there was miserly, good for nothing except potatoes. Maria liked everything she saw around her in Lazistan: blue sea, colorful mountains, fresh fish and fruits, and particularly the sweetened nuts, halva, and baklava passed from the hands of street-traders, coming to do their business at the hospital entrance. I was telling her that our flounder was bigger and fatter, fruits sweeter, and there was an abundance of thickets of nuts around our town . . ."

"Did you tell Maria that we make our Armenian baklava with forty layers of pastry, representing exactly the forty days of Lent? That every Armenian family should have this on the Easter Sunday?"

"Yes, yes! Maria listened to my tales about our house, and our family's gatherings and weddings with such fascination. She was willing to go with me to my part of the world. I used to think and worry about whether my mother would like my Russian wife. Would she accept her smile and laughter and blonde hair? But then I assured myself that you, Pietzar, and my father would help her to recognize and appreciate Maria's smart hands and her kindness.

"How silly I really was. 'Durachok!' At that time we, the Armenians in the Russian army already knew that the new massacres of our people had begun in Turkey, more cruel and more persistent than ever. I, myself, talked with a couple of the Armenian men who managed to escape from their villages around Trebizond. So I knew that apparently my father and brothers were dead like the other Armenian men, and you

* "Your black-eyed dear has come!" (Russ.)

and mother had been driven with other women to nowhere. Sometimes, however, I forgot about that, and my mind kept showing me my family in our house and Maria and I coming in. My mind was troubled. After a sad talk with my Armenian fellow fighters I almost cried at night, remembering my father's face and thinking about his possible end. Then, suddenly, I would catch myself imagining how my father would play with my son—for some reason Maria and I were sure that she was bearing a boy—how much he would be pleased because Maria and I would give to our son his name, Pogos, and how much they both would look alike. Then, again, I realized that these two would never see each other because my father was dead."

"And now, my and Maria's son is also dead. . . . Did I not tell you, Pietzar, that such conversations could not bring anything but tears? You, my dear sister, make me as flabby as milksop. I should go and find those Russians on this ship. I need a drink. They will understand me."

"Who can understand you better than me? I am your sister, and sisters are for hearing and sharing pain, weeping instead of the brothers who cannot. God created us to be like sponges. I already came to like your Maria very much. Tell me more about her and you."

"There is nothing else to tell. Everything ended that morning in the waters of the Rizeh Bay. One month after the hospital ship with Maria was drowned our battalions took Trebizond. How long had we, the Armenians fighters, dreamt about this day? Now, it had happened. I was closer to my hometown, but I was not excited. I knew that none of my family was expecting me there, and I had also lost Maria. I was just angry that the Turks had left the city without a street battle. With their flight I lost the chance to have a face-to-face fight, to pay them back by myself—by my own bayonet, hands, and teeth—for all my losses.

"A delegation of the Trebizond Greeks came asking our Russian general to cease bombardment. Merchants, tradesmen, sorry kerosene shopkeepers; they were afraid of the destruction of their houses and stores. For me the entire world already had been destroyed because so many innocent people have been killed—not only soldiers, who, of course, might die during action and hopefully with valour and dignity, but also women, children, and nurses who did not carry arms. What kind of world is this if the children and women are being destroyed? *Pooch ashkhar paitel'e*!*

* "The world has exploded like a soak-bubble!" (Arm.)

"However, for the kerosene shopkeeper it does not matter. Such people can tolerate anything. Like cockroaches after the harsh winter, they crawled out onto the streets of Trebizond. Their routine life continued. Soon, even a few such Armenians began appearing in the city, patching the deserted dwellings, getting small trades, or just pottering around."

"Life is life, Haroutiun-djan. So you also have to move on . . ."

"No, I cannot. During those days in Trebizond, the Greeks opened tables on the streets and greeted the Russian liberators. On the main square of the city, photographers made pictures of happy crowds of soldiers and civilians. People posed waving the Allies' flags. They dragged me in too. So, if there, somewhere, is a picture showing only one sombre face in the crowd, this face is mine. I still don't know how to 'move on.' I am not an indestructible cockroach. I am not a kerosene shopkeeper!"

That was what my Uncle Haroutiun said about Maria. He related it to my mother on the military ship deck between taking heavy drags of smoke from cigarette rolled by his hands. We saw them talking, but the wind carried away his smoke and words. When Haroutiun went in search of the Russians, my mother returned to our "gypsy camp." Retelling what Haroutiun had said, her voice made his love story more disturbing. At the end, she asked that we mention Maria in our prayers for our dead. We all nodded assent. Grandmother Iughaper said that she would pray also for her unborn grandson, Pogos, who could look like her late husband Pogos Aleksanian, but also have blonde hair like his Russian mother. Uncle Simon uttered something about his understanding of Haroutiun's sufferings and admiration of his brother's strength. One of the Lazes, difficult to say which one of them exactly, cursed infidels making "sheitan ships" that can run and fire from under water. As for Nargiz . . . well, that day young Nargiz understood that she should pray for her brother, Hakop. There, on the ship, it struck me that the same sea had taken up not only Maria and her son but my younger brother, too. Then I came to understand why there was so much fear in me, the fear of this otherwise beautiful greenish-blue surface, such deep repulsion for its salty smell and waves' gleaming. The thorny pieces of that hot day on the small dirty square near a mooring lane—the pile of naked children, the trembling of feeble Hakop, the zaptieh with his long, punishing stick—began to pop into my head. Then, for the first time, a nine-year-old Nargiz sensed the guilt and shame of abandoning her dying brother.

Pera Encounters

Have you been, professor, in Polis? I mean Constantinople. I cannot call it Stamboul or Istanbul as many others do now. For us, Turkish Armenians, that city has always been Polis. We used this name as a short one of the original Constantinople. Would you agree that short names or nicknames reflect the special bonding that people have with certain places?

One part of Polis was called Pera, where Armenians preferred to settle, live and die. Stamboul, at that time, was just another part of the city, across the long, narrow bay. Stamboul was almost entirely Turkish. There were also Galata, with its Greek quarters and cemeteries, and distant Skutari behind the Bosphorous. All these regions of that enormous city were crowded with various colorful folks. Now, this city became Istanbul.

I am curious, what do they call Pera now?

Do you know what our first impression of Polis was? Terror! Yes, we were stunned and terrified! In full daylight we slowly approached the city and were met by the high towers and thick walls of the ancient fortresses at the gate into the narrowing channel. These silent guards let us further in. Then we saw a gigantic panorama of the city, irresistibly unfolding before our eyes and surrounding our vessell from all sides. The frightening pile up of heights and terraces, the anthills colored by the walls and roofs of thousands houses, and myriad of people dashing about. All was unknown to us and nobody expected us. But there was also a great beauty in this picture we were seeing; the huge domes of mosques created an incredible harmony by mirroring the shapes of the hills and exclamation signs of the white minarets perfectly matched with the tall, green cypresses.

Our ship stopped because a big bridge crossed the waterway. Near the bridge, herds of sailboats, scows, caiques and bumboats were waiting for passengers. Soon our ship was surrounded by them. Boatmen shouted loudly offering a cargo ferry and a ride to the city's shores.

"Galata, Galata," "Stamboul," "Skutari"—we did not hear "Pera" where my mother and grandmother decided to go. They had heard a lot about Armenian churches and schools in the quarter. They knew that Pera was the first choice for any Armenian: *"Pera Haikakan'e."** But they did not know that Pera was situated behind Galata, on the hill.

We, the shipwrecked survivors, all bunched together. Even usually self-confident Haroutiun was overwhelmed by the city's size. However, the Lazes, our luckless smugglers, very soon discovered that many boatmen were of their own kind. These boatmen wore the same distinctive shawls with the flaps knotted around their foreheads like turbans. The boatmen and the smugglers talked the same language. They made a quick deal and the Lazes, now cheered up, went down by the narrow gangway to the rolling caique. On parting, one of them sparkled his eyes and grumbled something inaudible. His twin brother wished us luck. "*Bashariler delerim!* Good luck to you!" replied my mother. "Shams!" said Uncle Haroutiun. "Remember how one of them was pretending that they would be lost and all by themselves here, in Polis?!"

Then came our turn. The sailors hurried us up. We went by the trembling gangway to take the next caique to Galata.

Putting our feet on the Galata's quay, we had nothing. All our possessions drowned in the sea. Haroutiun still carried two pistols in his favorite jacket, Simon was clothed in the sailor's shirt given to him by our saviors on the military ship. He carried one sorry bundle of our rags and nothing else except his ghosts and fears. My mother saved a few photographs, and my grandmother, our treasurer, had on her last coins of the golden jug hidden in our garden. I had nothing with me. But then it was much easier for us to walk up and down and around in search of a refuge. Pera with its wide streets and mansions, was too good for us. We found a cheap room somewhere in its distant back streets, almost in Galata. Our quarter had more Greeks than Armenians. The tall house resembled a pregnant figure with the second floor's covered balconies, protruding into a narrow street and overhanging its always trashed footway. The low, sleeping benches were arranged along walls of our room which floor was covered by mercilessly worn rugs. Nocturnal legions of bugs inhabiting these and bedding of the benches were eventually defeated and destroyed after a long battle with my

* "Pera is an Armenian place." (Arm.)

mother and grandmother. The battlefield was divided with a rope and a couple of sheets into two halves: one for the men and the other for the women. From the previous tenants we inherited a long squat table. Around that table the women and Uncle Simon spent a great part of our more-than-three-year-life in Polis, earning copper coins by sewing for the entire neighborhood. Haroutiun, the most skillful among us (for better or worse, but for a few years he maintained a small tailor shop in Sukhumi set up with his father's money), could not remain seated at the table. He used to find any reason to get out of the room and then disappear for hours somewhere in the city.

No wonder that he always offered to accompany me to my school. With great difficulty, my mother succeeded in settling me in this elementary school, an absolutely ordinary one. A few Armenian schools, much prettier and with names, refused to take me in. We couldn't afford to pay their fees, but also I, myself, inspired a great deal of caution in the school administrators. I looked independent and stubborn, behaved impolitely and was even rude. So, I was a wild girl, one that by no means belonged to the pretty dressed "sweethearts" of those schools.

In the last such school I confirmed my reputation, and it ended my poor mother's attempts to bring her daughter into "high society." Blushing because of our appearance, she was talking with "Madam X," the head mistress of the school. The latter wore an impressive black dress with a corset and a white jabot. They stood at the entrance of the school building where the head mistress has chosen to see my mother. A few girls, the "sweethearts," played in the courtyard. I walked out of the yard and slowly moved down the street along the ornamental iron fence, waiting impatiently for my mother to end her hard conversation. One girl of my age approached the fence from inside the courtyard, apparently wishing to talk with me or ask my name. Who knows? I did not respond. The girl smiled and pushed her hand through the fence. Instead of giving her my hand I grabbed hers and bit it. The girl ran to the mistress screaming, with tears in her eyes, and a red mark on her white, tender wrist. Soon, the totally shocked mother caught up with me on the street. I did not say a word in my excuse, only knitting my brows and sighing convulsively, trying to suppress tears.

Why did I do it? I think I had grown up; I mean, enough to understand that we were desperately poor, poor as church mice, and that my mother, the "Lord" Pogos' daughter, was embarrassed by the pleading tone of her futile conversation with the inaccessible school head mistress. My mother was trying to remember and use some strange words and turns, those that she had not used for years, the remnants of her carefree past when she was the darling daughter of a successful man. And another important thing was that I was already able to realize that there were many Armenians in Pera strikingly different from us, poor newcomers. We had been the uprooted ones, leaves driven by the fierce wind. It seemed that those Armenians of Pera lived quite normal, comparatively of course, lives during all the war years. The husbands worked in banks or companies, the wives made their routine visits to friends and stores, and their girls studied French in the schools and gymnasiums. Of course, for them, people like us were very disturbing. What could we bring from those places where the wind had driven us? Nothing interesting, only the same sick, overburdening, and hard-to-believe life stories, guilty voices, and lifeless gazes, illnesses of soul and body. Often I felt unwanted there, in Pera.

My mother accepted my unspoken feelings. She did not blame me. When Uncle Haroutiun listened to this "Bite Story" he laughed loudly and to tears, praising me a lot. Uncle Simon looked at me with some respect.

At that time, twenty-year-old Simon was a tall, well-proportioned man with the clear features of the pale face and slightly curly hair and tuft. He walked with a little stoop, but that did not spoil the whole impression. Shortly after our settling in Pera, he became the subject of intent attention from the women's part of the quarter. There were girls ready for the first-time marriage, as well as those whose time was running out, and young women who had lost their husbands and children and were eager for a second chance to make a new family. However, there were not enough men for those Armenian girls and women: pretty or ugly, merry or sad, well-to-do or living entirely on sops. One could easily observe that the Turks had more thoroughly destroyed our men and boys. It was absolutely obvious that many more Armenian women had survived through the Yeghern than their men.

Uncle Simon was a picture of the women's hope. Even his oddities could not frighten them off. Haroutiun's rude remarks were effective, but only in relation to his own candidacy. So, our bleak room became a stage of continuous presentations and self-presentations of hopeful brides. Poor Simon was timid in the presence of new faces; he was afraid of the very thought of being separated from us. He was always eager to accompany me to school or bring me back just to escape another scheduled introduction. Thus, in my uncles, I had two personal guards available to walk with me along the city's streets. There were some places of vice in our neighborhood that terrified my mother such as madam Tsakalidis' "Funny House." So, we had to go a mile out of our way to avoid seeing her "girls" leaning out from the windows of that house.

My uncles were quite different guides. Sometimes, on our way to home, Uncle Simon and I would take a break, spending time in the Mussulman cemetery. When the skies were clear and the ground was warm, we used to find a secluded spot and recline there, looking into the distance from the waters of the bay. The silhouettes of ships on the water did not move. Everything was quiet. Only the figures of a few visitors inaudibly and unhurriedly passed here and there between stone and marble grave columns. A motionless shadow not so far from us suddenly livened up, changed its shape and turned out to be a man or woman, another silent observer.

Turkish tombstones were different from those on the Armenian cemetery. The latter were curved with emblems of the professions of the dead. The Turkish tombs had small holes through which the dead could hear what was going on there, outside of their graves. A dead man could hear whether his widow was lamenting long enough and with proper affectations when visiting his grave. Uncle Simon explained that through these holes the dead also received a piece of bread and some water from their visiting family members as a sign of remembrance. Later, Uncle Haroutiun told me that another possible purpose of these small holes was to convey family gossip to the dead. My mother and grandma listened to his words with loud disapproval. They became much more upset when I asked whether I could to speak through such a hole with my father or grandfather. Both women started to console me in all possible ways. Uncle Haroutiun could not stand up to their reproaching glances and tears and immediately retired out of the room, to the courtyard.

Our "Noah's Ark," I mean the big old house we lived in had an inner courtyard and open balconies wrapped around its upper floors. Refugees of all kinds lived in separate rooms; the thin walls and the doors continually opened by an army of swarthy hungry children broadcasted all the tenants' daily arguments to the amusement of the others in the courtyard. The courtyard had a water pipe and a large stone washtub with wide, flat sides. This place was a nerve center of our multilingual community, the show stage for the women gathering there for laundry work and gossiping about neighbors, and their husbands, mostly unemployed men, losers along with their former armies, out from their native lands and without language, who now spent their time by playing cards and *tavla* (backgammon), and obstructing access to the water.

Haroutiun gained respect among most of these men because he was independent—no wife, no children—and he knew not only Armenian and Turkish, but also Russian and some Greek. It helped him to defend the tenants' interests when the building owner, a short, fat Greek with a face like a cured olive, turned up to collect the rent. There were a couple Russian families in our "Noah's Ark" who, most of all, appreciated Haroutiun's skills. The Russian men, former officers of the tzar's army which was destroyed and thrown away by its own people, could not get into the landlord's head why exactly they had again delayed their payments, although the cunning Greek knew perfectly the extremely straitened circumstances of his suddenly impoverished tenants. Who else would take residence in his ramshakle, bug-infested place? However, some bygone pride did not let the Russians condescend to ask the Greek for more time. They only clenched their fists, catching the lustful glances he was pointing at their fair-skinned, blonde women. At such moments, Haroutiun's indifferent composure and sarcasm blew out the landlord's blatant threats. "Drink less rakia, former gentlemen! Next time, mark my words, I will throw you on the street. Noble beggars!" With such words the furious Greek used to let the Russians off his hook and went off to hunt for the next debtor.

So, there in this courtyard, noisy even in morning, Uncle Haroutin awaited me for the walk to the school. On the way back, he always asked me, as a joke, whether I would like to go by Madam Tsakalidis' "Fanny House" or another way. He never took me there where Uncle Simon did: to cemeteries. With Uncle Haroutiun, after school trips were much longer. We would walk along the fashionable main street of Pera, all the way down to the Galata Bridge—"To look at people." There, Uncle Haroutiun used to find a place aside from the endless human current and stand for hours leaning on something and looking at faces of the passing people.

Indeed, if one wanted to study human nature, there was no place on earth like the Galata Bridge to do so. At that time an enormous variety of human species would cross this bridge every day, creating before one's eyes an amazing procession of human races of all skin colors and face forms. Here, by the way, was the first time I had seen black people, tribesmen from Africa and soldiers of allied army occupying the city. There was a medley of religious beliefs belonging to Turks and Kurds, Greeks, Armenians, and Europeans, and other Mussulmans and Christians of Anatolia, Caucasus, Persia, and Syria, walking next to Jews, Bedouins, and strange Yezidis, devil-worshipers, and gypsies, who might have no belief at all. It was an exhibition of costumes and headgear consisting not only of the usual black suits, dresses, and veils, or red fezzes and bleak military uniforms of different armies occupying Constantinople, but also extravagant ones such as blue and white mantles and tunics of muslim and silk, wide robes of brown, purple, and yellow colors, turbans of green and white, and shawls of thin angora wool, and hats, pyramidal and conical, made from the fur of animals or camel hair. It was a show of various human trades and arts, for instance, one could see a sherbet-man with a can almost twice of his height strapped on his back and a set of tin mugs on his belt, and a cotton-beater with his bow, a spoon-seller, and famous *hamals* or porters carrying on their shoulders unbelievable bales and boxes of merchandise; two of them would have been glad to bring you a piano. Next to them, there were priests and friars, nuns and missionaries of all kinds who found their vocation in saving and feeding the legions of the city's homeless, hapless, crippled, and orphaned inhabitants, some of whom, in turn, held their own freak show on the same bridge, revealing bleeding wounds and ugly signs of diseases, and begging for small coins. They blended their sad songs with the noise of streetcars, automobiles, horse carts, and the shouts of the hurrying crowd "*Larga!*" "*Haydeh! Haydeh*!" "*Tazeh poonar sooyou!*"* that made my head spin and feet numb. So I used to sit down on the ground and look at the passing shoes and boots, dirty and sometimes foppish, with shiny buttons or small straps from the ankle to the knee, the shoes with blunt toes or bended up, with the embroidered stockings or just made of rough

* "Make way! Hurry up! Hurry up! Fresh spring water!" (Turk.)

sheepskin, until I was dazzled and demanded that Uncle Haroutiun and I return home. He promised to buy me a handful of popcorn and usually kept his promise if I whined long enough to tear him away from observing this parade of characters and vehicles.

Once, in the chaos of the Galata Bridge, his sharp eyes had noticed the lanky figure of his good friend Kilikia. Haroutiun fought with him and other Armenian volunteers in Lazistan and had driven the Turks out all the way from Artvin to Trebizond. With Kilikia, my uncle grieved the loss of friends and his only love, Maria. After the Russian revolution and the collapse of Tzar Nicolas's army, the remaining Armenian soldiers began their sorrowful path of retreat from Trebizond to Erzerum where they joined General Andranik's units. From there they continued their desperate resistance, leaving one Armenian town after another to the plundering armies of Turks. Only a few of Haroutiun's old comrades eventually reached the big city of Baku. Soon this was also surrounded by the Turks and the local Tartars. The Caspian Sea was behind the backs of the defenders. Badly organized Christian towners, a small detachment of English troops, and some separate groups of Armenian soldiers gathered in the city had no chance to stand against the enemies. In this last battle, Haroutiun and Kilikia lost their last comrades. They fought their way out and escaped behind the Persian border.

Among the fleeing Baku refugees, Kilikia noticed a lonely Armenian girl. He decided to marry her. After four years of battles he was tired. The girl was well built and obviously strong because could endure the long marches and hunger. Moreover, people were saying that the war was over in the place where he was from, and that it was now under the Allies' control. So, now three of them, Kilikia, his bride-to-be, and Haroutiun, headed toward Kilikia's village near the town of Marash. There Kilikia found his parents' home empty; his family, driven out by Turkish gendarmes, vanished somewhere in the Arabian deserts. Haroutiun could not stay with a couple. An idea, vague yet unsettling, of finding what had happened to his family, forced Haroutiun to continue his journey. Thus, one crisp morning that could only be in winter mountains of Marash, he said "*Hadjoh*!"* to his faithful friend Kilikia and left. One more departure, one more "farewell" in a long sad sequence of partings.

* "Good luck!" (Arm.)

Have you, my faithful listener, ever asked yourself how many partings a man's heart can take? Each time a bit of his heart is torn off. The places and people that became so close and so dear are left behind, most likely forever. It is particularly hard when one knows that he is leaving the place and people behind to the mercy of fate, abandoning them, completely defenseless against the coming calamity.

It turned out that Kilikia came to Constantinople just a couple of days ago. He was all by himself in this city, totally overwhelmed by its size and numbers. After a few days of staying with us, he took up residence in a dark box room in the same building, in our noisy "Noah's Ark." However, he usually spent a great part of the day in our room, helping our women in their tailoring "business" and telling and retelling the story of his life in Marash after Haroutiun left him and his young wife there. Very soon he started paying obvious signs of attention to my mother.

Haroutiun became perplexed. Unexpectedly, my uncle discovered that, although he spent four years side by side with Kilikia, and had got in and out of many serious situations with him, he did not know well this man, as well as he thought he did. All that time together they were on the front line, in the trenches, or on marches. Haroutiun never saw his comrade in his usual home life. Now he found such domesticated Kilikia annoying. It was not because his old friend repeated many times how he had lost his wife and infant son; Haroutiun co-experienced every word of that incredible story of Kilikia family's run from the Turks through high mountains and killing snowstorm. Also, it was not because the very next moment his friend would describe, for the hundredth time, how beautiful his native land was, the ancient Armenian kingdom of Cilicia, how fertile its soil was, and how remarkable was the taste of the fruits and vegetables from his village. Haroutiun's frontline friend had received his nickname (Kilikia) exactly because of these boastful speeches and excursuses. Also, Haroutiun was not annoyed because Kilikia, very soon but somehow naturally, assumed some of his, Haroutiun's, duties around our meager household. As a matter of fact, my uncle found this quite convenient for him since he could spend more time in courtyard or wandering along the streets. (My Uncle Simon was pleased by the emergence of Kilikia. For him it was suitable because the latter served as a shield, successfully distracting the peculiar attention of girls and widows still coming in alone or with meechnord and hoping to charm Simon into serious affairs.) Lastly, not even Kilikia's funny languid sighing in the presence of my mother, Pietzar, irritated Haroutiun because he was sure that she did not buy it.

Nevertheless, Kilikia annoyed him. The old friend, the comrade-in-arms, has changed, looked different.

I think that my uncle's friend, Kilikia, was always an ordinary and "down to earth" guy. Haroutiun simply had no chance, previously, to notice such characteristics in his comrade. Or maybe he did not want to see them. In great part, Haroutiun's irritation was a result of his friend's shallow ideas about time, past and future, and memory. I mean, my uncle was really disappointed and even felt ashamed of how Kilikia, former fierce fighter and the best shooter in their group, quickly and easily forgot bygone things, even some major events, and moved in with his new, light-minded plans. Haroutiun, who by himself was unable to stop his persistent examining of the past and questioning of the future, could not accept such "*tadarg datum*"* from his friend.

Of course, it is so easy for me now, in my old age, to look back and reflect upon the two such opposite characters. However, at the time, I just racked my little brains over Haroutiun's criticisms, often quite sharp and bitter, that made the genial Kilikia fall silent or sometimes retire to his box room, deeply insulted. Each time, the joint efforts of Simon and my mother brought back Kilikia, who could not bear grudges.

I remember Kilikia perfectly, as well as our conversations about him and with him. It often began with my mother or grandmother asking the question: "Haroutiun-djan, why have I not seen your friend, Hetoum, today?" They always preferred to call everybody by the name given to this person by his parents. Haroutiun's friend, Kilikia, was named at birth as Hetoum. It was an old Armenian name, a royal, handsome one. However, Haroutiun did not split hairs and would answer: "Apparently His Highness is still asleep after the stormy night. This morning, I passed by his apartment; it was quiet as a cathedral!" The women would pursue this further, until the reason for Kilikia's reclusiveness became clear. In this or that way it was always because of Haroutiun.

* Empty thinking. (Arm.)

"This man is crazy!" exclaimed Haroutiun. "Yesterday, the two Russians invited us for a party. You know them, both are from our building; Evskiy and Vania. We had a very serious dispute. However, my friend did not even listen to it. In heated arguments, I was backed into a corner, but he did not care. He was busy; a few times I caught him staring at Evskiy's wife. So, I said a few words to him . . . and he left."

"I can imagine what kind of words they were." My grandma tried somehow to excuse the absent Kilikia. "This woman is much younger than her husband. And believe me, she can stare herself when she wants. When? When she comes here asking for a couple of liras for the next week, she looks at me like at the blank place. Such cattish green eyes! Then you listen as they throw parties. It is not your friend who is crazy, but these Russians!"

"Why indeed do you go to their noisy gatherings?" joined in my mother. "When sober, Mr. Evskiy seems to be a quiet and taciturn man, and Vania is always is a polite and kind person. However, judging from your own words, dear Haroutiun, the same Evskiy after two, three glasses of vodka, shockingly changes; he bursts out with insulting speeches and his words turn to acid, burning and leaving scars."

"This acid has the ability to clear things; it burns all the superficial and borrowed, and exposes the truth." Haroutiun tried to evade any long discussions with the women.

"Besides, why do these men and their wives scorn the idea of finding jobs?" Grandma persisted anyway, and her daughter followed her.

"We cannot comprehend the way these people live here. Do they care about their own future? How can they survive in a foreign land if they don't even care about learning its language?"

"My sober-minded mother! My prudent sister! You cannot understand the Russians, simply because you never met them before. They are not like the Armenians. They live by today. Vania sells his wife's jewelry, and he will not seek any job until he sells off the last diamond. By the way, the yesterday's binge was an obligatory 'bathing' of the sum he made from such a sale. Evskiy does not work because he receives some money from his sister in Paris who was lucky enough to leave Russia before the revolution. So, his only job is to go to the Russian Red Cross on Grand Street in Pera each month and pick up the next envelope containing his sister's francs. However, you cannot imagine, that even doing only this, Evskiy manages to be late in meeting the right clerk in Red Cross office."

"Haroutiun-djan, you are saying all this in a tone suggesting your approval. Don't forget, Vania and his wife have a young daughter," anxiously mentioned my mother.

I liked this Russian girl. She had long golden hair and pale skin, so delicate that I wanted very much to touch her dollish face or hands to find out if they were real. Unfortunately, she never left their room nor went out to the courtyard fountain alone. She was always with her mother. Both looked alike and had the same, slightly sad smiles. It was a very kind family. A few times, especially during the first months of their residence in our "Noah's Ark," this woman gave me small presents, such as an embroidered handkerchief and muslin ribbons. She used to say some strange, funny-sounding words in Russian to me. I did not understand. My mother, recalling some French phrases she learned in school, thanked her instead of me. My mother and grandmother wondered how to repay those unexpected presents. However, the other day the Vania's wife would pass us barely recognizing. My mother and grandmother really had problems with the unpredictable Russians.

Meanwhile, the talk again turned to Kilikia. "I found nothing disgraceful that your friend wants to have a new family," said my mother. "After all the horrors he has experienced, he needs a safe harbor, a place where a man can warm his soul. Mother and I would be very happy if you, Haroutiun-djan, also began pondering this."

"Oh, no, sister! I am not such a forgetful person. One moment he is telling us about how his child and wife were frozen to death in the blizzard over Marash mountains, and the very next he is livening up when seeing a woman entering this room. He becomes flirtatious, this old he-goat. I think that snow storm blew out his mind."

I giggled over the end of my angry uncle's tirade. The mother and grandmother looked at me with reproach. Our simple breakfast was already over and, my mother, grandmother, and Uncle Simon were worrying about poor Kilikia confining himself in his dark, windowless box-room. Of course, we all knew perfectly that Kilikia was not asleep, but ardently waiting for our call. He could not stay alone for long; he was a man of company.

"Why did not you think that Hetoum wasn't following your discussion with Evskiy and Vania yesterday simply because he could not understand their Russian as well as you did? He could not learn much of

Russian on the front line. Meanwhile you, Haroutiun-djan, had lived years in Sukhumi before the war started. It's a big difference . . ."

"Don't tell me, sister! When these Russians talk I also have troubles understanding every word they blurt out. They shoot them like 'Maxim' machine-gun. However I try hard to comprehend their points. Sometimes, I also try to explain these to Kilikia in Armenian, but in vain; he does not want to get into it. Their words turn my heart upside down and make my hair stand on end, yet here is my front line friend, sitting next to me and blissfully smiling and staring at the mistress who is just proffering him a cup of tea. By the way, the same smile sticks to his face whether you hand to him a cup of tea or coffee. I say, what a charmer!"

"For today I managed to find a little coffee," my mother tried to appease her angry brother.

"Coffee would not be a bad thing for this morning. These Russians drink only tea, kettles of tea in an evening, nothing but the tea. Rakia is the only exception."

"There is enough for both of you." The mother seized the apt moment to try to reconcile the friends, at least temporarily. "It would be very kind of you if you called Hetoum by yourself. Please!"

Reluctant and sarcastic, Haroutiun was slow to go for "His Highness," so Simon and I rushed, almost racing one another along the balconies and stairs, to bring the good news to "kermit" Kilikia. He did not make us beg him for long, nor did he mind yesterday's bitter words of Haroutiun. This man forgot easily, indeed.

Sipping coffee and smoking; for men in the Orient this combination takes time, demands no words, and allegedly brings peace of mind. Haroutiun turned over his emptied cup first and rolled cigarettes for himself and Kilikia. The latter tried to delay parting with his cup, hiding it behind his clutched fingers as if trying to preserve this bit of warmth. Seemingly, his long fingers, with black and purple spots of frostbite, enjoyed this. When catching people's glances at those awful spots, Kilikia used to explain in great detail how he got them. It took from him a while to tell about the desperate winter march of the Armenians of Marash away from the pressing Kemal Pasha's Turks, through high mountains, deep snowdrifts, and killing blizzard; a French detachment with its horses, camels, and wagons in front and a few thousand Armenians dragging themselves after them. Stretched behind for miles, women and children could not keep with the French soldiers. They died, more and more, and quietly felt onto the snow. The others did not stop; the blizzard would bury the bodies soon anyway, and crows and jackals would not begin their feast before spring.

Kilikia's infant son had no chance. It was so windy and cold that Kilikia's wife could not feed the child. Kilikia's shovel-like palms and long fingers could not help. During the stops he tried to warm the son's face and lips, and he rubbed the wife's breasts to enable her to feed the child. He told us that her breasts were cold like marble statue. "*Havatatsek indz, sarats khari pes. Hehch mankikeh cher untunum ir moreh. Kateh saratsadalel er mor krtskoum, katil ankam chkar.*"*

Our joint sigh and quickened puffs of tobacco smoke from Haroutiun's side encouraged Kilikia to continue his story. "I did not leave him just on the side of the path as the others did with their dead. In a crevice between two rocks I dug out a deep hole in the snow, to the ground, and put him in there. I did all of this with own hands; that was when I damaged them so badly." Kilikia again showed us his crippled fingers. "You remember, Haroutiun Eghbair, how well these could handle the rifle? When my finger pressed the trigger I did not miss; one more Tachik disappeared from the earth. Now, look; I cannot even hold this small cup with one hand. Thank God, the war is over!"

Simple-hearted Kilikia actually believed that breast milk could freeze in a live body. He did not blame his wife for their son's death. There were so many little bodies scattered on both sides along the path through the snowy mountains. What he was unable to forgive her for was that she refused to live after that loss. While he burnt his hand digging the hole for their son, she stood by, numb and silent. She did not cry. Besides, who could make tears under such mad freezing wind? Tears are not like milk, they are water, just salty water, and water freezes. Kilikia was strong; hard peasant's work and military hardships had schooled him to endure. He dragged his wife forward, passing one slowly hobbling figure after another. He knew they should be as close as possible to the French detachment at the head of this endlessly long column. Kilikia hoped that after stopping for the evening, when the soldiers set bonfires for the night, he would be able to find a place for him and his wife near one of them. To dry little the hoar-frosted clothes, to rub and warm their almost dead feet and hands, and maybe to have a couple of gulps of hot water—this would give them a chance to survive the next day.

* "Believe me, cold like stone. The poor baby did not recognize his mother. The milk had frozen in her breasts, not even a drop came out." (Arm.)

Kilikia did everything to reach this goal. He brought his wife out of the snow whirlwind, sometimes overcoming her jerky movements of turning and going back. During the evening, they were lucky enough to squeeze themselves into a circle around the fire, where a kind French nurse gave them a hot drink. Here, Kilikia became weak from the heat and fell asleep. He woke up in the morning when his side, where his wife had been leaning on him, felt cold. He did not see her around. He could not find her anywhere in the camp that was about to go forward again. She was gone.

"Why did she leave me?" a perplexed Kilikia asked us. "She was so good to me, always complaisant; young and strong, and we could have had children again. Do you remember her, Haroutiun Eghbair? She had such a funny Baku accent?"

Haroutiun nodded, but did not know what to say. Both our women sighed again, this time with an obvious understanding, as if expressing their solidarity with that unfamiliar woman, a young Armenian who made a long journey from the sunny city of Baku at the Caspian Sea to find her end in the snowy mountains of Cilicia.

"Young or not, Hetoum Eghbair, she was a mother first of all. It is much more painful for mother to leave her child . . . in any circumstances. She went back to her son. Mothers always do return." My mother's voice acquired that "ringing" tone which used to fill my heart with agitation. I knew why there was so much guilt in her breaking voice. I just could not express, at that time, that I loved her in spite of everything that had happened in our life. I loved her because I was sure that I always, even as a Turkish girl, Emine, firmly believed that my mother would come back for me.

Anyway, Kilikia thought that his wife's act was wrong. If the frost didn't kill her on her way to her son's grave, then the Turks would have. Besides, she had no chance to find the grave, since the thick snow covered up all the traces. "Now," he grieved, "it is very difficult for me to find a new wife. Women look at my hands and see these terrible spots. They look at my face and notice that my cheeks are red, blazed in flames. So, they think that I have consumption. How could they possibly know that my skin was burnt in the blizzard? That's why they don't like me, particularly if they see me next to Simon Eghbair." He jokingly stretched out his neck so we could compare Simon's face with his own, which, to tell the truth, was long and rectangular, had heavy lips, and most of all resembled that of a kind, slogger horse.

At that point, the morning conversations used to take a twist. Kilikia would skip to another subject. He would thoroughly weigh the merits and disadvantages of Simon's potential brides. Some of them were seriously being considered by my grandmother and mother, others had no objection to finding out in practice what was in the mind of my young uncle, and one, a shopkeeper from Psamatia, was quite persistent in her bids. I did not like her: she never brought a present, but was loud and had a birthmark above the lip that moved graspingly when she tired to bill and coo with Simon. Haroutiun cautioned against this woman growling out something like, "Shopkeeper! She will eat him alive." Nevertheless, my grandmother and mother, they were both leaning more and more toward this woman's candidacy. "*Depi tooneh,**" explained they, her obvious miser. "This woman knows the value of hard work and earning money. She has been managing her shop all by herself since the death of her husband. She says that she needs a reliable man to help her around." Then Kilikia used to make his points. He asked Simon to take notice of the Psamatian shopkeeper's prominent forms, indicating her physical capabilities, as well as of the age difference between her and my uncle, so the younger Simon could comfortably rely on her experience not only in business—here Kilikia used to make a significant pause, causing Simon to blush—but also in more intimate family matters.

For Haroutiun, such conversations were like the last straw that broke the camel's back. They exhausted his patience and he headed for the entrance door. In vain, my mother tried to stop Haroutiun, reminding him of the unfinished orders and the angry clients waiting for a long time to have their trousers or coats fixed. Haroutiun had the ability to break free from the room before his customary, "Say them to come tomorrow" reached us. Reading the minds of the women, I rushed after him to see if he was again going to one of our Russian neighbors' apartments.

Grandmother Iughaper's major concern was the time—the time, she thought, her Haroutiun had been wasting in the company of the Russians—"idle talkers." She was always shrewd and practical, you know, but there, in Polis, her sense of time became even sharper. Perhaps, this was because she was the oldest among us, most close to the end of life. My grandmother wanted her elder son to see reason and

* Toward-home-(woman). (Arm.)

settle down. My mother dreamt about the same things for Haroutiun. For her, Haroutiun's heated discussions with Evskiy were not just "empty talks"; she felt they were some threat to her brother. Neither Kilikia, who a couple of times sat at the table with our Russian neighbors, nor Haroutiun, could dispel her fears. Kilikia tried hard to interpret for her the nature of lengthy debates Haroutiun had with the Russians. However, speaking thickly even in his native tongue, Kilikia used to give some incomprehensible explanations. He was much better in showing vividly how Evskiy, his eyes and face strangely becoming more and more pale with each glass of rakia, burst out with speeches that made Haroutiun's face grow darker until he, Haroutiun, choking with emotions and because of his lack of Russian words, interrupted Evskiy by contending and protesting. The kind host, Vania, used to resort to exhortations of Evskiy and to beg Haroutiun to calm down. Sometimes he needed the intervention of his wife to bring Haroutiun from the threshold back to the table. Apparently, with rakia on the table, Evskiy was a very unreasonable man. Very soon some of his remarks would ignite a new eruption of my uncle's indignation. Not even scornful glances from his younger wife, of whom Evskiy was usually rather afraid, could stop him from having his pleasure.

"Oh, this Russian, he was hissing his words as a snake!" exclaimed Kilikia, and diligently repeated the sound. However, he was unable to explain the exact meaning of the Evskiy's words roughly translated into Armenian, strange words, such as, for instance, "*Hintsats, unpetk azger.*"*

My mother was also seeking the reason that kept bringing Haroutiun back to Evskiy, the source of his "incomprehensible attraction to this indecent man," in spite of the fact that every time the words of this Russian maddened her brother.

She found her answers after that our family had one more unexpected encounter, when a person from the past re-entered our life. Until then, I should admit, our routine life in Pera was quite uneventful. With *Her* appearance everything changed. Can you guess right whom I am talking about?

* "Obsolete, useless nations." (Arm.)

Crossing Places and Bidding Farewells

I will give you more time to guess her name. Don't give me the name now. You should better go and make your wife happy. Tell her that everything has been arranged for your family's departure. You see, my grandson, Movses, is waving his hand from his car window.

Yes, my dear, I am going to accompany you all the way to the border between Abkhazia and Russia. In my grandson's car it will take a couple of hours. There, in the big Russian village, not far from the boundary, my grandson's in-laws live. They will arrange the rest of your trip home. They should already have secured plane tickets for your family.

I have to go with you. We figured out that having me in the front passenger seat would help to avoid possible troubles on the route. We may encounter many bellicose groups of local men. However, whether they are Abkhazians or their adversaries, the Georgians, they all still have respect for old women like me.

Now, professor, tell me her name.

You are right. It was Takouhi Libaridian, a darling guest from the past. Oh, you really did not listen to my stories idly. You remember this girl's name. Actually, when I saw her in our apartment, she was a young woman, a young European lady. It was not only her clothes and light eyes that distinguished her from other Armenian women. There was something else that came from inside. Her eyes radiated quiet dignity and freedom. Sometimes sorrow shadowed her eyes, but nevertheless her motions and step always remained naturally gracious and confident. The name, Takouhi or Queen, was indeed in keeping with all her merits. My mother recognized Takouhi in crowd of the people gathered in an Armenian church in Psamatia, after not seeing her for about ten years!

For quite a long time before that, my mother had been planning a trip to that church. It had the best choir among all the Armenian churches of Constantinople. There was also a famous orchestra in Psamatia. My mother also wanted to visit that widow who was very much willing to get a hold of Uncle Simon as a husband. Many times this woman invited our family to come and see her house and her small shop. Shy Simon hesitated. So, such a combined trip to Psamatia could be very efficient. My mother was so excited. Everybody praised the choir and the orchestra, and she had not listened to any music since the outbreak of the war. It also gave her an opportunity to create a romantic bond between her brother, Simon, and the widow of Psamatia.

My mother had difficulties recruiting her family members for this "musical journey." Uncle Simon was scared by the pressure the Psamatian widow applied on him every time she saw him. He did not know how to handle her now languishing, now unconcealed lustful looks. He wanted as much protection and supportive advice as possible; he wanted his mother to be with him. Grandmother Iughaper wanted to stay home to look after me and to give Haroutiun the opportunity to join his sister and brother. "The older brother's appearance would be a very respectful gesture."

Haroutiun refused brusquely. He considered his sister's venture as genuine female craziness. Marriage, family life, children—all these would not change Simon into a man. He, Haroutiun, had given Simon a real chance to become a man that day, at the moment Missak the Traitor's execution, and Simon had failed. Besides, now, it was not the time for a man to burden himself with simple family concerns. A real Armenian man should find out how to continue his fight for justice, even in this incomprehensible, mixed up city of Constantinople, or somewhere else. Such were the thoughts of Haroutiun. "Armenian men should forget the word 'family,' " insisted my uncle. "Families always were fetters for the Armenians."

My patient mother did not surrender. She reminded Haroutiun that he used to like listening to music played by his perished brother, Levon. "Music, choir, all such stuff is good only for squeezing out tears and weakening people's spirits." Haroutiun was unyielding. "I would never cross the Galata bridge, not to see this woman, 'a shopkeeper,' nor to listen some gospel songs. They are all about brotherly love and forgiveness!"

It is a fact that during our more than three years in Polis, my stubborn uncle never crossed Galata Bridge. In order to get to Psamatia one had to cross this major bridge by foot or tramway, and then proceed further through Stamboul. Stamboul was different from Pera or Galata. It was Turkish. I mean, it was full of Turks. That is why my uncle never went there. That is why he spent hours at the Galata side of the bridge, watching people on the bridge, but never crossing it. This was despite his professional habit and passion for reconnoitering unfamiliar places.

Because of Haroutiun's stubbornness, Kilikia got his chance to join our family's embassy to Psamatia. This man burnt with desire to be involved in such kinds of endeavors. He tried in all ways to hearten Simon and persuade him to be "like a man" with the Psamatian widow. Kilikia shared his own expertise of dealing with women which, by the way, confused Simon more than it inspired him.

Haroutiun grew angrier with the unfolding of my mother's venture. However, his sarcasm did not sway her determination. She desired to see her younger brother happy and at peace with himself. She thought that there was a good chance of helping Simon with his fears and insecurities, self-reproach and absence of any confidence by fixing him up with the older woman. The widow seemed experienced and successful in her shopkeeping. *Hopefully*, thought my mother, *she would be the same in family matters.*

So, the group was assembled. A bottle of wine and a box of sweet delights were bought for the first official visit to the widow's home. As you already may have understood, I was not included in this group. The adults considered me too young for such an important event. All the last preparations were carried out secretly from me. One morning, Haroutiun took me for a walk. When we returned, our room was empty. It had never happened before that everybody was out. Such a strange thing immediately aroused my suspicion. Haroutiun did not even try to fool me further. I became quite furious, not as a result of missing the Psamatian widow's shop and sweet delights from the beautiful tin box my mother had been hiding from me all these days, but because all this time I had been cherishing the hope that I would ride on the tramway. I had never had the chance to do this before. I also wanted to listen to the music in the church. It had such a precious for me name—St. George's church. You remember, of course, my St. George with a scarlet cloak, don't you?

I cried a lot, so much that I became totally exhausted and fell asleep early, well before my mother and the others returned from their eventful trip to Psamatia.

Your wife thinks that it was wrong what the adults did to me that day, doesn't she? Even brutal?! Well, I am not a great educator by myself and cannot argue with her. It happened so many years ago, and people did not know about "open, honest talk" with children. My mother and grandmother did not deceive me by hiding something from me or by not telling me everything, they just wanted to protect me. Everything they tried to keep secret was intended to be in my best interest. This was how they understood it at the time.

To her last days, my mother kept the entire horror of her "death march" and the circumstances of her survival in the Kurdish village deep inside herself. Shame and guilt! She did not want to disturb or embarrass me, her daughter, even though I was not little Nargiz anymore, but already a mother of two children myself, actually older than she was during her exile.

What my relatives told me or what I managed to hear them talking about comprised only a small part of their experiences. The rest they took with them; the worst parts were buried with their bodies, not in my memory. I should thank these people for how they treated me!

I woke up in the morning, heard the joyous voice of my mother, and immediately forgave her. She was very excited, and even tried to croon. However, each her song was bringing sweet sorrow. She stopped, sighed, said something to Grandmother Iughaper, and then tried another song. My mother's voice was joyous but trembling. How could I not forgive her?

The uplifting mood prevailed throughout our room. Everybody smiled. A smile touched even the features of Haroutiun's face, usually serious and pensive. It seemed that the news about his family's total unexpected encounter with Takouhi Libaridian excited him, too. He went out of the room to the courtyard gallery to smoke, but then returned and asked my mother the same question he had asked ten minutes before. "Did you tell her that Ara's death was avenged?" My mother nodded incomprehensibly and switched the conversation to "more tender" subjects.

My poor Mayrig! She believed that good things were going to happen to her brothers. The trip to Psamatia inspirited her. The Psamatian widow showed herself to be very prudent and efficient. She suggested that Simon visit her house sometimes and help her, "a single, needy woman," around the shop. Kilikia, who during that morning was rushing by the corridors and stairways of the gallery carrying out my mother's and grandmother's errands, had the time to give a somewhat different definition of the widow's words—"the woman took the bull by the horns"—but, hey, he was Kilikia, a former peasant and then a soldier.

Simon asked for my forgiveness because I missed everything: the tramway to Psamatia and back to Pera, Saint George's church with its choir, and the encounter with Takouhi Libaridian.He seemed to be perplexed by the widow's invitation. The ubiquitous Kilikia instilled confidence into Simon by affirming that Simon could—and should—stay with the widow right yesterday, so impressed was she with Simon. He, Kilikia, would definitely stay if he were lucky to be in Simon's position. However, later, when Simon's "affair" with the Psamatian widow turned out to be a total flop, the same Kilikia claimed that he was the first one who felt that the widow was not right for Simon. "Too greedy; this woman did not lay a proper table for such an occasion, and even managed to conceal the bottle of wine which her guests had brought with them."

Nevertheless, that particular morning my mother believed that not only Simon but also Haroutiun had the chance to change their fate. That is why she was crooning.

What is happening? Why have we stopped, my grandson? Oh, a checkpoint! It is probably the Abkhazians; they control this area.

Don't worry, my dears. These guys will not harm us. They are looking for the Georgians who lost their minds to travel here during this troublesome time. We are Armenians, and your wife and you are Russians, so they should not bother us. However, when my grandson and I go to talk with them, you and your wife, and even your kids, step out of the car, so Abkhazians could see that we are really accompanying our guest family from Russia. I hope these people have not lost their natural gallantry to guests, in particular to a woman with children.

You see, I was right. They have seen your faces and have let our car proceed. I also used a little Abkhazian I learned while living in Sukhumi. It is a terribly difficult language, a scream of birds, really, but I managed to utter a couple words here and there. These "patrolmen" or "national guards," I don't know what to call them, are mostly young guys. So, I pretended to know some of their grandparents. I don't know about your city, but here, around villages and small towns, such knowledge almost always works. Later on our way, we will be crossing some places with Georgians living there. And I will tell the Georgian "national guards" that I know their grandparents. God will forgive an old woman for her lies.

Well, well, my dear! I understand that I am wasting our precious time. We do not have so much of it, so I have to finish my story. So, now, we are going back in time again! To Constantinople!

Where did I stop, my thrifty listener? Simon and the Psamatian widow, Haroutiun and Takouhi Libaridian, my mother's hopes . . . though it does not matter! Today, I mean, the exact order of those past events is not so important as what really happened with these people at that time.

My mother's hopes did not last long. I remember very well when Takouhi Libaridian came to our small flat for the first time. I already mentioned that she was different. A Queen! Her visit made quite an impression on the neighbors. The noisy, gypsy-like crowd at the courtyard fountain grew quiet. All heads turned toward her, and their inquisitive eyes examined everything from her well-cared-for face to her nice clothes and clean shoes. The Russians, Vania and Evskiy, foppishly snapped the heels of their shamelessly worn out boots and showed her our door on the second floor of the building. They talked with her in French: "Madam, madam, Le Le this, Le Le that." I, who was sent to the courtyard in order to meet Takouhi and accompany her to our flat, became totally confused. I did not make a sound, and mutely followed the guest to our door. However, I was not the only quiet one. Poor Kilikia, usually garrulous in the presence of women, became numb as soon as Takouhi entered our room and looked throughout her entire visit like he had a poker up his butt.

My mother cherished the hope that the "special feelings" young Takouhi used to have for Haroutiun could flare up again, ten years after their separation. She also hoped such emotions would embrace Haroutiun, too. However, more than ten years had passed, not just of separation but also of living in absolutely different worlds. For almost all those years after that memorable summer marked by Ara's death, Takouhi had lived in Paris. (She had relatives there—"Frank" Markar and his madam Zabel. You should remember them.)

So, to the point. I remember my mother's momentary glances at Haroutiun and Takouhi when they both happened to be next to each other. Such glances continued from their first encounter in our flat, through each Takouhi's following visits. There were many such visits during her stay and work with a charitable mission that had come from France to help the Armenian refugees and orphans gathered in Polis. One could notice that the emotions caused by the initial surprising encounter with the witness of youthful times, the days long gone and almost forgotten, quickly subsided in Haroutiun. He returned to his routines. So, my mother's searching, wistful looks did not find in his face what she wanted. Neither my mother nor Grandmother Iughaper noticed any promising changes in him, not even a hint of tenderness. "*Kharatseleh, Kharee n'man dartseleh,*"* whispered they in despair. Kilikia and I could not grasp how one would be unable to fall in love immediately with such a beautiful and kind human being like Takouhi and marry her as soon as she deigned to.

"What about Takouhi?" I am repeating your question, but am unable to give you an exact answer. One can never see into another's heart. Our Haroutiun was no mystery to us. He almost never bothered to withhold his emotions. So, for my mother, his feelings were as clearly visible as if they had been spread out in the palm of her hand. With Takouhi, who had come from another world, it was different. It seemed that she had matured more than Haroutiun. In Polis, my mother saw in front of her not a confused young girl who had come to her house ten years ago and bashfully prattled about her feelings to Haroutiun, but a young European woman with polished manners. ("*A la franca hanum,*" described her Kilikia in his own way.) Whatever feelings this new, calm and reserved Takouhi might have had for Haroutiun, she did not show or express them. We could only guess and hope.

Today, looking back from the height of the years and experiences I have lived through, I can assume that the love the former shy and fragile Takouhi had felt for Haroutiun had faded away and given its place to her sense of guilt and pity. All these terrible years we endured in the hands of the Turks, Takouhi and her family had lived in Paris. Her father had committed suicide there, when the first reports and pictures of the destruction of the Turkish Armenians were published in Europe. Even so, she and her family were spared of that Turkish *yataghan*** which fell down on our heads. Takouhi Libaridian felt indebted to its victims. That is why she came to Polis to help the Armenian

* "Turned to stone, became like a stone." (Arm.)
** A Turkish saber having a doubly carved blade.

refugees and orphans. She felt indebted to us, too. What do you think, can guilt and pity become a source of true love? Personally, I doubt it, especially in the case of a person such as my Uncle Haroutiun.

All right, all right! Let's focus on what did happen with my family in Polis. I am perfectly aware of our "time shortage." It is exactly what makes me nervous and inconsistent. The rush throws me off track and makes me digress. From now one, no more lengthy screeds about "feelings." You just stop me if I go astray again.

My mother's plans had collapsed. On both sides. Both her brothers, each in his own way, proved themselves incapable of dealing with women. They ruined my mother's hopes. Grandmother Iughaper was more realistic than her lofty daughter and seemed prepared for the sad endings. Nevertheless, when they happened both women grieved with same bitterness.

Simon's experience with the Psamatian widow happened to be a very short-lived one. The widow pressed Simon to come to her house and "help around." This woman had no patience to carry out any further prologue for the ultimate man-woman relationship, a prologue that in ordinary times supposed to be, or at least pretended to be romantically tinted. My mother and grandmother, whom the widow was mostly communicating with, clearly understood her intentions. The woman wanted to see for herself some weighty evidence that Simon could be the one she foresaw for the roles of husband and worker in her shop. Apparently, the order of importance for these roles puzzled neither my mother nor my grandmother. Only its bluntness disturbed them.

"Polis, Polis! What a rotten city! Has anyone in our town ever heard of such a thing as a man and a woman being allowed to be left in private before the marriage?" grumbled Grandmother Iughaper. With much understandable hesitation Simon was sent to Psamatia with a new mission. It was said that the widow needed a man's help; some heavy stuff had to be moved in her shop, such as bags of corn-cobs, cucumbers, or marrows, and maybe baskets of grapes and pomegranates—whatever this woman asked Simon to move for her use. Such was the general meaning of the parting words which Simon and Kilikia got from Grandmother Iughaper before their trip to Psamatia.

Kilikia was included to make sure that Simon would definitely reach the assigned destination. Our family's treasurer, Grandmother

Iughaper, furnished Kilikia with a sum enough for a tramway ride and to buy "something" in the widow's shop. This move was an idea belonging to my mother; it should partly explain to the widow Kilikia's escort of Simon, and also please her with his buying a product from her small shop.

Between you and me, only the Armenians after such long elaborations can reach such intricate, but quite clumsy ways of expressing respect and politeness. To make an impression! You, I mean, the Russians, are more straightforward. Accept it as a compliment!

From the morning the men left for Psamatia to the evening of the same day, both our women were on edge. If everything in the house of the widow had gone well, then Kilikia should have already returned. Alone!

It was not happening. The women were lost in conjecture. Eventually, Kilikia and Simon appeared. They came back together. Simon looked tired and preferred bed to supper. The anxious women did not take the risk of questioning Kilikia in the presence of Haroutiun. After a simple meal, they followed Kilikia to his room. I sneaked into that kennel, too. We were packed like sardines in there. My mother and grandmother showered Kilikia with questions. A peasant and a soldier, he clumsily defended himself against their perplexities, which more often sounded like reproachful exclamations. The greater responsibility for the failure of the second expedition to Psamatia Kilikia laid on Simon. It was Simon who took the official cover up of their visit to the Psamatian widow too much word for word. Simon started to work really hard in her shop. Here, Kilikia lost the chance to disappear. Somehow Simon's zeal drew him in. They cleaned up and rearranged the entire shop, moving around heavy bags with nuts and other similar produce. The widow seemed impressed. She served a light meal and even brought out the bottle of wine she had received during our family's previous visit. This fact heartened Kilikia so much that he wasted his second chance to make off and leave Simon all alone with the widow. My grandmother and mother could clearly imagine how loud Kilikia was around the table and in the presence of a woman, and the length of Kilikia's reflections upon his beautiful homeland, heroic adventures while fighting with the Turks, and unfortunate attempts at finding a new "soul mate" after the tragic loss of his wife and their little son. It was obvious that he did not give Simon any room to utter a single word with the widow. Kilika, this simpleton, ruined the entire mission.

I lost my interest. So, I left Kilikia's small room. For me, it was clear from the beginning that the Psamatian widow was not even worth Simon's little finger. I was sad that my grandmother and mother were trying to fix them up together. I sat down on the wooden stairs outside. "Why do adults sometimes become so blind and dull?" I was wondered this while looking down at the weakly lit courtyard. "Why do they behave so strangely?" It was night. Everybody had already left the courtyard. Only our Russian neighbor, Vania, was still there, curled up on the flat edge of the fountain. "Tipsy again." I liked this man; he was harmless, even when drunk. "Go down and wake him? Or maybe go and tell his wife? How could his 'friend' Evskiy leave him in such a foolish position?" Then Vania's wife herself appeared in the courtyard. She suddenly arose from the darkness of the passageway to the street.

Rumors had been roaming for some time around the neighbors that she came back home late at night because she had begun to work for Madam Tzakalidis. Of course, eyewitnesses came forward with stories of seeing her in the notorious "Funny House." We preferred to sweep aside that terrible gossip. My grandmother's verdict was that none of all the accounts of those "eyewitnesses" were worthy of serious consideration, simply because a person who hung about near haunt of vice such as of Madam Tzakalidisis could not be a decent person. You know, dirty pigs like slinging mud at others!

Meanwhile, snuggling up to the banisters of the stairway, I saw how Vania's wife knelt next to him and embraced his wilted head. Faint audible sounds reached me from the fountain. They were not the murmurs of water spurting. The sounds had no rhythm. It was not the echo of conversation between Vania and his wife. It was wordless. Suddenly, I realized that both of these Russians were crying. For some reason, I joined them. It was not just my eyes that became wet. No! The streams of salty fluid ran down my face, flooding my nose and mouth. I tried to wipe my face by my hands. I tried to do it quietly in order not to give away my presence. However, my nose let out nasty sniffing sounds, and while sobbing, my teeth chattered like in a fever.

I got bogged down again. I mean I did not finish with Simon and the widow. For some reason, my tongue gets sidetracked. Nevertheless, I think that during that night in Pera, I grew up all at once. There was no doubt that I had already experienced and learned much more than any normal girl of my age. I was pretty realistic in my expectations of the surrounding people, as well as in what I was capable of when dealing with them. I knew the Turks and what they had done to us. Although very young, I already had an attitude of staying away from them. In any place, or at any occasion, I could meet the Turks in Pera. Don't talk with them, don't even look at their faces, nor, God forbid, in their eyes. I also knew that my small family was my only safe shelter and its four adults were my only reliable protectors. However, that night in Pera was the moment when I began questioning my family's strength along with the wisdom of their deeds.

My always-wise grandmother looked just exhausted and let my mother proceed with this silly idea of "fixing up" Uncle Simon with the widow from Psamatia. I understood that all my mother's actions were driven by her deep devotion to the brother, but sending poor, obedient Simon into the hands of the widow seemed more like a brutal order than an act of love. Even my hero, Uncle Haroutiun, seemed to be not as invincible as I innocently was sure about before; he obviously was afraid of dealing with a kind and beautiful woman, Takouhi Libaridian.

So, suddenly, I saw how confused and irrational my family members were. How vulnerable they were! The recognition of this fact made me sad. Strangely, I had never had such sad feelings before, even during the worst of our hardships. That is why I said to you that I grew up that night in Pera. Young Nargiz lost her innocence.

Now, my exhausted, but patient listener, I will try to finish the story of my Uncle Simon.

So, about Simon. My mother made one more attempt to put her brother's life into "normal order." She spent a couple of days, at every possible moment (actually, all Haroutiun-free time) inspiring our shy Simon. My mother pointed out the higher goals and God's behests of family life, not forgetting, however, to enumerate also the prosaic advantages of having an able wife such as the Psamatian widow. She spoke affectively about "family" as an Armenian way of surviving through troubled times. "Would it not be wonderful if your children bore the family name of Aleksanian, continuing our father, Pogos Aleksanian's, heritage?" exclaimed my mother. Simon heartened along with his sister. He loved his sister and wanted to please her. He loved everything about his father. Unfortunately, very soon after such excitement, doubts and fears occupied his mind again. He had no idea how he could live outside of our family. He was afraid of it.

However, one day Simon left for Psamatia. He had a fictitious errand for the widow. Simon went on this trip alone. Kilikia was banned from accompanying him because he had caused the failure of the previous such mission. For two or three days there was nothing from Psamatia. No news, no messengers. In turn, my mother and grandmother were on duty at the street gate, expecting Simon back or, preferably, Simon and the widow as a couple They worried about how Simon had passed through Turkish Stamboul, how he had found the widow's house in Psamatia, and how she had met him there this time. Kilikia volunteered all the time to go and check this out. Haroutiun was very angry because of Simon's trip to Psamatia. He threatened to go there and bring back his brother by himself, even if that meant walking through Galata Bridge which for him, as I told you before, was a barrier dividing us and Turks. He glanced at his sister and mother really angrily and measured the length of our room with heavy steps, so the floorboards cracked and squeaked.

That evening, one of our Greek neighbors noticed Simon wandering frantically not so far away from our house. Simon had almost reached the safety of his family. He had become completely entangled due to exhaustion; he had been walking from Psamatia since dawn, losing and finding his way many times. The Greek brought Simon with him, leading him like a child by hand. Simon was on the verge of tears. His trembling lips could not utter a single word. He was completely not himself. Nobody made an attempt to ask him anything. Even Haroutiun was moved to pity. He helped his brother to bed and took off his shoes. Simon wrapped himself in a blanket, refusing to take off his clothes. Something bad had happened with him in Psamatia that had thrown him back to his former ravings—visions and ghosts of the past and old self-reproaching speeches. It was all that terrible nonsense which my mother thought he had left behind him. They were back. That was how Uncle Simon's "love story" ended. Never again after that did my mother attempt to introduce him to a woman.

My dear, you are asking me a question I have asked myself many times. However, I do not know what exactly happened with our Simon in Psamatia. Why, for years after, was he afraid of going to a public bath? I don't know! Talking about his trip to Psamatia immediately became one more forbidden subject in our family, like many others that my mother and grandmother guarded silently.

Of course, I heard something: these women's "ah's and oh's," their sudden disdain of the Psamatian widow, and scraps of their secluded conversations. You know, it is very difficult to keep anything secret when many people live in one room. What I, a young girl, managed to pick up at that time, was that, apparently, this woman from Psamatia made some vulgar remarks disparaging our family. She might have ridiculed Simon and said here and there that we were not the people we pretended to be. She also might have threatened my mother and grandmother to disgrace them if she had seen them in a public place. Poor Simon! She apparently had something terrible to say about him.

The details are less important than the fact that Uncle Simon was seriously hurt. One more unhealing scar had been added to his fragile soul. His mother and sister were not much help. They could not deal with the widow's harassment; they were simply intimidated by the very possibility of a public scandal and humiliation. They already felt guilt and shame.

During this hard time, Kilikia became our "savior." He undertook a new crusade to Psamatia. He left there to find, as he struggled to put into words, "peaceful ways of shutting up blatant woman's mouth." Kilikia left and did not return for a couple of days. It was exactly as it had happened before with Uncle Simon. Again my mother and grandmother were lost in conjecture. I guarded the courtyard gate to be the first to catch sight of Kilikia's lanky figure.

When I saw Kilikia entering the courtyard I began to tear along the stairs to my mother and grandmother. Poor Kilikia was maybe hoping to sneak into his box-room unnoticed, but I ruined his plan. He approached my mother and grandmother with an embarrassed smile. He talked with Simon in an apologetic way. Clumsily as always in dealing with words, Kilikia explained that he had just come to say "Good-bye" to us and to pick up his belongings. A very few items barely filled his bag, the same one he was carrying when he appeared for the first time in our lives. He uttered that "the woman will not bother anybody," and that she "deserves some understanding, too." We understood, that the Psamatian widow had won him over.

My mother and grandmother reassured the guilty Kilikia. "*Halala, halala,*" they exclaimed. "You deserve it. Such a good woman!" They said it too loud and too many times. However, the simpleton Kilikia took in their enthusiasm unconditionally. Simon also expressed joy, thinking that "his story" had come to the end which satisfied everybody. The only person who could ruin this moment, Haroutiun, was somewhere outside. Kilikia made a very good guess when choosing this time to come. He was afraid of his comrade's sarcastic remarks like the plague. Haroutiun's words could definitely prevent him from returning to the Psamatian widow. That is why Kilikia was in a hurry to get out of our room before Haroutiun's appearance. Thus, it happened that we, not Kilikia, heard a full cartridge of gibes from Haroutiun. My mother and grandmother were not able to say many words to excuse the absent Kilikia. My mother only said mildly: "Each good man deserves his portion of a happy life."

The story with the Psamatian widow did not end with Kilikia's departure. For almost a month we did not see our friend or hear any news from him. So, imagine our happy surprise when one day Kilikia entered our room. This time he came when Haroutiun had not left yet. The women made a huge roll of lavash stuffed with cheese, boiled eggs, and fresh herbs for Kilikia. Then they gave him a cup of a thick black coffee. Haroutiun lit a cigarette for him. Then, between the sips and inhalings, Kilikia related to us that it was all over with the widow. He understood that a man like him could not live with such a "*zhlat aghves*."* We all let out a joint sigh of relief. Vying with one another we asked him to stay with us again. Haroutiun was ready to convince our landlord, a porty, pot-bellied Greek, to give back to Kilikia his previous box room. However, with tears in his eyes Kilikia refused. He could no longer look in our faces because he had done a wrong, shameful thing when he left us, the only people dear to his heart, for that unworthy woman in Psamatia. That was what he told us. Our attempts to persuade him had no effect. Stubborn peasant Kilikia! Besides, he also said, that it was boring and "stuffy" for him to live in the big city. He wanted to go back to his native land, to his beloved Cilicia, where the sunrise was clear and the morning air crisp, like an apple the second you bit into it. He begged Haroutiun not to dissuade him from returning to Cilicia. He had heard that somewhere down there the French troops had taken over the Tachiks and had let the Armenians come back and till the land. Here he might find a local girl or woman, pure and simple, opposite to the Polis women. My Uncle Haroutiun's warning, that the French

* "Stingy fox". (Arm.)

would again be fooled by the Turks and would eventually abandon Cilician Armenians as they did it in 1920, did not discourage Kilikia. He had already made up his mind. He almost hated Polis.

My mother and grandmother, sad and tear-stained, silently began their routine actions as they had done many times over those turbulent years. My mother prepared some provisions for Kilikia's journey and darned his socks and clothes, while my grandmother thrust her hand into the family's scanty cache and dug up a few coins for Kilikia. Haroutiun decided to part with his most valuable possession—big pistol "The Cannon." Kilikia did not take this enormous gift; he was going not to fight but to work on that land. I could give Kilikia my icon of Saint George. I loved this man so much. I would have, if I had not lost it during the night of our escape from our town.

But then, I was allowed to accompany our dear Kilikia with my two uncles to the Galata Bridge. There we bid farewell. Kilikia and Haroutiun stood for a long time long embracing each other for the last moment of their brotherhood. Tall Kilikia was hunched down to reach the shoulders of his rather short comrade. Then, a few minutes later, his figure vanished in the waves of people crossing the bridge. That was how the story of the Psamatian crusades ended.

We never saw Kilikia again and never received a letter or a word from him.

Now, I will finish the storyline, "Haroutiun and Takouhi." Some experienced reader of romantic novels and fairy tales might expect a great story of resurrected passion. Yes, indeed! Two young persons separated from each other under tragic circumstances, with everything needed for such stories: first innocent love and sweet dreams, malicious jealousy and murder, true friendship and just revenge. Then, by the will of fate, after many years of wanderings and adventures, these two meet again and eventually find their happiness in embracing each other.

Oh, how much all of us in Pera wanted it to happen! How desperately we waited to see the first sparks of passion between Haroutiun and Takouhi! However, it wasn't fated to happen. Pera wasn't the place for fairy tales to occur.

I think Haroutiun's character, with all his oddities, has become familiar for you. Well, he had very good traits; for instance, he was very brave, honest, straightforward, and devoted to his friends and ideas. However, he was "too much" in everything of these, to the degree of annoying rigidity, stubbornness, and even fanaticism. He never changed, my uncle! It made him very difficult to deal with. He was no lump of sugar!

Haroutiun avoided any new feelings. He did not tell Takouhi about his Russian woman, Maria. Of course, he could have said a few words about Maria and that he could not forget his first and only love, in order to make it clear that he was unavailable for a new relationship. However, he did not do it, simply because he was sure that talking about such an innermost subject was completely inappropriate for a real man. There was no doubt Haroutiun regretted that he once broke his own rule and did talked about Maria to my mother, Pietzar. Of course, my mother did not share this secret with Takouhi; she hoped to the very end that these two would somehow find the keys to each other's hearts.

So, Haroutiun considered it unnecessary to let Takouhi into his past. He avoided telling her about the great passion he experienced with another woman. It seemed like he did not care anymore about such "ridiculous" things as human feelings.

If so, why did Haroutiun persistently avoid being alone with Takouhi? Every time he managed to keep us or other people around him and Takouhi. When we, on various pretexts, left our room so they could be alone, he used to invite her to our Russian neighbors, Evskiy or Vania, to help him during heated political discussions. Usually, Takouhi came back after these disputes that were alternated by loud proclamations in all available languages—Russian, Armenian, French—with her slender fingers pressing to her temples.

Sometimes, Takouhi, by herself or through my mother, asked Haroutiun to meet her in the central part of Pera, where she lived and worked, and to escort her to other places. You know how it works! It was enough for Takouhi just to mention that tomorrow she would need to go to some place, for my mother to turn to her brother: "Haroutiun will accompany you, my dear! No questions asked. A young lady should not go there by herself. Harout will do it right, Harout?"

Haroutiun could not avoid such courtesy actions. However, each time he took me with him, even if my mother displayed obvious disagreement. We usually met Takouhi at the bookstore near the Grand Street of Pera. I still remember the name of its owner, "Dirmikis," as well as garden nearby and a cemetery behind the garden. This was not the same Turkish cemetery we used to go to with Simon; that one was in Galata in the lower part of the hill. By the way, a few times Haroutiun took Simon with him, too. "He spends all day in the room; he needs fresh air."

Another trick Haroutiun used was that while walking with Takouhi and me, me a few steps behind or ahead of them, he always brought up the name of their friend, Ara. "Do you remember Ara's thoughts and predictions regarding the future of this country?" he asked Takouhi. "It is interesting to hear what our friend would say now, seeing all the current events?" Poor Takouhi sighed and shrugged her shoulders. Ara's name made her uncomfortable; she remembered the past and hesitated to talk with Haroutiun about their future.

I think that Haroutiun did all these things without any clear planning, perhaps, unconsciously. If someone were to say to my uncle that he was afraid of being left alone with Takouhi and talking with her about their feelings, I am sure he would laugh at this person. He, Haroutiun Aleksanian, was never afraid of anybody in his life! However, I think he had a fear of commitment to another person.

With regard to Takouhi, it is difficult, after so many years, to say anything for sure about her feelings for Haroutiun. Haroutiun was much more clear for us; he was one of us, an Aleksanian. Well, my uncle was spontaneous and explosive, and living with him was like living on the slopes of a volcano which could erupt any time. However, we all learned to do it. Takouhi Libaridian was completely different; very calm and polite. She always spoke quietly, pausing to wrap her thoughts in the most appropriate words. She was a good listener, and people in their turn made sure not to interrupt her. Takouhi was an Armenian like us. My family knew her from a long time ago, but there was something that differentiated her from all of us. That "something" I cannot explain or describe, that subtle, almost indistinguishable "something" which nevertheless made it hard to understand her as fully as we understood each other.

Perhaps it was because she never had the same experiences that we had. Being in Europe for ten years, she was spared of that treatment by the Turks we went through. She had no personal issues with the Turks.

Am I repeating myself?! Yes, of course! Can you imagine? I totally forgot that some time ago I already told you about Takouhi's character "distinctions." Why is this so? The more I try to tell you during these last hours the more I waste valuable time because I keep getting distracted.

Moreover, I cannot fully vouch for my explanations of all my heroes' actions and thoughts. "What a brain-wave!" one may say about me. "This old woman is just wise after the event."

By the way, you should share the blame. You rarely prevent my "distractions." You have to control me.

Thus, Takouhi accompanied Haroutiun to the evening discussions in Evskiy's apartment, and Haroutiun sometimes walked with her (and me as a free supplement) along the streets of Pera. There and there they mostly talked about politics.

"Oh, these politics!" my mother used to exclaim. "What did they talk about today?" she would ask me about Haroutiun and Takouhi.

"About Kemal Pasha, about the Franks and Ingelzis," I reported habitually.

"Again this Kemal Pasha!" sighed my mother. "Nargiz, you should not go with them. Next time, please stay home. Maybe they would like to go to other places, like a park or concert, or visit Takouhi's friends or colleagues. Understand, your presence prevents them from doing this."

"No. 'Auntie' Takouhi likes to see me. She is never angry." I was countering my mother's attack. I spoke the truth; Takouhi always showed sincere joy when seeing me.

"She is too polite," growled my grandmother at my words. "What we cannot say about you. Don't pretend you don't understand what we are telling you about."

Of course, I understood, but when Haroutiun took me with him the next time, I could not resist. Even the reproachful glances of my mother and grandmother could not stop me. I wanted to be around Takouhi. I dreamed of being like her: pure, beautiful, and noble. My childish dreams did not come true.

What kind of politics? At that time everybody in Constantinople was talking about Kemal Pasha. He was the hero of the day. News and rumors of his victories over the Greek army agitated all the people of this huge, ill-assorted city. Inhabitants of Stamboul openly celebrated his advances and anticipated his capture of the city with pleasure. Crowds of men in black suits and coats and fezzes were becoming thicker and louder. People in Pera waited for the inevitable fall of the city with great fear. They criticized the Greek army for its lack of determination and, at the same time, the Franks and Inglezis for abandoning the Greeks at the most crucial moment.

There were no more joint patrols by these armies' servicemen in their beautiful uniforms, strolling proudly and lordly along the main streets of Pera with a confused looking Turkish zaptieh coupled to them. The French soldiers had already left the city, and their missions were preparing to do so, too. The refugees who had barely found any shelter in Constantinople started to consider running away again from "the coming Turk."

However, Takouhi still continued her work with the Armenian orphans, arranging for some of them ways out to France, Lebanon, or Egypt. Our Russian neighbors still could not find their way to Europe, although Takouhi was helping Evskiy and his wife to obtain visas to France where he had a sister. Evskiy's wife was already asking Takouhi about the Parisian lifestyle and what the ladies were wearing there.

Another Russian, Vania, had no relatives who could help him. He sold all his wife's valuables and now he and his family lived in poverty. They were desperately behind in paying rent, even after moving into that box-room which Kilikia had occupied before, the cheapest room in our building. Actually, Vania's family did not need more space. He wandered around all day trying to make some money, but whatever little of it he was able to earn or collect from missionary agencies he squandered on drink before bringing it home. His wife came back from her wanderings much later. Their daughter, a girl with a pale, sad face, spent her days in Evskiy's apartment reading books. Whenever my mother or I invited her to eat or play with me, she refused by shaking her blonde head.

Poor girl! Perhaps she had the feeling that a bad end was awaiting her family. One summer day, hot and sultry, rare for breezy hills of Pera, Evskiy and his wife invited us to celebrate their long-awaited French visas. Of course, it was a sign of observing decencies. Even with those miserable conditions in which we all lived, some people tried to follow old rules. So we knew that in fact the invitation extended only to Haroutiun, since the rest of us could not speak Russian. Takouhi was invited too, and with particular pomp because of her assistance in securing these visas.

The Russian table was served, including the usual whole boiled potatoes, fried fish, big pickled cucumbers, wine for the ladies, and vodka for the men. Evskiy and Vania preferred only Russian vodka in smaller turbidly green bottles. They both hated Turkish rakia, especially the habit of pouring water into the glass with rakia and making it look like milk. They ridiculed the Turks who, in their opinion, were just fooling their Allah who prohibited them from using strong drinks. "If we Russians drink, we drink. We don't play games!"

Takouhi did not like such Russian "devotion." What Armenian woman would? She usually left the Russian parties in the middle before Evskiy became too bilious and Vania began to smile without any reason and talk out of place. Takouhi never appeared in our house empty-handed. She knew what to bring so as not to offend us or our Russian neighbors. So, she usually brought some sweets for the coffee table. However, with the Russians, she was never able to sit until dessert; she usually had coffee in our room. Here, she made comments to my mother about some of Evskiy's numerous "shocking ideas."

Unfortunately, that last evening did not proceed as usual. Before Vania had reached his state of bliss our landlord, a short, fat Greek appeared. He was not in a good mood; he was sweating profusely and breathing heavily, and cursing "the damned Russian" who did not pay his rent on time and made him, a respectful person, climb the stairs to collect a "miserable sum of money." The sight of Vania, his persistent defaulter, sitting at the party table, infuriated the Greek even more. The arguments immediately became personal. Here, the Greek made some vulgar remarks about Vania's wife and reason for her absence. Realizing, maybe for the first time, what exactly the short sweating man was saying him about his wife, Vania chased his landlord down the stairs to the courtyard and then further to the street. The Greek, despite his fatness and short legs, escaped almost unharmed. He shouted from the street and promised Vania an immediate and terrible punishment.

The celebration was ruined. Vania did not come back to the table. A stunned Takouhi left us and went back to her place accompanied by Haroutiun and Simon. Evskiy finished his drink alone, angry at losing his audience.

Neither Vania nor his wife came back that night. In the early morning the landlord appeared, as he had promised, flanked by two of his associates looking rather like ordinary burglars. Despite the neighbors' pleas, they threw out Vania's poor belongings from his room and put a new lock on the door. Haroutiun and Simon helped Evskiy to store Vania's things in his apartment. One more day passed, then one more, but the missing Russian couple did not show up. Everybody in the building was suggesting explanations of their own, one gloomier than another. Women pitied Vania's daughter and brought simple dainties to her, but she refused them by shaking her head. She sat in Evskiy's apartment on her family's suitcase reading a book as always. Local authorities and Russian church and organizations were notified, but nobody really could help to find the refugee couple. Haroutiun and Evskiy went everywhere, including port markets, hotels and taverns, but in vain. Nobody in those cheap and dirty places could say anything intelligible to them.

Eventually, Vania's and his wife's bodies were found by a boatman ferrying people at Galata Bridge. They had risen to the surface of the water at the place where these both apparently ended their lives. Evskiy, who went to identify the bodies, said to Haroutiun that there were no signs of a struggle on them. He also said that they both ended their lives amicably, "had just stepped over the line." At that time I was too young to understand what "line" this unpleasant man was talking about. His comments were interpreted in my family like he had known perfectly beforehand about that "line," but did nothing to stop his neighbor and countryman. We even got the impression that Evskiy considered Vania's act a logical one or one that might be excused.

Despite being unruffled by Vania's and his wife's end, Evskiy was visibly irritated by his new duty, taking care of Vania's daughter. However, his own wife, usually ignorant and strutting around the neighborhood with her scornful smile, blankly refused to leave the girl. She threatened Evskiy that, otherwise he would go to Paris without her. So, Evskiy was forced to stay in his apartment, by his words "surrounded by barbarians of all colors," much longer than he had planned, until he could obtain a travel document for Vania's daughter, too. Then, one day they were all gone.

Takouhi was also about to leave Constantinople along with her French colleagues. Their mission was over. She had mentioned this a few times already in the presence of Haroutiun, sounding casual. He did not react to her words. It seemed that Haroutiun did not care that he was parting with Takouhi and might be forever.

However, Takouhi could not vainly let go of everything that tied her to Haroutiun and, in this sense to her own past, those bittersweet days she spent one distant summer in our cozy seaside town, all those memories and feelings of her first love, unanswered and interrupted. That is why, I think, she wanted eventually to clear "the fog" surrounding her relationship with Haroutiun because of their failures to communicate. Call it speechlessness, numbness, or other words. The fact is that for so long a time seeing each other in Constantinople, they could not find time and resolution for one earnest talk. She also maybe considered herself somehow obliged to help our family and was looking for a practical way to do so.

So, one day, Takouhi came to my mother with "a suggestion" or, better to say, "an idea." Very soon, she explained, all the French would leave the city. The Greek army was defeated. The small English garrison would not be able to stand against Kemal Pasha's troops. All the Turks in Constantinople were his sympathizers. Open or hidden, they saw him entering the city in their dreams. Any judicious person would have expected nothing good for the remaining Armenians in the city after the appearance of Kemal's nationalists. In order to help us to escape from coming hardships, Takouhi continued, she would try to do everything possible to relocate us to France. It would be a difficult thing to do, and maybe not all of us could go at once. The easiest way to begin would be with Haroutiun. There was a certain possibility that he could go with her to France almost immediately. So, could my mother, asked Takouhi, talk with him about "this possibility"?

Takouhi Libaridian was too polite to say directly what she was implying by that "certain possibility." However, my mother understood exactly what Takouhi meant. Haroutiun's and Takouhi's marriage!

However wonderful it was for my mother to realize this, she hesitated to promise Takouhi her assistance. She did not want to mix our family's interests with Haroutiun's personal feelings. Our safety should not, in any way, affect his own decision regarding Takouhi, whether he already had one or was going to come to one eventually. However tender my mother was, she could not trespass against her major principle that love between man and woman should be genuine, free of any conditions and agreements. By the way, such pure love existed between her and my late father, Nishan, may they both rest in peace?

The situation with Simon and the Psamatian widow was completely different; Simon needed rather care and support, while Haroutiun should regain ability to love.

Thus, in that situation, my mother did not want any self-sacrifice from her brother. We were not an issue in this matter. She assured Takouhi that everything would be just fine with us; we would be safe and sound and very happy anywhere, just knowing that she and Haroutiun were together. Clearly, my mother preferred direct talk between Takouhi and Haroutiun.

After Takouhi, pale and perturbed, left us, my poor mother paced around our room for a long time. "Don't reproach yourself, my daughter," said my grandmother. "What can you possibly do? It is not your fault. It is your brother who has forgotten or might have never learned how a man should talk with such a lady as Takouhi. I understand her perfectly. Why should she start the talk? After all, she is a woman. This is an unseen and unheard of thing to do." Grandma tried to comfort my mother.

"What to do? What to do?" continued my mother. "Is he really unable to see and appreciate her kindness and intelligence, and, after all, her devotion to him? Only profound feeling could force such a noble young woman like Takouhi to the conversation she just had with me. On the other hand, is it her love that has survived through all these years of separation or just pity and duty of her honorable soul? I am not sure. I only know that my brother will not accept any pity; it will completely discourage him."

"Let me talk with Uncle," I suggested. I could not bear to see my mother's troubles. I also very much wanted to go to France, which Takouhi had promised in the event of her marriage with my stubborn uncle. "He never gets angry at me!"

"No, no, I must find a way by myself," said my mother, embracing me and pensively caressing my hair. "I must help them, but without hurting anybody."

Eventually, my mother chose a roundabout way of dealing with Haroutiun's habit of brushing aside all discussions about regular subjects. He called these "women's talks." He broadened their range quite enormously, including all the topics he did not like to talk about. Women, by themselves, and everything related to them, for instance, marriage, family life, children, and a myriad other ideas, plans, and problems that would excite and occupy the minds of any other common inhabitant of the city of Constantinople, were excluded from his considerations.

So, my mother initially struck a rather innocent (from Haroutiun's point of view) conversation and then began telling him a parable. Presumably, she had heard this from her father, "Lord" Pogos. She knew that their father's name would make her impatient brother listen to the story to the end. For the same reason, by the way, she had chosen a very short story.

"There was or there wasn't a fisherman. He was a very religious and devoted person. He lived his whole life following only God's behests and checking all his steps and deeds against God's directions.

"It happened once that this man's boat began sinking when he was fishing far away from the shore. However, the man was not afraid. He prayed and put his trust in God. He was so sure that God would help him that he even declined to be rescued by a boat floating by. He continued to pray and also refused to go with a second boat. This man was so sure that God's miracle would save him.

"Unfortunately, his boat sank and he died. When this fisherman appeared before God he was very disappointed that God had let him die despite all his prayers. Upon hearing the fisherman's complaints and perplexities, God wisely pointed out that he had heard the fisherman's prayers well and it was he who had sent those two boats to save the man. It was the fisherman's fault for refusing God's help twice!"

Haroutiun shrugged his shoulders. "God I cannot be, fisherman I never wanted to be; I am Haroutiun." He did not find any instructive line for himself in this story. My mother was glad to interpret it for him.

She began explaining to him that the story hinted at not expecting miracles from God. Haroutiun noted that he had stopped doing so a long time ago. My mother continued her argument, pointing out that God reveals his wisdom through such events in people's lives that may seem to them rather ordinary. Haroutiun said that he did not know about other people, but he always took care of his matters by himself.

"God wants us to make our own decisions and take our own actions. That is why," persisted my mother, "he does not perform miracles, but helps and shows right directions through simple, everyday-like occurrences. Unfortunately, many people cannot properly interpret God's directions."

Haroutiun glanced at his sister with an inquiring look. Does Haroutiun remember, asked she, a situation very similar to the story of the fisherman? Does he remember us on the boat belonging to the two lousy Lazes, sinking in the middle of the sea, and the two ships passing by our doomed boat? The second ship saved our family and brought us, instead of Batum, to Constantinople.

So far, Haroutiun followed my mother's words without interruption. She continued making her point. "One day, here, in Constantinople, where our family did not plan to come, a few of us, after a long discussion with you (worthy to note, by the way) went to the Armenian church in Psamatia, just an ordinary thing to do, and met your dear friend, Takouhi Libaridian. Isn't all this Providence? Why don't you listen to God's advice? Why don't you talk with Takouhi about mundane matters such as love, family, and home, instead of arguing in her presence with Evskiy about abstract, political ideas? These ideas spoke neither to the mind nor the heart . . ."

At this point, Haroutiun realized where his sister was leading their conversation. At first, he was serious. He said, "I like Takouhi, like a sister, like a 'dear friend' of my late friend, Ara. I cannot feel another way. Even if you are right and God shows us ways and options, in the end we humans have to choose one by ourselves. Right? So, I cannot choose the one you all expect from me."

However, then, seeing my mother's chagrin, Haroutiun turned to his "crazy" arguments. "Besides, what an 'excellent' time to create a family and children. Do we, the Armenians, have our own land to live on? Do we have a good army to protect our women and children and to punish our enemies? Our remaining soldiers should concentrate their efforts on more important tasks. The 'gallant' French have already left us, and soon the Britons will follow them. Kemal Pasha will come here and the Armenians will ran away from him again. I walk around Pera and Galata, and there are only a few of us who are ready to resist somehow. All the others think exactly like you, my sister, about homes, wives, families, and children.

"By the way, what is wrong with our race that we always occupy our minds with such issues? For instance, the Russians, they do not care much about these banal things. They live day by day, and are not crazy about making themselves at home. Remember our neighbors, Vania and Evskiy? They even didn't care about learning Turkish. That is why the Russians are so quick off the mark to fight and defend themselves. They are absolutely right saying that if a couple of Armenians were given some small space and a little time, they would build a shop there and produce a bunch of young snivelers. The people say that we are a race of shopkeepers, kerosene shopkeepers! And a kerosene shopkeeper would never leave his nest for joining freedom fighters. He would rather endure daily beatings and humiliation to the very end. Believe me, my tender sister, it is true! I have seen it!"

My poor mother could not allow herself to retell Takouhi everything that Haroutiun had said about "love" and "marriage." She tried to explain to Takouhi that her brother's self-restraint as a negative result of his hobnobbing with the Russian neighbors, especially the caustic-like Evskiy. My grandma quite noisily backed her up.

Their apparently clumsy attempts could not cover up the stern fact that there was no need for Takouhi to talk with Haroutiun about their relationship. Takouhi Libaridian was a clever person. She read well between the lines of my mother's lengthy, sometimes disconnected explanations of Haroutiun's behavior. Takouhi's face, first pale and tensed, just blushed slightly when she said that she had come to a decision to talk with Haroutiun by herself anyway. It was her duty, she said firmly. She added that even though Evskiy was a "dangerous man," a cold and cynical man, one thing he repeatedly proclaimed was, perhaps, correct: there are "invisible lines" in human's souls which they are unable to cross even it is crucially important to do so. For instance, one cannot step over one's own "pride" nor another over his "aloofness," even knowing that it could make a huge difference in their lives as well in the lives of others.

Obviously, these words were not exactly those spoken by Evskiy, but Takouhi's own interpretation of one of his slogans.

What do I know about this "dangerous man," Evskiy? Oh, I remember very well his light-colored eyes and his heavy, immobile stare which this man looked through me with, as if I were not a young, live girl, but a glass statue. He was a really scary figure, believe me . . .

What do I possibly know about his ideas? I don't think it is a good idea of yours to distract me now from the major line of my story. It is because, my dear, we are approaching the boundary between Georgia and Russia and soon we will be at the place of our destination. There I will not have enough time to finish my story. . . .

Well, if you think that Evskiy's ideas are very important, I will try to recall something I heard about his thoughts from the others.

Haroutiun used to repeat some parts of Evskiy's utterances, especially when arguing with my mother. Then, my mother would try to interpret them with her mother, Iughaper. Something very vaguely was retold by Kilikia when he was still with us. However, the most reliable source was Takouhi, who was present a few times during the heated discussions between Haroutiun and Evskiy in the latter's apartment.

Takouhi told my mother that Evskiy teased my uncle by claiming that the Armenians were a "second grade" race. In his categorical opinion, the Armenians, as well as other similar peoples (such as the Greeks and the Jews) were very well-suited, with all their special talents, only to serve other, higher races. In this higher group Evskiy included, of course, Russia, America, at a stretch some European countries, and, to the fury of my uncle, Turkey.

When Takouhi, who often assisted impulsive Haroutiun in his arguments, noted that Armenia was a civilization with many great achievements a long time before the Russians, the Turks, and even the Europeans were able to establish their states, Evskiy did not deny those things. He just called them "past glories, rotten beliefs, cemeteries of collapsed monuments," and other similar ridiculous names.

For him, the old civilizations were doomed. In order to survive, their folks, "pitiful remnants," must serve the young, "hungry for power" races, such as Russia and Turkey. Evskiy became excited by his own words when foretelling the might of Russia. That was when we heard his loud voice even in our room. He declared that during the war and revolution he saw, with his own eyes, "The Advent of a New Man," one who could reject at once all the fetters of old human beliefs and norms.

When Haroutiun sarcastically mentioned that Evskiy and Vania, both monarchists, could not even protect their tsar, Nicolas, against the New Men of Russia, and ran like rabbits from a wolf, Evskiy readily admitted it, saying that this fact only confirmed his point: those (here he pointed to himself and to half-drunk Vania) who could not bid farewell to their old, useless beliefs, were doomed to a miserable vegetation in a foreign land.

What else? You know, it is extremely difficult for me now to give you a coherent account of Evskiy's philosophy, trying to remember some disconnected fragments of his speeches, actually sentences or even words, later reverberating in Takouhi's and Haroutiun's conversations with my mother. You should help me by giving my recollections a proper form and sense.

It was Takouhi who called Evskiy "a homespun philosopher." She accused him of being very much conducive to his comrade Vania's last fatal action. It was Evskiy's constant praises of man's impulses to break "ancient, decayed rules of humanity" that could make for desperate Vania end his own life and that of his wife by jumping together from the pierce into water. After their bodies had been found floating in the sea, Evskiy admitted to Takouhi that he did not expect his weak comrade would find enough spirit to do such "a noble thing" as overstepping the pierce edge.

"Just think, Madam Libaridian, one step forward and you are free," envied Evskiy. "These words are upsetting you, Madam Libaridian, but to no purpose. After all, who ordered us to cling to our lives? Survival is such a primitive idea; it enslaves simple people and makes them look like animals. Self-destruction is for really creative individuals, an ultimate victory over all primitive forces of nature, a total liberation!"

Takouhi argued with Evskiy. She had a personal reason. If you remember, her father also committed suicide. So, she opposed Evskiy quite strongly. My mother was simply terrified just knowing that her brother, Haroutiun, heard such ideas from Evskiy.

My mother worried a lot about Haroutiun because she thought that his meetings with the notorious Russian neighbor would bring only harm to her brother. She was afraid of this despite knowing that her brother was not just a passive listener of Evskiy. He argued fiercely with Evskiy and she heard their voices flushed with opposition.

However, she also knew that Haroutiun's major objection to Evskiy was not that this man used to disparage all human qualities—love, kindness, pity, compassion, to name just a few—all those, that by her opinion, had been keeping our family together and alive. Haroutiun would be mostly obliged, she thought, to prove to Evskiy that the Armenians were not "a bunch of pitiful refugees whining for help" or "a wandering merchant tribe," but people who were still able to produce zealous patriots and unyielding warriors. My mother was afraid that in order to prove this, perhaps not only to Evskiy but rather to the most merciless critic inside himself, Haroutiun would get mixed up in a new dangerous adventure. Apparently, she was right about that . . .

Oh, my God! Look through the window. We are already near the boundary. After we cross it, we will be in Russia. We were so lucky, after that stop outside of Sukhumi, that there were no more Abkhazian or Georgian patrols on our way here.

We have reached the boundary faster than I expected. I have not even finished the story. So, I will try again until we reach our in-laws' house.

The end of the story is sad, like any other when the people dear to your heart leave you.

Kilikia left us in Pera first. We missed his conversations which were as ungainly as his tall figure. Then, our Russian neighbors. Of course, nobody cared about Evskiy. However, Vania's family was friendly to us. We remembered Vania's kind, apologetic smile, his pensive wife, and their daughter's beautiful golden hair.

Next it was Takouhi Libardian, the Queen whose appearances brightened our gloomy room. She gave us hope. It wasn't her fault that it faded so quickly.

She kept her word. Before leaving Constantinople, she had a talk with Haroutiun. One to one. However, we all knew the result beforehand. After the talk, Haroutiun seemed to be more disturbed than Takouhi. Her calm face was just a little more pale than usual. She spoke and moved as smoothly as always.

After her departure, our life in Pera became monotonous and boring. The main topic of conversation was the inevitable coming of Kemal Pasha. My mother and grandmother were afraid of new troubles for the Armenians. They were seriously considering a final escape from Turkey. They were talking about it and preparing, but before they could do something the Kemalists took Constantinople.

Well, their victory was not celebrated by the massacres of Armenians in Pera. There were no killings of infidels, no burning of their houses as Kemal's troops had done previously with the Armenians in Cilicia and the Greeks in Smyrna. Kemal was too smart to do it in Constantinople, in full view of Inglezis and Franks. He needed peace with them.

There was enormous celebration among the Turks. The eternal city was again in their full possession. We, the Armenians, felt like unwanted guests at this feast. Very soon, Kemal made it absolutely clear. Turkey for the Turks only! The Armenians and the Greeks had to leave. So, we were paying with hangover for the feasting of others.

We were lucky to find cheap tickets to a steamboat for Batum. I was very sick during the whole trip! The smell of the sea caused the nightmarish days and nights. I did not see anything, even our former town and its surrounding mountains, when the ship was crossing its bay. Those places where we were born, lived happy and sad days, and at the end tried to escape the death. Strangely, I remember only a tall imposing passenger in an all-white suit and hat. "A famous Armenian actor!" people said then, or my mother told me later.

Another thing was hiding the crosses hanging around our necks. A rumor among the passengers was that the Soviets did not like religious people. The same about firearms. With tears in his eyes, Haroutiun threw his pistols into the water of the Batum harbor. (Later, under unfortunate circumstances, we discovered that he had thrown "The Cannon," the big one, but could not depart with the small "Maria.")

A custom checkpoint. Two young smiling Russian women in black leather jackets. Their penetrating glances. However, they did not check for our crosses. They asked questions. Haroutiun cracked jokes in Russian. The girls laughed. And that's all. We were in Sovietland. A few days later we were in Sukhumi and I have been living in this city since.

What else? What else? What else should I tell you?

"Haroutiun's adventure?" In Constantinople? Oh, yes! I mentioned it before. It was not adventure really. He had no time for that because we left the city. However, there were signs of his next obsession, this time with Kemal Pasha. Haroutiun hated this leader of the Turks enormously. "Too smart for a Turk," used to mutter my uncle. He thought that if it were not for Kemal, then Turkey as a state would have collapsed. Kemal saved Turkey, and the Armenians lost their chance for an independent Armenia. Haroutiun acknowledged the meaningfulness of Kemal's new name, Ataturk. Father of Turks!

The destruction of Kemal became Haroutiun's favorite topic. "If somebody would do it" or "If somehow it would be done." Those were just the wishes of a desperate man. He had nothing real in his mind. Otherwise he would not have talked about it in our presence. However, it was enough for my mother, an additional, important reason for her to leave Turkey.

I do not think that Haroutiun was connected with other Armenian patriots. Nobody came to our flat, except our regular customers, and I did not see my uncle outside spending time with other men. I am sure that he would not obey to strict rules of any secret organization. He would like to play a lone hand. Besides, we, our family, tied Haroutiun's hands and feet.

To this point, I am going to tell you one of my secret thoughts. It sounds crazy. However, sometimes it comes to my mind. Perhaps, I ask myself, Haroutiun would have felt happy and proud by continuing to fight against his enemies, instead of wasting the rest of his life with us. Maybe, Simon would have been happy and felt safer if he had continued to live with Kurd Bakro in his mountain village.

In the dusk of my life, I am questioning everything, even seemingly clear ideas. If a person survives through a terrible ordeal but then is unable to be happy, where is the sense in staying alive? Was anyone among us, survivors of our family, really happy? I doubt it.

Hey, at least I am telling you about them. And you are going to write a book about them. Many people can read it and learn about Grandmother Iughaper, my mother, Pietzar, my two uncles, such different brothers, Haroutiun and Simon, and "Lord" Pogos, my grandfather, and maybe me, Nargiz.

I feel guilty because I could not tell you about the others, even about my father, Nishan. I didn't have time to tell about his beautiful passion for my mother. He met her in my grandfather's garden. Petals of blooming cherries were falling on her shiny black hair.

Look at this picture. It's him. It's the only one I have of my father. Look at what an intelligent man he was. He knew many languages. He studied in America, in the city with a very gentle, feminine name.

Philadelphia? Yes, maybe. Here, on the back is his inscription to my mother. Neat letters!

Take this picture. I brought it with me today. I always thought that I would never be able depart with it. My mother managed to save only this, his picture. Now, you take it and put it into your book. At least the readers will see his face. Sorry, Father, I did not tell your story.

Take my mother's picture, too. They should be together, side by side.

There were so many others to talk about, but I couldn't. There were seventy people in our clan there, on the opposite side of this sea. Only a few survived. Do you know what such a number means? Every young one could have had a family of his own. Then their children, too. Thus, today, they could have put together a village. An entire village!

The ultimate tragedy, and crime, is that there is no such village around this sea. Never existed. Nobody saw the faces of its people, I cannot tell you their names, and you cannot write a word about them. The Turks killed them all before they were born!

So, promise me to write the book about those who survived. At least, keep those few alive. It is the best we can do.

Promise it in the presence of this sea. Seemingly indifferent, it contains—I believe so—the bodies and souls of the perished Armenians, the drowned and unborn, their tears and cries felt through the salt and bitterness of the dark water and nightly laments of its waves, and their pains and fears which still drive me mad if I dare to come close to the sea after so many years! Promise, please!

My father, Nishan Zhamkochian. The only photograph that survived the "death march" along with my mother. He presented this portrait to my mother just before their marriage in 1910 with the inscription on the back: "This is a present for my beloved bride. Nishan Zhamkochian."

This picture of my mother, Pietzar Zhamkochian (Aleksanian), was taken when we lived in Constantinople from 1920 to 1924.

A Letter Instead of an Epilogue

To: Prof. Vitali Ianko
19 Memorial Street, Apt. 15,
North Providence, Rhode Island, USA

How do you do, much-esteemed professor. You probably do not remember me because you saw me only once, in passing. One day, almost four years ago, you arrived at my parents' house in Krasnaya Poliana, together with my husband, Movses, and his grandmother, tikin Nargiz. I remember that you, and particularly your wife, were very anxious to get tickets and fly back home.

In the first lines of my letter, I am sorry to inform you that our dear Grandma Nargiz died two years ago. When the real war started between the Abkhazians and the Georgians, we (all the Armenians of Sukhumi) were forced to leave our houses and seek refuge anywhere else where we had relatives or friends. At that time, my husband's family came to live with my parents because Krasnaya Poliana was inside the Russian territory.

As you know, Grandma Nargiz was very old and always had bouts of fever which made her feel like she was suffocating and losing her mind. Do not think, dear professor, that I am being disrespectful toward Grandma Nargiz; she told me about such feelings herself after these bouts had happened to her two or three times in a row right in my parents' home. Soon she died, but before that asked me to take down her words in writing, and then forward them to you (at that time she could not have known that you and your family went to live in America). Nargiz chose me because she did not believe that her son or grandson, my husband, would have been interested and patient enough to sit by her bed, listen to her, and write. She was right, Grandma Nargiz, but who could blame our men? After the collapse of the Soviet Union and because of the war in the Caucasus, they had no time for such things as writing letters; all of us here have been running around the entire time just for daily bread. Sorry that it took me years to find your address in America, and then the time to sit and write this letter. I am doing it out of respect for our Grandma Nargiz, and because I promised her I would. I only want to warn you that I have never written such an important and lengthy letter before, so I will try just to convey the facts exactly as Grandma Nargiz described them before she passed away.

She told me about what happened with her family in Sukhumi—I mean, her mother, grandmother, and uncles—after they escaped there from Turkey. Nargiz also said that you knew all of them very well and would not need any explanations about who was who. She remembered that they had come to Sukhumi through Batum, and that it was the year Lenin died. The first years in Sukhumi were very hard for them because Haroutiun's former companion, an Armenian, to whom Haroutiun had left his tailor shop before joining the group of the Armenian volunteers for the war against the Turks, totally swindled him, claiming that he lost the shop with all its materials and machines during the Revolution and the Civil War. Haroutiun realized that his companion was lying because this man opened another shop and had a nice house he could not afford when they worked together. This man did not even respond to the letters which Haroutiun's mother was sending to Sukhumi in order to find out what really happened with her son. So, Haroutiun beat him up, but could not receive his money back. He spent a few days in jail because of "an assault on a Soviet citizen." Nargiz told me that from the very beginning, her uncle could not find himself in the changed Sukhumi and often broke the Soviet laws. He drank and talked too much of what he really thought. The people in Sukhumi had changed; there were many informers and slanderers everywhere, in any factory, shop, tavern, or even family. These were the first years of Stalin's repression, but Nargiz said it was a miracle that her Uncle Haroutiun, with his independent character, was able to survive so long—almost ten years—in the Soviet country. Eventually, one day, some people in a black car came to the house where Nargiz and her family lived and took him away. During a search of the house they found his small, almost toy-like pistol and charged him in a plot to assassinate a Communist party leader of the city. Haroutiun was sentenced to ten years without correspondence and sent to Siberia, from which only very few came back alive. Nargiz and her mother never received a word from him; he vanished there without a trace.

I am sorry, but I am running ahead. Haroutiun was not the first loss in Nargiz's family because a few years before, her Grandmother

Iughaper had passed away. Nargiz said that her grandmother, who never complained of tiredness and continued to do everything she could to help her family, somehow lost her will and strength and died calmly and silently. She just finished her mission on Earth and expired—I am repeating Nargiz's words. Nargiz also said that her grandmother's end was "as fair as her entire life." I do not know exactly what this meant. Nargiz did not explain her words. She had no time, and I did not dare to ask her for an explanation. By the way, Nargiz also met her end without moaning or whining; rather, she was totally ready.

Iughaper died less than three years after moving to Sukhumi. After her, the rest of the family continued to live together. Nargiz's family always lived together; her mother and both uncles did not marry. It seemed that they could not separate from each other. Even when Nargiz grew up and married, her husband did not take her away. Instead, he moved in with her family in their tiny house. You, dear professor, stayed in this house during your vacation, but almost nothing remained of that original, tiny, hovel-like house. It was rebuilt many times and expanded to accommodate the families of Nargiz's daughter and son. Then the rooms for vacationers were added and mandarine garden was developed behind the house for an additional income. You know that almost all inhabitants of Sukhumi had such rooms and mandarine trees. Now, everything in the city has been abandoned and ruined. Sukhumi as you saw it does not exist anymore.

I should continue with Nargiz's marriage, as I have already mentioned it. Nargiz found a young Armenian, Grikor Amirian, a man with the same family story; he and his parents lived in Van where they ran away from the Turks in 1915. All the same escape stories, all the same sad memories. Nargiz's husband was a simple, taciturn man, who had very good hands and worked very hard as a mechanic in the port. I am enclosing their only photo together, which Nargiz also asked me to send you. They had two children, a daughter and a son, and the son was born just before the war with Germany started in 1941. Grikor went to the front and did not return; Nargiz never even received one letter from him. Perhaps he had no time to write, because after just two months, she received a small piece of official paper, a short standard text with the inserted handwritten name of her husband, informing her that Grikor Amirian, a member of a tank crew, had fallen at a battlefield as a hero. She never learned whether her husband's body was buried or burnt inside his tank.

My husband and I after our wedding in Sukhumi. I did not take his family name, Amirian; I retained my own, Zhamkochian.

Later, Nargiz's other uncle, Simon, the last man in her family, was also driven into army and sent to Crimea. Unavailing were Nargiz's and her mother's entreaties to the chief officer at the army draft center. He did not care that Simon was mentally unfit to bear arms, even though everybody in Nargiz's neighborhood knew perfectly that Simon was "a little crazy." After his brother's arrest, he was even afraid of his own shadow. With other men, many of them either very young or very old, he was put into a cattle wagon and shipped to the front because Stalin needed more and more cannon fodder. Simon did not return home. Nargiz and her mother never even received that official piece of paper about his death like they got about Nargiz's husband, Grikor.

However, in contrast with Nargiz's husband, they learned much later what did happen to Simon. Sometime during the 1960s, a Russian man came to their house. He was a miner from Siberia, but not a regular vacationer. He claimed that he had been Simon's comrade-in-arms and had witnessed the last minutes of Simon's life. The Germans had surrounded and crashed their division, and the last desperate groups of the Soviet soldiers had been pressed against the seashore. Those who could swim dived into the water, and many went down to the bottom under the bullets of German machine guns. (I am describing that moment in this way because I saw something like that in our Soviet movies and I can imagine what happened there with Simon and his comrades.) The Armenian soldiers could not swim, so many of them were captured by the Germans. The Germans decided the fate of the prisoners right on the spot. The communists and the Jews were shot and their bodies thrown into the sea. The others were driven to a concentration camp. However, before that, the Armenian soldiers with their black hair and hooked noses, were forced to unzip and show their private parts in order to prove they were not Jews but Christians. When Simon's turn came he refused to do so. The German officer shoved him to the left side into a small group consisting of a commissar and two Jews. The Armenian prisoners who temporarily saved their lives dared to shout to him to do what they did, but it was too late, and the Germans gunned him down with the three other men.

The Russian who told this story after more than twenty years swore that he had seen all this with his own eyes from a distance of maybe just five to six meters. He even recalled a tranquil smile on Simon's face, so strange for the moment. Then the Russian was taken to one camp after another before he could escape and join partisans. However, his escape and fighting with the enemy as a partisan did not save him from Stalin's labor camp in the Siberian gold mines where this man spent years until the dictator died. The man had no family, so he chose to continue his work in the same mine. After the years of slave labor, he was paid for his grave work and paid well. Nargiz recalled that when he came to her house he had a small dirty suitcase full of rubles. It was his first vacation and he had decided to travel to Sukhumi because he still remembered the strange name of street, Djuguburia, which Simon had given him when they, like all other soldiers, had exchanged their addresses before the battle in case one died and the other survived.

This man was a terrible drinker. The empty space under the veranda floor was filled with bottles of a cheap port he drank off during his stay in Nargiz's house. He drank and cursed Stalin, the Germans, and his own fate. At the end, he asked Nargiz to buy him a ticket back to his Siberian mining town. Her neighbors warned her and her mother not to believe his stories, but they were sure that this man was telling the truth about Simon. Nargiz told me that at that time, she and her mother believed that Simon had finally "found his peace of mind." At the same time, Nargiz was upset because her uncle's body was thrown into the water of the Black Sea. Maybe you, professor, know what her words meant, and why she was still upset about "the sea" after so many years had passed since her uncle's death.

Today, I am continuing this letter after breaking for almost a week because I was very busy with my home errands. I re-read these few pages I have already scribbled and I realized how sad they might appear because of all those hardships that befell Nargiz and her relatives. Of course, the time they lived in was very hard for them, but they did not choose it by themselves. However, even during those hard times, Nargiz had some happy days and hours, too. She mentioned some of them, such as her own very simple wedding when her uncle, Simon, and her mother, Pietzar, were with her, and then the more elaborate weddings of her son and daughter when her mother was still beside her, and also the births of her grandchildren and her grandson's wedding. You may not known that Nargiz, on special occasions, could amuse herself and others in such ways that nobody would expect from her. During my wedding, when I was marrying her grandson, she got up from her chair among the most honored guests and entered the circle of dancing people. I never saw such a dance as the one she performed that day.

On all her ten fingers she had very small vessels which our men usually use for drinking vodka, and she danced and tapped the rhythm with those vessels so skillfully and with such grace that we all just stopped dancing and stood around her in total amazement.

Most of all, Nargiz told me, she was fortunate because her mother, Pietzar, lived long enough to share some of these happy moments with her. This woman even saw the birth of her great-grandson, i.e., my future husband. He does not remember the old lady, but everybody in his family attests that she was an extremely kind human being. She, like her daughter, Nargiz, lost her husband very early, so she was a great example and inspiration for Nargiz to be strong and resistant as, by the way, almost every Armenian woman was destined to be. (I am realizing this now myself and am trying to follow their example each single day.)

One more event I should write to you about. Apparently this was very important for Nargiz because she reminded me a couple of times about reporting it to you. In short: it happened when Nargiz's uncle, Haroutiun, was arrested by *NKVD* "bloodhounds," and Nargiz and her mother did not know what was happening with him in the prison. Almost each day they would go to the prison building where the arrested were interrogated, and they would stay there in a long line with the same kind of women whose husbands or brothers had been taken away a few nights ago, and they would wait on the street for two to three hours before reaching a small window in the wall just to hear again and again the same short answer: "there is no new information about the accused, Haroutiun Aleksanian." Then this blind iron window would close with heartrending gnashing. There, in that long line of women who looked alike in their black clothes and shawls, Nargiz and Pietzar heard about a young Armenian who had recently appeared among the NKVD officers and was one of the interrogators. Pietzar decided to see that man and tell him that her brother was just "a garrulous toper, but had never been in any terrorist organizations, and had only kept his small pistol as a memorial present from a Russian nurse, his late fiancée." Nargiz insisted on going with Pietzar because her mother did not know Russian at all, and all the official papers were in Russian. On bending feet they entered the waiting room of secret police headquarters, the most feared building in Sukhumi, asked for an appointment with the officer, Kazanchan, and waited for him as they sat on the edges of their chairs. Poor women, they could never have suspected that that officer, Kazanchan, was actually a son of their old enemy, Missak Gazanchian, or, as Nargiz strangely called him, The Crooked Cucumber. Apparently, the young Gazanchian, along with many other Turkish Armenians, had immigrated to Soviet Georgia, slightly changed his family name to sound more Russian, found his way into NKVD school, and was assigned to Sukhumi. Knowing nothing about him, Nargiz and her mother were shocked when he self-importantly walked through the waiting room. His head was shaved clean like a billiard ball, but they both recognized him immediately, even without his red hair standing on end. They recognized his grinning smile revealing rows of small sharp teeth. As soon as he entered his room they stood up and left, barely keeping themselves from running away. The guards at the gate would not have failed to shoot them on the spot, Nargiz told me. Many nights after that she and her mother expected a black car would stop at their house and NKVD servicemen would knock on their door. For years they wondered if the scion of The Crooked Cucumber had played some, if not a crucial, role in Haroutiun's arrest. They could only pray for Haroutiun and nothing else. Their own lives became wretched after his arrest; until Stalin's death, Nargiz and her family were ostracized as relatives of "an enemy of the people." As for Kazanchan, he soon disappeared. Maybe he was transferred somewhere, or perhaps was destroyed by his own colleagues during regular "cleaning" practices inside the Stalin's secret police.

Dear Professor Ianko, this is all I was told by Nargiz. I feel good that I could keep my promise to her and write such a lengthy letter. I hope it will be of some use for your book. We all here, especially my husband and his parents, send our most sincere greetings to you and your family. We think you found America a much safer place than here, in the Caucasus. We wish you a great success in all your matters!

With respect, Susanna Amirian.

Russian Federation
Krasnodarskiy region,
Krasnaya Poliana.
April, 1995

The Additional Chapters

The Lamentations and Tribulations of Blackie (aka Sevouk), The Rats Destroyer

We, dogs, do not know dates. We are only able to distinguish between days and nights. Thus I know that many days and nights have passed since the people I lived with disappeared. There have been so many of those lonely days and nights that I understand: my people will not return. *So why do I still come to the gate of our house? Just to see again and again that other people are now occupying it? Is it because my thoughts are short like my tail and I forget easily? Or because there is still some faint hope at the bottom of my small dog's heart?*

These new people are very bad. I sniffed around them to their last bone. Dogs can sense the difference between bad and good. If only I could have taught my master to do the same? Many of his former customers smelled of jealousy and concealed hostility. The newcomers who have taken over his house smell dangerously of iron and fire, and also of being cheaply fed. They are all men and wear similar clothes. They also carry with them the heavy sticks that have sharp knives at their ends. These people are always ready to fetch a hard blow to my ribs or to prod me with their sticks. They can also make these sticks belch forth smoke and fire, which can kill from a distance. I have seen it.

If only I could have warned my master against bad people! We could have run away together. Unfortunately, right now, I should run instead to find something edible; it is difficult to lapse into daydreams and hopes on an empty belly.

* * * *

Did not find anything; not even the smallest crust of bread. Wandered for a long time through our quarter. There is nothing here because the people who lived in our quarter left their houses and shops. With them vanished the captivating aromas of cooking food and the leftovers for us, the dogs of the quarter. Recently, some new people began to occupy the emptied houses. They are men, women, and their children. They wear plain clothes, not like the men who stay in my master's spacious house. However, they are all very similar in their hatred of us. Some of them brought animals: sheep, cows, donkeys and mules, hens and roosters, but no dogs. So, these people like animals and know their usefulness. But we are different. We, the dogs who remained in the quarter after our owners' disappearance, became the street pariahs. Nobody wants us.

Their lads are the worst. They would not fail to kick me on an encounter and would not hesitate to smash my head with a stone if I lingered for a moment.

My belief in humans' wisdom and friendship, which I took in with my mother's milk, has been shattering. *Did not we, humans and dogs, make a pact many, many years ago?* People will give us shelter and food, and for that we will serve them unreservedly. That was the pact! (However, I always felt happier when my master was stroking my head and scratching behind my ears than when his wife was putting a couple of juicy bones in my bowl. It is true that a full bowl does not mean a full life!)

I am wondering what I would do if one of the newcomers threw me a bone. However, it's better not to think about.

I am just afraid of thinking about such a situation.

* * * *

Today, I ran into our stallion. He stood on the street, harnessed to the same carriage in which he used to carry my master and his family. Now, he serves other people—those with fire-throwing sticks, the people who took away his master.

The stallion pretended that he did not recognize me. To tell the truth, I never liked him. He was always jealous of me, apparently because of my freedom. I could run anywhere, hunt the rats and greet the incoming guests, even bark at the moon if I were as stupid as some of the other dogs in our neighborhood. The stallion spent his free time in his barn chewing hay. He used to shake his head and mane and chuckle scornfully when he saw me running near the open doors of his barn. Nonetheless, the stallion had his own lodging, and our master's sons took great care of him by washing and polishing his shiny skin. *So, why be jealous of something that you cannot do?* After all, I was the family dog, the rats destroyer, and he was just a horse.

The stallion pretended that he did not see me. Maybe he was embarrassed when I saw him subserving to other people. I just wanted to know any news that he might have had about our master.

The other day I met a man wearing a long black robe. There was a familiar scent of poverty. I knew him. A few times he had visited my master, during those happy days when our house was full of people and food. They had sat at the table in the garden talking for hours; only humans can do this for so long. Dogs need only a short moment to sniff around the ears and under the tails to learn everything about each other. However, we have no such serious problems with each other as people do.

So, this man, unlike our stallion, recognized me even though he was wearing spectacles. He dismounted from his donkey and talked to me for a while. His voice was very sad; he obviously was telling me about my master. *How could I, a dog, understand him?*

* * * *

I am shaking. Have barely escaped death. At the dump of the ravaged butcher shop. People with fire-throwing sticks got two of us, Fat Lady and Sniffer. They were both big dogs, an easy targets. I am the smallest from our dwindling pack of dogs. These people missed at me. I ran away with all my might. Now, I am hiding in some bushes that happened to be on my way, and I am not leaving here before nightfall. I will never return to the dump again.

Many days ago we finished pilfering all the bones from that place. Some had dried out completely under the sun, while others had decayed under dust and refuge. These bones are disgusting thing to eat, but what else could we find? Hunger is not a kind woman, and will not treat you to a plate of lamb stew!

That place was becoming dangerous. The new people who occupied the nearest houses drove us away by throwing stones at us and shouting as loudly as crows. However, the smell of meat that penetrated the walls and grounds of the butcher shop continued to draw us in.

Um-mm-m! I still remember what a delicious smell emanated from the open door when my master entered this shop! My eyes managed to glance upon shining cutlets of lamb and veal and, separated on the counter, small hills of kidneys, hearts, and washed intestines, skinned carcasses of sheep and calves soaring in the air, and a giant butcher waving his huge ax. I patiently waited for my master at the door and nobody dared to drive me away. For my patience, upon returning home, I received a generous present, not just a bone, but a couple of shins of lamb, boiled and with big pieces of juicy meat on their ends. I did not rush, instead waiting for the steam to subside, while enjoying its aroma and licking clean all the warm juice from the plate. Then I ate the meat, not forgetting to polish the gristly ends of the shins. Some gluttons fall upon the bone at once, crushing it for marrow and making a mess all around. I preferred to extract the marrow (undeniably the best part of the bone) at the end, in order to keep its sweet taste in my mouth for a long time after.

Is it not a shame that I am dreaming about bones just a short while after seeing the deaths of two of my own? Perhaps humans are right, thinking disparagingly about us, dogs, as always looking to fill our bellies?!

Sniffer, a pointer, was a fool as, by the way, are all hunting dogs when they do not work. He could use his sense there on the dump to warn us of people with sticks. I am more sorry for Fat Lady. This bitch was round like a barrel because she kept bringing puppies. She did it in a good order indeed. Some of her cubs were from me: had the same black hair. When she was in heat, she went with all the dogs of our quarter. However, because she lived next door to my house, I, despite being of not imposing build, was the first to be in her good graces. Fat Lady was not notable for her brains. In no way could she understand that because of my shortness she needed to bend under her rear paws. So, I had to stretch myself up.

Now, she is gone. And Sniffer, the silly, but good-natured, pointer. And Sissy, a puffy lap-dog, who lived in the house of my master's sister.

That's it, I am crying! I am crying because I cannot whine or howl. I must not make a noise. *Do humans know that we can cry and even have tears?*

* * * *

I have a strange feeling that most of all I am upset and disheartened by the disappearance of my master, even more than by the brutal killings of my own. Sissy, Fat Lady, Sniffer, and other dogs whose ends I did not witness but heard when hiding, just a squeal from a distance, and a whining for a mercy cut short. Sissy, a delicate small ball of white hair, was the first victim I saw dead.

She was smaller than me. With her it would be much easier to play some amorous games than with tall Fat Lady. To my disappointment, however, Sissy never left her owner's hands when she visited our house. My master's sister never allowed her favorite to go down to earth, needless to say, to go out of the house with me. "Sissy, my princess, stay away from this terrible mongrel, the rats destroyer!" I believed this woman used to say that about me to Sissy.

When Sissy's owners vanished like all the other former human inhabitants of our quarter, she was devastated by their "betrayal." I found her trembling hysterically with terror, her white hair dirty and tangled. At that time, the former "princess" recognized me at once. However, I did not reproach her, for we were relatives through our owners. I found her a burrow in which to hide from the new dangerous people moving into our quarter. Later, I brought Sissy something to eat. With difficulty, I sacrificed a portion of my stocks I still had at that time. It was for no use, however; "princess" Sissy was doomed. She was not able to survive more than a couple days after more new people arrived to take over empty houses and more of their children started roaming around streets and orchards. The next time I saw Sissy, her small body was buried under the stones these savage children had thrown on her. I could descry the pink ribbon around her broken neck, a present from her former owner.

Did I immediately regret the small portion of my stocks I had sacrificed for hapless Sissy, or do I only feel it right now, when I am much hungrier? It is difficult to say.

It does not matter! The point is that I do not feel as sorry for dead Sissy as I do for my master, even though he may be alive and may return one day to his house. . . .

Wait a minute, Blackie! "Return!" "Stocks!" *How are these two connected to each other? Why am I so excited? Am I feeling that this connection is very important? How? Or am I just crazy because of hunger?*

My canine thoughts are plain and straightforward. So, the connection should be quite simple. I need to calm down and find an explanation for my sudden agitation. In any event, I have nothing to do until darkness falls and allows me to crawl out trying to find food. I need to find a distraction to quiet my stomach a little bit. Otherwise it will gnaw me to death.

Well, I was struck when thinking about the "return" of my master. I oftentimes think about this; sometimes believing in miracles, but other times think about him with a despair. However, this time, I was reminiscing about Sissy and how I gave her a little of my food supplies. At that time, I still had pieces of deep friend lamb hidden in a hole in our garden. Before leaving her house my master's wife had taken me to that place and showed me what she was putting there. It was a big bundle of flat bread containing many slowly fried pieces of lamb. Neither she nor even my master had ever given me this delicious food before. I had only seen how it was prepared for the coming winter. Tender pieces were thoroughly fried in hot oil made from the fatty tail of sheep, and then when ready, they were put into a clay jug. Next the meat was covered by hardening oil, very diligently, in order to fill all the spaces between the pieces, so it would keep them fresh through the entire winter. Really delicious! Now, I know.

My master's wife made these supplies for me because she and her daughter were going to leave me alone. And they did it so, the very next morning, carrying only two bags with them. I stayed behind as they ordered me. I don't know where they went. Maybe they went after my master?!

There were so many pieces of lamb in that bundle of bread that I thought I would feast on them forever. I even shared them, a little, with Sissy. However, within a short while, newcomers with fire-throwing sticks completely occupied our house and garden. I could not prevent this. They did not find my supplies, but getting into the garden through the gate became very dangerous for me. When, after a couple of days, I discovered a safe way to my supplies, through the opening for our brook flowing out of the garden, I found that the supplies had disappeared. The rats, my deadly enemies, had robbed me. It was such a blow! In spite of how carefully I had always filled up the hole with earth and leaves, the rats had found it anyway. Their sickening sour smell was all over the place. Not even a single piece of bread had been left. Since that time I have been hungry.

It was my fault. I had allowed them to escape from my fangs. Many strange things were happening that had diverted my mind, so I had stopped my rat-hunting. Rats are like a disease. If you stop destroying them your home will be swarmed with these ugly creatures. I killed them because somebody should stop them.

There is one, a big Father Rat, with a pulpy nose and dense long mustache. He is the smartest and fastest of them all. When he was young I almost got him, but he managed to sneak into a wall crack leaving half of his tail in my fangs. Since that time he has become more keen in his dirty tricks and steals. Soon, he took over his crowd. He ruled it with unseen brutality; corpses of unruly males he carried out of his underground world and placed on all my routes as if showing me who owned and dictated the entire place. With his females he produced an army of thieves. However, while sending them outside to steal and damage food, he preferred to hide from me behind them. I could contain their noctural raids well. Almost every morning I used to bring a couple of strangled rats to the back steps of my master's house for his review and approval. For some reason my master's wife and their daughter did not like that. However, I continued my job as the rats destroyer. These women, like, by the way, many other people, did not understand that rats should be destroyed. Rats are not like other animals. They cannot be trusted. They are invaders who bring only terrible disease and devastation.

Now, I know, Father Rat is laughing at me, bristling his mustache and exposing his sharp teeth. He thinks that I will never return to my home and get him. He is wrong, this bastard; I will break his neck. I just need a little food to restore my speed and strength . . .

What a silly dog I am! Why again do I think about food, about my enemies? My thoughts should not stray from my master.

Before, I remembered that my master's wife had hidden supplies of food for me in the garden. Now, I am also remembering that before that, she had hidden something else in the garden as well. A heavy clay jug. I don't know what was inside that jug. Apparently, not food, because she had buried it in the bed of our brook, actually under the water. It must have been very important thing to have been concealed in such an unusual place. I also hide some things, usually bones which I cannot finish gnawing because I am full or very busy. I always conceal them under a thin layer of earth, but never bury them under water. It is easier for me to make a mark on the ground in order to come back and unearth my hidden treasure.

However, it's me, Blackie. Humans are smarter. Apparently, they can remember places better than dogs do. Obviously, that my master's wife, a wise woman, will not forget the spot under the brook where she buried her heavy clay jug.

That's it! Finally, I understood what has been disturbing and at the same time exciting me all day. They will return! My owners will come back for this jug! Surely, if they concealed the jug with such precautions, then they were thinking about coming back and digging it up, exactly like I always did with my hidden food.

Oh-ho-ho! What a great heaviness is off my back! Now, everything for me becomes clear and simple. I must wait here for my dear people's return. What a happy, beautiful day it will be!

I just need a little food to survive here alone.

* * * *

Is it strange that I can reflect upon something important or just things from the past only when I am idling here, in my secret refuge? When I am out during the night, rummaging through all the rubbish heaps, such thoughts do not enter my head.

What about other species? Does our stallion think about his past life or future fate when he moves his legs pulling a carriage? Or does he only care about his portion of hay? Does something glimmer in the small heads of birds during their chase of flies and mosquitos?

Stupid birds! I could not catch a single one of them, even the fat pigeons; every time they took flight before my very nose. I had the same lack of success with small fish darting in and out of the stones in a fresh water stream. I just became soaked through to no purpose. I lost my previous quickness because of starvation. At the end, to my great shame, I satisfied my hunger with a frog. It had the smell of slime, but the rear legs were quite meaty.

I did this for the first time in my life. Before this frog I had never killed to eat. I killed hordes of rats, but I never ate them. I never even tasted their blood. I still think about it with disgust. That is why I simply strangled them.

What about chickens? A couple of days ago, Lop-Eared, a mongrel like me, but much bigger and stronger, suggested we work together to steal a chicken. During the day some of these birds carelessly swarm on the sides of the streets. They are afraid maybe only of kites, but not of us, house pets. In days of old, just for fun, we sometimes chased them a little bit. In confusion, these birds run; they forgot how to fly a long time ago. So, together it would be much easier for us to catch one of them than it was for me alone with the pigeons. According to his plan, Lop-Eared lies in ambush while I am driving in a chicken, closer and closer to him. Then he bounds, and here we are both clearing out with the prey.

At that time, I did not agree with Lop-Eared. First of all, we both were raised and trained to protect people's dwellings and all their belongings, up to a fallen apple in their garden and an egg in the hen house. That was our agreement with people. However, Lop-Eared had his point, too. He pointed out that it was not our fault that for some unknown reason the old agreements had been broken. People broke it first. Our owners had left us and did not allow us to follow them, although we would be happy to accompany them anywhere they went. The new people who came later and occupied their houses hate us, and instead of giving us a little food, they are ready to destroy us. Many of our friends and relatives, even cute puppies, are already dead: stoned, drowned and killed by fire-throwing sticks. Now, to survive we have the right to break the old rules, said Lop-Eared.

It was true! My heart has been smarting since that day when my master abandoned me, even though, I felt that his sudden disappearance was somehow connected with the people who had visited his shop that unlucky day. They had been very loud and rude. Strangely, my master had not allowed me to snarl back at them. Instead, he had shooed me away from the shop to the garden, though I could not bite through their rough boots anyway. However, he could not stop them from striking me with sharp knives mounted on their fire-throwing sticks. Later, when I sneaked back into the shop my dear master was not there. He could have taken me with him, but he chose to leave me.

Now, I am remembering that my master's wife and her daughter had left their house after they, too, had the same rude and loud visitors. I recognized the smell of a particular one, a sour smell of sweat and a rancid oil. My master's wife heard my growl. She sent me out of the house and closed the door. When she let me back the visitors were gone. However, soon after that visit my master's wife and daughter also left, leaving me absolutely alone in this now dangerous place.

Yeah! It was not characteristic of Lop-Eared, but he made a good point. However, I hesitated to join him in his venture. It was very risky because if we were seen even just chasing a chicken, never mind killing it, the newly arrived people, as ruthless and hateful as they were toward us so far, would immediately launch an organized hunt upon us and destroy all of us still barely surviving here. I agreed that our existence was on the edge and that it was terrible and unfair, and most likely we would all soon perish anyway, but at least we were not dead yet. I also told Lop-Eared the story I heard from Sissy. I told this unbelievable, really sickening, story to him just to explain that we were now living with a very new type of people than we had encountered before. These people are very dangerous because they would do everything with us, even unimaginable, to establish their order in our quarter. You cannot mess with them, namely because their cruelty is unseen and unimaginable, and nobody can deal with something if he has never seen it before.

Pure-bred Sissy was born not in our quarter, not in our town, but very far away, in a huge human settlement where long streets and rows of buildings stretched as far as the eye could see. This noisy place was crowded with different looking people, as well as big and small carriages drawn by horses, donkeys, and people, and believe or not, by themselves. Young Sissy never put her little paws on the street. She heard this awful story from her mother, who, in her turn, heard it from an acquaintance. It was a trustworthy source, a foreigner, a middle-aged bulldog who used to accompany his owner during the morning exercise walks along the streets of this city.

This city was famous for its dogs. These dogs were not like Sissy and her mother who lived with their owners, but rather totally independent creatures. They might have thought of themselves as free spirits, but others might have preferred to consider them nothing more than arrogant loafers. These filthy, tattered street-walking vultures rummages the city searching for food. They scared people, new in the city, when engaging in fierce group fights for a territory or for a love of their bitches. The old inhabitants were used to tolerating the city's dogs. People did not pay any attention to dogs' internal affairs. People did not notice dogs lying about on the corners of the streets; they just went around them. If a dog chose to sleep at the steps of a shop, its customers routinely stepped over the dreaming dog when entering or exiting the shop. Apparently, the dogs in this city always had fascinating dreams; even the loud sound of an approaching carriage could not arouse them, and they would simply bend in their legs at the very last moment, just enough for their limbs not to be crushed under the wheels of the carriage. So, the dogs of that place really believed that they had been sharing this city with people from the time immemorial.

Then, all at once, the old order changed. A very new breed of people took over the city. They established their own order. Among other very new things it was also decided that there was no place in the city for its street dogs anymore. "They are filthy, useless, and dangerous for the nation's health." In a short time, all the dogs were rounded up and sent to a small island near the city. The new leaders of the city decided that killing thousands of dogs would be very difficult to organize and some of them could escape the execution. They found that it would be much easier to let the dogs die by themselves on that barren rock surrounded by salty water.

I told Lop-Eared that I hope the sun and thirst killed those poor creatures before crazy hunger could drive them to committing atrocities upon their own, the smallest and weakest ones. But even if that did happen, who can blame the dogs?

Scared, Lop-Eared retracted his idea about stealing chickens. Instead, he decided to join two sheepdogs, two shaggy brothers, Archo and Boorcho, on their trip to the mountains in search of a village where they could serve people in return for food and shelter.

* * * *

Today, I took a risk. Because of the hunger. I could not bear it any longer. I felt like my belly was stuck to my spine.. So, actually, I risked my life just to prolong my misery. Stupid!

However, I got lucky. On my way to the bazaar and back, I received only a couple of kicks, though heavy ones. At the main gate I was fortunate to spot that man in a black robe and his sad donkey. This man again talked with me at length and with pity. For a long time I had neither heard nor seen pity, and I needed it. I also needed something to choke my hunger. Apparently, I looked at him with such pleading eyes that he finally understood me. This man gave me some cheese rolled into a piece of flat bread. Could have been his breakfast. I swallowed his generous alms instantly. I don't remember if I waved my tail in appreciation.

Cheese! That pungent, salty stuff which I had turned up my nose at in the past. Today, I did not hesitate with it even for a moment. This man's donkey nodded his head in approval.

* * * *

Today, another frog. Gradually, I will turn into a stork or a heron. Nevertheless, it is better to eat frogs than rats. Never!

* * * *

What happened with Lop-Eared? I did not see him for a while. *Was he able to make it to the mountains with Archo and Boorcho?*

“One Problem Solved. The once-famous dogs of Constantinople, now destroyed.” From: F. G. Aflalo, Regilding the Crescent. L: Bell & Sons, 1911.

To tell the truth, I never liked those brothers. Both rude and primitive chained dogs, they always plumed themselves on their strengths. Yes, they were very powerful, and for that reason their owner, a jeweler, had brought them from a mountainous village to our town. They were so powerful that they could break loose and leap over fences when they learned about Fat Lady's "times of passion." However, these heaps of muscles could not achieve anything because they could not court with her. These boors only hurt and frightened her when fighting with each other.

I don't think that the good-natured Lop-Eared will be able to find any common ground with Archo and Boorcho.

☼ ☼ ☼ ☼

How ravishing was the smell of my master's socks! When, for some reason, upset and sad, I used to sneak into the laundry room and take out his sock from a pile of clothes prepared for washing. I liked to sleep with it under my snout. Many times I was caught in the act. My master's wife was the most difficult to outwit. She would burst out with unusually long tirades while smacking my nose by the sock. Even if I had been able to speak with her in her language she would not have understood my addiction. The smell of my master's socks had a secret power to soothe me and dispel all my daily chagrins.

Oh, how much I need them during these sleepless days and nights!

☼ ☼ ☼ ☼

Already quite a time has passed since my last talk with Lop-Eared. His scent marks in the places we hung around almost has totally disappeared. However, I am not yet the last dog in our quarter. I am still finding scent marks of Snow, a bitch with thin high legs and white fur, who has been hiding in the ruins near a round, stone building in the square, the big building that my owners and other people of our quarter used to visit for singing. I never talked with Snow, since she was always very reserved. Interestingly, how is she surviving now?

Maybe I will go and find her! Maybe tonight! Just one thing. I don't like the smoldering smell of fire coming from that big building.

☼ ☼ ☼ ☼

When I reached the ruins of dwellings around the building the moon was throwing light on some of their still standing walls, but the holes and crevices between their collapsed parts were dark like my hair. I don't know how Snow discerned me while I was standing in the shadow of a wall. The weak breeze brought her scent. Then her pale body suddenly appeared on top of the pile of debris. From there she silently jumped in front of me.

Snow did not say much to me. She had no news, and had not seen Lop-Eared or other dogs. As she was sitting in front of me and not moving away, I realized that she was not going to invite me into her hiding place. It was her territory and I did not intrude. I left Snow still in her guarding position.

What did Snow want to prevent me from seeing? Is it possible that she had some food there? A few bones hidden in the secret passages under the ruins?

For some reason, I doubt such an explanation. Standing there in the shadow of the big building, I sensed that there was somebody else in those ruins. I had some vague feeling which I cannot explain now to myself. Nevertheless, there, near Snow, I felt that we were not alone. I also felt that she wanted me to leave.

Does she have puppies? If so, how could she survive so long?

No, her lean body did not show any signs of a feeding mother-dog. She smelled of smoke, fire, and dust, but not of milk.

* * * *

I just realized that Snow and I are apparently the last two dogs remaining of all that lived here not such a long time before. It was so strange that we could not relate with each other.

Should I try to see her again?

I am too tired. I have to reserve my strength and wait for my master. This is only thing I should do now. So far I have not given up hope.

* * * *

I was wrong about just the two of us still surviving here. Lop-Eared is back. He is sleeping right next to me. His legs, the soles bloodied by the long rugged roads, are twitching as if their owner is still trying to escape some danger.

Lop-Eared's story completely broke my heart. The world I live in now has no meaning anymore, no justice. I simply don't know what to do. Everything seems senseless. Even my clinging to life.

It's amazing that Lop-Eared still has plans after all he has experienced during his trip. With the two brothers, Archo and Boorcho, he had strayed in the nearby mountains looking for the village from where his road-fellows had been brought from to our quarter when they were very young. Big, but stupid, the brothers did not remember anything, and could not find the right direction. After spending their entire lives chained, they had only learned to bark, growl, and bare their teeth. It did not help in hunting at all. Without any difficulty, birds flew away from them and small animals took refuge in their burrows. The brothers became so angry and frustrated that poor Lop-Eared worried for his own life. Sometimes, he really felt that Archo and Boorcho were ready to have him as a snack. Somehow, he persuaded them to stage an ambush and succeeded in driving a young hare on them. The brothers caught the bare and gobbled it together momentarily, not leaving even a bite for Lop-Eared. That was when he decided to leave them at the first appropriate opportunity.

Finally, the luckless travelers came across a village. The scents of people, their animals, and, best of all, of food being prepared, teased them. This was a chance to find jobs as guard dogs or shepherd dogs. Suddenly, another dog appeared on their way into the village. It confronted and stopped them. According to Lop-Eared, who saw this creature from a close distance, it was not just a dog, but rather a frightening monster. With its unusually long striped trunk of yellow and muddy brown this beast most of all resembled a snake with a huge canine snout. It was a mother-dog; her loose-hanging teats suggested that maybe an army of similar ugly young creatures were following her. However, that was not the reason for Archo's and Boorcho's hesitation. The powerful jaws of the mother-dog and ferocious hatred in her eyes froze the brothers. They understood that the beast in their way did not want them in her village and that it would attack them immediately after their very first step forward. Confused, they growled. That was like a bubble burst in comparison with the monster's replying growl, a thundering roar coming from her mouth. Terrified, Lop-Eared turned around and hit the road. Behind him he heard the beast's jump; there were sounds of heavy bodies hitting each other and the ground, and then screams of pain and terror. When, after running for a while, he finally stopped and found the courage to look back, he saw Boorcho not far behind him and the badly limping Archo following them at a distance.

Lop-Eared was surprised by the deep wounds Archo and Boorcho had sustained during their very short fight with the beast. The snake-dog was not just protecting her territory, but intended to kill both brothers. Dogs never try to kill intruders or challengers, especially the defeated ones already leaving the scene. Archo and Boorcho, experienced fighters by themselves, were stunned by the vicious attack of the beast. Archo was in worse condition. Blood was dripping from severe cuts on his neck and shoulders. Nevertheless, fear continued driving the trio away from the village with its beastly guard. Later, they found a secluded place looking like a hollow and stopped there for a rest. It was a very quiet place; the only sound was the dark sand squeaking under the dog's paws. In exhaustion, Archo and his brother fell to the ground. Lop-Eared did not follow their example. He sat looking around that strange place. Its gloomy appearance, unusual quietness, and most of all awful odor made Lop-Eared very nervous. He did not want to stay in such a place any longer and decided to leave. Boorcho was able to get up and follow him, but Archo did not respond to their call and remained on the ground in the same position. When Lop-Eared and Boorcho approached, they found him dead. A foam was bubbling on his mouth. Lop-Eared and Boorcho left the place with a firm certainty that Archo died because of poisonous bites by the snake-dog.

After many hours of wandering in the inhospitable mountains, Lop-Eared and Boorcho came across a big road coming from their town. On the side of this road they came across another gloomy place. In big shallow graves, they found human remains. Jackals and vultures had visited that place long before them. Human ribs and skulls were scattered around and pieces of human clothes were hanging on thorny bushes. Hungry Boorcho lost all his domestic dog's dignity. Like the very last shameless jackal who had never lived with people, he began rummaging through the human remains. Bones were crackling under his teeth. Lop-Eared could not stop Boorcho. Apparently, the beast's poison had also affected Boorcho and made him mad because he, like his brother, had been bitten by the snake-dog. Disgusted, Lop-Eared left Boorcho in that grisly place and headed to the town which he had left days before in an attempt to save his life. He did not know any other place to go.

Now, he is sleeping next to me, and in his sleep my poor friend is again seeing all the terrible things he went through during his sad journey.

* * * *

I cannot sleep. I am wondering, again and again: *What could kill all those people and bury them in those shallow graves along the road?* I think I know the answer and I am afraid of it.

This is a mass murder. There are no other species in the entire animal kingdom who dare to commit such an act against people. The answer comes into my mind: another group of people must have done it.

However, this obvious answer troubles me even more. *How can humans kill their own? Why would one group of people destroy another one? Just because they are different? Would white dogs like Snow destroy all black dogs like me or hairy shepherd dogs exterminate all smooth-haired hunting dogs?* Never! It is against the major laws of nature: live and give a chance to live to others, even to the smallest or most strange creatures. Yet people are destroying these laws. From now on, the world will be different. I see it tumbling down.

* * * *

Lop-Eared had a plan. He wanted me to take him to meet with Snow. He thought he would be able to convince her to leave the town with us and find some better place outside, a vacant place, far from people's hostilities, a place where the three of us could set up our own colony. He assured me that we could survive by hunting hares and other small animals. Poor Lop-Eared sincerely believed that he had learned good hunting tactics during his journey with Archo and Boorcho.

Lop-Eared's venture of a "union of free hunters" did not live long. Snow refused to go with us. She did not argue with Lop-Eared, but simply declined his offer. This time she seemed to be more affable, but again I felt somebody's presence behind her.

Lop-Eared was disappointed by Snow's refusal. He really thought that with her our colony could thrive. However, he did not abandon his plan, even when I also decided to remain here. Lop-Eared, who had become such a dear friend of mine, left the town alone. It was a sad departure because both of us knew we would never see each other again.

Sometimes I regret my decision not to leave with my friend, Lop-Eared. Then, I think that as weak as I am now, I would have been a burden to him. "Hunting hares!" I even postpone from night to night my battle with the rats who—I can imagine how much—are enjoying the basement, courtyard, and back garden of my house. I always feel obligated to protect my master's property in his absence. Now, I deceive myself by repeatedly thinking that tomorrow night I will feel stronger. Instead, I am becoming weaker.

* * * *

The thoughts in my head are all mixed up. Sometimes I am confused and do not know what to do. Like today, I went astray far from my quarter, although I should not even be outside of my refuge. It seems that I completely forgot that it is dangerous to wander on the streets in broad daylight. Accidentally, I met a young child with a piece of bread in his hand. That was a strange moment; the street near his house was empty, and the young human was standing in front of me all alone, looking at me, sometimes bringing his hand holding the bread to his mouth. Maybe he was seeing a dog for the first time in his life. The human face was serene. His eyes did not show anger or fear, and only his lips moved silently when the child chewed bread.

Bread! In the small child's hand it was so close to my mouth! However, I stood there fascinated and continued to look in the young human's face. Then, somebody, maybe the child's mother, called from inside the house. The child turned around and entered the open door, vanishing inside along with his piece of bread.

* * * *

Who were those people buried along the road? For some reason, I forgot to find out from Lop-Eared. Maybe he recognized some of them. I would. I could always sense and distinguish my master and those of his big family. Even from a distance. They all had one common scent, that of a well cared for house: freshly baked bread and pastries, coffee and tea with cardamom, and clean linen soaked with a lavender aroma. Each of them also had a scent of his own. My master's shop scented the air with a heady tobacco and hints of distant places coming from the carpets hanging along the walls. I liked all of his scents, even the smell of his cigarettes. His young grandchildren had a more simple scent, milk and honey, and, sometimes, medicinal powder. I remember all the happy scents of that family. We dogs never forget scents of the past.

Can it be that my master and his family were buried in those graves alongside of the road leading from our town? I only knew for sure that they all left the town and did not return. *Is it possible that they cannot return because they are dead and their bones are scattered along that road? Thus, my waiting has no meaning?!*

* * * *

New people, new laws, and new order. Our stallion serves new owners, I eat frogs, Boorcho dares to gnaw human bones, rats are taking over my house. End of the world!

Why am I still alive? What is inside of my body that stubbornly drags me to find food and water? Why can I not stop everything by my will? I hate my body! It is small, filthy, a nest of fleas, it cannot run and jump, but it does not die either.

* * * *

I was wrong. My body could run. My stupid body betrayed me. Apparently, it was just not scared enough before. Until today, everything it had seen and heard had happened to others. It was different when it ran for its own life today.

How did it all begin? Was it today or tomorrow? Well, I remember it was a bright day. I was on the street, somewhere near the bazaar. Somehow, again I came across that child. I met him once before. This time he had no bread in his hand. This time he was with his mother. She was talking with other women. I thought the child recognized me. He again was looking at me with some interest. Maybe it just seemed to me. His interest. Then something happened with him. Maybe it was my fault. It could be that I remembered the piece of bread he had in his hand the first time we met. It could be that I licked my mouth and showed him my teeth. Or maybe he just did not like my purulent eyes. In any event, the child's face suddenly frowned and he started howling. His mother turned around and saw me standing near her child. She shouted, other women joined her, and the chase began.

Oh, how did I run! The women and the child were left behind, but other people, men and boys, joined the hunt. They persistently chased me from one street to another. They shouted and urged on each other to pursue me. These people thought I had really bit that child. Stones were whistling past my head and some hit my back. I was limping, I was tired, and it felt like their sticks were already lashing my sides. In total desperation, my body turned to the ruins near the big building in the square. I did not know what I was doing at that last moment. I did not think about bringing my chasers to Snow who could be in her place either. My legs just turned there, because it was the last chance to hide my body in some burrow under the pile of the debris.

So, why couldn't I stop this chase? Just turn around and meet my end? I wanted the end even before the chase happened. However, my short legs were still running and my body making sharp moves I never knew before to avoid my chasers' sticks and stones. I lost my mind. On my last breath I reached the square. I saw the opened entrance to the big building and I rushed into it. I had no strength to run further. The shouting people followed me into the building. Now, in a big and completely empty hall I had no chance to escape their rage.

Suddenly, from nowhere, a man's figure appeared in front of me. I could barely discern his face, some pale spot, open mouth twitching in scream, and big terrified eyes. The people chasing me apparently recognized him better, because I heard behind me a burst of even more excited shouts and hallooing. In panic, the man took off to the entrance of the building through the strikes of stones and sticks which a moment ago were intended for me. My persecutors rushed onto the square after their new prey; they completely forgot about me. Noise of the hunt moved away. I stood shaking and at the same time frozen to the spot. Then a new triumphant burst of shouts reached me from a distance. They got him!

I still didn't know who that man was and can only guess what they did with him, my unexpected savior. Later, when I came to my senses, I found Snow hiding in her underground refuge. She disclosed that she had befriended that man since she had begun hiding in the same ruins. In the half-collapsed basement of his former house, he had a burrow of his own and a quite good stocks of food and water. He even shared it with Snow, sometimes, when she was too hungry to keep her distance from him. (Such a reserved dog was that bitch Snow!)

She had been keeping all this in a secret from me and Lop-Eared. She explained that it was her obligation to assist that man in his hiding to somehow repay for his kindness. She used to warn him about anyone approaching their place of refuge. Lately, when his supply of food had expired her friend became less cautious. He started to visit the big round building on the square during the day; he did it before only crawling into the building at nights. Snow said that in the building her friend used to kneel down near the wall and sing. Strange humans! I knew that people of our quarter and my owners too went to that building to sing. However, to risk his life for singing was not wise thing to do. The last time Snow's friend had done it she had no time to warn him because I had burst in the building so suddenly. The man could not reach his burrow unnoticed.

Now, without this man, Snow has no reason to stay in the town. She is going to trace the steps of Lop-Eared and, if lucky, will join him sometime soon. She is not angry at me. Maybe she is not just reserving her bitter feelings for me, but really thinks that what happened today was not my fault. Or was it yesterday? Whatever. The world is crazy now, and terrible, unfair things happen to everybody.

* * * *

I did not go with Snow. I think my left leg has been broken by a thrown stone. I can barely move it, although I do not need to anyway. There is no place to go. I am alone. I am the last dog of this quarter! I do not need to wait for my master anymore. He was a good man, a real pal, and it was a great pleasure to serve him, but he is not coming back.

* * * *

One thing I have to do. The rats. They should not take over my dear home. If I continue crawling through the night I may reach my home. My jaws are still strong enough . . .

* * * *

Here, they are coming. Dark shadows. Everywhere. Where is Father Rat? I see his grey mustache and ugly teeth. This fight will continue to the end!

Eat to Live,
or
Some Useful Recipes of the Survivor

Now, my insatiable listener, you are asking for the recipes of the dishes I prepared during your vacation stay in my home! It is not enough that you have spent almost the entire vacation scribbling down my family's story. Now, you want my family's recipes, too. You really want to know all our secrets!

I understand. It is your wife. Are you sure that she will prepare them for you?

I, myself, never used to write down any recipes. I learned everything by watching, standing next to my mother at the oven, or glancing from behind my grandmother's shoulder at what she was preparing for the table. Also, I helped them to wash and cut the vegetables or to stir the sauce, doing all the same things they did when they were girls like me. Their recipes were very simple. Just put together a couple of edibles; that was all. When we lived in Turkey, we did not have a variety of provisions. We were poor refugees. These days people become really "crazy" about serving fancy meals. Wedding parties turn into a theatrical shows. Families compete by offering more and more courses and presenting more and more elaborate dishes. It is not just gluttony but also a shameless boasting of wealth and power—shameless because so much of the remaining food is discarded afterward.

As long as I knew my grandmother and mother, they looked at food in another way. They were indifferent to it. Of course, they always wanted my uncles and I to eat well: "to be healthy." God forbid if they ever thought I did not have enough or I was hungry! Then they would force me to eat more or they would prepare for me a dainty. However, for these women themselves, food was just the fuel they needed in order to move on.

Their indifference was strikingly strange considering the fact that my grandfather, "Lord" Pogos, by their own admission, was very fussy about the food on his table. Not only did he refuse to eat alone—bringing with him friends, acquaintances, and even strangers, in accordance with his slogan that, "whoever eats alone may die alone from choking on the last bone"—but he also demanded from my grandmother no less than a dozen different dishes on the table. Sometimes he was pliable to count as a dish a plate with cheese and scallions, but anyway, my grandmother very often had to exercise her culinary talents to impress his guests. As a cook, my grandmother was very famous around our town. No wonder why! A couple of times she accompanied her husband on his business trips to remote parts of the country. During those journeys among Arabs, Persians, Kurds, Jews, Assyrians, and other inhabitants of the former Turkish empire, while her husband searched for rare carpets and kilims, she picked up many local recipes for the future amusement of his guests upon their return home. During one such trip in Urfa, my grandparents met with a rug dealer, Mousa Agha by name, and were well-entertained in his big house. Who could have imagined at that time that after a few years my grandmother would stand again at the gate of this house, but this time as a dirty, starving exile? And that namely her culinary skills would save her life?

I already told you—a little bit—about my grandmother's escape from her group of exiled Armenian women and children who had managed to reach Urfa. She was able to sneak out of their encampment near the rail station unnoticed by the escorting Turkish gendarmes. Apparently, the gendarmes did not believe that any of those completely exhausted women, "walking skeletons," could move any more without being whipped and struck by their rifle-butts. Grandmother Iughaper could. Somehow. She was also lucky to find the gate of Mousa Agha's house; she remembered its ornament—blue and white tiles composing a picture of stars on the sky. There, in the shadow of the gate, she sat to gather her strength and thoughts before daring to knock on the door. Suddenly, the wooden door opened wide by itself and a frightened man burst out. His head was uncovered and his forehead was bleeding through his fingers pressed to the wound. Then his chaser, a man of a medium height but with a huge belly, appeared at the door, cursing loudly and waving a long spoon which, to all appearances, was the weapon that had been used to make a gash in the victim's head. It was Mousa Agha by his own self!

As the pursued man disappeared at the turn of the street, Mousa Agha threw after him something he had been holding in his other hand. It fell in the dust near Grandmother Iughaper. She looked at it and realized that it was a crust of rice that usually forms on the flat bottom of the vessel in which pilaf is made. A crisp crust of golden or pale brown color, usually broken in pieces and placed on top of the mounded cone of rice, shows the guests the mastery of the cook. Grandmother Iughaper noticed that the crust thrown away by Mousa Agha was dark brown, apparently burnt by his negligent cook. She knew the old rule: "an unattended pot boils immediately." The curses of Mousa Agha confirmed her assumption.

"You, stupid, lazy, drowsy bastard, you have ruined my dinner! What will I show to my much esteemed guests? From this day on I, Mousa Agha, will be known around Urfa as a person who dared to serve burnt garbage instead of pilaf. Oh, what shame is expected! What laughter there will be around my table! God is witness, I will find you and stuff this piece of your lousy work in your mouth so you can choke on it!"

(I am not surprised. In the Orient, such a terrible mistake as spoiling the central dish of a big dinner, for instance, wedding or circumcision, has always been considered a catastrophic event. It might became the talk of the town for years to come. Sometimes the unfortunate cook might not only be cursed, chased, and beaten, but also murdered by the enraged dinner-givers. Believe me, cooking is a very dangerous profession since, for many people, eating is a great passion and the knives are right there, in the kitchen.)

My grandmother picked up the burnt crust of rice from the dust and said, "Mousa Agha Effendi, I think I can help you to save your dinner."

"How do you dare to speak with me and how do you know my name, dirty beggar-woman?" asked an infuriated Mousa Agha.

"I am not a beggar-woman, I am the wife of Pogos Aleksanian. He was one of your carpet-buyers. We have eaten pilaf in your house. Before this war. The pilaf and your hospitality were great!"

As my grandmother was speaking to Mousa Agha, he was peering at her emaciated, darkened face and rugged clothes. My grandmother told us that time slowed for her at that moment. Her heart almost stopped, awaiting Mousa Agha's reaction.

"What can you do? My guests may be here in a hour; you cannot make a new pilaf." He did not ask about "Lord" Pogos at that time and never asked her about her husband during her three year refuge in his house. Successful merchant and careful moneylender, Mousa Agha did not need to ask questions which had evident answers.

Grandmother Iughaper did not have a clear solution for Mousa Agha's problem, even when she followed him to the kitchen in the back of his house. She was still clenching the rice crust in her hand, managing at times to bite it behind Mousa Agha's back. In the kitchen she asked for a skillet that was the same size as the bottom of the pot used by Mousa Agha's cook to prepare the pilaf. She warmed it well on the fire, melted in it some sheep fat, and then spread a portion of the rice prepared before by Mousa Agha's unfortunate cook around the skillet mixing it with egg yolk. At the end, she pressed the thin rice layer tightly to the bottom of the skillet and kept the covered skillet on the fire until Mousa Agha's guests were ready for pilaf. The rice in the skillet formed a perfect golden brown crust which was broken in pieces and proudly placed on top of the rice mounded on the huge plate. An anxious Mousa Agha offered these pieces of "fake" crust to his guests—a couple of Turkish officers, some provincial officials led by a judge, and a couple of wealthy landlords and merchants—and nobody among them complained about the pilaf. Only the judge asked Mousa Agha if his cook had prepared it in a Persian way. "Yes, yes!" assured Mousa Agha, "you are so perceptive, Hakim Effendi!"

At that time, the creator of this "Persian pilaf" was sitting on the floor of the kitchen slowly eating up her piece of the rice crust, dark and burnt one. She thought about the women and children of her exile group who apparently had already left their encampment and were being driven further to their final destination.

That was how my grandmother survived. Pilaf saved her. She did not leave Mousa Agha's kitchen for three years. Filling his unbounded belly with delicious food, amusing his guests, spicing, seasoning, and remembering scents of happier days . . .

Rice Pilaf

So, my dear, why do we not start with pilaf? Pilaf is the king of all dishes. It is not for an ordinary dinner serving only a couple of people. As the king it is supposed to preside over a big crowd. Also, like as a king, pilaf can be unpredictable and punishing. Just think about a master cook who is making pilaf for a wedding of 300–400 guests. *What would happen to him if he burned the pilaf and wasted hundreds of pounds of rice, meat, and oil invested in it?*

About the ingredients. Remember, to prepare an excellent pilaf you, first of all, must have the best rice and oil. For really good pilaf you should find a special sort of rice. It has to be long-grained and aromatic. (I prefer rice from Iran, or at least from Middle Asia. The Persians, Uzbeks, and Kazakhs are crazy about pilaf and they have very good sorts of rice.) Next, the rice should be thoroughly cleaned. Pour the rice grains, portion by portion, onto the surface of the table and sort them out. Discard all grains with an irregular size and color. Ask your kids to help you and your wife. This is a great opportunity to seat at the table together and to talk about this and that while cleaning the rice. When buying rice ask the seller about its age. If you buy aged rice, which is hardened by time, it is a good idea to put it in water for a few hours before making the pilaf. Some folks, the Turks for instance, fry the rice to make it easier to prepare. *Ha, what do the Turks know about pilaf?* I agree with the Persians and Uzbeks that frying changes the natural aroma of rice.

For the meat part of pilaf the best is mutton. Some people use hen or turkey, and I even heard about cooking pilaf with sturgeon. However, stick with mutton; it is the traditional choice. Mutton also has a strong aroma which mixes well with spices and vegetables and penetrates into the rice, making a nice combination. Poultry is not as aromatic as mutton.

Different kinds of oil are used for pilaf: melted and refined butter, olive and sunflower oil, or any other vegetable oil which is available. However, the best is oil extracted from the fatty-tails of a special breed of sheep. In the rural areas of Caucasus and Middle Asia, on Saturday mornings, behind the last rows of the bazaar, men gather to buy such sheep. The quality of the sheep is determined by the weight of their fatty-tails. The buyers take the heavy, roundly shaped tails in their palms and push them up, trying to determine their weight. After many tries they may choose a sheep that will be perfect for a pilaf. It is a very strange thing to watch. There is even a joke about one such man. This man went to a bazaar with his young son to buy a sheep. The son watched with amusement at how his father was treating the fatty-tails of the sheep: "Why are you doing these things, father?"

"I am choosing a good sheep to buy," answered the boy's father.

Then the boy exclaimed, "So what's wrong with our mother? Our neighbor was 'choosing' her the other day when you were out, but he did not buy her."

For a traditional yellow color use carrots or the more expensive saffron, and for red color—tomatoes. For additional aroma and taste some folks use dried apricots, quinces, raisins, and spices, for instance, such as cinnamon. Too many aromatics and fruits may confuse eaters and "beat down" the main aroma and taste of the rice and mutton. I personally prefer to keep the recipe simple. Salt and black pepper will do their job.

Remember the main principle of pilaf—each rice grain must be separated from the others, but be well done. The rice grains must be saturated with meat, vegetable, and fruit juices, but not stuck together in a mass like the Russian kasha.

If you and your wife invite four guests to dinner, for a total of six people, you will need: 600 grams of lamb meat, 600 grams of rice, 300 grams of carrots, 300 grams of onions, 150 grams of beforehand melted and refined butter (I doubt that you will be able to find the fatty-tailed sheep in your city), salt and black pepper to taste, and maybe a little bit barberry and cumin.

My recipe for doing pilaf is close to the method used by Uzbeks who simmer rice with meat. Persians braise meat and simmer rice separately, putting them together at the very end, on the plate. Afghans and Tadjiks use both these methods. I think that the rice in the Uzbek pilaf is the most flavorful because after the long simmering it comes up fully saturated with the complex juice of meat, vegetables, and fruits, if the latter were also used.

Cut the meat into small, mouth-size pieces. Heat half of the melted butter in a pan and saute the finely diced onions and carrots until the onions became golden in color. Add the cubes of lamb and saute it together with onions and carrots for a few minutes. Add twice as much glasses of water as there are glasses of rice, then salt, pepper, and the spices to taste and bring it all to a boil for 5 minutes. Then let it simmer. Meanwhile, in another pan (preferably with thick walls and bottom), heat the remaining butter and place on the bottom a layer of half of the rice that has been thoroughly sorted out, well-soaked in water, washed, and drained. On this layer of rice put the meat, onions, and carrots from the first pan, place the second layer of rice on them, and press well. Next, very carefully pour the remaining liquid from the first pan over the rice. The level of liquid should completely cover the rice. Close the pan with the rice and meat very tightly and leave it on medium heat until all the liquid has been absorbed by the rice grains.

If all the liquid is gone but the rice is not yet ready, your wife may make a couple of holes in the rice to the bottom of the pan and pour 1 to 2 spoons of water in each hole to continue cooking. This will give the rice more time. For a novice who is not confident about producing, at the end, a proper crust of rice at the bottom of the pan, it is a good idea at the beginning to place a piece of lavash on the bottom of the pan. This thin flat bread will protect the rice from burning.

Your wife may serve the pilaf by piling it on the platter, putting the pieces of meat on top of the "hill," and arranging seeds of pomegranate around the sides of the platter. The best way to eat pilaf is by hand. People in Middle Asia use their fingers to form mouthful size pyramids of rice and manage not to drop a single grain of it. In this way they can fully appreciate the fatness and tenderness of the pilaf.

Bulgur Pilaf

The Armenians do not like the rice as much as their neighbors, the Persians and the Azeris. They never cultivated rice. The Armenians prefer wheat. They were great ploughmen. From the wheat their women produced their famous bulgur. After harvesting the wheat, groups of women gathered to help each other while doing the hard work of washing and boiling the wheat. Then they dried it and broke it into groat by beating grains with sticks or using stone grinders. Then the bulguar was sorted by different sizes. The coarse fraction was used for bulgur pilaf and finer bulgur for mixing with ground meat and stuffing vegetables.

Why did the Armenians work so long and hard to process the wheat? This method made the wheat tender, preserved its flavor, and allowed it to be stored for a long time. The Armenians always lived in such conditions where they had to think about preserving their food supplies from spoiling in case of long sieges or exiles. They learned to prepare special types of bread, meat, vegetables and fruits, and even dairy foods that could withstand destruction by time. Bulgur is just one of them. It is also heartier than rice and very good with stews and soups. Bulgur pilaf is definitely not from a royal family; it is a simple, very filling dish.

For this pilaf, your wife should prepare: 1 cup of coarse bulgur, 4 tablespoons of olive oil or melted and refined butter, 1 diced onion,

2 cups of beef or chicken broth, salt, black pepper, and dried and crushed basil or ground coriander to taste.

In a pot and on moderate heat saute the onion in the oil until it becomes golden. Add bulgur and saute for 2 to 3 more minutes stirring constantly. Pour the broth inside the pot and then add salt, pepper, and spices. Bring to a boil while still stirring. Then lower the heat, cover the pot tightly, and let it simmer until all the broth has soaked into the grains. After 20–25 minutes the bulgur should be tender, but not mushy.

You see how simple bulgur pilaf is. It takes less than a hour and may fill a family of four. It is particularly useful when one has broth remaining after boiling a big cut of beef or whole hen.

We all liked bulgur pilaf, but I doubt that my grandmother could have served bulgur pilaf for Mousa Agha. He would have turned up his nose at such "a peasant meal." However, using bulgur, my grandmother made another famous dish for Mousa Agha which should have definitely satisfied this gourmand's whims. *Kiufta!* Each Armenian community has its own way of making kiufta, which is not just a food product, but to put it better—a beautiful and delicate creation by the hands of women. Imagine this: kiufta may be of various shapes and sizes (usually about 5–6-centimeter balls); it may also be boiled, broiled, baked, stuffed, and eaten hot, cold, or even raw! And the most amazing thing is that the balls of kiufta actually consist mainly of bulgur and lamb meat. No extraordinary ingredients. However, it is not so easy to make these balls because they should be made hollow for stuffing. Women's hands are best suited for such passionate and delicate work.

Ishli Kiufta

This kind of kiufta was prepared by the Turkish Armenians, mostly in and around the big city of Kharberd. The fertile plains of this province and people's hard work produced great harvests of wheat. In cold winters, the hot kiufta warmed up families gathered around the tables and helped them to live through the hard times. During the genocide, this province of Kharberd was called "The Slaughterhouse," because so many Armenians were butchered there by the Turks. The blood and flesh of the Armenian peasants fed the plains they had ploughed before for centuries. These plains became even more fertile, indeed. Somewhere there my mother and grandmother were separated. My mother was taken in and saved by a Kurdish family, while my grandmother proceeded with her group of exiled Armenian women and children further to Urfa. There, my grandmother lived for about three years in the kitchen of Mousa Agha. Later, she recalled some dishes she had cooked for Mousa Bey to extend her stay under his roof. My mother never explained what she did to survive those years.

You see, I began explaining to you the recipe of ishli kiufta, but then the name of this dish brought back very sad memories. Some Armenian words are like scars of deep wounds; you touch them and you suddenly feel old pains.

I know, I know; I should not be distracted by any other things from the past other than my family's old recipes.

The stuffing for kiufta is the first thing to make because when prepared it should be left for a few hours "to rest and ripen." Your wife will need the following: 350 grams of ground lamb, 2 tablespoons of melted and refined butter, 1 onion, 1 tablespoon of parsley, 1 tablespoon of basil, and 2 tablespoons of green pepper, all finely chopped; salt and black pepper to taste, and ½ tablespoon of cinnamon.

In a skillet and on moderate heat saute the onion in the butter, stirring frequently. Add the ground lamb and continue cooking and stirring for a few minutes. Then add the green pepper. When the meat is browned and the green pepper is soft, add salt, black pepper, and herbs and stir well. Remove from the oven, allow it to cool, cover, and put in a cold place for a few hours.

After this long break your wife should return to the kitchen to prepare the kiufta balls. She will need: 500 grams of very finely ground lamb, 1½ cups of bulgur (fine size), 1 ground onion, and salt and black pepper to taste.

Prepare the bulgar by soaking it in water for 10–15 minutes. Then drain off the water by squeezing the bulgur in a piece of cloth. In a bowl, thoroughly mix together bulgur, meat, onion, and spices. Note that your wife must knead the mixture well before it becomes very smooth. For this, she must work really hard, periodically moistening her hands in a bowl of cold water. Her hands must always be moistened so that the mixture does not stick to them.

Then, she must take a small portion of the mixture and shape it like a ball, approximately 4 centimeters in diameter. Holding this ball in the palm of one hand, she should place the thumb of her other hand into the center of the ball and press to make a hole. She needs to continue pressing with her thumb on the inner wall of the ball and rotate the ball slowly in the palm of her other hand. Doing it gently she will be able to make a hollow ball with thin walls and a bigger size. Through the opening she then fills the ball with the stuffing. She closes the opening with her moistened hand and smooths the surface of the ball. She has to repeat this difficult procedure again and again until the stuffing and the bulgur have all been used up. I doubt that you or any man would be willing to prepare this dish!

However, the preparation is not yet over. The stuffed kiufta should then be boiled in broth. For this, take: 8 cups of lamb broth, 4 fresh tomatoes, and salt and black pepper to taste. In a large pot mix the broth with tomato puree. Bring to a boil and add spices. Lower all the kiufta balls into the broth and keep on a low heat. After a few minutes the balls will begin to rise to the surface. Spoon them out and put them immediately into the guests' soup bowls. (Do not be afraid to handle the kiufta balls, since their walls will have been thickened and strengthened in the boiling broth.) Pour a couple of spoonfuls of broth over the kiuftas. Some people like this very much, particularly after cutting the balls into pieces and letting some of the stuffing mix with the broth.

Hmmm, you are not sure whether your wife is going to devote so much of her time to preparing just one meal. This sounds familiar! I tried to teach my son's Russian wife to prepare some of my recipes, but she said that life was too short to stuff mussels and eggplants. So, when he wants to eat something really tasty he comes to me, my boy!

Well, let's go for an easily made dish. What about deep-fried kalkan? This flatfish of the Black Sea has less bones than many other fish, so its cleaning is not a problem, even for a busy woman. And the meat of this fish is so tender and its fat so flavorful that it is quite difficult to ruin this fish. Not without reason, it is prized by all folks living around the sea. (Except maybe for the Abkhazians and the Georgians.) However, nobody, and I am sure about that, is as fond of fried fish as much as the Greeks. No matter what side of the Black Sea they live or used to lived, the moment you enter their houses you will probably recognize the smell of fish and frying oil. In summer, this smell emanates almost constantly from the outdoor kitchen of my neighbors, the Mouvrakis. For them, to clean a kalkan, season it, and throw it on the skillet takes only a couple of minutes. The mistress of the house, kiria Mouvraki, does not even care about rolling the fish in flour; she just sprinkles it well with oil and spices. You would not find more tastier fish in the most prestigious restaurants from your city to Moscow! All my vacationers from the northern areas always turn up their noses: "Phi! This smell! Phi! It is too salty and spicy!" Oh, please! Fish must be salty! It is not veal nor pork, nor even poultry; it likes salt. Salt is natural for fish because they both come from sea water! Isn't it true?

Well, if you are afraid that strong fish smells will cause you trouble with the neighbors in your building, you may roll the fish pieces in flour. I recommend that you use rice flour which is finer than wheat flour. Rice flour creates a thinner crust on the frying fish that prevents it from being drenched in grease. You may do that for frying barbunya (red mullet) or kefal (grey mullet), which are fattier and smellier than kalkan. According to my neighbor, kiria Mouvraki, kalkan does not need flour. Saying that, I am going to tell you the exact recipe for fried Kalkan or "kalkan a la Mouvraki." Because you are writing it down in your notebook and somebody may read and use it, the recipe must be told as much accurately and truthfully as possible.

Fried Kalkan

First, clean the kalkan by cutting off its head, belly part, and fins. Then cut off the small bones located along the sides of the fish. Just move your knife around its flat body. Rinse and dry well with a cloth. If water remains on the fish it would cause the frying oil to splash during the cooking. If the fish is big, cut it into portion pieces, but if your skillet can accommodate it whole, do not bother. Frying the fish in its skin reduces its smell. However, cut the skin of the fish in a few places so the whole fish or its pieces will not bend during frying. Sprinkle well all sides of the fish with olive or sunflower oil. Rather generously rub in salt and black pepper and a mix of dried and crushed tarragon and thyme. Place the prepared fish into a well-preheated skillet sprinkled with oil. Fry the fish on both sides until the crusty skin has reached. Because the fish is flat, it will be easy to turn it over. If you are frying many pieces of this fish it is a good idea after a while, to use a second skillet. The expense of the frying oil will be more, but you will avoid excessive blackening of the fish skin in the accumulating grease.

Another important thing about fried fish is that it must be fresh and the exact amount must be bought and prepared. It has to be fried as soon as possible after it is taken from the sea and should be eaten up to the last piece immediately after is taken from the skillet. No leftovers! Even kalkan, very forgiving as it is, loses its wonderful flakey texture and excitingly unblemished aroma if left cold. Also, never drink water with fried fish. You may have headaches afterward. Any light, simple wine which has no strong aroma is the best way to accompany fish. Like Doctor Isakovich, my old vacationer from Minsk, said: "A fried fish, to taste right, must swim three times—firstly, in water, then in oil, and at the end, in wine!"

Of course, oil is better for frying fish than butter, even melted butter. This is the correct method used by the Greeks, the unsurpassed fish masters! We, the Armenians, prefer melted butter in our cooking. Apparently, we invented this method of refining and preserving commercial butter. You will find a stock of melted butter in any traditional Armenian household from any Armenian community or neighborhood. It is very easy to make. Place some briquettes of butter bought in a store into a pot. Shower the butter well with a coarse salt and put it aside for a while until the salt has drained out all the water from the butter. Then, pour out all this waste from the pot and put the pot on a slow heat. While the butter is melting and boiling, periodically discard the spume appearing on the surface. (This is dirt added by the butter manufacturer just to increase its weight. Believe me!) Turn off the heat when the surface becomes clean of spume. Let the hot butter rest for a couple of minutes. This allows the remaining waste to settle at the bottom of the pot. Carefully pour the clean melted butter, trying not to disturb the sediment, into jars up to their very necks and close the jars tightly. The end product, when cooled, acquires a pleasant yellow color, becomes smooth like cream, and has the distinctive scent of natural unspoiled butter. This, in my opinion, resembles the aroma of freshly cut grass. The most important feature of such melted butter is that it does not lose its color and taste for a very long time.

Tell me, why is that? Why have the Armenians developed so many kinds of foods that can persist against the destruction by time? I agree that almost all nations, small and big, even the very powerful and safe, have similar products for a rainy day: sausages and spiced meat cuts, dried fruits and pickled vegetables. However, I think that no folks have so many and so varied long-lasting foods as the Armenians! We not only have *sudjukh,* a sausage of oval form made from the spicy ground meat of veal and pork stuffed in animals' intestines, but also *kaurma,* fried pieces of sheep tightly packed into a clay jug and sealed by melted fat from sheep tail. A pile of Armenian flat bread, *lavash,* can be stacked under a cloth for months and fully revived just by pouring a little water over its sheets. *Targhana,* consists of small flat pieces of dough made from mixing flour, salt, eggs, matsoon (yogurt), and yeast. These pieces are dried outdoors in a windy place and then stored in air-tight jars before their use in various soups. The kitchen walls of Armenian houses are often decorated with beautiful dry plaits woven from bunches of wild plant *avelook* (sorrel), much prized by our people as a refreshing winter meal when boiled and braised with fried onions. We should not forget our *chortan* or dried matsoon, which can also be stored for a long time (for instance, during an exhausting trip or hard work), before being diluted in water and drank to slake thirst. There are hundreds of other such kinds of food products used by the Armenians from time immemorial. I can go on and on by naming them one after another.

One may say that the Armenians learned to preserve their food because they too often were forced to leave their old haunts and migrate to new, quite distant places. Of course, it was wise to have something in their bags like dry lavash and matsoon for when the time was came to take a rest at a roadside spring. These light and easy-to-carry marvels—may they be blessed forever!—were converted, within a minute, into a honest meal, just by adding some water.

To see for yourself, just open any sheet of lavash, look at its intricate pattern of dark spots left by a baking oven fire, and you can see the routes and read the history of the Armenian people's wanderings! Imagine how many of them survived because of having a piece of lavash. Hidden from the enemy's eye under a shirt or dress, it warmed a refugees' heart and instilled it with a little hope. Rolled with the dusty leaves of wild plants, this piece of lavash gave other poor souls the strength to drag their exhausted feet a little further. Survival tool, indeed!

However, I think that the Armenians' obsession with food preservation speaks also about their peculiar attitude toward the time. For the Armenians, in general of course, the main idea is that there is no "End" ahead; life, as well as time itself, does not end. Putting so much effort into preserving and stocking up food, we, Armenians, demonstrate that we are going to be around, here or there, for a very long time. It looks like we firmly believe that nothing and nobody will be able to end our history, which by itself is an endless story of survival. Apparently, there is something important which we have been carrying inside us, so crucial for the Lord's ultimate plan, that he has been supporting us through all our misfortunes and catastrophes, and even our own failures! Crying and laughing, we again and again rise from the ashes, build *odjahs,* which in Armenian means both "home" and "oven," and bake lavash for another journey. Sure, our lives are in the lap of our Lord, but also in the hands of our cooks!

I am sure that simple lavash and matsoon are not what your wife is interested in. She definitely would like to have a recipe for a much more showy dish. Well, let's talk about "Imam Baialdy," perhaps one of the most famous among all dishes of the East. In Turkish, "Imam Baialdy" means "Priest Fainted." There is an abundance of tales explaining this curious name. One tells that Imam, or holy man, fainted when he sniffed the strong garlic aroma of this dish set before him. Another claims that Imam lost consciousness from gorging too much on such a rich dish, while a third explains Imam's fainting as a result of his sudden realization of how much fine and expensive olive oil has been used by his wife for preparing this dish. May I suggest my version? I think a glutton, for instance, like Mousa Agha of Urfa, may have fainted when his eyes saw such a gorgeous dish and his nostrils sniffed its extraordinary fragrance, but his belly could not take in one more mouthful. My grandmother recalled the moments when Mousa Agha mournfully sighed, sitting alone at the table, and his black oily eyes were ready to shed tears over an unfinished pot of a meal.

"Imam Baialdy"

For this dish, you will need: 8 small (long and narrow) eggplants, 4 medium-size ripe tomatoes, 3 medium-size onions, 8 garlic cloves (finely minced), 1 cup of olive oil, ⅓ cup of water, 1 cup of chopped parsley, mint, dill, celery, and coriander, and salt and pepper to taste.

Peel the skin of the eggplants, making a few strips on each of them. Sprinkle well with coarse salt and leave them for 30–40 minutes in order to force out their bitter juice. Then rinse well under running cold water and dry. Make long cuts lengthwise in one skinned strip of each eggplants and scoop out as much as you can of their insides.

Chop the scooped out flesh of the eggplants and mix well with the herbs, onion, and garlic, adding salt and pepper. Fry this mixture in half of the olive oil and then stuff it inside the eggplants through the cuts you made before. Place the stuffed eggplants in one layer on the bottom of a deep skillet with the rest of the preheated olive oil. Arrange the eggplants with their cut sides facing up. Cover them with chopped tomatoes, sprinkle again the salt and pepper, and then add the water. Cover the skillet tightly and cook on rather low heat until the eggplants are tender. This dish is better when served cooled to room temperature.

Even cooled it emanates the strong, complex aroma of stuffed herbs and garlic. Each cook uses his or her own combination of herbs for stuffing, so their "Imam Baialdys" may have various aromas. My grandmother, for instance, used to add fried ground meat of lamb to her stuffing. She recalled that once, when she prepared this dish for Mousa Agha, one of her master's guests, the local judge who considered himself to be a gourmet and the only one who might to challenge the host's superiority (of course, not in the amount of consumed food, where Mousa Agha had no serious contenders, but in appreciation of the culinary craftsmanship), claimed loudly at the table that he could bet his fez that Mousa Agha's cook was "an Armenian." The judge argued that the scent of the dish was different from the traditional one. "It definitely smells of an infidel!" Mousa Agha, always cautious around his useful, but dangerous table companions, had chosen not to deny the judge's claim. Instead, to avoid any further mention of the existence of "an Armenian" in his kitchen, he rushed into praising the judge's "exquisite taste and undeniable acumen which allowed Hakim Effendi always to advance witty thoughts and to exercise just decisions both in civil matters and at the table of friends." His guests joined him in praising the judge and then they all returned to their previous conversations. Grandmother's luck! Sitting at the table, the judge could easily have exercised his "justice" and ordered Mousa Agha to get rid of his "infidel cook" immediately, and then I would never have seen my poor grandma again.

Later, Mousa Agha told my grandmother about the judge's remark and demanded she stop making dishes for his banquets in her "Armenian ways." What did that mean: "Armenian ways"?

Well, the Armenians usually over-salt their meals. Even their melted butter, which they like so much to use, is made with salt. True, all those who live and sweat in hot climates also prefer more salt in their cuisine than northern folks. Nevertheless, our neighbors, the

Greeks and the Georgians, nicknamed us as "the salty ones." We Armenians even manage to put salt in water of the fonts when we baptize our infants.

There is also an astonishing amount of edible grasses and plants cooked and eaten by the Armenians. I heard many times that there are about 300 of them, not just herbs and garden grown plants, but also wild plants which many other folks, for instance, the Russians, firmly consider to be weeds, useless and poisonous. It is hard to dispute that there is a lot of vegetables in regular stores that is much easier to prepare and better to fill the stomach. However, for many Armenians, their intimate knowledge of wild plants and grasses turned out to be life-saving wisdom. For months, flocks of Armenian refugees survived on this green food; a small bundle of *pipert* (marshmallow leaves), picked up straight along the march, blunted one's hunger, and the juicy pitch extracted from the thick stem of *byldyrhan* (sort of like horsetail) quenched one's thirst, just a little bit, but enough to stay alive for another day. These Armenians were able to survive if diarrhea did not finish them off.

Another peculiar characteristic of the Armenian cuisine is our habit of stuffing. We stuff almost everything: grape leaves, onions, and green peppers; squashes, eggplants, and pumpkins; fish, mussels, and fruits; animals' intestines and heads. If necessary we could stuff a soldier's boot and it would taste good! Why this obsession? Well, despite of all the bumps and lumps through our long history, we Armenians still believe that we can improve the world. Show me a perfectly round, ripe and fragrant quince and I will immediately proclaim that it will be much better if you cut off its head, cut out and discard its inner stem with seeds, insert the stuffing of ground meat and herbs and spices, close it again by replacing its head, and braise the fruit slowly in broth.

What is wrong with us? Why do we always bustle? We tear our navels to make additions to our houses, plant more trees in our gardens, strive to improve this and that, as if we have not learned enough already that our houses may be destroyed and our gardens may bear fruits for not for us but for our enemies. *Do you know how the Turks used to find Armenians among the crowd of wanderers?* If there was a bonfire and a bunch of people sitting around it, just enjoying rest and warmth, and only one man was poking the fire to arrange the logs better, the Turks would seize this man at once. And they would never be wrong!

Who else except the silly, fidgety Armenian would play with the fire when all the others would just sit around and not come out?

Stuffed quince with stuffed apples are called "Ashtarak *dolma*." Ashtarak is a town in Armenia which produces big juicy apples. However, the traditional Armenian dolma is made not from apples, but from fresh grape leaves.

Of course, almost everyone knows about Armenian dolma! Let me give you a detailed recipe, and don't interrupt me with "I know this" and "I know that." You don't want to be like the famous "know-all" Manoosh from that joke.

Oh, you don't know this story! Listen!

Manoosh came to her neighbor and requested the recipe for dolma.

"Ground piece of lamb." began the neighbor.

"I know, of course, meat," proudly replied Manoosh.

"Mix with chopped onions and herbs, then add . . ."

"I know, I know . . . ," interjected Manoosh.

"Roll the stuffing into grape leaves and put into . . ."

"I know this too," again interrupted Manoosh.

The angry neighbor could not take it anymore and snapped: "Take a flat-cake of dung and put in on top of the dolma in a pot."

"I know, I know," continued silly Manoosh.

"When the dung begins to smell, your dolma is ready! Enjoy it, but don't say that it was my recipe, you pumpkin head!"

Believe me, there are so many women like Manoosh around. They did not see a hundredth of what I have seen, but they try to teach me. Willy-nilly you may snap at them.

Grape Dolma

For dolma, begin with the following: 1 pound of ground lamb meat, ⅓ cup of rice, 1 large onion (chopped), 2 tablespoons each of chopped mint, basil, coriander, savory, and marjoram, salt and black pepper to taste, 50–60 young and fresh grape leaves, and meat broth.

Preparation of the grape leaves is the most important part of the recipe. The leaves must be of a proper size. If the leaves are too small, they demand more work: they need to be doubled for each dolma and may be torn in the process of rolling. Leaves that are too big may have tough veins. Anyway, put each leaf into boiling water for 1 to 2 minutes just to make them more tender. Rinse the leaves under cool water and drain them on some paper. Cut off the stems, if there are any.

For stuffing, thoroughly mix the ground meat with the rice, onions, herbs, and spices. Take one leaf and place it on a plate, dull side up and stem end toward you. Put one spoon of stuffing mixture near the stem end of the leaf. Fold the end of the leaf over the stuffing and then fold both sides of the leaf on it. Then roll the leaf firmly to its other end. You should make a small cylinder. This is dolma. Continue until you have used all the stuffing. All dolmas must look uniform, like cartridge-cases. It is laborious work. Every young girl from a decent Armenian family learns hard to acquire this important skill of making dolmas before her wedding. Nothing instills in men the false belief that their homes are in order like one pot of perfect dolmas!

Making dolma: On the bottom of a pot place a few lamb bones, followed by about 10 grape leaves on top of them. This layer will prevent the tender dolmas from burning. Arrange all the dolmas in rows, rather tightly and with their folded sides down. Pour in the meat broth and cover the dolmas with a heavy plate upside down to keep them in place while boiling. Cover the pot and simmer on low heat until the stuffing becomes tender and the rice is fully cooked. If the leaves were sorted precisely for one size and rolled properly, all the dolmas will be ready at one time. The leaves of perfect dolmas must be shiny and not tattered. I am sure your wife will manage to prepare such dolmas for you!

Dolmas are better eaten when they are still hot, dipping them into matsoon with minced garlic or with sugar and cinnamon.

Which of my other recipes do you want to write down, my dear? There are perhaps hundreds of them. Some I imitated after my grandmother and mother, who brought them from Tachkastan. Others I learned here, in Sukhumi, from my Russian, Greek, Georgian, and Abkhazian neighbors.

Unfortunately, there are very good meals which your wife will not be able to make for you because they need crucial ingredients she will not find in your city. For instance, soup *kharcho,* a pride of the Georgians, cannot be made without *tklapi,* pulp from a special sour cherry-plum which is dried out in the form of a thin sheet. I doubt that your wife can find tklapi in any stores. Without this mandatory flavoring, her kharcho will taste like regular soup, even if she follows all the other instructions from the original recipe, such as using brisket of veal and ground walnuts. It takes days to prepare tklapi sheets, and only one hour to make the soup. Thorough preparation is the main secret of cooking craftsmanship!

Another meal that demands the long preparation is *hashi.* Cow feet are cleaned repeatedly and washed in "seven waters" before being boiled in a huge pot for hours. My grandfather used to put the cleaned feet into a small net which he then placed into the cold stream of the brook running through our garden. He kept the net in the water for two days to eliminate the unpleasant feet odor.

Oh, your wife hates hashi! I really feel sorry for you, my dear. In the early chilly morning, being surrounded by the entire family and close friends, and having a big bowl of hashi seasoned with plenty of salt and garlic, accompanied by a small glass of mulberry vodka is a simple, but beautiful thing to do. It is maybe one of the oldest customs we Armenians are still eager to follow. Especially our men. A hashi table brings a sense of unity without the usual long and verbose toasts. Having strictly only one dish on the table helps to create a feeling of equality and mutual respect among eaters. This it not a banquet; they are not encouraged to sit too long. They come, eat, and leave for their routines. A good bowl of hashi will keep their stomachs full and spirits high for the entire day. Oh yeah! The men will also smell! Garlic and mulberry vodka, exactly what your wife does not tolerate. Well, let's give her something she will be glad to use in practice, not just as a record in her kitchen notebook.

Spas or Tanabour

To make this dish, your wife will need a few simple things: 4 cups of matsoon, 1 egg beaten, a half-cup of rice, 2 onions chopped, 5 tablespoons of flour, a half-cup of chopped mint, a half-cup of chopped coriander, 2 tablespoons of melted butter, and salt and black pepper to taste.

Making spas: She should mix the flour with the egg very thoroughly, so that no lumps are left inside the flour. Then, in a pot, she has to dilute the matsoon in an equal volume of water and add in the flour and egg, constantly stirring this mixture while bringing it to a boil on a heat. Next she adds in the pot half-cooked rice with its remaining water, followed by the fried onion, mint, coriander, salt, and pepper, and continue stirring until the soup boils again. The spas is ready. What is good about spas is that it may be eaten hot in winter, or cooled during summer. It is always very refreshing and is famous as a cure to renew appetite and strength in people after illness.

Mousa Agha often ordered my grandmother to prepare this light soup on days following his long bouts of gluttony. This man was digging his grave with fork and spoon. For him, a large breakfast was just a prelude to a dinner that would last for hours. Then he would stay in his bed for long hours, surrounded with pillows, but unable to find a comfortable position among them for his "suffering" belly. So, my grandmother's spas helped him a lot to recover. However, when my grandmother left Urfa, shortly after the French army entered the city, Mousa Agha was still able to give banquets. He followed the rule that givers of great banquets had no enemies. His dinners were not as long and splendid as before, and the guests around his table changed completely. The defeated Turks disappeared, replaced by new "friends," officers of Allied army. Mousa Agha changed too. He declared that he was actually "a subject of Persia and always felt oppressed by the Turks." With knavish modesty he never failed to mention to his new guests that all those years he had been hiding "a Christian woman, the wife of his former business partner, from certain death at the hands of Turkish barbarians." At that moment, Mousa Agha used to screw up his oily eyes and clasped his hands to hide a cunning smile under his big hooked nose. For my grandmother, this man's exact extraction was and remained vague, but she always was very grateful for his hospitality and protection.

To continue about spas, it is worthy to warn you that it is a very light dish. It is so light that there is even a joke about it. Spas, hashi, and pilaf meet somewhere and talk about their qualities. Hashi boasts: "A man who has eaten me in early morning will feel absolutely full until night!" Pilaf says: "I can easily keep him full until midday!" And spas goes "As soon as he is off the table I am not responsible!" So, keep this in mind, my dear.

Chicken Tabaka

This is another simple, but very rewarding dish. No wonder it is so popular around the Caucasus. The Georgians claim it as their national dish, and they have been so persistent in this case that it is now listed in all the menus in the Soviet Union as belonging to "the famous Georgian cuisine." The Armenians are sure that it is an Armenian dish, arguing that the very word "tabaka" comes from "tapak," which in Armenian means "flat," precisely describing the form which is given to the bird before roasting it. And "roasted" in Armenian sounds "tapakats!"

"Georgian chicken" or "Armenian chickens,"—it does not matter, as long as the name of this dish is not stolen by the Turks. I would like to remind you again of how they contrived to misappropriate the black coffee name from the Arabs who invented this drink hundreds of years before they, the Turks, began to use it. Now, all other folks refer to black coffee as "Turkish coffee." Total nonsense!

It is true, I am obsessive. Sorry for the distraction!

Flattening chicken: clean well and rinse a chicken, cut along its chest and paunch, unroll both sides (crushing the ribs), and place it on the cutting board with the bird's back up. Using a wooden kitchen hammer, flatten the bird. Apply salt and black pepper on both sides of the chicken.

Roasting: Pre-heat some melted butter in a skillet large enough to accommodate the whole flattened chicken. Place the chicken on one side and cover with an upside down plate. Put some weight on the plate in order to preserve the flat form of the chicken throughout the entire duration of the roast, which is 15–20 minutes on medium heat. Then turn the chicken over, cover with plate, don't forget the weight, and roast its second side, this time for 10–15 minutes. When ready, "Chicken Tabaka" shines like a small sun!

As you see, it is really a simple dish. You can do it without your wife. The only secret is its sauce. Grind a few cloves of garlic, mix with two teaspoons of salt, and add this mixture into a cup with hot chicken broth. For good taste and flavor, pour the sauce over each portion of chicken; this makes all the magic because salt and garlic match perfectly with the roasted chicken meat.

Chikhirtma

This is undoubtedly a Georgian dish! It is quite complex in preparation, but unusual and tasty. Your wife may try to make it to impress her friends who have never been to the Caucasus. All the necessary ingredients may be found in the food stores of any big city.

For this dish she will need: one fat hen, 4 onions chopped, 1 tablespoon of flour, 4 tablespoons of lemon juice, 4 eggs, salt and black pepper to taste, 2 tablespoons of fresh, finely chopped coriander, ½ teaspoon of diluted saffron, and 1 teaspoon of vinegar.

Firstly, your wife puts well cleaned and medium cut pieces of the hen into a pot and adds cold water to cover all them. She boils the hen for approximately 2 hours, frequently skimming off the scum from the top of the water. She then removes the meat from the pot and strains the stock into another pot. She collects the melted fat from the top of the stock and uses this to fry the onions in a skillet. Next, she sprinkles the onions with flour and cooks them, stirring for one more minute. She adds one glass of stock, stirs well, pours this mixture into the main stock, and cooks until it begins to boil. She adds salt, pepper, and vinegar, brings the stock to a boil again and takes the pot off the heat. Then, in a small bowl, she beats the eggs well and slowly pours them into the stock, stirring constantly. She puts the pot on the heat again and once more brings it to a boil. As soon as it starts to boil she should immediately remove the pot from the heat to prevent the eggs from curdling. Finally, she flavors the prepared chikhirtma with lemon juice and saffron. She should serve the soup immediately, sprinkled with coriander. Your wife may use the meat of the hen for another dish, but she may also add small slivers of the meat to the finished soup, too.

Gata

Finally, for desert, I will give you the recipe for traditional Armenian fancy pastry, otherwise known as the famous gata. This pastry is not like pakhlava, which belongs to many Eastern people. Greeks, Turks, Arabs, Persians, Azeris, and Armenians, with small variances in their recipes, all make good pakhlava. Gata is different; nobody except the Armenians make these sweet flat cakes. All its ingredients are very simple—flour, eggs, milk, butter, and sugar—and can be found in any food store. Tell your wife: the work involved is lengthy, but the final result is more than worthy.

First, she should prepare the leavened dough. In a glass of warm water (200 grams) she dilutes 10 grams of yeast and mixes it well with a glass of flour. The prepared dough should be placed in a warm place for 2 to 3 hours for fermentation.

When the leavened dough is completely ripened, it is time to prepare the main dough. Very thoroughly, she mixes 200 grams of melted butter with a glass of sugar, 5 eggs, a pinch of salt, and just a little vanillin powder until she has created a smooth cream-like mass. She pours this mass into the leavened dough and mixes it well. Then, while continuing to mix, she adds one portion of flour after another (750 grams in total) and puts the prepared main dough in a warm place for 30–40 minutes.

For the filling, your wife should take 350 grams of butter and mix this very well with 400 grams of flour and then with 300 grams of sugar powder. Then she places the main dough back on the kitchen table. She must knead the dough really well or as my mother used to say, "work heartily to leaven up the dough." Then she divides the dough into portions off about 250 grams each. She rolls them out into round shapes 4–5 centimeters thick, and places layers of filling (200 grams each) on the surfaces. She joins the edges of the portions by pinching them together over the fillings, then turns them over and rolls them out to be 2 centimeters thick.

At the end, she puts the gatas on the oiled griddle with their seams down. She brushes the gatas' surfaces with beaten yolk and makes lines on them with the blunt side of a knife. Each Armenian woman uses her own pattern of lines, sometimes quite elaborate, but usually those that she learned from her mother. Making gata is a very old tradition, so in some families the patterns on the surfaces have been running maybe from ancient times. There were, of course, many more Armenian families who were wiped out from the surface of the earth due to wars or massacres, and their patterns have been lost forever.

To let the steam out, pierce each gata with a fork. Bake the gatas for 30 minutes: 15 on medium heat and 15 on low. Gata emerges from the oven with a beautiful dark yellow, almost brownish color, and adorned with an ornament carved into its surface.

Enjoy your gata with a cup of black coffee. After the last sip, turn your cup upside down and place it on the saucer for a while. The black sediment will run down along the sides of the cup and form a pattern of its own. Somebody, a "sagacious" one sitting around the table, may read this pattern and interpret events from your past and present, as well as reveal dangers and predict fortunes facing you in the future. If the cup sticks to the saucer, do not use force to separate them. It simply means that you are not ready to see your fate! You will, maybe next time.

Glossary

(of the Turkish words, if otherwise not specified, frequently used in the text)

Agha—a title; "master, elder," commonly used for rich landlords or merchants
arshin—meter; also in Russian
asker—soldier
Ataturk (Father of Turks)—Mustapha Kemal Pasha (1881–1938) was Turkish general who inspired and organized Turks in defeating Greeks and later became first president of Turkey (1923–38)
Bey—a courtesy title for high Turkish officials
chavush—sergeant; topal chavush—lame sergeant
Cilicia—ancient Armenian Kingdom (1080–1375) in SE Asia Minor; later a part of the Turkish empire and currently within the contemporary Turkey
dervish—a wandering beggar; a devoted member of a Muslim order
djan—dear; "soul" (Armenian)
druzhina—military detachment of volunteers (Russian)
Effendi—a title of courtesy; "master"; Beyeffendi was equal to "Sir"
Eghbair—brother (Arm.); rather hail-fellow-well-met for addressing a good friend
fez—the cone-shaped Turkish headgear
giavour—an infidel
Hak Dini—True Faith or Islam
hammam—bathhouse
hanum—lady
Harab Caravansaray—Abandoned Inn
Haroutiun—"resurrection"; the Armenian male name
hent—crazy, daredevil, foolhardy (Arm.)
Iughaper—"bringing oil" or bringing prosperity; the Armenian female name
Jart—"destruction" (Arm.); was commonly used by the Armenians in the reference to their massacres in Turkey in 1894–96 by sultan Abdul Hamid II; in 1909 and 1915–18 by the Young Turks; and in 1920–22 by Ataturk

jiins—evil spirits
kadi—judge
kaimakam—governor of town or region administrator
kalkan—flatfish of the Black Sea
kiria—missis, madam (Greek)
kiz—girl
lavash—Armenian flat, thin bread
matah—sacrifice (Arm.)
matsoon—Armenian curdled sour milk, similar to yoghurt
mayrig—mama, mother (Arm.)
meechnord—"go-between" person or matchmaker (Arm.)
meidan—square, central place
midia—mussel of the Black Sea
mollah—priest
mudir—chief
narghile—water pipe for smoking
Nargiz—Armenian female name; from the Persian "narcissus flower"
NKVD—People's Commissariat for Internal Affairs; this organization's major aim was to carry out the Stalin's purges of the regular Soviet citizens in 1930s
para—small coin
paron(er)—polite form of addressing man or men (Arm.); equal to "gentleman(men);" derivative of the French "baron" after many years of cooperation and socialization with crusaders in the Armenian Kingdom of Cilicia
Pasha—title for higher ranks of military and civil hierarchy
Pera—hilly part of the European part of Constantinople
Pietzar—"bright, pure;" the Armenian female male
Pogos—the Armenian form of Paul
Polis—derivative of Constantinopolis i.e., Constantinople (vernacular)
rakia—anise vodka
Sheitan Delik—Devil's Hole
Tachkastan—Turkey (Arm.)
Tachiks—Turks (Arm.); from the general name given by the Armenians to the Seljuk Turkish tribes who from XI century began migrating from the Central Asia into the territories of the current Turkey; incorrect name given after the Tadjiks, Turkish-speaking Persians, also living in Central Asia
Takouhi—"Queen," the Armenian female name
tikin—missis, madam (Arm.)
tondir—a large, urn-shaped underground oven (Arm.)
tsavet tanem—let me take away your pain, anguish; the Armenian soothing or consoling saying

vali—governor of a province
yayla—a summer shepherd's campground at highland plateau
Yehern—"slaughter, carnage" (Arm.); commonly is used in reference to the Armenian Genocide in Turkey; see also Jart
Yeni Koy—New Village
zaptieh—gendarme
zabit—officer
zoravor—a hero (Arm.)

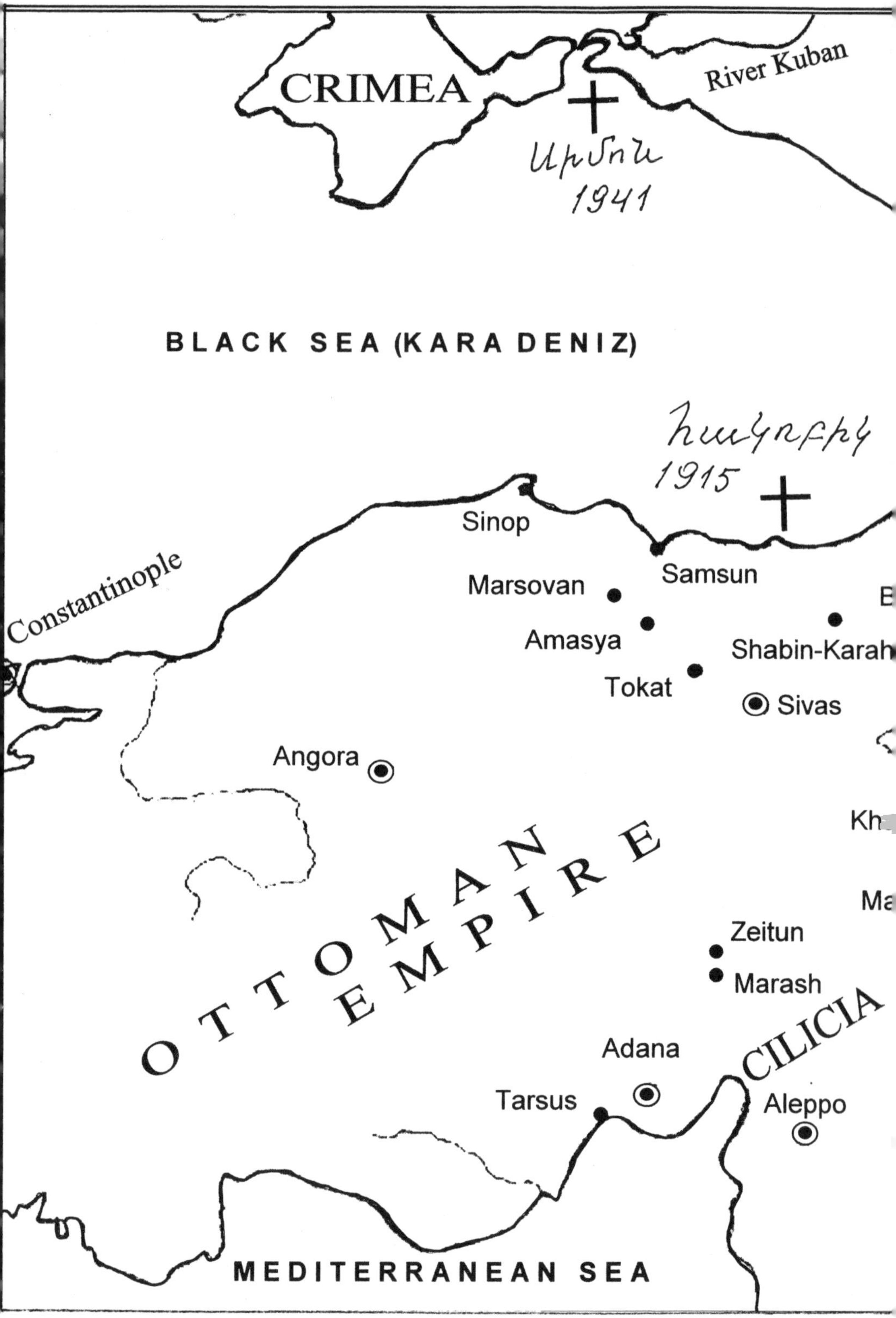
CRIMEA
River Kuban
Արմոն
1941
BLACK SEA (KARA DENIZ)
Հակոբիկ
1915
Sinop
Constantinople
Samsun
Marsovan
Amasya
Shabin-Karah
Tokat
Sivas
Angora
OTTOMAN EMPIRE
Zeitun
Marash
CILICIA
Adana
Tarsus
Aleppo
MEDITERRANEAN SEA